MW00619065

PRAISE FOR INCARNADINE

"When I picked up your books and started reading, **I was blown away.** Finally, some books I can get into and it feels like the author put some thought into their brilliant work."
Marion C. posted on Facebook

"I've just finished reading your first three books to my wife. **We both enjoyed them enormously.** The Homestead communities sound **fascinating**."
James B., Clansman

"Filled with action and adventure and suspense, **it's the characters who make this story.** I care about what happens to these story people almost as much as I care what happens to my friends. **I'm hooked on the series!**"
Clio B., Kindle Reader

"Your writing is so **clever and so masterful.** I'm truly on the edge of my seat keeping up with your plots. I've read other mystery writers and **outside of Agatha Christie your page turning novels are the best!**"
Holly A., Amazon Reader

"**Thank you** for your wonderful writing!"
Wendy D. Amazon Reader

PLEASE JOIN US!

You are cordially invited to join the Loch Lonach Homestead Community.

All Members will receive insider news, Scottish lore, and entertaining details about life on the Homestead. New members will also get a **FREE** Short Story.

Come join Ginny, Jim, Angus, and all the Scottish Texans as they make the world a happier, safer place.

SIGN ME UP!
https://dl.bookfunnel.com/et9yw1y0qw

Click or copy the link to join the Loch Lonach Community.

Incarnadine

Loch Lonach
Book Five

TM

DEDICATION

This work, the fifth in the series, is dedicated to the champions of justice, the foundation of all civilized behavior, for without justice, there can be no mercy.

In addition, I wish to thank:
- The Firewheel Fictionistas Writers' Group for their continued support and assistance
- Members of the Scottish community here and across the world who have given generously of their time and encouragement
- My content experts, beta readers, and ARC team
- My long-suffering editor and brainstorming partner, Mary Foster Hutchinson, without whom none of these books would have been possible

ACKNOWLEDGMENTS

The Mackenzie Dress Clan Tartan is listed as WR1981 on the Scottish Tartans World Register.

The quote, "Be careful what you wish for," is attributed to Aesop's Fables (c. 260 A.D.), but may be even older.

Macbeth was written by William Shakespeare and is quoted here numerous times. Many thanks to the Bard of Avon for his keen insight into human nature.

"Good fences make good neighbors" is a line in Robert Frost's *Mending Wall* published in *The Poetry of Robert Frost* by Robert Frost. However, the origin of the sentiment, that clear legal boundaries reduce contention between neighbors, is ancient.

"Bread and circuses" is attributed to Juvenal, a Roman poet active in the late first and early second century A.D.

The quote, "I'm a politician, which means I'm a cheat and a liar, and when I'm not kissing babies I'm stealing their lollipops," is from *The Hunt for Red October*, Paramount 1990.

The proverb, "The enemy of my enemy is my friend," is attributed to a Sanskrit text dated to the fourth century B.C.

The phrase, "Sumer is icumen in" is from the *Cuckoo Song*, written in Middle English and put down on parchment sometime during the mid-thirteenth century.

Apologies to Rudyard Kipling for mangling the first line of his poem, *If*.

The prayer, *The Only Son of a Southern Mother*, was handed down in my family and is, as of this writing, untraced.

All three of the epitaphs exist on old Scottish tombstones and the compilations and reproductions are in the public domain.

The candlestick referred to in this text and depicted on the cover exists. It is located in the Metropolitan Museum of Art in New York City, NY, Accession Number: 13.135.2a. To the best of my knowledge, it has never been used as a murder weapon.

SCOTTISH DIALECT

Some of the characters in this series speak with a broad Scots accent.

- For those with paperback or hardback copies, you will find a GLOSSARY at the end of the book.

- For those with ePub versions, hovering over an unfamiliar term usually brings up a dictionary with translations and explanations.

- For those with an audiobook, there is a comprehensive GLOSSARY on the website: https://www.maggiesmysteries.com/glossary

PR UNCIAL FONT

The Celtic font used on the covers, in the titles, and for the chapter headings in this series is PR Uncial, created by Peter Rempel. It has been a continuing source of delight throughout this endeavor and I am happy to have this opportunity to tell him so. It is free for personal use. You can download it here: https://www.dafont.com/pr-uncial.font

INSTALLING PR UNCIAL

Starting in 2018, Amazon released an update to its Kindle e-readers allowing the user to install custom fonts. Here is the link to the article with instructions on how to do that:
https://the-digital-reader.com/2019/01/02/how-to-use-kindles-new-custom-font-feature/

For Kobo e-readers, the instructions are here:
https://goodereader.com/blog/e-book-news/how-to-add-custom-fonts-to-your-kobo-e-reader

DISCLAIMER:

Dear Readers:

This is a work of fiction. That means it is full of lies, half-truths, mistakes, and opinions. Any resemblance to any actual person, living or dead, is unintended and purely coincidental.

Similarly, the businesses, organizations, and political bodies are mere figments of the author's overactive imagination and are not in any way intended to represent any actual business, organization, group, etc.

Some of the locations mentioned actually exist, but the reader is warned that the author has re-shaped Heaven and Earth and all the mysteries of God to suit herself and begs the reader, for the sake of the story, to overlook any discrepancies in fact.

Incarnadine

Loch Lonach Scottish Mystery Series
Book Five

by Maggie Foster

"Will all great Neptune's ocean wash this blood
Clean from my hand? No, this my hand will rather
The multitudinous seas incarnadine,
Making the green one red."

Macbeth, Act 2, Scene 2
William Shakespeare

Cover design by M. Hollis Hutchinson

Foster, Maggie.
    Incarnadine: Loch Lonach mysteries, book five / Maggie Foster

ISBN (pbk)
    ISBN-13: 978-0-9989858-8-6

ISBN (epub)
    ISBN-13: 978-0-9989858-9-3

Fonts used by permission/license. For sources, please visit lochlonach.com

NEMESIS

Whose name means "to give what is due."
For thousands of years, goddess of justice. Still her whips
she wields.

Colonel Mustard, in the Conservatory, with a Candlestick

CAST OF CHARACTERS

Ginny Mackenzie	An ICU nurse
Jim Mackenzie	An Emergency Room physician
Angus Mackenzie ("Himself")	The Laird of Loch Lonach, Jim's grandfather
Ian Hunter	A state senator from Texas
Maury Patterson	A state senator from Illinois
Rita Patterson	Patterson's third wife
Lorenzo Scala	An investigative reporter
Patsy Olafsson	An old woman with a secret
Hue Tran	Dallas Police liaison to the clan

Loch Lonach is a Scottish community established before Texas became a Republic in the geographic region that would become Dallas. It has retained its culture and identity. Loch Lonach boasts its own schools, police force, churches, and other civic institutions. The head of the community is the Laird, currently Angus Mackenzie.

CΠΛΡΤΕR 1

Tuesday Morning
Mackenzie residence

Newlywed Ginny Mackenzie had promised her brand-new husband, promised him faithfully, that she would do her *very best* to give up murder. So far, so good. It was Day Two of their new life together and not a body in sight. There should have been one, of course. She rolled over and reached for him, finding his side of the bed warm, but empty.

There was no reason for her eyes to fly open or for her to sit up suddenly or for her throat to close. He couldn't be far.

She slid out of bed and into her robe, her ears pricked to the sounds coming from the back of the house. Voices—tense and angry, one step below violence.

She found him in the den, his arms stretched along the back of the sofa, watching the morning news. It was an odd side effect, she thought, of getting one's heart's desire to find that, even in sleep, one was terrified of losing it.

She took a deep breath, then padded up behind him, slid her arms around his neck, and bent to his ear.

"Gracious husband," she breathed, "and source of all earthly delight, I beg thee, of thy bountiful mercy, to silence that pestilential machine."

He grinned at her over his shoulder. "Oh thou love of my

life, and fount of all wedded bliss, your wish is my command!" He reached for the remote and turned off the program, plunging the room into peace.

"I thank thee, kind sir!" She bent to kiss his cheek, but didn't get the chance. He twisted around, put his hands on her waist, and somersaulted her over the back of the sofa onto his lap.

"Good morning, wife!"

They had been married for slightly under forty-eight hours. As neither had any vacation days available, instead of a honeymoon, they were getting used to their new furniture. Jim wrapped his arms around her.

"You don't have to listen, you know. You can ignore it."

She fought down a shudder. "It's not that easy. Rioting and arson in south Dallas is too close to home." Much too close.

"True, but you're safe here. Grandfather would never allow such bad behavior on Homestead property."

Ginny laughed. "An autocrat of the old school."

"It's a good thing he likes us. Imagine what a tyrant he could be if he didn't."

Ginny wrinkled her nose. "I don't want anything spoiling our honeymoon, not even your grandfather!"

Jim sighed. "Too late! I'm summoned to a meeting and he said it was urgent. Can you find something to do to amuse yourself for a couple of hours?"

Her lips curved in a mischievous smile. "I might be able to, if I put my mind to it."

His smile matched hers. "What are you up to, wench?"

There were lots of possible answers to that question. She had a home to make for him and the care of him, and her new job at the hospital, training ICU preceptors. Also, as soon as they settled into a routine, she would begin her own training for the job of Homestead Matron. When Jim became Laird, she would be his good right arm, running the distaff side of the massive undertaking that was the Loch Lonach Homestead. And she had other, equally important duties to perform.

"Opening and recording wedding presents, in preparation for writing thank you notes—the ones that haven't been done already. Mother and Caroline are coming over to assist with what I hope will be the last of them. Also I have agreed to help poor Mrs. Olafsson set up her genealogy files. I was supposed to get it done before the wedding, but that pesky corpse interfered."

Jim's brow furrowed. "How is she doing? Mrs. Olafsson, I mean." As a precaution, and because Jim was an Emergency Room physician, his grandfather kept him abreast of situations that might arise in the community.

"I'll know more after I see her." Ginny grew stern. "But don't let Himself keep you too long. I have something special planned for dinner."

Jim's eyes lit up. "I'll be there, and probably early. Unless you want me out of your hair?"

She dimpled. "Not just yet. I still have a use for you."

His smile grew wider. "And I for you." He bent to kiss her again.

Ginny felt a warm glow spread through her body. All the old, empty words had taken on new meaning in his arms. She had been afraid of him, at first. Now she was afraid for him, because she could no longer live without him. She hugged him tightly, then pushed herself to her feet.

"Breakfast first. What time is your meeting?" She held onto his hands, not wanting to let go completely.

"Noon."

"Perfect." She led him away to the kitchen.

* * *

Breakfast over and coffee in hand, Ginny surveyed the mess. Every surface in the house was covered with wrapping paper and ribbon. She hadn't really considered how many people would be affected by her marriage to the heir of the Loch Lonach Homestead.

Loch Lonach was only one point in the network that linked the Scots throughout the North American continent. Fully half of the Homesteads had sent a representative to her nuptials. Many had been strangers, but she'd been delighted to see friends as well, including both of the Gordons, and Mrs. Lauder. Those who could not send a human representative, had sent a tribute. All had to be acknowledged.

Not all the presents were from officials. Ginny'd had no trouble identifying the source of one of the gifts—a fishing lure adorned with a plastic toy giving her a very sly wink. The lure was for Jim. The wink was for her.

She smiled at the memory, then answered the doorbell, opening to her mother with Caroline just behind her.

"Come in!"

Ginny wrapped her mother in a big hug, then relinquished her hold to allow her husband to do the same. Sinia Forbes took it in stride, giving them both a kiss. She smiled at her daughter. "Happy, dear?"

"Delirious! I'm the luckiest woman on the face of the planet! I have the best husband, and I'm going to have a perfect life!"

Both of the other women started laughing.

"Not likely," Caroline said. "Not with your record."

"Oh, but I've reformed!" Ginny said. "No more bodies, except at work, and as few there as I can manage."

"Even if you aren't presented with any more murders," her mother warned, "there will be other challenges. Married life is full of them."

"I know." Ginny steered the group into the kitchen. "Plumbing breaks. Children get sick. I get it. I'm just not going to let it upset me!" She was pouring coffee and handing the cream around when the doorbell rang again.

This time Jim went to answer it, returning with another gift. "Where did that one come from?" Ginny asked.

He set it on the kitchen table. "Jean just dropped it off. She said it was found in the corner of the Cooperative Hall."

Ginny looked at the attached gift tag, her brow furrowing. "It's addressed to Ginny Forbes. Why would anyone use my maiden name on a wedding present?" The other three peered over her shoulder at the oddity.

"It would be unusual," her mother said.

Caroline reached around and turned over the tag. "There's no name. I wonder who sent it."

"Maybe there's a card inside." Jim proceeded to unwrap the package. The box that emerged was another oddity. Instead of a shimmering cube of white, it was a heavy-duty brown cardboard container, stuffed with packing material. He pulled the wadding out, looking for an envelope, but found none. At the bottom of the box, shrouded in plain white tissue, was an object—heavy, and of a vaguely familiar size and shape. He handed it to Ginny. She was required to tear the tissue and it took her a minute to peel enough of the wrapping away so they could see what was inside.

"It's a candlestick."

They all stared at the gift.

"Is it supposed to be black?" Caroline asked.

"No." Ginny shook her head. "It's silver. Very old silver."

"Is there another?" Mrs. Forbes asked. "Candlesticks usually come in pairs."

Jim checked the box, then shook his head. "Just the one."

"Who would send a bride a dirty old piece of silver?"

Caroline asked. "And only half a set at that?"

Ginny frowned. "That's a very good question." She lifted the candlestick, holding it by the tissue to keep from getting the tarnish on her hands, and looked at it closely. "It has lovely lines. Seventeenth century, I think. It's too ornate to be earlier. I wonder if it's marked." The symbols pressed into the finished product could tell the material used, the geographic area of origin, and sometimes the individual maker's name.

Ginny took the candlestick over to the sink and set it on the counter then hunted up some silver polish.

"Don't tell me you're going to clean that thing," Caroline said.

"Not just yet. What I'm looking for is information." Ginny dipped the sponge in the silver polish and gently applied it to the base. "Candlesticks are typically marked along the edge, so as not to interfere with the design." She drew the sponge across the surface, then began to rub. The tarnish came off, revealing a series of tiny impressions in the silver.

Ginny peered at them. "I don't recognize these." She got her phone out and took several careful pictures, then examined the images, enlarging them to show more detail. "They're not English. If I had to guess, I'd say French."

Mrs. Forbes' eyebrows rose. "French! If so, and it's genuine, it's valuable. Most French silver was melted down to replenish the state coffers. Not much survived."

Ginny nodded. "That might explain why there's only one."

"But not why it's black."

Ginny looked up and smiled at Caroline. "Silver tarnishes if it's not protected, and it's hard work to clean it. I often find silver in the antiques stores in this condition."

"And she's a miracle worker when it comes to polishing them," her mother added. "No tarnish left behind!"

Ginny protested. "That's not true and you know it!" She

turned the candlestick and rubbed gently along the next edge, hoping to find more marks. "The more intricate the design," she explained to Caroline, "the more difficult it is to get the cracks and crevices clean. So it's both accepted and a mark of authenticity to see an old piece with black lines edging the design."

"What's that?" Caroline asked, pointing at the sponge.

Ginny glanced down, then stopped, staring at the pad. She expected to see brown, the dust of ages being removed, and black, the corrosion that comes with oxidation, but she did not expect red. She looked more closely. Not bright red, a dull rust color. She frowned.

"Maybe there was something spilled on the candlestick." She rinsed the sponge and dabbed at the spot. It came away red again. She looked up into her husband's face. His mouth was shut, but his eyes were dancing. She set the candlestick down and went into the master bathroom, returning with a bottle of hydrogen peroxide. "Let's try this."

She pulled a clean paper towel off the roll and wet it with the peroxide, then touched the sponge. It foamed.

She looked up and found Caroline's eyes wide, her mother's narrowed, Jim's speculative.

"Is it blood?" Caroline's voice was hushed.

Mrs. Forbes answered her. "Not necessarily. It will have to be properly tested."

Ginny nodded, then blotted the candlestick dry and wrapped it back up in its tissue paper. "I'm going to put this back in the box."

The other three watched as she repacked the candlestick, then Jim took the parcel into the living room and set it aside. He returned to the kitchen and gathered up his keys, a smile still playing at the corner of his mouth. "I'm off. I have a couple of errands I want to do before the meeting starts."

Ginny accompanied him to the garage, her brow furrowed.

"Jim, I'm sorry—" She started to apologize, but he pulled her into his arms and kissed her, grinning.

"Don't worry, my love. I won't hold this against you."

She shook her head. "It's a good thing you were here when the package arrived."

He climbed into his car, still smiling. "One thing about marrying you—I'm not going to be bored."

"Give my love to Angus." She waved as he pulled out, watched until the garage door closed, then led her guests to the living room.

All three women sat down and stared at one another. Mrs. Forbes broke the silence.

"It's probably nothing. Old silver always comes with a history, and we don't know where this piece has been."

"The police lab will tell us what it is," Caroline said.

"If they're willing to waste time on it," Ginny said.

"Why wouldn't they? It's blood on a wedding present! Aren't you curious how it got there?" Caroline almost bounced in her chair.

"Someone may have cut her finger and bled on it."

"And not wiped it off? Who would do that?"

"It may be jam or paint or something else organic, not blood. Or not human blood."

"Maybe," Caroline said. "But that candlestick would make a good murder weapon!"

Ginny frowned. "Even if you're right and it's human blood, it's not recent. The red didn't show up until *after* I'd cleared away the dirt and tarnish."

"So it's a cold case!" Caroline's eye were shining. "Someone wants you to solve a cold case that the police couldn't!"

"Don't be silly! The police aren't fools! It's obvious they never saw this candlestick!"

Caroline went over to the box, picked up the tag, and held it out toward Ginny. "She used your maiden name. Everyone knows Ginny Forbes has solved four murders."

Three. The fourth hadn't needed solving. "How do you know it's a woman?"

Caroline blinked, then looked down at the tag. "From her handwriting, I guess. Though I could be wrong. But it doesn't matter. The point is you've been sent the murder weapon in a cold case as a wedding present! The media is going to have a field day. Imagine the headlines! *Laird-to-be's new wife sees red!*"

"You wouldn't dare!" Ginny felt the blood draining from her face.

"Caroline, that would be neither kind nor wise." Mrs. Forbes was frowning and Ginny knew that quiet comment covered the sound of a serious warning.

Caroline put the tag back in the package, sighing. "All right. I won't tell anyone, but you have to admit it would be a great story."

Ginny relaxed a bit. "Maybe so, but let's see if there's any reason to be worried before we go public."

Mrs. Forbes picked up a clipboard and lifted an eyebrow at Caroline. "Shall we get to work?"

Caroline grinned, not the least bit discouraged. She turned to Ginny. "I will work, but only if you promise to let me know what you find out."

"I promise. You'll be the fourth person I tell."

"Fourth? Who before me?"

"Jim, Himself, and my mother, in that order."

"Oh." Caroline nodded. "I guess I can live with that."

It took them two hours to list the remaining gifts and address the envelopes then Ginny glanced at the clock.

"Thank you both for your help. My husband and I would like

to invite you to come to dinner one day next week so Jim can show off his wife's cooking, but for the moment, I have an appointment at the library." She saw Caroline out the door, then turned to her mother. "I promised Mrs. Olafsson I'd help with her genealogy. I'll drop the candlestick at the police station on my way over."

"That sounds like a good idea."

They looked at each other in silence for a long moment, then Ginny shrugged. "It's probably nothing and—even if it is—I don't have to do anything about it. I can still keep my promise to Jim."

Her mother held out her arms and Ginny gratefully accepted a hug and a kiss. "It's a bit early to worry about what may or may not come of this."

Ginny nodded, then let her mother out. She gathered up the materials she would need at the library, then went to collect the unwelcome wedding present. She hefted the box thinking it seemed heavier than it had on arrival, as if it had taken on more importance while it sat in her kitchen.

She shook off the impression, telling herself not to be a fool. Things like that only happened in fiction. This was her real life, her true and genuine and happily ever after with Jim life and she wasn't going to let any old candlestick ruin it! She tucked the box firmly under her arm, locked the door, and headed out.

* * *

CRAPTER 2

Tuesday Afternoon
Dallas Genealogy Library

The old woman was waiting on the bench outside the entrance to the genealogy section of the Public Library. Ginny smiled in greeting, then walked over and offered her hand to help the old lady to her feet.

"Good afternoon. How are you today?" Mrs. Olafsson was suffering from metastatic breast cancer. She had good days and bad days. On a bad day, an effort of this sort, coming down to the library, would have been impossible.

"Good, thank you." Mrs. Olafsson reached over and patted Ginny's hand. "You're such a sweet child. You always ask as if you mean it."

"Of course! What's the point of asking a question if you aren't willing to hear the answer? Let's set up over here." Ginny guided her charge to a computer desk, made sure her pupil was comfortable, helped her locate her glasses, and opened the genealogy program.

"What we're going to do today is set up a family group file. You'll add to it as we go along. The software we're going to use was created by a genealogist specifically for this purpose, so it's pretty user-friendly."

Ginny followed her words with action, creating a new

database, giving it a title they could both remember, then pulling up the family group sheet for the primary researcher.

"This is where you put in information about yourself. You start with the name you were given at birth." She showed Mrs. Olafsson how to position the cursor and watched as she typed in her name and birthdate. *Patsy Bryant. 17 March 1951.*

"Patsy. Is that what the birth certificate says?"

The old woman shook her head. "No. My real name is Martha. Patsy's just a nickname."

"We want this database to match the documents, so let's put Martha in front and put parentheses around Patsy. That will make it clear to everyone that you had a nickname."

"Why is it asking me for a source?" Mrs. O. asked.

"Because it assumes that a newborn isn't capable of remembering her own birth, and that you got the information from someone else, usually a birth certificate."

Mrs. O. laughed. "Well, the machine is right. I don't remember being born."

Ginny smiled. "This is one of the most important principles of genealogy. We use witness testimony to establish the truth of whatever it is we're asserting, and we know from experience that people can make mistakes. So there are some rules. If the information is supplied by adults who were present at the time—actually there and paying attention—we usually believe them."

"What if they're lying?"

"There are some things we can do to test the veracity of the statements, but we'll leave that for another lesson. Did you bring your birth certificate with you?"

Mrs. Olafsson dug it out of her bag and handed it over. Ginny placed it on the scanner and made a digital image of the document, then showed Mrs. O. how to attach the image to her source file.

"Now you have a fact and a picture of the document you're using as proof."

Mrs. O. was peering at her birth certificate. "There's a lot of information on this."

"Yes, and we're going to use all of it. Here's where you type in your mother's name and here's where you'll put your father." They worked for twenty minutes in this manner, adding names, dates, and locations, then linking those bits of information to the image of the birth certificate.

Mrs. O. looked over at Ginny and smiled. "I had no idea I could do this!"

Ginny nodded. "Once you get all your information into the program, you can share it with other researchers. When you're ready, you can print a book right from the computer."

"You mean like the books I see here?"

"Yes, indeed!"

"What do we do next?" Mrs. O. asked.

"Your husband."

"He died a long time ago."

"Well this is one of the ways we can make sure no one forgets him." Between them, they pulled the raw data off her marriage license.

"What's this question?"

Ginny smothered a smile. "One of the possibilities is that a couple had children without being married to one another."

"You mean like adoption?"

"Well, that's one possibility. The database is flexible enough to cover all the ways a human being can come into existence, and all the ways we can link them into family groups. Did you have any children?"

Mrs. O. shook her head regretfully. "No, none of our own, and Hubert died before I could talk him into adopting. I wanted to, though. It got lonely at times."

Ginny nodded again. "Here is where you put the rest of Hubert's information." She walked Mrs. O. through adding the death record for her husband. "This field allows you to type in anything you want. I usually copy what's on the gravestone and any obituary I can find. Every word matters so I always put it all down, exactly as it appears, mistakes included."

Mrs. O. typed diligently, then sat back and sighed. "He was a good man. Strong and brave and handsome." She turned to Ginny and smiled. "I hope you and Dr. Mackenzie will be as happy as we were."

Ginny felt a tiny thrill at the thought of her future. "Thank you. I hope so, too." She walked Mrs. O. through the steps for recording data and the source documents for each of the bits of information, including short biographies for herself, her husband, and her parents.

"It's asking me if I had another set of parents."

Ginny reached over and chose the correct setting from the drop-down menu. "Remember I said it was flexible. It allows for deaths and divorces and second marriages. It's a little harder to manage, but you could also put blended families in, those made up of several families all living together. The thing you have to remember is to always tell the truth. If there is a child born out of wedlock, for instance, you put in the biologic parents, then link them to the adoptive parents using the option provided. No one is judging. In genealogy all we care about is the truth."

"That's very high-minded of you."

Ginny shrugged. "People aren't perfect, and some of the stories are fascinating. It took me many years, but I finally found a horse thief among my ancestors! "

"My goodness! How did you find out about him?"

"You read everything, legal documents and histories of the area, family letters, and local newspapers. Anything you can find. One day the missing piece fell into my lap and I was able to follow the thread and figure it out."

"How exciting!" Mrs. O.'s smile faded. "I won't have time for anything like that."

Ginny felt a stab in the region of her heart and hurried to soften the truth. "No genealogy is ever finished, and you're in a very exciting moment of your research since you're just getting started. It's all new and there's no telling what you may find!"

Ginny opened a browser window and navigated to a genealogy website. "This is an open source (that means free) site with a huge amount of information on it, most of it primary source documents. Those are the best since they were made at the time by the people who were present and had a reason to write it down." She typed in Mrs. O.'s maiden name and birthdate then hit the search button. The official birth record popped up at the top of the list. "Here you are, and here are your parents."

"That's right. That's what it says on my birth certificate."

"And that's what we're looking at. See? Here's a picture. This is the same document you have in your file. And here's the same information written down a little differently because this record was created after the fact. The farther you get from the event, the less you can rely on the documentation. That's why tombstones are not considered good sources of birth information, but they're excellent at recording death dates." Ginny scrolled down the list, looking for other examples of the public information genealogists use to build databases.

"Here's another birth record. This one is two years after you were born and it looks like a boy. This must be your brother."

Mrs. O.'s forehead wrinkled. "I don't have a brother."

Ginny looked from the old woman to the screen, then back again. "A sister?" The sex might have been recorded incorrectly.

"No. I was an only child."

Ginny frowned at the computer screen, then dug deeper, switching to the census records that would have covered Mrs. O.'s birth. Two children, a boy and a girl. "This looks like you. That's your name, right? And your parents? And the dates fit."

Mrs. O. peered at the screen, adjusting her glasses. "Well, it certainly looks like me, but I didn't have a brother."

Ginny went back to the birth records. Same parents, same name, same address. "Could you have had a brother who died, or who was raised by someone else?"

"I suppose it's possible, but I don't remember my mother ever mentioning another child."

"Well," Ginny said. "One of the things genealogists have to do is keep an open mind. Let's put this boy in your database and see if we can find out what happened to him."

"Okay." Mrs. O. typed in the data for the male child, and Ginny attached the images of the birth certificate and the census to the source links.

"So I have a brother I never knew about?" Mrs. O. asked.

Ginny shrugged. "It looks like it." She smiled. "It's a bit surprising, but that's one of the things I love about genealogy. It gives me an outlet for my insatiable curiosity!"

* * *

CHAPTER 3

Tuesday Afternoon
Mackenzie Residence

When Jim got home, Ginny met him at the door, drink in hand. "Welcome home, darling!"

Jim smiled, taking the drink in one hand and his wife in the other. He kissed her swiftly, released her, then stood sipping the scotch, eyeing her expression. It was too soon to tell how sneaky she was going to prove to be, but he'd had a taste of it already. This was just the married version of the same behavior.

"Do I need softening up for some reason?"

"Heaven forefend! I just thought you might like a drink after a hard afternoon at the office. How was the council meeting?"

"Very interesting."

"I want to hear all about it, but you'll have to follow me into the kitchen. I'm cooking."

Jim settled down in one of the kitchen chairs and watched as she opened the oven and examined a large piece of meat.

"Are we expecting company?"

"Not tonight. I've promised to have everyone over next week, but I've already had to share you today." She closed the oven door and turned to face him. "I want some time alone with you."

Jim licked his lips. "When will the food be ready?"

"Quite soon. You have ten minutes to wash up."

Jim rose and crossed the room, coming up behind her and wrapping his arms around her waist. He bent down and planted a kiss on the side of her neck. "I don't have to go to work tonight."

Both of them were used to working the graveyard shift at the hospital, which meant the main meal of the day was timed for four-thirty in the afternoon, so they could be done, dressed, and at work by six-thirty.

She turned in his arms, smiling up at him. "Would you rather eat later?"

He considered his options, then shook his head. "No, I'd rather eat now and hear what you've been up to."

"All right. I'll get the plates."

When they had taken the edge off their appetites, she opened the conversation. "Tell me about the meeting."

Jim dabbed at his lips with the napkin. "Well, the first surprise was that most of the lairds who came to our wedding were present. Grandfather must have decided it was too good an opportunity to miss. We started with congratulations and toasts."

Ginny smiled. "And then?"

Jim sighed. It had been a sobering afternoon. "The discussion was mostly about security and how to strengthen it."

Ginny looked up from her plate. "Are we in danger?"

"The consensus seems to be, yes. Some of the lairds have received threats."

He watched her put down her fork, her eyes troubled. "What kind of threats?"

"Hate mail, graffiti, a dead animal tossed onto someone's lawn."

"Oh, Jim! That's awful!"

He nodded. "Most of the discussion was about what it will take to make a gated community out of each of the Homesteads."

Her eyes narrowed. "We have the Children's Wall."

This was a reference to a physical barrier, a rampart actually, that surrounded a large part of the core properties of the Loch Lonach Homestead. It was pierced by wide gates that could be closed at need. They never had been.

The practice of painting memorials for fallen veterans on the outside of the wall had begun after the First World War This continued, but the custom had expanded to include the children of the Homestead. Each made a pilgrimage to the Wall, to add his or her voice. The messages were typically of peace.

"Which puts us ahead of the game." Jim sighed. "Most of the Homesteads don't have anything to protect the residences, only the museums and living history sites. Anyone who wants to start a firestorm can."

Their new house, the one he and Ginny had been given as a wedding present, was not new. It was situated on a hill behind a lawn that sloped up to the foundation of the house. There were mature trees out front, positioned to allow an unobstructed view of the lake, and any visitor who might be approaching.

The original log cabin had been sited further up the hill, and the dwellings that had replaced it had been designed to protect the inhabitants from wild animals, weather, and the occasional unprincipled human.

Jim's grandfather had deepened the ditch out front, improving the drainage and leaving a channel no sane driver would try to breach in anything less than a military assault vehicle; upgraded the entrance and exit to the sweep drive, and the bottom of the stone steps that led to the front door with electronically controlled barriers; replaced the wrought iron fencing with taller, stronger, more deeply rooted decorative railing; and installed a state-of-the-art security system for the entire property. The back of the house had been similarly updated. Jim had not questioned the improvements at the time.

Ginny frowned. "Why would anyone want to attack us?"

"Jealously. Fear. Hatred."

Her eyes widened. "Why should anyone hate us?"

"Because we're different."

"But this country was founded on the idea that different cultures could live in peace, side by side."

"Unfortunately, some people don't want to live in peace. They want to wipe out anyone who is different from them."

Ginny's face was stricken. "Our Highland ancestors were burned out of their homes and sold into slavery. If that happens again, where are *we* supposed to go, the moon?"

Jim shook his head. "We don't have many options, but the vote today was against giving in to bullies. We'll stand our ground, and fight for our homes." He sighed. "If we have to, we'll retreat to the caverns and ride it out." He looked at her and smiled. "Don't start packing yet. It may not be necessary."

She nodded, still frowning. "You said there was a first surprise. That implies a second."

"You remember Ian Hunter?"

"Wally's father, yes."

"He's got someone opposing him for his state senate seat."

"That's not surprising. Who is it?"

"You may not know him, but he's one of us. I mean, one of the Loch Lonach Homesteaders."

He saw his wife smile. "It's okay, Jim. You were born here, and you're here now. You can include yourself."

Jim rubbed the back of his neck. His time away from Texas had left a mark and he was being careful not to presume his return was universally welcome.

"It's Maury Patterson."

Ginny's eyebrows rose. "Didn't they just bury old Mrs. Patterson, about a week ago?"

"Yes. He's been living in Illinois, but he came back for the funeral, and he's inherited the house."

"Oh! Let me guess. He's moving home."

Jim nodded. "And wants to continue his political career. He was a state senator in Illinois. It's a lateral move for him."

"If he can win the seat."

Jim made a face. "He's running on the *Bread and Circuses* ticket, promising everything to anyone who wants to live well without having to work for it."

"That doesn't sound like Homestead."

"Grandfather seemed very put out."

"Were there any other surprises?"

Jim shook his head. "Not that concern us." He smiled at her across the table. "As a matter of fact, I was dismissed and sent home to my wife, to do my duty by her." He caught her eye, and Jim was tickled to see the color rising in her cheeks. "Your turn," he said. "How is Mrs. Olafsson?"

"We had a pretty good day, but there was a surprise there, too. We found a birth record for a brother she didn't remember. Apparently, he died as a child. I suppose she might be losing her memory, from the cancer, or the chemo, or some other form of dementia."

"It's possible."

"But it seemed strange to me. Surely her parents would have mentioned a dead brother at some point."

"People do funny things, to protect themselves, including pretending a dead child never happened."

"Maybe her mother did all the usual things to remember a lost child, but Mrs. Olafsson suppressed the whole thing. Maybe she was jealous of her brother. Either way, whether her mother did the suppressing or Mrs. O. somehow forgot to remember, it's suspicious."

The corner of Jim's mouth curved up slightly. "Am I going to have to share you with Mrs. Olafsson during our honeymoon?"

Ginny's face cleared. "No. We're booked for a family dinner with Sandy on Wednesday evening, but the rest of the clan will have to wait."

"We, huh?"

She dimpled. "Yes, my love. Alex isn't in town often and this is an opportunity for you to get to know him better."

Jim rose and helped clear away the meal, then leaned up against the counter while she filled the dishwasher. "And the candlestick?"

"I dropped it by the police station on my way to the library, with a note to Detective Tran telling her the circumstances, and that I was washing my hands of the whole affair."

Jim burst out laughing, caught his wife as she went by, pulled her to him, and kissed her. "Aren't you even a little bit curious?"

She wrapped her arms around his neck. "Well, of course, but I expect Tran will let us know what she finds. It's none of my business, anyway."

"None of your business? You're sure of that?"

She smiled up at him. "I've got the Homestead, my job, and a husband to train. I don't need any more trouble. The police can have it."

* * *

CHAPTER 4

Wednesday morning
Loch Lonach

Early the next morning, Jim rolled over and stretched, delighting in his health and youth and the warm bundle beside him. He had no trouble sleeping, day or night, on a featherbed or the floor. This day he woke rested and eager to begin his third day of married life.

He went up on one elbow, and looked down at his still-sleeping wife. She lay curled on her side, one hand tucked under her pillow. Her cheeks were flushed with sleep, her lips rosy, her cute little nose white beneath its dusting of pale freckles. The Nordic bloodline showed also in the red-gold braid that followed the line of her shoulder, falling across the blanket, then cascading onto the mattress, while the fuzzy tendrils of new growth that framed her face glowed in the first light. She was lovely to look upon and Jim's heart swelled within him.

Much as he hated to wake her, he had a treat planned. An early bird treat. He bent down and kissed her cheek, murmuring to her, rousing her gently from slumber. She was not a morning person, but there would have to be some accommodations made in light of the change in her status. He promised himself he would make sure she got enough sleep, just not right this minute.

"Wake up, my love. We have places to go and people to see."

She sighed, then stretched, her eyes still closed, but it was enough. Jim leaned down and kissed her, gratified to see a smile appear, followed by drowsy eyes opening to his voice.

"Wake, my love," he said, "and rise. We've got a date with a horse."

She nodded. "I'll be right there." She closed her eyes and rolled over, snuggling into the bed linens.

"Nope. Now." Jim pulled back the covers, exposing her to the cool air in the room. She protested, but sat up, rubbing her face.

"I'll start the coffee. You get dressed," he said.

Jim rolled off the bed and into his riding clothes. He was just dishing up the scrambled eggs and bacon when she appeared, dressed and ready to go. The two of them ate swiftly, leaving the dishes in the sink, and hurried out to keep their appointment.

It wasn't far. The stables were on the north side of the loch. The sun hung just above the eastern horizon, throwing golden streamers across the lawns. The sky was still pale from the night, but growing bluer with each passing minute. There were fluffy white clouds scudding across the face of the heavens, promising a cool breeze to whisk away any early summer heat. Ginny rolled down her window and stuck her nose out, breathing in the air.

"What a beautiful morning!"

Jim nodded, then turned onto a private drive, parked, and came around to hold her door open for her. The proprietor was already approaching, two saddled horses in tow.

"Good morning."

"Indeed it is!" Jim settled his ball cap on his head, feeling out of uniform without a Stetson, and shook the owner's hand. "This here's Lulabelle. The stallion is Rhombus."

Jim looked at the mounts. Both appeared well-bred and well rested. Combine that with the fresh breeze and they were likely to have a frisky outing. He'd ridden before, as all good Texas children do, and at camp in Virginia. He had the basics and a bit more.

Ginny had shown nothing but enthusiasm for the idea when he'd suggested it, claiming proficiency and a love of horseflesh. She projected self-confidence. Cockiness, even. He looked forward to seeing what she could do.

The proprietor gave Ginny a leg up and watched with approval as she gathered in the reins. He adjusted her stirrups, checked the girth on her mount, then turned to Jim and did the same for him. When he was satisfied, he pointed along the back fence. "The trail starts on the other side of the road. It's well marked and dry at the moment. You shouldn't have any trouble." He pulled the gate open and looked for traffic before stepping aside. "I assume you have your phones with you." Both of them nodded. "All right, kids. Have fun!"

Jim turned his horse's nose in the direction of the woods and headed out, Ginny following. She looked back over her shoulder. "He's not coming with us?"

"Nope. It's just you and me for a couple of hours." He smiled at her expression. It was a tremendous compliment to be allowed to take another man's horse out without supervision and she recognized the implication.

"Pulled some strings, did you?"

"I know a man."

She laughed out loud, coming up beside him. "Daddy, I want a pony for my birthday!"

He grinned. "No paddock at the house."

"Darn! Well, I guess I'll just have to make this do!"

She trotted forward. The trail wound its way through meadow at this point. He watched as she urged her mare into a canter, then left the trail, turning a wide circle through the tall weeds, startling a pocket of butterflies and kicking up dust behind her.

"Whee!"

In her gingham shirt and faded jeans, scuffed boots and battered straw hat, she could have passed for a barrel racer at the Stock Show. She cooed to her mare, then urged her into a full-out sprint to the end of the meadow and back.

Jim held his mount still, watching her. The exercise brightened her checks and sparkled in her eyes. The braid flying out behind made her look young, a teenager, rather than the mature professional she was. She was laughing, grinning, and Jim could not have been happier.

She trotted up to fall in beside him, reining in her exuberance and her equine companion in plenty of time to enter the shaded woods at a decorous walk.

The animals paced through the woods, familiar with the route and undisturbed by the shimmering brook that appeared on their left. It was still running full. Later in the season, it would be a series of shallow pools. At the moment, Jim could see carp rising to snatch the insects resting on the surface of the water.

The canopy of leaves moved in the air above them, too thick for much sun to penetrate, but what light did make it through was the color of clover. Every now and then, there would be a gust of wind and the top branches would sway, letting shafts of sunlight fall momentarily on the earth and riders.

It was quiet in this refuge, but not silent. There were birds calling to one another, and the sound of the water in the middle distance, and the whispering wind in the tops of the trees, far enough away to be another world, close enough for a benediction.

Jim breathed deeply, letting the horse lead the way. It was soul-restoring out here, with just himself and nature and the one companion he wanted in all the world. She had paused to look at the water. When she turned back, she smiled, and Jim felt his heart sing. Now, *this* was what a honeymoon should feel like.

They had seen no one since leaving the roadway. He dismounted, led his horse over to an oak, and tied it to a low hanging bough. When Ginny caught up with him, he took her reins, did the same for her mare, then caught her as she dismounted. He set her gently on the ground, then turned and headed up the path, his arm around her waist.

"Let's walk a bit."

She leaned into him and tried to match his stride, giggling when he lengthened it and she had to be hauled along to keep up. He stopped abruptly and pulled her into a kiss.

"I adore you, Mrs. Mackenzie."

She returned the salute with enthusiasm. "And I, you, Dr. Mackenzie." She smiled up at him, then put her head down on his shoulder, breathing deeply. "This was a wonderful idea! Thank you!"

"It's my pleasure." .

"How long do we have the horses for?"

He consulted his watch. "Another hour. Let's ride to the top of the hill and see what's on the other side, then head back."

They remounted and followed the path, still going slow, savoring the morning.

"I'm having a ball," Ginny said. "But I'm going to be sore tomorrow. I can't remember the last time I was on a horse."

Jim smiled at her. "Most people don't know that you have to use your knees."

"And thighs."

Most people also thought Dallas was flat. They climbed the hill, emerging from the trees onto a vast sweep of prairie grasses, thoughtfully mown by the park department. They trotted across the field, then continued the climb to the summit, stopped, and looked around.

There were cliffs and ridges and valleys all over the area. From their vantage point, Jim could see down over a section of the watershed that fed the loch, then, turning, across the slope crowned with a carefully preserved patch of old growth hardwoods, then, turning again, the skyline of downtown, clearly visible, glittering in the sunlight. He could also see movement in the air above them. He shaded his eyes and looked up. Herons.

Loch Lonach was on the North American Flyway. They got migratory birds from all over the two continents. They also had swans and ducks and gulls who made their homes on the lake. The fishing was good and the water clean. The pioneers who had claimed this spot had chosen well. It was a lovely place to call home.

Something caught his eye and he turned to look again at the Dallas skyline. On the southern edge, black smoke was rising into the air in a billowing column. Too big to be a trash fire, and brush wouldn't be that color. A burning car looked like that, but wouldn't be so broad, or so tall. He watched it for a minute, trying to pinpoint the direction and estimate where it could be coming from, then pushed the puzzle aside.

"You ready to head back?" he asked.

She nodded. They rode back slowly, spinning out the hour, then turned the horses in and climbed back into the car. From there Jim took her for BBQ, then home to wash the horsey smell off.

He had promised her a nap and was as good as his word, stretching out on the bed and tucking her up against his heart.

She closed her eyes and yawned, relaxing into his arms, then drifting off to sleep. Jim bent down and kissed her, very gently. It had been a good morning, therapeutic, and neither one of them had anything on the calendar for the rest of the day. He pulled the cover over them, but didn't close his eyes.

He had turned on the news while she was in the shower. The column of smoke was on every channel. It was big, all right. Protestors had torched the oil refinery in southeast Dallas, citing 'green energy' concerns and ignoring the EPA's support of recycling used oil.

The experts were shaking their heads. The processing plant was a total loss and the fire would have to be allowed to burn itself out, spewing thick smoke over a wide swath of the area until it did, destroying air quality, jobs, and the associated tax base in the process.

Jim tried to recapture the peace of the morning, but it was gone, replaced by a growing fear that this incident would not be the last of its kind in Dallas.

There was historical precedent. There had always been too many people in the world willing to use force to get what they wanted, and not afraid to destroy lives in the process. Especially if they'd been told those lives were a threat to their own. *Good fences make good neighbors.*

The council was right. They needed walls and too many of the Homesteads hadn't seen this coming. Jim frowned and tried not to imagine what an armed mob could do to his new found happiness.

* * *

CҺAPTER 5

On Wednesday evening, there was a merry family group gathered around the Laird's table, with Mrs. Forbes cooking, assisted by her daughter, and the Laird pouring the whisky, assisted by his grandson. The true guests were the five Forbes family members visiting from Atlanta—Ginny's brother, Alex, his wife, Wendy, and their three sons, Alex, Jr. (six and one-half years old), John (coming up on his fifth birthday), and George (three and a half). Ginny couldn't help noticing that they were very close in age, and that there had been no more since George's appearance—not yet, anyway.

When Jim had bent down to whisper in her ear, "Why are you staring at the boys?" she had whispered back, "Just thinking ahead."

She'd done some thinking ahead already, having child-proofed Angus' den and laid in a variety of games for the older boys to play after dinner, while the adults caught up on family news. George was settled on the kitchen floor with age-appropriate (too big to swallow) building blocks and over-sized crayons that were guaranteed not to stain the floor if he ran off the page.

Jim was the curiosity, being the newest addition to the

family. When the visitors had finished interrogating their new brother-in-law, Ginny was required to fill in details of her adventure in New Orleans, suitably modified for young ears. She was astonished to find it was less than a week ago. So much had happened since.

"And what's this I hear about a murder weapon among the wedding presents?" Alex was grinning at her from across the table.

Ginny stared at him. "I'm going to have to strangle Caroline."

He shook his head. "Mother mentioned it."

Ginny gave her mother a withering look, then answered Alex's question. "I handed it over to the police, but it's probably a dead end."

"Hah! Caught you!"

Ginny was startled, then sheepish. She'd forgotten this particular game. Jim turned to look at Alex. "Caught her in what?"

"Subconscious punning. She's really bad about it. Half the time she doesn't even know she's done it." He was grinning. "We used to make her pay forfeits."

Jim was smiling, too. "I like that idea."

Ginny almost stuck her tongue out at him, then decided she was too old for that.

"There must be a story behind it, the candlestick, I mean," said Wendy.

Ginny shrugged. "We might be able to figure out who sent it, then ask them why, and why now. But that may be all we get. We'll just have to wait and see what the police find." She closed the door on the subject and turned the conversation to family matters.

While the men retired to the living room to talk sports, the women cleaned the kitchen, then followed the two older boys into the den, taking George with them. Sinia settled down with her grandsons, having been invited to join their game. Ginny hung back, feeling shy about her lack of maternal experience. She watched as Wendy settled George in a nest of small blankets on the floor at her feet, his thumb planted firmly in his mouth, marveling that anything as innocent-looking as that sleeping cherub could wreak the havoc a three-year-old can produce.

Wendy looked up, caught her eye, and patted the cushion beside her.

"You look as if you have questions."

Ginny flushed, then accepted the invitation. "I do."

"What do you want to know?"

Ginny was a nurse and she had reference books, but reading about something was not the same thing as going through it. "I want to know what it's like to be pregnant."

Wendy smiled. "Two ground rules. One, it's different for every woman and every pregnancy is different, so stay in touch with your obstetrician. And two, call me anytime. I'm still in the stay-at-home phase and will be happy to have an adult to talk to."

"Thank you!" Ginny took a deep breath and plunged in. An hour later, Alex stuck his head in the door and looked around.

"What are you two talking about?"

His wife smiled at him. "Souvenirs. The boys want cowboy boots and hats and six shooters."

"And I know just where to get them," Ginny volunteered. "Would tomorrow be a good day to go shopping?"

"Works for me," Wendy said.

"We'll all go. I need new boots."

"We'll all go where?" Jim asked, adding his head to the crush at the door.

"Boot shopping, which you don't need, having just

purchased a rather expensive pair of custom boots for yourself." Ginny smiled at her husband.

Jim nodded. "But I neglected to get a hat, so I do have a reason to go with you."

"You just don't want to be left behind."

He slid past Alex, settled down beside Ginny, threw his arm around her shoulders, and pulled her to him. "Absolutely right. This is my honeymoon and I don't want to miss a minute of it."

Alex snorted. "Some honeymoon! Here you are eating family dinners, and going shopping with small children, which is *not* supposed to happen on a honeymoon!"

They all laughed, but Ginny thought herself lucky to have affectionate family to eat with, and her own bed to sleep in.

There was nothing said of the danger to the Homesteads in front of the children, of course, and all three had to be taken away and put to bed soon after the arrangements for the next day had been completed, George, thoroughly asleep, carried to the car by his father.

Ginny waved goodbye from the door, then returned to the kitchen. The departure of the Atlanta contingent left the four of them free to talk for a bit longer, this time about Alex and his family and how well everyone looked.

When she and Jim took their leave, it was with a sense of deep contentment. She was sure she was right. Her married life would be a charmed one, full of love and happy times like this one. She slipped her hand into Jim's and his closed around hers. Home. She had a home of her own. And, if it came to it, that was something to fight for. But not tonight. She put the thought away and concentrated on not spilling the remainder of the apple pie onto the floor of the car.

* * *

Thursday morning
Boot store

Ginny was kneeling on the carpet of the boot emporium, surrounded by stacks of boxes, helping Wendy locate the right size for George. The bright lighting at the back of the store was doing a good job of displaying the options, but George was having trouble sitting still. Alex was talking to the clerk about John, and they seemed to be choosing between red or blue leather. Jim was shepherding Alex, Jr. through the hats, eliciting cheerful protests as he dropped adult-sized Stetsons onto Alex's head.

Wendy shook her head. "They're all going to grow out of them in six months. I don't know why we're doing this."

"For the fun of it, and the boots will last long enough to be hand-me-downs."

Wendy lifted an eyebrow. "We're going to need pictures."

Ginny nodded. "We can do that. It's a beautiful day. We'll grab lunch and have a picnic in the park." She shoved the boot in her hands onto George's left foot and rocked it back and forth, checking the toe space. "There! That should last for a while. And you can use double socks until he grows a bit more." She wasn't aware she was the object of a stranger's attention until she saw the expression on her sister-in-law's face. She turned, following Wendy's gaze.

The man who stood at her right shoulder was the picture of a Dallas businessman in the time of her grandfather, from his bolo neck tie to his silk vest, pocket watch, boots, and gray felt hat, which he raised when he addressed her.

"Good morning, Mrs. Mackenzie. I was grieved when I found myself unable to attend your nuptials. Allow me to offer you my wish for all possible happiness."

Ginny climbed to her feet, her social smile in place. As far as she knew, she'd never seen this man before. She had certainly not invited him to her wedding.

"Thank you, Mr.—"

"Senator Patterson." He shook her hand, then Wendy's, then extended his hand to George, who ducked behind his mother. "What a fine tyke! I see you're buying him boots. An excellent decision. Bring them up right, I always say."

The bonhomie rang false and Ginny was suddenly reminded of a line in one of her favorite movies. *"I'm a politician which means I'm a cheat and a liar, and when I'm not kissing babies I'm stealing their lollipops."* George's instincts seemed sound.

The Senator's eyes strayed from Ginny and she turned to find Jim approaching. He was in the process of handing off Alex to his father. That done, he came to stand beside Wendy, giving her an opportunity to excuse herself and join her husband, taking George with her. That left Jim and Ginny to face the intruder. Jim reached over and took Ginny's hand, his eyes on the Senator.

Ginny was delighted. Not only was Jim presenting a solid front, protecting his new family from outside interference, but he was doing it with her help. She wanted to hug him, but contented herself with squeezing his hand, and an introduction.

"Jim, you may already know Senator Patterson. He was just introducing himself to me."

Jim nodded. "I know of him, of course. Please accept our condolences on the loss of your mother."

"Thank you. She lived a long, full life, but it was time."

"I understand you'll be moving into the house. That must be quite a job, coming from Illinois."

The Senator waved his hand, brushing the trouble aside. "We'll manage. It's a good house for children."

Ginny's eyebrows rose ever so slightly. "Children?"

"My third wife and I have three, two girls and a boy." He looked around. "I'm here to buy a new hat. My wife says this one is too frivolous. She recommends black."

Jim nodded in the direction of the desk. "I'm sure one of the clerks will be happy to help you."

Ginny hurried to soften the dismissal. "It was so nice to run into you like this. Perhaps we'll meet again. In church, on Sunday?"

"It's possible." He tipped his gray felt again. "Good day to you, to both of you." He turned and headed for the front desk.

Ginny turned to Jim, her smile relaxing into something closer to a grin.

"So that's the man your grandfather mentioned. I'm delighted to have met him."

"As am I," Jim said. "Now, come help me decide on a hat so we can move this herd of cattle on to greener pastures."

He led her toward the Stetson section, where they found the Forbes family making final decisions about their purchases, assisted by a salesclerk dressed as a working cowboy (sans spurs).

It appeared he moonlighted at the rodeo and the boys were begging their parents to stay in Dallas long enough to attend the show. Their father shook his head. "I'm sorry, boys. I have to go back to work on Monday, which means we have one more night here, then the airplane ride home tomorrow."

"But we're going to have a picnic and you'll all be coming to the ceilidh tonight," Ginny said. "Just as soon as your father pays the ransom on your souvenirs."

Alex handed his credit card to the clerk, then smiled at his wife. "I remember my first pair of boots. I may still have them, somewhere."

Ginny laughed. "Have you checked Mother's attic?"

"No. I should do that this afternoon, though we don't have

space in our luggage to pack what we already have."

"If you find something you can't live without, we can ship it to you."

"It's a deal."

* * *

They reconvened at the lake armed with fried chicken, lots of napkins, and the camera. Ginny followed the children around the grass taking pictures as they held a mock gunfight at the O.K. Corral, and, in the case of the older boys, fell to the turf with regularity and realistic groans. She eyed her brother.

"Sign them up for theater classes when you get home."

"They're already enrolled at Stone Mountain," Wendy said, "but we can see what else is available."

Ginny finished her photoshoot and came over to join the grownups. Jim handed her a box of chicken fingers, with dipping sauce, a container of cole slaw, and a cup of iced tea.

Ginny sat on the picnic blanket, looking out at the surface of the lake as she ate, and decided she had never been more contented. Let the rest of the world worry. She was on her honeymoon. The cares of real life could wait.

Jim slid an arm around her waist, then bent down and whispered in her ear, "Do you still want children?"

She smiled up at him, her heart fluttering at the look in his eye. "Yes," she whispered back. "As long as they're yours."

* * *

CHAPTER 6

Friday morning
Mackenzie / Olafsson residences

The honeymoon was over for Ginny. Oh, not her besotted adoration of her husband, just the holidays devoted to getting to know one another. She pulled the door of the bedroom shut and left him alone.

It had been great fun seeing Alex and his family and she and Jim had stayed as long as they reasonably could yesterday, but they'd had to leave early to make sure Jim could get to work on time. He was still at work the next morning when Ginny and her mother collected the Atlanta contingent from the Homestead guest quarters and delivered them safely to the airport, with hugs and kisses all around.

Jim would continue to be assigned to the night shift until he'd served his first full year at Hillcrest. Ginny had fed him, and made sure he was dressed, and kissed him goodbye yesterday, as a good wife should, then let him go.

He'd called her just before eleven, to check in and wish her goodnight, and to let her know he was thinking of her. A nice gesture, but she'd be glad when he moved to day shift, so they would be able to settle into something more closely approaching normal life. In the meantime she had some late nights of her own to serve before her schedule would convert to daylight-only hours.

Knowing his schedule, she had made arrangements to visit Mrs. O. this morning, to help her get the genealogy set up on her home computer, so she could work on it without having to go to the library. Jim would sleep until midafternoon so this was a perfect opportunity to get that done.

Ginny wrote him a note, in case he woke and had forgotten where she was, then slipped out and drove over to the Olafsson house.

* * *

Mrs. O. sat in front of her computer, staring at the evidence Ginny was laying out before her. She shook her head repeatedly. "No. I don't recognize him. I don't remember that. I don't understand."

Ginny was being careful not to insist.

Mrs. O. swiveled her chair around and faced Ginny. "The death certificate says the dead boy had the same parents I did. That's proof."

Ginny nodded. "If we don't find any evidence to the contrary, yes."

"I feel terribly guilty, as if I've failed him somehow."

"These are just pieces of a puzzle. We may not have all of them and we may not be able to figure out what they mean. So, for the time being, we record them, and set aside worrying about them."

"This looks like I knew about him, before he died. I should remember." Mrs. O. caught Ginny's eye and held it. "I'm always forgetting things these days. Is there anything I can do to jog my memory?"

Ginny thought for a moment. "I don't suppose you have any scrapbooks?"

"This old house has rooms I haven't been in for decades. There's no telling what we might find."

"Well, let's start there." Ginny rose and helped Mrs. O. to her feet. Together they searched the bookcases and cupboards in every room, but found nothing to shed any light on the missing boy.

"Do you have an attic?"

"Yes. I keep Christmas decorations up there."

"Can you manage the stairs?"

Mrs. O. shook her head. "Not anymore. It's got one of those pull down stairs that take up the entire hallway. Even has railings, but my knees won't cooperate."

"Is it all right with you if I go up alone?"

"Of course, dear."

Ginny pulled the cord and the attic stairs descended smoothly, popping into place when she put her foot on the bottom tread.

"There's a light switch on the wall at the top. I'll make some tea while you look around."

Ginny's first impression when she reached the top of the staircase was of a deep, dim space, lit by an exceedingly dirty window in the gable at the far end. She hunted for the light switch and found it, but the bulb must have been as old as its owner. It burned out immediately and Ginny hurried to switch it off.

She waited patiently for her eyes to adjust to the feeble sunlight, then looked around. She'd been right about the size of the place. It stretched across the entire top floor, a vast retreat for the discards of a lifetime. The floor was solid planking, unvarnished, with a thick coat of dust that rose under her feet.

Ginny peered down at the floor, noticing footprints in the dust. She followed them to an old-fashioned steamer trunk, then lost them again in the gloom. The trunk's dust didn't appear to have been disturbed, but she opened it anyway, and carefully withdrew each item. Old clothes, including a Cub Scout uniform, a broken toy train, books for boys, accented with crayon marks, and a photo album.

Ginny returned all the other items to the trunk, then took the album and descended to the kitchen. She put the book down in front of Mrs. O. and sat down next to her.

"Those are my parents," the old woman said. "That's their wedding picture." She turned over the pages. "Here's Daddy in his uniform." World War Two vintage. "Here I am, in my mother's arms." An infant Christening photo. "The dress was silk, with Belgium lace." Mrs. O. smiled, then shook her head. "Mother used to talk about that dress, but I don't think I ever saw it, not to remember."

Ginny waited and watched. If the boy was there, it might jog Mrs. O's memory. It might also bring on a stroke.

Mrs. Olafsson turned over another page, then stopped, staring at a picture of a man and a woman, with two children, standing in front of a Christmas tree.

"That's me and that's my parents. And that must be my brother. What did you say his name was?"

"Tommy. Is that the only picture?"

Together they finished going through the album, finding pictures covering the boy's birth, baptism, toddlerhood, and pre-school years. There the record stopped. Not just pictures of the boy. All pictures. The remaining pages were empty.

Mrs. Olafsson closed the album and sat with her hands clasped upon it. "I don't understand," she said. "How could I have forgotten?"

Ginny sighed. "We protect ourselves from the tragedies of life as best we can." She hesitated. "I found footprints in the dust up in the attic. Did you go up there recently? Or did someone else?"

Mrs. O. shook her head. "I haven't been up there in years and I'm the only one who has access. Everyone else is dead."

Ginny lifted an eyebrow, a half-smile playing at the corner of her mouth. "Maybe your attic is haunted." She had meant it as a joke, but at the sight of Mrs. O's suddenly pale face she hurried to apologize. "I'm sorry! I didn't mean to upset you."

Mrs. O. was frowning. "You didn't, it's just that I remembered something."

"What did you remember?"

Mrs. O. took a breath, then faced Ginny. "You're far too young to understand, but things get a bit muddled as you grow old. You don't know if you've done what you were supposed to do, or just dreamed you've done it." She shook her head. "I'm all alone here. So either it's me, or my memory, or the Broonies." She smiled. "I have a lot more respect for those old stories now than I used to. The old wives tales, I mean."

Ginny nodded, unsure what to make of this confession. "Is there something specific going on?"

Mrs. O. shook her head. "Who can say? There are things that seem to move in the night. I find clothes on the floor as if someone pulled them off the hangers, and food gone from the refrigerator, when I was sure I hadn't eaten it. But then I'd find dirty dishes in the sink."

She frowned. "I know it's an imposition, dear, but do you suppose you could help me sort out which is fact and which is fiction? I'd feel better if I knew the truth."

Ginny sucked in a breath. "Of course I'll help you, in any way I can."

Mrs. O. smiled and patted Ginny's hand. "Thank you, dear. It's a great comfort to know you're looking out for me. And now, I'm sorry to do this to you, when you're being so kind about coming over and helping me, but I think I need to lie down."

Ginny nodded. She escorted Mrs. O. into her bedroom and helped her stretch out on the bed, then pulled a comforter over her. She was just straightening up from this task when her eye fell on the bedside table and the medication bottles that stood on it. She picked them up, looking through the collection. "Are you in pain?" she asked.

Mrs. Olafsson shook her head. "Just tired and a bit dizzy."

"From the stress, then. Just lie quietly for a bit. If it doesn't get better, we'll let someone know."

She slipped out of the room, collected the picture album from the kitchen table, took it into the library and set it down next to the computer. She turned the pages, studying each of the images. It fit. It was all here. The child had lived, and died, and everything having to do with him had been tucked away in that steamer trunk. The bereaved mother had done that.

But the pictures showed a boy and a girl old enough to remember one another. Even if her mother had denied Tommy's existence, little Patsy Bryant would have remembered. Even if the living child had been forbidden to speak of the dead one, she would have remembered. There was something else at work here.

Ginny peeked into the old woman's bedroom and watched for a while, to make sure she was all right, then let herself out. A faulty memory might be responsible for the missing food, or things moving around the house, but it didn't explain those footsteps in the dust. They were too big to have been made by Broonies.

* * *

Friday afternoon
Mackenzie residence

Ginny set the plates on the table, then settled down to dinner. Jim smiled at her.

"Several people asked about you last night. I told them what your plans were. I hope that was all right."

Ginny nodded. She was not going back to straight nights in the Medical ICU. There had been many changes as a result of losing the ICU Head Nurse and it had given Ginny an opportunity to suggest an experiment.

One of the continuing sources of dissatisfaction was the lack of support for newly hired nurses. Most didn't have enough experience to fit seamlessly into the ICU routines. Not without a mentor. Ginny had stepped up to the challenge of creating a training program, with schedules, homework, and oversight. For the rest of the month she would be interviewing potential mentors. Once the slots were filled, the training would begin.

"What did you do while I was asleep today?"

"Visited Mrs. Olafsson, remember?"

"I remember. Anything new?"

Ginny nodded. "The poor thing has been invaded by Broonies." She rolled the "r" to emphasize the Scottish origins of the beasties.

Jim laughed. "The little people are tearing her house apart at night?"

"Well, playing tricks on her anyway." Ginny described the symptoms.

"Sure sounds like Broonies. Anything else?"

"Yes. I found a photo album in a trunk with some boy's clothing and toys. The mother must have collected all his possessions, put them in the trunk, closed the lid, and turned her back on the memory."

Jim frowned. "That's not the most productive way to get over the death of a child."

"There was no sign of a boy child anywhere in that house. I would have expected Patsy to have at least one family portrait on the mantle." Ginny poked at the remnants of a scalloped potato, then set her fork down. "Jim, there's something else."

"What is it, my love?"

"I'm afraid I was rather rash today."

Jim gave her a stern look. "What did you do?"

"Mrs. O. asked for my help in sorting out what's going on with her."

"And you gave her your promise."

"Yes."

He sighed. "Well, I have to admit I'm a little curious myself. Will you promise to stay out of trouble, if I ask very nicely?"

Ginny felt a rush of warmth from the region of her heart. "I promise. Will you promise to waltz with me tonight, even though we're not supposed to book dances ahead of time?"

He laughed and she could see the crinkles at the corners of his eyes. "That's only for the balls and then only to make sure the hosts dance with the visitors." He crossed his arms on the table and leaned forward. "Besides, it doesn't apply to the waltz. The privilege of holding the loveliest woman in the room in his arms is reserved to the man who brought her."

Ginny could never remember afterward how she got from her chair into his arms, or how long she had been too busy to notice the passage of time, but eventually he spoke. "Time to get ready, my bonnie lass, or we'll be late to the ceilidh, and that would never do."

* * *

CHAPTER 7

Friday evening
Cooperative Hall

Jim poked his head around the doorframe. "What am I supposed to do with the cupcakes?"

"They're for the refreshment table tonight."

Jim shook his head. "Too much sugar on that table."

"Always! But we do burn a lot of calories, so maybe it's not so bad."

The Cooperative Hall where they met every Friday evening was a gymnasium-sized multi-use facility with up and downstairs, a stage, a kitchen, and storage for event equipment. It was kept cool year-round, to prevent heat prostration among the dancers, so there were racks for the on-again, off-again sweaters and jackets, many of them a permanent fixture, which gave the entrance a homey, lived-in look. Ancillary rooms were available for smaller gatherings, but most of the activity occurred on the sprung wood floor.

Ginny left the cupcakes with her mother, who was doing hostess duty, put on her dancing ghillies, and headed into the sets. They were just in time for *The Black Mountain Reel*, followed promptly by *Monymusk*, and *The Bees of Maggieknockater*.

During the first intermission, Angus mounted the steps to

the stage and took possession of the microphone. "Clansmen, may I ha'e yer attention, please?"

The hall fell silent, all eyes on the Laird.

"This nicht I tak' great pleasure in welcomin' hame ane o' our own. Chris was born here and grew up in Loch Lonach. He's been awa' many years, but ha'e decided tae come back and settle wi' us. He'll be fillin' a long-standin' vacancy an' I ask each o' ye tae help him feel welcome as he tak's up his duties. He comes tae us highly recommended an' I ha'e nae doubt tha' he'll prove a boon tae the clan. Please welcome Dr. Christopher Urquhart."

Ginny looked around, spotted her mother, and grabbed Jim's arm. "Come on." She hustled her husband over to the chairs and they sat down, one on either side of Sinia. "Did you know about this?" Ginny asked.

Her mother glanced at her. "Yes. Himself said he was bringing someone to the dancing tonight."

"A doctor. I wonder what kind," Ginny said.

"A psychiatrist," Jim answered. "And not just any psychiatrist. One of Greg Gordon's protégés."

"Oh!" Ginny smiled to herself. Perfect timing! Someone who could shake Patsy Olafsson's memories loose. She'd been worried about having to ask Dr. Gordon to come all the way back to Texas from upstate New York after he'd just been down here for the wedding. "I wonder if I can get close enough to have a word with him."

Her mother seemed interested, too. She was staring at the psychiatrist with a puzzled expression on her face.

Ginny's eyes flicked from her mother to the new arrival. "Born here. Grew up here. How old is he, do you think?"

Sinia Forbes' face changed—her eyes widened and her smile disappeared. She took a breath, then answered. "Old enough to be your father!" She looked from her daughter to her son-in-law and made shooing motions. "Go. Dance. We can talk later."

Ginny followed Jim back out onto the floor, her mind on her mother's expression.

"Did you hear? Old enough to be my father! And did you see the way she changed color?"

Jim was smiling. "I did. An old beau, do you think?"

"I sincerely hope so!"

That was all the time they had for talking. The dance swept them away and Ginny had to concentrate to prevent making a mistake. When the next break came, Ginny went in search of the psychiatrist.

"Dr. Urquhart?"

The new man turned to face her. "Yes?"

"I'm Ginny Mackenzie and I would like an opportunity to come ask you about something. Could you spare me half-an-hour tomorrow?"

"I can, with pleasure. What time would you like to come?"

"Would nine o'clock be all right?"

"That would suit me very well indeed."

They agreed that Ginny would come to his office. He gave her the address, cautioned her she might have to sit on the floor, and took his leave, melting back into the crowd waiting for an opportunity to speak to him.

That settled, Ginny took a minute to admire the doctor's general appearance (from the back), including the breadth of his shoulders and the hang of his kilt, before rejoining the dancers. No wedding band. She would undoubtedly learn more about him tomorrow, but, on first impression, her mother could do a whole lot worse.

* * *

Saturday morning
Dr. Urquhart's office

Ginny knocked on the unmarked office door and was invited in. Dr. Urquhart met her with an outstretched hand and a gesture at a folding chair set up for her use.

"I apologize for the lack of creature comforts, but I'm still moving in." He sat down in the other folding chair and fixed his gaze on her. "Now, what may I do for you?"

Ginny found herself a bit tongue-tied. Close up, the man was even more impressive than he'd appeared last night. "We—"

He interrupted. "We?"

"Yes. I'm speaking for Angus Mackenzie and my husband, as well as myself."

"Go on."

"We would like for you to evaluate a member of the community, in your professional capacity."

"Has this potential patient been consulted about your wishes?"

"Not yet, and I reserve the right to broach the subject to her myself, if you agree to see her."

Ginny saw the ghost of a smile appear at the corner of the doctor's mouth.

"I see she has people who care about her."

"Very much."

"And you are concerned about her."

"Yes." Ginny paused. This was proving harder than she had anticipated. "Look. I know I don't count as the patient in this situation so patient-physician privilege won't apply. But I'm asking for your discretion. She's a sweet old lady and something disturbing has surfaced. We'd like to find out what actually happened."

"And you think I can help?"

Ginny sighed. "It's worth a try."

Dr. Urquhart sat back in his chair and crossed his arms on his chest, his eyes on her. "You're Sinia Forbes' daughter?"

Ginny nodded.

His eyes narrowed slightly. "Newly married and saddled with a reputation for solving mysteries."

Ginny felt the blood rise in her cheeks. "Correct."

"Dr. Gordon described your wedding to me. I wish I'd been there."

Ginny's lips thinned into a very polite social smile. "If I'd known you were coming to us, I would have included you."

His eyes narrowed, studying her, and Ginny began to think this had been a bad idea.

"You've piqued my curiosity and I have a suggestion."

"Oh?"

"There's an easy way to guarantee I cannot reveal anything we discuss, except under orders from the court. You said it yourself. All we have to do is list you as a patient. That would cover everything except imminent threat to life and limb." He leaned forward, rested his arms on his thighs, lifted his chin, and smiled at her.

It was as if the sun had come out. Ginny smiled back. She couldn't help it. A warmer, more infectious, more reassuring smile she had never seen, not even on Jim. This man had charm to spare and knew how to use it.

"What do you say?" he asked.

Ginny weighed her privacy concerns against Angus' need to know, and came down on the side of cautious cooperation. She didn't have to reveal anything to this man. Unless she wanted to, of course. "All right. You have my permission to list me among your charges here at Loch Lonach."

"A responsibility, yes, but I suspect you will also be a

pleasure to get to know." He leaned back in his chair. "Now, tell me what's worrying you."

Ginny recited the circumstances, starting with finding the dead brother and ending with the Broonies and the mysterious footprints in the attic dust. "Can you visit her at her house? She has good days and bad days, but she'll be more comfortable at home."

He nodded. "Do you want to be present?"

The question took her by surprise. "Would that be appropriate?"

"It could be useful to have a witness. You can introduce me and offer a familiar face."

"Then, yes, I do want to be there."

"My schedule is open for most of the coming week. When would be a good time?"

"I'll have to talk to Mrs. O. and make sure I haven't promised to be somewhere else. Which reminds me." She glanced at her watch, then sprang up. "Got to run, but thank you." She held out her hand. "I'll call you. Goodbye."

Ginny hurried out to her car and headed home, thinking the psychiatrist had left a good impression. Now, if she could get Mrs. O. to cooperate, they might be able to solve the mystery and ease her distress. That would be a blessing for an old woman facing death and, possibly, the ghost of a small brother she had forgotten she had.

* * *

Saturday afternoon
Alan Bean Memorial Auditorium

Ginny had left Dr. Urquhart's office and hurried to the market. Delivery was available, but she preferred to select the meats and vegetables herself. Once her shopping was done, it was back to the house to get the perishables into the refrigerator (or freezer, as needed), and update the ledger. Both she and Jim would be responsible for the Homestead budgets and part of Ginny's training was learning bookkeeping. She had been started on a much smaller scale—her own home—but was finding the subject a bit difficult. Jim caught her with the tip of her tongue sticking out the side of her mouth, trying to make the columns add up. He bent over her shoulder.

"Here, and here. You've flipped them."

"Oh! Thank you!" Ginny made the correction, then smiled up at her husband. "What have you been up to while I was dealing with mental, physical, and fiscal health issues?"

"I've been trying to talk myself into going back to my gym routine." He pulled her out of her chair and into his arms. "But I find I have more distractions than I did a week ago."

She patted his chest, wholly satisfied with the muscles evident beneath his shirt. "Well, the dancing is fairly serious aerobics, so all you need is weight training, and maybe a yoga class for balance."

"Wench!" He scooped her up into his arms and pressed her to his lips, kissing her, and counting the repetitions.

Ginny threw her arms around his neck, to make sure he didn't drop her, but otherwise let him have his fun. "When you are done with this session, may I remind you that sword fighting is on the afternoon's agenda?"

"Huh?" He lowered her to the floor. "I don't recall signing up for fencing class."

"We promised to go help Alan and Caroline."

"Help them do what?"

"The auditions for *Macbeth* are this afternoon. Alan is producing and he's hoping to break the back of it today so they can start rehearsals."

Jim made a face. "I am *not* going to be roped into play acting! Nope. Not me!"

Ginny started laughing. "That's what I've been telling them. But I promised we'd show up and give them any advice we might have."

Jim sighed heavily. "Oh, all right. I can give him a few hours. When are we expected?"

"Two and we don't have to stay long. This is more to show support than anything else."

"You'll have to feed me first."

"With pleasure, my lord."

Sandwiches and sodas behind them, Ginny and Jim slid into seats in the front of the Alan Bean Memorial Auditorium. The Loch Lonach Summer Repertoire tended to focus on Scottish playwrights, stories, and themes, which sometimes posed more than the usual amount of difficulty, and this year would be no exception. "The Scottish Play," as it was known in the industry, was cursed. It was considered very bad luck to speak the name of Shakespeare's masterpiece. There had been so many "accidents" during production over the years that some repertory companies refused to produce it at all.

Ginny leaned over and whispered in Caroline's ear. "How's it going?"

"Not bad. We've got the crew set and we've been able to cast about half of the roles."

Ginny smiled to herself. Caroline had been urging her to play one of the three weird sisters, citing the aptness of the new Lady of Loch Lonach playing one the Three Fates of classical mythology. Ginny was resisting.

Caroline continued. "We got lucky. The school has agreed to do virtual reality and digital images for the backdrops, battle scenes, ghosts, and witch's dance. That will allow us to use fewer people on stage."

"Makes sense. Who's going to play Macbeth?"

"Alan, of course. This is his baby and he reserves the right. The good news is that he's done it before so he doesn't have to memorize all that dialogue."

"And Lady Macbeth?"

"I am that lady. And I've got my work cut out for me. She was something else!"

"Aye, that she was!"

Alan was looking at his phone. "Where is he? He's late."

"I'm sure he'll turn up," Caroline soothed.

"If he doesn't, we're going to have to re-think the casting. There's no one else—"

The door to the auditorium burst open and a man strode down the aisle. "Where do you want me?"

Alan sucked in a breath, then got to his feet, gathering up a pair of broadswords. "On stage, please."

Ian Hunter climbed the stairs, then grinned down at them, shrugging into the padding and doublet he used when demonstrating to the fascinated masses at the Homestead Living History Display. He accepted a blade from Alan, examined it, flexed the steel, then nodded. "Nice choice."

He looked down at Jim and Ginny and made a small, apologetic gesture. "I hadn't meant to make a grand entrance. I was held up downtown. You would not believe the crowd Patterson has assembled." His smile faded. "The streets were filled with them. Carrying signs, chanting. All of them thinking Patterson can make them rich."

Ginny sighed to herself, but she had no time to spend on the political battle between Ian Hunter and Maury Patterson. Alan was ready.

"Lay on Macduff!" he cried and attacked Ian.

It was a thrilling exhibition of skill. Alan was the better swordsman, the instructor for the clan, and had longer arms.

But Ian had more muscle, and years of experience. The blades sang as they connected. From where Ginny was sitting, she could hear grunts and slaps and the creak of the wood floor beneath them.

The two men seemed unconcerned about drawing actual blood, and Ginny gasped in spite of herself. Caroline had both fists pressed to her lips. Jim was leaning forward, his eyes fixed on the combatants, looking as if he was reconsidering his refusal to accept a role in the play.

The two swordsmen struggled, locked together, chest to chest. Alan twisted to the side, to break the hold. In doing so, he leaned over backward, momentarily exposing his throat. Ian closed the distance, his blade suddenly against Alan's skin. And then it was over. Alan stood up, shook hands with Ian and turned to the audience.

"Blackout."

* * *

Saturday evening
Ian Hunter's house

Ian Hunter stood in his front yard, his arm around his wife's waist. She was weeping.

"When did this happen?"

"During the game. I waited for Wally and brought him home with me. When we turned into the driveway, we saw this."

"Did you see anyone, a car, something that looked out of place?"

"No. Just the damage. Oh, Ian! My rosebushes!" She turned her face into his shoulder.

The front door opened and Wally came out to join them. He stood on the other side of his mother, dwarfing her, and gazed at the damage. "It's not just the roses. You should see the backyard. Remember the oak we used to climb when we were kids, the one with the tire swing? They took an ax to it. And there are dead animals on the lawn, front and back. And they broke a window. Used a brick, with a note tied around it."

Ian looked at his son. "Did you read the note?"

Wally nodded. "It said, '*Withdraw from the senate race, or we'll break more than a window.*' I've called the police."

"Have you touched anything else?"

"Just the doors."

Ian nodded. "We'll wait until they get here." He sighed. "I'm sorry to ask this, but I would like both of you to keep this under your hat for a while, until I see what I can do about it. Can I count on you to cover for me?"

"The police will know," Wally said.

"And the neighbors are sure to notice the damage," Lola added.

"Wally and I can clean up the carcasses, and replant the roses tonight. Tell the police the truth, but If anyone else asks, tell them it's drunk teenagers pulling a prank that got out of hand, and don't mention the threat. It won't help me at the polls. I'll tell Angus." He turned to pull the two of them into a hug. "This is one of those times we need to take the high road. I promise, this will not be tolerated. Not here. Not in Loch Lonach."

The other two nodded, then broke free as a squad car pulled up to the curb.

"We're with you, Dad," Wally said. "We trust you."

Ian smiled. "Thanks, son. Now let's go talk to the police."

* * *

Chapter 8

Kirk on Sunday was an opportunity for everyone to show off their best clothes and their best behavior. Fellowship in the Parish Hall afterward was a different matter.

Jim and Ginny had appeared together at Sunday service for the first time as man and wife, then lingered to chat with everyone who wanted to congratulate them again, which appeared to be everyone in the community. Someone had arranged a brunch, complete with more cake and more champagne.

Ginny sipped coffee, her eyes on the crowd. Second only to the Friday night ceilidhs, coffee after church was the place where information was exchanged, business affairs were settled, and gossip was disseminated. On this particular Sunday morning, there was a lot to keep track of.

Chris Urquhart was surrounded by churchgoers eager to get to know him better. Ginny had already cornered him and settled on the next day, Monday, for their meeting with Mrs. Olafsson, so she was able to leave the field open to the rest of the congregation.

Senator Patterson was trying to lure parishioners from their loyalty to Senator Hunter with sly suggestions that their lives would be rosier if Patterson replaced Hunter in the Texas Legislature. Senator Hunter was displaying his good breeding by not doing the same.

Jean Pollack was dealing with the larger-than-usual crowd and loving every minute of it. She marched up to Ginny and handed her a wrapped package.

"I rescued this for you. It's wedding cake. I found it in the freezer at the Cooperative Hall and wanted to make sure you got it."

"Oh! Yes, thank you! We would have been desolate if we couldn't find it on our first anniversary." Ginny hugged Jean, carefully not letting on that she already had the top layer of her cake in the freezer at home. "Do you know if anyone took a piece to Patsy? She was having one of her bad days and missed the party."

Jean shook her head. "I'll ask around. Everyone knows about the cancer, of course, and her absence was noted, but we were all pretty busy that day."

"Cancer? Patsy has cancer?"

The two women jumped, then turned to face the speaker. Jean recovered first.

"Senator Patterson! How lovely to see you again. We met at your mother's funeral." She held out her hand.

He took it and kissed her knuckles, smiling at her and making her giggle. "I remember you, dear lady. And I'm grateful to you for all your kindness to myself and to my mother during her illness."

"But of course. She was one of us, you know, as you are, because you were both born here."

"You know the family history, then?"

Jean nodded. "A Homestead Matron is required to keep up with her charges." A shadow crossed her face. "It will seem strange not to have your mother around anymore." Her face brightened. "But you're moving into the big house and bringing new life to the old place. That will help."

"I sincerely hope so. But back to Patsy. She's my cousin."

Jean nodded.

"If she's ill," he continued, "Courtesy demands I visit her, ask her if there is anything I can do for her."

"If she's well enough to receive visitors, of course."

"Of course. I shall look into the possibility."

"That would be a kindness, I'm sure. Her memory's not what it once was. She gets confused. But she should remember you."

Senator Patterson looked grave. "You think so?"

"You were children together. Those are the memories that come back to us as we age. We can't remember what we had for breakfast, but we can sing the songs we learned at our mother's knee. That sort of thing."

Senator Patterson seemed to be considering her comment, his brow furrowing. "Yes. You're quite right. Well, thank you for letting me know." He tipped his hat to the two of them and took his leave.

Ginny was spared further conversation with Jean by the arrival of another parishioner in need of the Matron's help. She excused herself and drifted back to Jim.

"What was that all about?"

"Senator Patterson was claiming kin with Patsy Olafsson and Jean confirmed that they were cousins. He wants to visit her."

Jim eyes narrowed. "To pay his respects?"

"That's what he said, but from what I've seen of his behavior so far, I'm inclined to think Patsy doesn't need any of that sort of attention."

Jim sighed. "If he's really her cousin, he may be the last surviving family, and her heir."

Ginny frowned. "I'll see what I can find out. In the meantime, I need to get this cake into the refrigerator. Jean insisted."

Jim smiled. "And we can't ignore a mandate from the Matron."

"Not if we want any more cake!"

* * *

Sunday afternoon
Loch Lonach

"I forgot to tell you. We have an appointment," Jim announced. "In one hour."

Ginny blinked. She had been looking forward to doing nothing for the rest of the day. She looked at her husband's face and found his eyes sparkling, which was good enough to change her mind.

"Where are we going?" She thanked her lucky stars she had set up the slow cooker and *Good Brown Stew* for the main meal of the day. It would keep.

"To the lake."

Ginny slid into work pants and shirt, grabbing her sunglasses and a visor. She turned to find Jim in shorts and a polo shirt, his eyes on her.

"Will I do?"

He nodded, then tossed her a pair of running shoes. "You can change the sandals for these in the car. Come on."

He swung through the burger joint on their way to the harbor.

"You didn't fill up on party food?"

He shook his head. "Cucumber sandwiches can go only so far. I need protein to face the ordeal ahead of us."

"Ginny ate while Jim drove to the far side of the lake where the water was deepest and the sailing club had established piers and moorings. He pulled into one of the parking spots, glanced at his watch, then inhaled his own meal, his eyes on the water.

"There he is." Jim brushed his hands, then climbed out of the car and headed across the parking lot to the gate. Ginny followed more slowly, watching as the two men met and shook hands. Jim turned and motioned for her to join them.

"Ginny, this is Mr. Bryant."

The old man touched his cap. "Ma'am."

Ginny had never seen a better example of an old sailor. He had a permanent squint, sun wrinkled skin, gnarled hands, a short gray beard, and pale blue eyes. All he needed was a pipe to complete the picture.

"I expect you want to see her in action," Mr. Bryant said.

Ginny was momentarily confused, but the object of the comment was explained in the next exchange.

Jim nodded. "Is she seaworthy?"

"She is. You'll want her inspected, though, before you decide."

"Yes. I trust you, but it's best to be thorough."

"I agree." He opened the gate for them and ushered them onto the dock. Ginny followed the two men along the wooden pier to where a sailboat sat in the water, tied to the dock.

Mr. Bryant stepped into the boat, then turned and offered his hand to Ginny. It was at that moment the truth struck her.

Jim had been talking about buying a sailboat for as long as she'd known him. That sparkle in his eye meant he was considering buying a boat. Buying *this* boat. Today.

"She's called *Saorsainn*. 'Tis Gaelic for 'freedom'." Mr. Bryant smiled. "There's nae freedom like the wind in yer sails and yer cares at yer back."

Ginny climbed gingerly across the rail and sat down on the bench, her mind flying to last October. Jim had offered to teach her how to sail. In December he had taken her to look at sailboats. Today he had brought her with him, to be included in this decision, because the outcome would affect her.

"Keep your head down, Ginny, and your eyes open. The boom can swing around really fast and knock you unconscious and into the water."

Lovely! His new toy was deadly. Well, there were a lot of things Ginny would do for her husband and ducking seemed a reasonable addition to the list. She nodded and slid further down into the cockpit of the boat.

She watched as the two men set the mainsail, then raised it halfway, shifting the position until it caught the breeze and started to pull away from the dock. Jim cast off, then took charge of the lines while Mr. Bryant manned the tiller.

They pulled away from the dock slowly, Jim and Mr. Bryant talking about the fittings on the ship, the age of the sails, and other details of maintenance and upkeep. The next item on the agenda was hoisting the mainsail, followed by the headsail, which, when filled, sent them scooting along the surface of the loch at a pleasant clip.

Ginny could tell Mr. Bryant was watching, letting Jim demonstrate his expertise. She understood only one word in six of the language they were using. But she had no trouble following Jim's instruction to move from one side of the boat to the other, on cue, while ducking.

They sailed back and forth across the lake, tacking and jibing, in light wind and with not much speed, but it was enough to show her that the fresh air and sense of forward motion took away the uneasiness in her stomach and allowed her to relax and enjoy the experience. Also, that she was going to need long sleeves and gloves and a better hat.

"Will you take the tiller, Mrs. Mackenzie?"

Ginny looked around to find Mr. Bryant eyeing her.

"Oh! I don't know how to sail."

"Well, then it's high time ye learned."

For a breathless fifteen minutes Ginny was instructed in where to sit, how to move the tiller, and the importance of not making sudden changes, as that could send Jim over the side and into the drink. She stayed at her post for the remainder of the cruise, following instructions, until Mr. Bryant took over the steering to make sure they got safely back to the dock.

Once the boat was back in its slip, there were sails and lines to stow, life jackets to put away in the lockers, and covers to tuck into place. Ginny took a cursory look around the cabin, thinking that the bunk space wasn't going to be comfortable for anyone as tall as Jim, but it would suit her just fine, once she got some thick padding in place. The lockers were large and deep and would need to be emptied before she would know what could be stored in them. And there were other amenities she might ask Jim about—later—but she could already see the possibilities of a starlight sail, cuddled up on the deck, just the two of them.

Before she could talk to him, though, there was the keel to inspect. This took longer than Ginny had anticipated, requiring, as it did, the two men to raise the boat, then crawl around underneath, with flashlights.

"I've kept her in good repair, for the most part, though she could use some updating."

Jim nodded. "I've got someone coming to look her over and advise me. Samuel Boatwright. Do you know him?"

Mr. Bryant nodded. The old man patted the railing. "I'm sorry to let her go, but I can't handle her alone, not any more. And, now that the missus is gone, the kids want me closer to them. I expect they'll take me out now and again, so I won't have to give up sailing entirely." He turned to face Jim. "I'm glad she'll be going to a good home. You take care of her. She's a true lady."

"Yes, sir, I will. I promise."

"Once the paperwork is complete, the club'll change the owner's name and give you the combination to the gate. Should take about a week." They made their way to the gate and the parking lot, then the old man held out his hand. "If I don't see you again, fair winds and following seas."

Jim smiled. "Thank you. The same to you."

Ginny watched the old man turn and walk over to his car. She smiled and waved, thinking about the immutability of change and the cycle of life. If they lived long enough, the day would come when she and Jim would have to do the same thing—give up the boat to a younger couple. But not today.

Jim controlled himself until they were in the car with the windows up and the air conditioner going, then he whooped.

"I'm a sailor again!"

Ginny burst out laughing. "You sound as excited as my nephews with their popguns."

"Bigger boys, bigger toys." He grinned at her. "We got a deal, and there'll be some sweat equity to pay before she'll be truly back to her old self, but she's a beauty and perfect for me—for us." He smiled at her and reached for her hand. "For us, Ginny."

"Yes my love, for us."

* * *

CHAPTER 9

Monday noon
Mackenzie residence

Monday was Ginny's first day on her new job. It hadn't been bad, and she'd only had to put in four hours, but the tension and first day jitters had wrung her out. She went in search of her husband and found him in the kitchen, laying out lunch. He looked up at her step. "Welcome home!"

She threw her arms around his neck and kissed him, then broke away and headed for the bedroom. "Give me a minute. I'll be right back." She stripped off her scrubs, sluiced off, and slid into fresh sweats.

Jim smiled when she reappeared in the kitchen. "Go ahead. I'll be right there." He finished chopping onions, washed his hands and joined her at the table.

He had prepared egg salad wraps, with fruit. Ginny tucked into the meal and thanked her lucky stars she had married a man who could cook. She smiled at him. "This is delicious, and a wonderful surprise."

"I thought you might like a break after your first day on the new job. How did it go?"

Ginny had to remind herself not to talk with her mouth full. "Quite well. There were a few glitches in the schedule and some items missing from the training materials, but nothing major. Everyone seemed pleased to see me, though I got some ribbing from the staff."

"About deserting them?"

"Yes, but they were just teasing. I got the impression most of them were in favor of the preceptorship idea."

"They should be. The board is in favor and so are the company lawyers."

Ginny nodded. "Angus told me the same. Speaking of lawyers, there was one sour note. You know how hospital rooms all have TVs in them, to help amuse the patients?"

Jim nodded.

"Half of them were tuned to the news. Which meant I was forced to listen to Senator Patterson announcing he was running for Ian Hunter's state senate seat, and the interviews that followed. He must have bought time on every station in town."

"Well, he can afford it."

Ginny made a face. "I know, but he makes my skin crawl." She gave an exaggerated shiver that made Jim laugh.

"I doubt if he'll get much traction in Loch Lonach. Ian Hunter is popular," Jim said.

"And why not? He's tall and handsome and he can handle a sword." Ginny felt her eyes widen. "I had no idea! I was afraid Alan was in real danger there for a moment."

"You can see why Alan didn't want to trust that scene to anyone else."

"I can, indeed. Even choreographed, it wouldn't take much for something to go wrong."

"Let's hope it doesn't. How to reattach a severed head was not something covered in medical school."

Jim wiped his mouth, then leaned back in his chair and smiled at her. "You got a phone call today."

"Oh?"

"Detective Tran asked you to drop by to discuss the candlestick."

"Oh!" Ginny's brow furrowed. She looked at Jim and found him watching her, a smile playing at the corner of his mouth.

"Jim, you know I didn't ask for this."

"I know."

"And I have no intention of getting involved."

"So you said."

"And I don't want to break my promise to you."

Jim leaned forward, resting his arms on the table. "Detective Tran is the official police liaison to the clan. That makes her almost one of us. I think you should talk to her."

Ginny's eyebrows rose. "You do?"

He nodded.

"And I think I should go with you, as grandfather's agent."

Ginny's lips twitched. "I agree."

Interesting. He had specifically asked her to give up investigating once they were married, but he hadn't said a thing about himself. So either he was exerting his authority as her husband and the laird-to-be, or he was stepping in to relieve her of the burden, out of the goodness of his heart. Either way, the visit was going to be entertaining.

* * *

Monday afternoon
Police substation

They pulled into the visitor lot and parked the car, announced themselves to the receptionist and were escorted back. Detective Hue Tran of the Dallas Crimes Against Persons Division rose to greet them.

"Miss Forbes! No, I must call you Mrs. Mackenzie now. And

Dr. Mackenzie."

Ginny smiled as she and Jim took the seats indicated. "The name has changed, but I'm just as much of a nuisance as before, I'm afraid."

Detective Tran resumed her seat. "If by that you mean you have brought me another intriguing little puzzle, you are correct."

"I thought you might find it interesting." The candlestick lay on the detective's desk encased in an evidence bag.

"The lab tells me there are many interesting things about this object. Refresh my memory, please. How did it come to be in your possession?"

"It was a wedding present." Ginny recounted the story of how the package had been delivered, addressed to her maiden name; how she had opened and examined the candlestick in front of three witnesses; and how cleaning the base had revealed what appeared to be blood. "So I brought it over and left it for you."

Detective Tran nodded. "The base had a sufficient quantity of blood and scalp tissue for the lab to obtain a DNA sample. I must caution you that running these tests is not a priority. I am assured the blood is of such a vintage that it cannot be related to any of our active cases."

"I understand." Ginny said.

Detective Tran continued. "On examination, we found several layers of fingerprints, yours on top."

"My prints are on file, however, because I'm a nurse, so you had no trouble eliminating them."

"Correct. The set of prints underneath yours turned out also to be on file. They belong to an elementary school teacher in the Loch Lonach Independent School District system. All teachers are fingerprinted, as you know, for security reasons. Her name is Olafsson."

Ginny blinked. "Patsy Olafsson?"

"Yes."

Ginny glanced at Jim then back at the detective, her brow furrowing. "If her prints were on the candlestick underneath mine, that means she handled it before I did."

"And recently, yes."

Ginny frowned harder. "Does that mean she sent it to me?"

"It is possible."

"Why on earth would she do that?"

"There is other evidence on the candlestick that might suggest a reason." Detective Tran pulled two images out of her file and slid them across the desk. They were both pictures of fingerprints, blown up, and laid side by side.

"Underneath Mrs. Olafsson's prints we found another set, of a size a child might make. They matched the larger set and belong to Mrs. Olafsson."

Ginny stared. "Mrs. Olafsson's fingerprints are on the candlestick twice?" She tried to compare the two fingerprints in the pictures, but could make nothing of them.

"Yes, as an elementary school-aged child and again as an adult."

Ginny screwed up her face, trying to think. "If she handled it as a child, then handled it again as an adult, then—what? Was it in her possession all these years?"

"I believe so."

"Why did she send it to me? And why now?"

"Let us return to that subject in a minute. All three of the sets of prints mentioned were aligned in a manner that indicated the candlestick had been held, for the most part, with the base toward the floor, in the usual orientation for candlesticks."

Ginny nodded and waited. There was clearly a *but* coming.

"There was, however, another set of child-sized

fingerprints. These have not been identified. They appear toward the top of the candlestick and were inverted, indicating that the child who left those fingerprints was holding the candlestick with the base closer to the ceiling."

Ginny felt her skin crawl. "Closer to the ceiling. As if he or she was planning to use that heavy base as a club."

"That is correct."

"So Caroline was right!" Jim's voice startled Ginny. She'd almost forgotten he was there. "What Mrs. Olafsson sent us wasn't a wedding present. It was a murder weapon!"

Detective Tran looked at him and lifted an eyebrow. "It is premature to assume this was a deliberate homicide."

"But it's human blood?"

She nodded to him. "Yes."

Ginny reached over and took Jim's hand, for comfort, or support maybe. He gave it a squeeze. She turned back to the detective. "You think Mrs. O. wanted me to bring this to your attention." It was a statement, not a question.

"Which you did, although I would have been just as happy to hear her story from her own lips. She has been invited to come in to explain her actions to me."

Ginny drew in a breath. "There's something you should know about Mrs. Olafsson. She's dying of cancer. If her doctors are right, she has fewer than six months to live."

"Is she able to travel?"

"Most days, yes."

"I appreciate the warning and will use all due care."

"Thank you." Ginny's brow furrowed, returning to the puzzle. "You said scalp tissue. That implies a head wound." She was thinking of Tommy Bryant.

"Correct."

"Two sets of child-sized fingerprints suggests two children fighting over something—maybe the candlestick. But if one child hit another with it, would that be considered a crime? I mean, children fight all the time and they don't usually land in jail for it."

"There are a variety of possible scenarios. If the attacking child was old enough to fully understand the consequences of her actions and did it anyway, there is precedent. There are cases of children as young as nine years old being tried for murder."

Ginny blanched. "If a child died from such a blow, would it be murder, or manslaughter, or some other version of homicide?"

"That would be a question for the District Attorney. The police would investigate any killing the same way. The age of the suspect might make collecting testimony a bit challenging, but the forensics procedures would remain unchanged."

Ginny was fascinated, in a horrified sort of way. "Do they put children on death row?"

"No. They do not go to adult prison and they do not serve life sentences. They are usually released from a juvenile rehabilitation facility when they attain the age of eighteen years. Many are then given new identities and allowed to start over."

"So we could have the grown-up version of a child ax murderer walking among us!"

"Yes."

"You're giving me the willies."

Detective Tran's mouth twitched. "I apologize. To go back to your question, why did this object of interest surface now, rather than sooner? There is usually an incident, something that sets the process in motion. If you see Mrs. Olafsson, you might find it useful to ask her about changes in her life."

"Other than the cancer, you mean."

"A diagnosis of terminal cancer might be the trigger, of

course, but my instinct suggests there was something else."

"All right, that addresses the why now, but not the why me."

Detective Tran leaned back in her chair. "This woman is one of the Homesteaders, is she not?"

"She is. Born and bred." Ginny had reason to know. It had been on the birth certificate.

"And you have just married Mr. Mackenzie's heir." She smiled at Jim, who nodded. "Which, if I understand the situation correctly, will make you Matron. That, combined with your experience, might impress a member of your clan."

Detective Tran lifted an eyebrow. "I think she has brought her problem to you as a matter of right." She glanced at Jim, then back at Ginny, her eyes twinkling. "I also believe she is counting on the fact that, in the matter of murder investigations, you have never yet been known to say no."

* * *

Monday afternoon
Mrs. Olafsson's residence

Jim pulled out of the parking lot at the police substation, his eyes on the road, his mind on the candlestick. "I think we should pay Mrs. Olafsson a visit." He glanced over at Ginny. "Do you have her number?"

"Yes." Ginny pulled out her phone and dialed. "Mrs. Olafsson? Ginny Mackenzie. My husband and I were wondering if we might drop in on you for a brief visit. Would this be a good time?" Ginny smiled, then nodded. "Yes, ten minutes. Thank you." She looked over at Jim. "She's expecting us. And you can be sure she'll have hot tea waiting."

"Hot tea? In May?"

"It's a ritual with her. And you may not like how it tastes, but I'm relying on you not to offend her."

Jim wrinkled his nose. "Thanks for the warning."

The house was situated in the old section of the community, and was easy to identify, being a classic Victorian three-story, complete with pastel siding, white gingerbread, and turrets. The first and second floors sported bay windows, designed as reading nooks. By contrast, the dormer window half-hidden behind the tower appeared furtive, out of character with the rest of the house.

Jim paused for a moment on the sidewalk to examine the building and grounds. The house was large and surrounded by at least a half-acre of lawns and garden. There was a wrap-around porch with white wicker rockers in need of a fresh coat of paint, but the grass and hedges were neatly trimmed, and the fence was in good repair. Ginny seemed to read his mind.

"Angus makes sure the yard is clipped and nothing is broken."

Jim nodded. He would have the same responsibility when his turn came.

Mrs. Olafsson met them at the door. "Come in. I'm so pleased to see you. I wasn't well on your wedding day so I missed all the fun. Now I have a chance to wish you both joy." She ushered them into the kitchen and there, sure enough, was the tea. "May I offer you some refreshment?"

"Yes, please." Ginny smiled and handed Jim a cup.

When the ritual had been completed, and Jim had tasted the tea, which turned out to be drinkable, Ginny took the reins of the conversation.

"We're imposing on your hospitality, I know, but I've thought of some more questions since I was over here the other day. I want to poke around in the attic again, and I want to change that lightbulb while I'm at it."

"Yes, of course, dear. Whatever you want."

"And I," Jim said, "would like to talk to you about your medical care, if you'll confide in me."

Mrs. O. looked at Jim and hesitated. "Dr. Weisbrod is my oncologist. I refer everything to him."

Jim nodded. "A good man. Would you be willing to show me what medications he has you on?"

"Why, yes, if you want."

Ginny rose from her chair. "And, if you'll let me have a lightbulb, I'll just pop upstairs and replace the burned out one."

Jim watched as the two women hunted among the cabinets and drawers, eventually locating a bulb Ginny could use. Mrs. O. moved carefully, as if her balance was untrustworthy, or it hurt to move. Either could be true. As soon as he could politely do so, Jim took her arm and steered her into the bedroom.

He didn't have to do more than touch her to know the cancer was in control. Her skin was paper thin, her color waxy. He decided it might be prudent to contact Weisbrod himself and see if there was anything else that could be done for her.

He sat Mrs. O. down in an armchair beside her bed and pulled up a hassock. The room was warm and well lit. It was easy to observe her out of the corner of his eye while he picked up each of the medication bottles and asked her about her routine and possible side effects. There was nothing unexpected in the collection and she seemed to have a good handle on how to take them correctly.

"Is this everything?"

"I've got a couple of bottles in the medicine cabinet, but I only take them when I need them."

"Let's look at those as well." Jim rose and went into the bathroom. The cabinet had the usual over-the-counter remedies for headaches, stuffy noses, and skin irritations. It also had two prescription bottles. He took them back to the bedroom and sat down where he could face Mrs. O.

"What about these two?"

She took the bottles from him, one at a time, and examined them through her bifocals. "This one," she handed the first bottle back, "is a pain killer I use only when nothing else works. I'm told it's addictive and I don't want to be dependent on narcotics."

The second bottle had only a few pills remaining. "I have trouble sleeping, so Dr. Weisbrod prescribed these for me. They seem to help. I usually sleep until late in the morning when I take one."

Jim nodded. "Do you keep track of when you take a sleeping pill?"

"Write it down somewhere you mean? No. Should I?"

"When was the first time you took one?" Jim heard a soft step and glanced over his shoulder to find Ginny standing just inside the door. He turned back to Mrs. Olafsson.

"Well, let me see." Mrs. O.'s forehead creased. "How many pills have I had from that bottle?"

Jim counted, then looked at the label. "Fifteen. You've been on them for two weeks."

She nodded. "I'd been having trouble getting the pain under control." She waved her hand at the array of pills on her bedside table. "Dr. Weisbrod changed some of the combinations and I think it's working."

"Did you ask Dr. Weisbrod about mixing the new medications with the old ones?"

She nodded. "He said it should be all right, as long as I watched out for allergic reactions, and reported any new symptoms."

Jim nodded, then swiveled around and motioned for Ginny to come join them. He handed her the bottle of sedative-hypnotics, then smiled at Mrs. O.

"I think this explains the Broonies." He heard Ginny catch her breath.

"Of course."

Mrs. Olafsson looked from one to the other. "The Broonies?"

"All those funny things that have been happening around the house," Ginny said. "These pills, these sleeping pills can cause sleep-walking, and other surprising side effects, like sleep-eating."

"Sleep-eating?" Mrs. O. laughed. "Well, that would explain the dirty dishes. But how could I eat if I was asleep?"

"You were partially awake," Jim explained. "Someone meeting you would have been fooled into thinking you were fully awake. People under the influence of these drugs have gone to parties, and to the casino, and driven on the streets, all while still technically asleep. And they never remember any of it."

"That sounds dangerous! Why would Dr. Weisbrod put me on a pill that does that?"

"Most people don't have a problem. He asked you to report anything unusual, but I'll bet you didn't tell him about the Broonies."

Mrs. O. colored. "Well, no. He's not Homestead. He wouldn't have understood."

"You were afraid he'd think you were losing your mind?" Ginny asked.

"Well, I *am*. My memory, anyway. Which reminds me, what about my brother?"

Ginny reached out and took Mrs. O.'s hand. "Patsy, we have news for you and it may not be pleasant to hear, but you need to know." Ginny glanced at Jim, but they had discussed this in the car on the way over. He nodded.

Ginny took a breath. "Someone sent me a wedding present

that bore evidence of an accident that happened a long time ago. We think you sent the present. It had your fingerprints on it."

"My *fingerprints*?"

Jim nodded. "You don't remember doing that, do you?"

She shook her head.

Jim lifted the bottle. "I think this is why. You took a sleeping pill and went to bed. In the middle of the night you got up, wrapped up a candlestick, put the box in the car, drove over to the Cooperative Hall, and left it in a corner for someone to find the next day, which is what happened."

Mrs. Olafsson stared at them for a full minute in silence, then frowned. "A candlestick?"

Ginny nodded.

"With my fingerprints on it?" She drew her hand out of Ginny's and looked down at it.

"On the box, and the tag as well," Ginny said.

Mrs. O. got a far off look in her eye. "Because I couldn't go to the wedding. My conscience was bothering me about that."

"We think you may know more than you realize about that candlestick. That your subconscious was telling you to send it to me," Ginny explained.

Mrs. O. frowned. "I don't remember any of this."

"We understand," Jim said, "but the police would like to talk to you about it."

Her eyes grew wide. "The police? Why the police?"

Ginny answered that one. "Because it appears you've had that candlestick up in your attic all this time."

"There's a lot of stuff in the attic, all over the house, really." Patsy's eyes grew sad. "I haven't had the heart to throw it out. It's just me and the memories these days." She sighed, then looked at Ginny. "Why should the police care if I sent a candlestick to you as a wedding present?"

Jim saw Ginny take a breath, then heard her soften her voice. "Because there was blood on the base of the candlestick."

"Blood?"

Jim had his eye on Mrs. O., watching to see how she took the news. He couldn't tell if she grew whiter, her skin was already so pale.

"The police have been able to identify the blood as human. They're running a DNA test on it, to see if they can identify the source," he said.

Mrs. O. frowned, her eyes dropping to her lap. "A candlestick with blood on it. And in my—" She looked up at Ginny, her pupils dilating. "Did you say you found that candlestick in my attic?"

"I found the place where it stood until someone moved it, yes."

Mrs. O. turned to face Jim. Her eyes, somewhat unfocused until that moment, had sharpened into Stygian pools of fear girdled in pale blue.

"You think the blood will turn out to belong to my brother."

"We won't know until we get the results of the test back," he said, "but, yes. I'm afraid so."

* * *

CHAPTER 10

Monday afternoon
Mackenzie residence

Ginny dropped onto the sofa and propped her feet up, closing
her eyes. What a mess! Mrs. O. had taken the news
exceptionally well, but that was probably because she didn't
understand half of it. Ginny had called Himself, and he had
arranged for twenty-four hour companions for Mrs. O. for as
long as she needed them, which would be until the cancer
killed her. She had also called Detective Tran to suggest Tran
hold off on interrogating the old woman until the DNA
evidence was back. But they were going to need more than
simple facts to find out what had really happened. Mrs. O. had
insisted she knew nothing, remembered nothing, and Ginny
was inclined to believe her.

"Ginny?"

"In here, Jim."

He came around the corner and joined her on the sofa,
pulling her into his arms. "Are you all right?"

She hesitated. "I don't know." Their meeting with Detective
Tran had unsettled her. It wasn't just that Tran had expected
Ginny to help in the investigation, it was that Jim hadn't
objected. He ran his hand down her back. "Talk to me."

What kind of child kills another? And where was that child

now? She pulled in a deep breath. "Do you believe in destiny?"

"You mean like predestination?"

She wrinkled her nose. "Maybe. That we're born for a purpose and can't escape our fates."

"I believe in free will. We can choose what direction our lives take."

Ginny squirmed. "Yes, but, having chosen, are we stuck with whatever those choices bring?"

His eyes narrowed. "I'm bound by moral duties in my chosen profession, and by promises I've made—like the promise I made to you. My conscience demands I fulfill those obligations, or die trying."

Ginny twisted around to face him. "That's what I'm afraid of!" They'd had this discussion before, but circumstances had changed. "Tell me you can walk away, if the price is too high. I can't think of anything worth your life."

"I can." He lifted her chin and kissed her, very gently. "And I'm not that easy to kill. Haven't you noticed?"

Ginny felt her chest constrict. What had gotten into her this afternoon? She nodded, then sat up and tried to smile. "It's just that I want to believe we have control over what happens to us, even though I know we don't."

His eyes radiated sympathy and compassion. "Come here, love." He folded her into his arms. "My destiny—freely chosen—is to be your husband and, probably, my grandfather's successor, whatever that may mean. That's enough for one man, I should think."

Ginny looked up into his smile and nodded. "More than enough."

"And yours, my bonnie wee lass? What's your destiny?"

Whatever her destiny might be, and however little control she had over it, Ginny knew the answer to that question. "You are my destiny. I will follow you to the ends of the earth."

It was some minutes before he released her and even longer before she remembered they both had other obligations. "You have to work tonight." She put her hand on his cheek. "You've got time for a nap, if you go lie down right now."

He shook his head. "I couldn't sleep and I'd rather spend the time with you. Which reminds me." He pulled the bottle of sleeping pills out of his pocket and set it on the table in front of them. "I didn't want to leave these with her. Did you find what you were looking for in Mrs. O.'s attic?"

"Part of it." She climbed off the sofa and retrieved her phone from her bag. "Here are the pictures I took today."

Jim flipped through the images. "Footprints."

"Some of which are mine, but there was a clear trail leading to the shelf where the candlestick must have stood. You can see the pattern it left in the dust."

Jim nodded. "The footprints go straight from the door to the shelf. She must have known what she was after."

"Her subconscious did anyway. I photographed the contents of Tommy's trunk, enough for Detective Tran to decide whether she wants to get a search warrant. I did *not* find the other candlestick, but I didn't open every box. It could still be there."

Jim's eyes narrowed. "The evidence suggests the other child, the one whose fingerprints haven't been identified, used the candlestick as a weapon, and that Patsy hid the bloody candlestick to cover up the deed."

Ginny nodded. "She may be an accessory after the fact, or she may be a witness and have seen the whole thing. Could that explain why she has no memory of the boy? Can you suppress something that traumatic so effectively?"

"That's a question for Dr. Urquhart." Jim looked at her. "And on the same subject, I have a question for you. Is

Detective Tran right? Do you feel obligated to solve whatever mystery comes up in this community?"

Ginny met his eyes. "I promised you I'd quit."

His brow furrowed. "It's not the investigating I object to, you know. It's the danger."

"You have every right to insist I stop taking stupid chances." She stuck out her chin. "From now on, if danger wants to tweak my nose, it will have to come to me."

Jim laughed. "I'm not sure that's any better. Do I need to wrap you in cotton batting and lock you in a tower somewhere?"

She spread her hands. "I can't avoid danger completely. Just being alive is dangerous. But I have more important things to do with my life than chase criminals."

He studied her for a moment. "You once told me that you will always follow your conscience. Is that still true?"

Ginny was silent for a moment, then drew in a breath. "Yes, but please don't make me choose between you and my conscience."

"How about if we work together?"

She blinked. "You'd do that?"

He nodded. "It's the best way to keep an eye on you."

Ginny was silent for a moment, thinking it through, then her eyes narrowed. "You know what that means don't you? You'll have to listen when I talk."

His dimple appeared, but otherwise he controlled himself admirably. "Well, it's a high price to pay, but I guess if that's what it takes, I can do it." He took her hand and drew her back to his side. "All right, partner, we investigate as a team. And if anything comes up, we turn it over to Detective Tran for action."

"Fine by me." Ginny closed her eyes and leaned against him. A team! It was more than she could have hoped for. She would have someone to share her problems with, and in exchange, she would be a good wife and a good citizen and leave the pursuit and capture of criminals to the professionals.

Besides, this particular crime—if it was one—was more than fifty years old. There was at least a chance the perpetrator was dead and buried, no threat to her and her happiness.

She smiled and snuggled closer to her husband. Yes, that would certainly be best for everyone. Dead and buried and nothing to be done but close the file, preferably before Patsy Olafsson succumbed to the cancer. She deserved to have her questions answered before she died, if it was possible, and if it could be done without hurting anyone else.

* * *

Monday evening
Mackenzie residence

As soon as Jim had taken himself off to the hospital, Ginny climbed the stairs and settled down in front of her computer. The new house was spacious and comfortable, with plenty of rooms to grow into. At the moment, Jim had appropriated a room on the first floor as his man cave, and Ginny had claimed this upstairs future bedroom as her office.

She started by sending Detective Tran the images from her phone. They were inadmissible as evidence, but showed why Ginny had come to the conclusions she had. Not that an indictment seemed likely. Possession of a stolen candlestick might be proved, or aiding and abetting a child murderer, but, considering her diagnosis, there seemed little chance Mrs. Olafsson would stand trial for anything.

More as a way of organizing her thoughts rather than laying out a case, Ginny opened the spreadsheet program she used in her investigations. She'd done this three times before. It was basically a Means, Motive, Opportunity table.

She took a moment to think about the problem. Tran had been very clear that one bloody candlestick did not a murder make. There was blood, certainly, and an old woman who had decided, after a lifetime of silence, to send that candlestick to Ginny. The same old woman who had no memory of a small brother, even though he had left a paper trail in the genealogical record. What were the odds those two events were connected?

Ginny started a fresh page and typed *candlestick* in the Means column. The other two remained empty. Was there any way she could fill either of those two blank fields?

She opened her genealogy software and setup a new database. It was essentially the same file she and Mrs. O. had created the week before. She was duplicating the family group they'd put together, using all the same source records. Once that was done, Ginny started researching Tommy Bryant. She had his birth record and the census file. Both gave her dates and locations. With those as a starting point, she looked for further evidence of the child's existence. She found it.

There were school records and medical records and pictures posted online. The boy appeared in a kindergarten class photo, then in images at the swimming pool, one taken at church, and another, in Cub Scout uniform, at a baseball game. That one included an older sister and a set of parents. A happy family group. What had happened to change that?

Ginny knew where to look. It took her no time at all to find the official record. The cause of death was listed as head injury. Male, aged five years eight months. Her brows drew together at the thought of that mother's pain. She knew what it felt like to lose a father, and she'd watched her mother cope with losing a husband. But it seemed worse, somehow, to lose a child.

Locating the obituary took more doing, but she found it at last, a short entry, posted more than a year after the incident. There was a cemetery record. The child was buried here, in Dallas, but not in the kirk yard, in a memorial park that had a special area for children. She wondered if Tommy's mother had ever visited the grave.

Ginny plugged all the information into her database, then went back and dug deeper. It took her another hour of concerted effort, but she found what she was looking for, the newspaper report of the child's death. It was small and buried at the bottom of a page of much more sensational news, but it was there. Small child killed in tragic accident. He and his sister and a cousin had been playing in a back room in the cousin's house. The rug must have slipped because the dead child fell onto the corner of the glass coffee table and hit his head. He had been transported to the children's hospital emergency room, but was pronounced dead on arrival.

Ginny paused. Opportunity. Another child, a cousin, was mentioned. And the accident took place in the cousin's house. Those inverted fingerprints on the candlestick, perhaps?

Ginny read the article through again, comparing the details to the death certificate. When she was sure she understood what was in the records, she sat back in her chair and stared at her computer. It wasn't what was in the records that concerned her. It was what *didn't* appear. In none of the documents had there been any mention of a candlestick.

So—according to the records—the dead brother *hadn't* been hit with the candlestick. But, if the blood on that candlestick didn't belong to the brother, whose blood was it? And where was the police record or newspaper article describing a deadly assault with a candlestick? If the candlestick had nothing to do with her brother's death, why was Mrs. O. in possession of that piece of silver? Why had she been hiding it all these years? And why had she suddenly decided to take it out and send it to Ginny?

A wider search for head trauma deaths around that same time came up empty. Ginny shook her head over the puzzle, then put it away. She locked up the house and went to bed, but lay awake for more than an hour worrying about Patsy and Tommy and the bloody candlestick. And the unknown other child, of course. The one who might be a killer.

* * *

CHAPTER 11

Tuesday morning
Mackenzie residence

When the doorbell rang the next morning, Ginny dropped her mixing spoon and ran. The last thing she wanted was for Jim to be disturbed. Before her marriage, her mother had run interference for her when she had to sleep during the day. Now it was her job to do the same for her husband.

She arrived at the front door out of breath and not knowing what she might find, but determined to prevent another assault on the bell. She swung the door open and confronted the stranger who stood on her doorstep.

"May I help you?"

The man was neither young nor old, late forties perhaps, dressed in casual slacks and a shirt open at the neck. His skin glowed with the rich, olive tones of the Mediterranean. He wore rimless glasses under blue-black curls, and a tentative smile. Ginny was sure she had never seen him before.

"Good morning. I'm looking for Mrs. Mackenzie. My name is Lorenzo Scala."

"I'm Mrs. Mackenzie. What may I do for you?"

"May I come in?"

Ginny's self-preservation instincts vetoed this immediately. "I'm sorry, no. Please state your business."

He nodded. "First, allow me to congratulate you on your recent marriage. I understand it was quite an event."

This statement did nothing to endear the speaker to Ginny. "Thank you. Your business?"

"The person I really want to talk to is Patsy Olafsson, but I understand she is ill and not receiving visitors."

Ginny nodded.

"You visited her yesterday."

Ginny nodded again, her brow descending.

"I was hoping you would introduce me to her."

Ginny crossed her arms on her chest. "Why would I do that?"

"She is, I believe, Senator Maury Patterson's first cousin."

"It's possible. You haven't yet told me what your business with her is."

"I'm sorry. Allow me to do that now. I'm an investigative reporter." He handed her a business card. "As a breed, we are the scum of the earth, as I'm sure you know."

Ginny found the corner of her mouth twitching. At least he had a sense of humor. "Go on."

"For many years I've been following the career of Senator Patterson. I'm interested in his family. His mother died recently, before I could interview her, but Mrs. Olafsson was her niece. I'm hoping she can answer a few questions for me."

Ginny's eyes narrowed. "How did you end up on my doorstep?"

"A charming but implacable young woman in a nurse's uniform suggested I apply to Mr. Mackenzie. He is, I gather, the local mayor. He suggested I speak to you."

Ginny's eyebrows rose. The Laird had sent this officious man to her? "I find that hard to believe."

Scala nodded. "He warned me you would, and told me I was to say, 'The enemy of my enemy is my friend,' and to give you this." He handed her an envelope with the Loch Lonach emblem stamped on the back. Ginny recognized the Laird's stationery and his handwriting. It was dated this morning.

Ginny, I've taken the liberty of investigating this reporter. He is who he says he is. I have further inquiries in hand, but if you can do it without giving anything away, perhaps you can find out what he wants.

Ginny tucked the note back into the envelope, then looked at the reporter. "Are you going to be in town for a few days?"

He nodded.

"And can I reach you at the number on your card?"

"You can, day or night."

"Let me make some phone calls and see what I can arrange. I will be in touch."

"It's very kind of you. Thank you."

Ginny watched him descend the driveway, get into his car, and pull away from the curb. Jim would sleep until midafternoon so he could not be consulted until then and she was due at Patsy's in an hour. Which meant she would have to look up Lorenzo Scala, Investigative Reporter after she got home.

She closed the door and went back to the kitchen, finished her preparations there, then pulled off her apron and headed for the Olafsson residence.

* * *

Tuesday morning
Olafsson residence

Ginny and the psychiatrist had arranged to meet at Patsy Olafsson's house. She arrived a bit early and found him waiting for her. They rang the doorbell together and were admitted by the caregiver.

"Good morning, Violet. How are you today?" Ginny smiled at the young woman.

"Fine, thank you, Mrs. M."

"And our patient?"

"She had a bad night. I'll let her tell you about it."

Ginny and Dr. Urquhart made their way to the old lady's bedroom and found her dozing.

"I hate to wake her."

Dr. Urquhart shrugged. "Can't be helped. We need to find out what's going on in that head of hers."

Ginny touched the old woman's shoulder. "Patsy, wake up. You have a visitor."

She came to with a start, then a gasp as she caught sight of the psychiatrist. Her face flushed and she stammered an apology. "I—I'm sorry. I thought you were—" She shook her head. "No. I'm wrong. You're not—"

Ginny's brow furrowed as she introduced them. "I'm sorry to startle you and even sorrier to have to wake you. This is Dr. Urquhart."

Patsy blinked, then took a deep breath. "Urquhart. I seem to remember that name." Her face cleared. "A pair of boys, rascals, as I recollect. The younger one, what was his name? Martin!"

Dr. Urquhart laughed. "Yes, ma'am. Martin is my younger brother. I'm Chris."

Patsy's color was improving by the minute. She smiled at Chris. "I used to come watch you play football."

"Well, that's been a while." Chris indicated a chair. "May I?"

She nodded, then turned to Ginny. "I'm happy to see you, dear. Would you like something to drink?"

"No thank you." Ginny took a breath, then plunged right in. "Dr. Urquhart is a psychiatrist. I've asked him to come talk to you to see if he can help us clear up this confusion about Tommy."

Mrs. O.'s face clouded. "I feel so guilty. Why can't I remember him?"

"I have a theory," Chris said. "But I'll need your help to prove it."

"What kind of help?"

"I need for you to trust me, and I know that can be hard, so I've asked Ginny to stay. Will that be all right with you?"

Patsy nodded. "I'll feel better with her here. I hope you aren't offended."

"Not at all." He smiled. "Violet said you had a bad night. Will you tell us about it?"

Ginny watched Patsy Olafsson relax and was struck again with the charismatic power Chris Urquhart seemed to have over women.

"It's so silly," Patsy said. "And you know my mind is going. Ginny will have told you."

"What she told me was that you have cancer and have been undergoing chemotherapy. That can addle anyone's brain."

Patsy smiled at Ginny. "She's such a sweet child. She's been helping me with my genealogy. I'm trying to get it all down on paper before I die."

"So what happened last night?"

Patsy's brow furrowed. "I think I was hallucinating, but it might have been left over from the—" She stopped and glanced at Ginny, who smiled at her.

"Don't worry. He knows all about the Broonies."

Patsy lifted an eyebrow. "You could call those hallucinations, too, I suppose, and caused by a sleeping pill of all things!"

Chris' face split in a grin. "Oh, but it's so much more fun to blame it on the Broonies!"

Patsy laughed, and Ginny relaxed, settling down in her chair to listen.

Chris led Patsy gently back to the night terrors. "You saw a face, looking in your window?"

Patsy nodded. "And I felt I should know him. As if I'd seen him before. Like when I opened my eyes just now and saw you. A face from long ago. The night girl checked, but didn't see anything, so I guess I imagined him."

Chris and Ginny exchanged looks and Ginny made a mental note to check the flowerbed for footprints before they left.

"Okay. Let's talk about the Broonies for a moment. When did they start? Do you know?"

"I can tell you exactly. It was two days after Mrs. Patterson's funeral. They buried her on Saturday and I didn't sleep for two nights after that. It hit too close to home, I think. Anyway, I went to the doctor on Tuesday, and that's when he gave me those sleeping pills, and the next day I noticed things had moved during the night. I didn't know what was causing it, though. Not until Dr. Mackenzie saw the prescription bottle."

Chris nodded. "That was the Saturday before Ginny's wedding?"

"Saturday week, because she got married on a Sunday, you see."

"So you started taking the sleeping pills on Tuesday, and the Broonies started showing up the next day?"

"Yes." Patsy sighed. "They tell me that sometime between that first pill and the wedding, I went up into the attic to get a candlestick, wrapped it up, and delivered it to the Cooperative Hall, but I don't remember any of it."

"That's okay. We're going to work on your memory. Can you describe the face in the window?"

Patsy shrugged. "An old man's face. Or a ghost's. It was white enough to be a ghost. And I couldn't see any clothing, just the head, floating there. Like Banquo."

"Didn't Banquo have a body?" Ginny objected.

Chris nodded. "He did. He sat down in Macbeth's seat." He looked back at Patsy. "Why did you mention Banquo?"

Patsy's eyes lit up. "Alan has talked me into playing one of the witches. Well, Hecate. She doesn't have as many lines."

"Banquo's ghost represents Macbeth's guilty conscience. You mentioned feeling bad about not remembering your brother. Do you think that could have caused a hallucination?"

Patsy nodded. "Oh yes. I feel terribly guilty. How could anyone forget she had a little brother, even if he's dead?"

"That's one of the things you and I are going to find out. But for the moment I want to focus on that ghost. Did he make any sound?"

Patsy's brow furrowed. "Yes. He did." She paled. "He tapped on the window. That was what woke me."

"Did you get out of bed to go investigate?"

Patsy shivered. "No, I was too afraid."

"Did you consider it might have been a real person, tapping at your window to get your attention?"

Patsy frowned harder. "Yes! I was sure it was someone I knew. Someone I didn't want to speak to. I pulled the covers over my head and tried to hide. Priscilla found me that way."

"Patsy," Chris said, "I don't want to frighten you, but I think there's something going on here, and that we need to get to the bottom of it. Your instincts are doing a good job of protecting you. Listen to them. If you feel uncomfortable about anything, let someone know. It may be important."

"Like what?"

"Like that face in the window. You said you didn't want to talk to him."

Patsy blinked. "It was more than that. He scared me."

Chris nodded. "See? I think that's important. When we

know more, we'll be able to deal with the fear, but I've got some digging to do before then. So chin up and be sure to let us know if you remember anything else." He picked up a pad lying on the table and handed it to her. "I'm going to give you a homework assignment. When you feel strong enough, write down everything you remember from last night. Every detail, no matter how trivial. There might be a clue in it. Can you do that?"

She nodded.

"I think that's enough for one day," Chris said. He looked over at Ginny. "Tomorrow?"

Ginny nodded. She still hadn't had a chance to talk to Jim and she had to swing by the hospital to pick up some files, but she wasn't scheduled to work tonight or tomorrow.

Chris turned back to Patsy. "Will that work for you? Tomorrow morning, around ten?"

Patsy nodded. "It's so kind of you to help me."

"That's what I'm here for." Chris smiled at her, then took her hand. "And I think Ginny can promise you no more nocturnal visitors."

Ginny nodded.

"So, I will see you again tomorrow."

"Thank you, Doctor."

Ginny bent down to kiss the old woman's cheek. "I'm going to go look at the flower bed under your window, so don't let that disturb you."

"I won't."

"Do you want me to send Violet to you?"

"Actually, I'm a little tired. I think I'll sleep."

"Good idea." Ginny pulled the shades, then found Violet and let her know what was going on. "I'll let Himself know. He'll want to follow up, I'm sure."

Ginny led Chris around the side of the house, to the spot

underneath Mrs. O.'s bedroom window, and pushed aside the holly bushes. She peered at the dirt, then stepped back. "What do you see?"

"Footprints, big enough for a man."

"And, look here. See the broken branches? He must have had to force his way in to reach her window."

"Look, here's something else." Chris pointed to a round indentation in the earth.

Ginny nodded. "I see it. What's more, I recognize it. Canes, the kind the elderly use, come capped with rubber tips that have ridges, for better traction. They leave concentric circles on the floor—just like those." She looked at Chris. "Do we mount a guard until the police can look at this evidence?" Ginny already had her phone out, dialing Detective Tran's number. "I'll stay, so you can go back to your office."

"If they want to talk to me, they know where to find me. But if anyone asks, I think Mrs. Olafsson was entertaining more than a ghost in her garden last night."

* * *

CHAPTER 12

Tuesday afternoon
Mackenzie residence

Jim was still asleep when Ginny got home. She slipped upstairs and into her office chair, pulling up Patsy Olafsson's genealogy first, and filling in the aunts and uncles and cousins. Sure enough, Patsy turned out to be Senator Patterson's first cousin, on their mothers' side. The ladies had been Killough sisters before their respective marriages.

There were two children born to each sister, a boy and a girl. In Patsy's case, the girl had come first. The opposite was true in the Patterson family. In each case, one of the siblings had died young: Patsy's little brother of the head injury, the Senator's sister of an unspecified accident in her early twenties. An odd coincidence, but not unknown.

Ginny put the genealogy away and turned her attention to Scala. A quick scan of articles about Senator Patterson turned up none with Scala's byline. There were a couple that had no author assigned, but that proved nothing.

Lorenzo Scala did, however, have a number of articles under his own name and published by respectable news outlets, all focused on politicians and suggesting some level of reform was needed to bring the subject's actions into line with his or her stated position. No surprises there.

Personal information on Mr. Scala revealed he lived in Springfield, Illinois, had majored in journalism, wrote a weekly blog on the evils of politicians, and had never married. His hobbies included photography, international travel, and musical theatre. Apparently he could sing for he was listed in the chorus of the Springfield Municipal Opera Association, better known as "The Muni." Ginny found this impressive. Not proof of anything, of course, but suggestive. She made some notes, then closed the files and slipped back downstairs.

She found Jim awake and in the kitchen, making himself a cup of coffee. "Hello, Husband." She reached up to give him a peck on the cheek.

"Hello, Wife." He set his cup down and addressed himself to a proper greeting, after which he went back to his coffee. He smiled at her. "What's the news?"

Ginny got herself a glass of ice water and settled down at the table. "When I left Mrs. Olafsson's house, the police were still taking measurements."

Jim started. "The police?"

Ginny nodded. "The poor thing was scared out of her mind by a midnight visitor. She thought she was hallucinating, but we found evidence of someone standing in the holly bushes below her window. Angus is engaging guards."

Jim frowned. "Is she in danger?"

"It's hard to say. Until we know what she can't tell us, we have to assume the worst."

Jim nodded. "Who was this midnight visitor?"

Ginny described the tale of the ghost in the garden, and of the terror the incident had caused. She frowned. "I got the impression Patsy's fear was based on something real, some incident from her past."

"It's possible, especially if she really did witness her

brother's death."

Ginny nodded. "Here's what I've been thinking. Imagine you're seven years old, and scared beyond anything you've experienced up to that point."

Jim grinned. "Okay. I'm a terrified little girl."

"Now imagine what you would do."

Jim considered this for a moment. "Run to mama, I suppose."

Ginny nodded. "Me, too, but there's no mention of what the little girl said, just that she was there."

Jim sat down across from Ginny. "It's officially a slip and fall, right?"

She nodded. "The report says the child landed on the corner of a glass coffee table."

Jim's brow furrowed. "Kids hit their heads every day and some of them manage to break their skulls. But to die from it, you have to either bleed into your brain or, if the swelling is bad enough, herniate the brain stem. Neither of those happens immediately." He looked over at her. "Hitting a coffee table must have been noisy. Where were the adults who were supposed to be watching these children?"

Ginny blinked. There was no way to tell from the written record which of the adults had responded, or when. But there had been no hint of delay in treating the child. He'd been taken to an appropriate medical facility and—the implication was—in a timely manner. "Are you suggesting the other children ran off and left him there to die?"

Jim shook his head. "I'm not suggesting anything. I'm just pointing out that it would have taken some time and, if the police had been called immediately, he would have arrived at the ER while still alive. Probably."

Ginny frowned. "Would the ER staff have noticed a delay?"

"I would expect so."

"Then they should have reported it."

Jim nodded. "If this child showed up in my ER, I'd be suspicious."

"Could you tell what really happened, if you saw the medical records?"

"Maybe. Maybe not. Can you get your hands on them?"

"Detective Tran may be able to, or Angus." Ginny frowned harder. Some disturbing ideas were forming in her brain. "Jim, could this have been a cover-up?"

"What do you mean?"

"Suppose the child was hit with the candlestick really hard, and he fell down which scared the other two children."

"How do you come up with two other children?"

"Mrs. O. was one and the unidentified set of fingerprints was the other, and there might have been more. Anyway, this boy looks dead to them and they get scared and want to hide what they've done. Could they have come up with the idea of the coffee table?"

Jim's eyes narrowed. "It depends. There might have been a teenager who was supposed to be watching them. If she comes in and finds the boy dead, she might want to make it look like a slip and fall."

"Only if she suspects one of the children of swinging that candlestick. Otherwise she has no motive for tampering with the crime scene."

"It's not a crime scene if it was really an accident."

"I know, but how else do you account for Mrs. O.'s hiding that candlestick?"

"I can't."

"According to the newspaper article, there was a cousin present. Patsy had two cousins at that point, the children of her mother's sister."

"Let me guess. Patterson."

Ginny smiled swiftly. "Yes, one boy and one girl."

"Where are you going with this?"

"Two cousins and one set of unidentified fingerprints on the candlestick."

Jim paused to consider the point. "That narrows the field."

Ginny nodded. "Yes, it does, and there's one more fact to be included."

"What's that?"

"The girl cousin is dead."

* * *

Tuesday evening
Mackenzie residence

"Jim, this is Lorenzo Scala. He's the man I told you about." The two of them shook hands.

It had taken her an hour to explain to Jim about their morning visitor and the message Angus had sent, then another hour to talk him into inviting Mr. Scala for dinner, so they could size him up and report back to Himself. Ginny excused herself to finish the dinner preparations, but kept the kitchen door open so she could hear their conversation.

"My wife tells me you have an interest in Senator Patterson."

"I do. I've been interested in him for many years."

"Yet you haven't written about him."

"Not by name, and I may never be in a position to do so. I'm trying to verify my sources."

"Verify. That implies less-than-complimentary content."

"And my publisher is not interested in theories."

"I understand that."

"You write?"

"In my own field, for peer-reviewed medical journals."

"Ah!"

There was a moment of silence and Ginny found herself unable to resist peeking in on them. The two men studied one another, like two strange dogs circling one another, looking for a weakness.

Scala broke the silence. "If you, in your professional capacity, believe the mainstream is wrong about something—a diagnosis, a treatment, an ethical decision—how do you handle it in your writing?"

Jim's eyes narrowed as he formed his answer. "I present the reason for my dissention, with solid arguments, based on facts. I go through why the current belief exists and show why I think that should change. And I invite readers to test my theories for themselves."

"And if no facts exist?"

"Then I don't write the article."

Scala nodded. "Investigative journalism is similar. With the exception that just one fact can be enough to start a serious investigation. That's what I hope to find here. One solid fact that cannot be erased, ignored, or swept under the carpet."

"Are you telling me," Jim said, "that you're trying to discredit Senator Patterson? And that you've been trying for years to get something concrete to use against him?"

Scala shrugged. "It sounds worse when you put it that way, but, yes, that's what I'm trying to do." He sighed. "And it looks as if I may not be able to."

"Why are you still pursuing him, then?"

Lorenzo Scala sat back, put his hands on his knees, and looked at Jim. "*That* I am not prepared to share with you. But I believe Mrs. Olafsson holds the key to the Senator's past, and that key will unlock the lips of those who have refused to speak until now."

"What's the urgency? He's almost at retirement age. Is there something in particular hanging in the balance?"

Scala shook his head. "Not that I'm aware of. Not of the sort you mean. But I will tell you this. The man should not be allowed to retire on a senator's pension. He does not deserve to be rewarded for what he has done."

"That you can't prove."

"That I can't prove—yet."

Ginny stepped around the corner. "Dinner is served."

There was no more said on the subject of Maury Patterson until the dinner was consumed and the group settled comfortably in the living room.

"Some more pie, Signor Scala?" Ginny asked.

"Yes, please, and please call me Larry." He finished the pie and settled back in his chair with a contented sigh, coffee cup in hand. Jim was doing the same.

"That was delicious," Scala said. "And now, in true Italian style, I must sing for my supper. Where to begin?"

"Why don't you tell us how you know Senator Patterson?" Jim suggested.

Scala nodded. He fell silent for a moment, a far-away look in his eye, then he drew breath and began. "It was a coincidence that I ended up at the same college Maury Patterson attended. We had no prior connection. I was ten years behind him, and by all rights, I should never have known he existed." His brow furrowed. "But I wanted to be a reporter, so I studied journalism, and I wrote for the school rag, and I was always on the lookout for an idea, something to write about. We met at an alumni dinner. It was a fund-raiser. He was a donor. I was a sophomore covering the event for the paper." He looked from Jim to Ginny, then back again. "I assume you know his father was one of the richest men in Illinois. That made Patterson news, even before he ran for the state legislature." Scala frowned. "Here I must confess to a very human weakness."

"You liked seeing your byline in the paper?" Jim's dimple flashed.

The reporter smiled at him. "Yes, but that's not what I was referring to. The man annoyed me. He condescended, and his manner seemed—" He searched for the right word. "—exaggerated."

Ginny exchanged glances with Jim, remembering the meeting in the boot store.

"And he had a following of sycophants." Scala's nose wrinkled, as if he smelled something unpleasant in the room. "I made up my mind that I would bring him down a peg or two. It would do his soul good and my career no harm." He took a sip of his coffee, pausing again to collect his thoughts.

"I dug up his school records, starting with a private and very exclusive prep school. I had to tread carefully, you understand, because he was important and very rich and contributed heavily to the endowment fund. So those first articles were all disguised." A smile spread across his face. "But that was what made it so easy. He thought he was bulletproof, even then."

"Do you have copies of the articles? May we read them?" Ginny asked.

Scala nodded. "I have copies of everything. Paper as well as digital. Notarized where possible, and accompanied by signed statements."

Ginny's brow rose. "Notarized?"

Jim echoed her surprise. "Signed statements?"

Scala's smile faded. "Yes, but it hasn't done me any good. I can't prove a thing."

"You suspect him of misbehavior," Jim said.

"And how! Let me get this out. Then we can talk about what it means—what it may mean."

Jim nodded. "Please, continue."

"I had my fun in school, but that's all it was. He didn't even read what I had written. He had no reason to. So, after I graduated and got a job, he became my hobby. I had regular assignments, but I spent all my free time following Maury Patterson. He wanted to be a senator and politicians are fair game. My boss even supported me. He had ideas about freedom of the press and our obligation to the voting public. His support did not extend to a photographer so I acquired a good camera and a long lens and learned how to use them."

Ginny nodded.

Scala shrugged. "For ten years, he did nothing worth reporting. I wasn't there every minute, you understand. I had my own life to lead. But when I could be there, all he did was go to church, or charity functions, or give innocuous speeches about saving the planet and a chicken in every pot."

Scala's face took on a troubled expression. "Then, one weekend I followed him to a cabin near the Hiawatha National Forest. That's in far northern Michigan, almost to Canada, and a long way from his usual stomping grounds. He was meeting a young woman. I took pictures of them both, expecting nothing worse than some unauthorized nookie."

Ginny smiled at the term.

"At the time, he was married to his first wife, the daughter of a very influential man. Any hint of impropriety could ruin his political ambitions. That was my angle. There were rumors, whispers really, that there had been other assignations, but nothing in the papers, not even the scandal rags. It would be a scoop if I could deliver the goods." Scala's eyes narrowed.

"The cabin was on private property, but that doesn't stop a determined journalist. I hid my car behind some bushes, then followed on foot. Patterson and the girl had driven their cars right up to the cabin. They were already inside when I got there. So I found a good spot to set up my tripod and waited.

"After a while, enough time for them to have a nice long chat, Patterson came out. His tie was no longer tied and his jacket was over his arm. The close-ups showed lipstick on his neck, which meant I had what I'd come for. I grabbed my gear and followed him. He went straight home and I went straight to my editor."

Scala made a sour face. "I wrote up the story, then went to hand it in, but I was too late. The woman had been found—dead—and no one cared if she and the Senator had been playing house. All of a sudden, it was murder."

Ginny's eyes widened, but she kept her mouth shut. Jim did not. "What happened?"

Scala sighed. "There was a back door to the cabin. They found her naked corpse in the woods. She'd been strangled." Scala ran his hand through his hair. "My boss suggested I call the police. They questioned me, and I turned over my photographs, and they checked my story, then let me go. They cleared Patterson as well. Couldn't find any forensic evidence to tie him to the corpse." Scala snorted. "Lipstick on his collar and they couldn't find any evidence!" He shook his head. "I was told it was probably a stranger who killed her. But it wasn't an isolated incident. There were others."

Jim's brow furrowed. "What are you suggesting?"

Scala lifted his eyes and looked at Jim, then Ginny, then back at Jim. "What I'm saying is that he'd done it before. Senator Maury Patterson is a serial killer."

* * *

CHAPTER 13

Wednesday morning
Olafsson residence

Ginny sat in the corner of the darkened room and took notes. It had been Chris' idea. He'd said it was useful to have an observer's point of view.

Patsy was out of bed and looked stronger than Ginny had seen her since that day at the genealogy library. She seemed pleased to have company. She was chatting with the psychiatrist, recalling his glory days on the gridiron, and some less glorious episodes involving the First of April one year. Chris and Martin had been ten and eight at the time and Patsy's memory of the episode was crystal clear.

Chris was attempting to hypnotize her and, in Ginny's opinion, it wasn't working. Patsy answered every question, but only as a distant memory, not as a recent event, fresh in her mind. He kept at it for an hour, then gave up, enquiring instead whether Patsy had been sleeping.

"Not well. Not since that face in the window."

"The guards are keeping everyone off your property. Does the pain wake you in the night?"

"Sometimes. Sometimes I can't get comfortable, and sometimes the coughing wakes me up."

"How would it be if I talked to Dr. Weisbrod about that?"

"I'd appreciate it. Thank you."

"I'll take care of it. Now," Chris rose from his chair, "with your permission, I'd like to look around the house, to see if I can find anything I think might be useful."

Patsy nodded. "Be my guest."

Ginny escorted Chris though the public rooms before heading to the attic. He climbed the stairs, then stood looking around. After a bit he spoke.

"Show me what you found."

She led him to the trunk that held the remnants of the boy-child's life. "Here are the clothes, toys, mementos, everything having to do with Tommy Bryant, except for the photograph album, which you've already seen."

Chris went through the contents of the trunk, examining each item, then replacing them, and closing the lid. "No blood on any of these clothes. I gather whatever he was wearing on the day he died was discarded."

"I got the impression that only the ceremonial clothes made it into the trunk."

"But she kept his cowboy hat and boots."

"The things he would have valued, yes."

Chris nodded, and climbed to his feet. "What else do you have to show me?"

"I think I know where the candlestick was hidden." She led the way to the back of the attic, to a dusty corner crowded with pieces of old furniture, most of it draped in dust sheets. She pointed at the top shelf of a low bookcase pushed up against the wall. "The pattern in the dust is the same shape as the base of the candlestick Patsy sent to me."

Chris leaned in to examine the spot, then nodded. "So where did it come from?"

Ginny went down on her knees beside an old sea chest that abutted the bookcase. "From here, I think." She lifted the lid, fighting the rusty hinges.

The chest held the artifacts of a sailor's life: a compass and sextant, a tattered ensign, old uniforms, scrimshaw, unfinished embroidery, a meerschaum pipe, a cap. She handed the items out to Chris, one by one, then removed a framed photograph. Someone had written names on it, and the date. It showed two men, one younger, one older, both named Bryant.

"Father and son, do you think?" Ginny asked.

"Ancestors, at any rate."

Ginny nodded. "Patsy said her grandfather was a sailor. This chest may have belonged to him." She emptied it completely, then peered into the depths of the box. "Look." She pointed to a black stain on the wood bottom. "If the candlestick was thrust into this chest by the young Patsy Bryant, with fresh blood on it, that could account for the stain."

"So how did the box end up here?"

"I'm guessing the sea chest, and the trunk with Tommy's things in it, were both in the Bryant family attic until the house was sold, then moved here for storage, probably without opening them."

Chris's brow furrowed. "Do we know why the candlestick was removed from the chest and placed on the bookcase?"

Ginny frowned. "Again, I'm guessing, but it looks as if Patsy dug it out and set it aside. Maybe she was looking for something else and realized it didn't belong in the box, but didn't remember what it meant." She looked up at Chris. "Could she have done that? Seen the candlestick and not recognized it?"

He nodded. "Certainly, but it appears her subconscious knew it was here and didn't want it to go back into hiding."

"I can believe that." Ginny looked at the contents of the sea chest. "What do we do with these things? Put them back?"

Chris nodded. "I think so."

Ginny pulled out her phone and took several pictures of the blood stain, then the two of them repacked the sea chest, and made their way downstairs. They took their leave of Patsy, and were let out the front door by the day nurse. Chris turned on the stoop to face Ginny.

"Thank you for your help. Those things in the attic give me a lot of ammunition to use the next time I try to jog Patsy's memory. I just need to decide how best to deploy them."

Ginny laughed. "You make it sound like a military campaign."

"That's not a bad analogy. Her memory is barricaded behind as stout a rampart as I have ever seen. It will take a full scale assault to get past those defenses."

Ginny's smile faded. "That sounds so violent. Is it going to hurt her?"

"Physically, no. Emotionally?" Chris sighed. "If she hadn't asked for help, I wouldn't be doing this. When her memory does return, I'm afraid she may find the truth very painful indeed."

* * *

Wednesday morning
Chancie Mor

Senator Patterson sat in the back seat of the dark blue sedan and stared at the Olafsson residence. He had seen Ginny Mackenzie and Dr. Urquhart enter only moments after he arrived and decided to wait for a bit to see if their visit would be a short one. If so, he was inclined to try to gain entry again. Perhaps there was a different nurse guarding the gates this time. He glanced at his pocket watch, then sighed, leaned forward, and addressed his driver. "Home, James."

"Yes, sir."

Patterson looked out the window as they made their way back to Chancie Mor. He had people coming this morning—supporters and donors. He frowned. He needed to have the place cleaned, and Rita would have to hire new staff. Most of those who had waited on his mother had been well past retirement age. He'd given the lot of them a vacation, at his expense, moved into a hotel, and hired a caterer to supply this meal. It would be wise to walk the rooms to make sure there was nothing that could offend his guests.

The car swept onto the road that edged the lake. It was a pleasant sight. The weather was a bit warm, of course, but seasonable for Texas. He remembered from his childhood how hot the summers could be. This morning wasn't so bad, and it was dry, with a light breeze. He watched a sailboat tack and come around into the wind. Very pretty. And people who owned sailboats had money.

Chancie Mor stood on a rise overlooking the water, its one-and-a-half acre of sloping front lawn verdant and inviting. The yard crew could stay. The sweep drive climbed to the porch, then curved around the side of the house to the garages. There was space for a dozen or so visitors out front and more behind, plenty to accommodate his guests. He waited for the driver to pull to a stop, then come around and open the door for him.

"Thank you, James. Ask whoever you find in the kitchen to feed you. I'll be going out again this afternoon."

"Yes, sir."

Patterson climbed the four broad steps to the porch, then turned and surveyed his domain. It was the biggest house on Homestead land, true, but not that big, really. It was only three stories and two smallish wings, plus the bedrooms. The front room had seen its fair share of parties, but the guest lists had been smaller when the house was built. He would find a new location and construct something that didn't have a historic marker or rules about renovations. Besides, this house was and always would be his mother's. Her ghost would walk the halls and hover over his shoulder as he slept. Much better to build one of his own. His eldest boy might want the place. He'd keep it, and keep it up. No sense annoying the neighbors.

He turned and let himself in, pulling the screened door aside to reach the heavy brass handle. The ancient oak creaked as he swung the door inward and the wood floor groaned as he stepped inside, setting off a cascade of memories, none of them especially happy.

He turned left and walked through the parlor, heading for the kitchen. Twenty minutes of inspection assured him that the food would be acceptable and the service correct. That done, he made his way to the guest bedroom he'd staked out as his office until further notice. He'd left papers in one of the suitcases. Old fashioned, true, but he liked to be able to spread out, which could not be done with a computer, and this room had a massive desk in the adjoining study.

He sat down in the armchair near the back window and examined his notes. The key to this campaign would be the popular vote. The districting was in his favor—it included the entirety of Dallas County. That covered a wide variety of communities, not just this old and out-of-date autocracy. He paused for a moment.

He'd been born here and into this community, this culture, but he'd never felt as if he belonged. He'd been relieved when his father had gathered up the family and moved to Illinois. No history there to get in his way. They had avoided the company of the Illinois Homesteaders, declining invitations to social events and resisting the efforts made to draw the Patterson family in. As a result, Patterson felt no kinship with the Loch Lonach citizens, even less with their leaders.

The incumbent, Texas Senator Ian Hunter, was an excellent example of the old order. His politics were fossilized, trapped in the ethos of the Texas pioneers, unable to move with the times. He still believed in Scotland's Calvinist ideal of hard work, thrift, and education. As a result, Hunter was tolerated, but only just. It would not take much to suggest to the voters that there was a better way, one in which they need not work, if they were willing to accept Patterson's leadership. It was time for Senator Hunter to step aside.

Patterson had sent representatives ahead to take the pulse of the various communities in the district. They were a mixed bunch, hailing from twenty countries and as many different ways of life. His agents had reported pockets of discontent, mostly drawn along social inequality lines, but there were culture clashes as well. The one thing they all agreed on was that their adopted country, in this case, Texas, should support them in whatever they believed was their right to have, do, hold, or say. Freedom from want was the battle cry. Freedom from poverty. Freedom from oppression. Freedom from having to pay bills. Patterson smiled. If that was what they wanted, that was what he would promise them. For a price, of course. Because there was no such thing as a free lunch.

He folded his notes and tucked them inside his jacket, then rose with the help of his cane, and headed for the front of the house. He had timed it perfectly. The first of the committee members was just climbing the porch stairs. Patterson put on his public smile and went to greet his guest.

* * *

CHAPTER 14

Wednesday morning
Mackenzie residence

It was Wednesday morning and Jim was restless. After Ginny left for her appointment with Patsy and the psychiatrist, he'd gone out to the lake to talk to the Corinthian Sailing Club officials, sign papers, hand over money, and in general waste as much time as he could on his new (used) sailboat. He'd been introduced to other members of the club, listened to their conversations, answered their questions, and made himself as agreeable as possible.

When he could think of no more excuses for hanging out with the other sailors, he had driven to the far side of the lake, climbed on top of a picnic table—*the* picnic table where he and Ginny had met by accident last October—and watched the sails on the water.

Jim didn't usually feel nervous, but he was feeling it now. In addition to a trailer, he would need a new car. His BMW didn't have enough horsepower to tow the sailboat. What's more, the garage hadn't been designed for larger vehicles. His sedan just barely fit as it was.

He hadn't thought this through. And he wasn't at all sure what Ginny was going to say when he told her. Money wasn't really a problem, but her Scottish instincts would baulk at unnecessary expenses. Well, he would just have to confess and throw himself on her mercy. Because the deed was done. He owned a sailboat and everyone knew that a boat was just a hole in the water into which you poured money.

It was a nice day, but *sumer* was *icumen in* and it was getting warm. He got down off the picnic table, drove home, dropped his keys on the kitchen table, and looked around.

He knew what he should be doing. He should be working on his article. He was a bit ahead of schedule, but that could change at any moment. Unfortunately, he couldn't seem to focus.

He prowled the house, poking his nose into each room in turn, fully aware that he wasn't going to find what he was looking for. He climbed the stairs and continued his prowling on the second floor.

Ginny had chosen the side of the house that faced the loch for her office. He leaned against the door jamb and let his eyes rest on the blues and greens of the shifting water. They had updated all the windows before moving in. Now they were pristine, double-paned, and larger than the originals, with sills, and blinds, and child-proof locks.

From his current position he could see the Cooperative Hall perched on the ridge across the lake, its white facade partially hidden by ancient oaks, in full leaf at this time of the year, though some were growing old enough for the limbs to fail of life. It was a bucolic and restful scene, but not restful enough. Jim turned from the empty room and examined the upstairs hall.

The afternoon sun danced on the polished wood floor, coming through the beveled glass octagon set high in the end wall. He headed in that direction, opening doors as he went. The floor creaked as he moved, reminding him of nights in Virginia spent trying to raid the refrigerator, only to find one parent or the other waiting for him in the kitchen. Those had been some of the best nights of his life, nibbling on pie or roast beef, talking, laughing, then returning to bed with a sense of comfort and security that made it easy for him to fall asleep the minute his head hit the pillow.

There were a number of potential bedrooms on this floor, all empty at present, with enough attic space to put beds there as well. In a pinch, they would be able to accommodate any number of visiting relatives. He opened the last door in line on the front side of the house.

This room was smaller than the rest, and filled to overflowing with wedding presents. Ginny must have stashed them here when she cleared the downstairs. Jim's brow furrowed. He hadn't even noticed, and hadn't been asked to help. He stepped inside and looked around.

This room, and the one opposite it across the hall, had windows looking out toward the neighbors as well as the front and back yards, respectively. Someone had planted red oaks along the property line, more than thirty years ago by the look of them. They spread a welcome canopy over the side of the house and would go a long way toward reducing the air conditioning bill.

The sun streamed in through the uncurtained windows, and lit the glittering dust motes which swirled across the room, then settled to the floor in the wake of his entrance. Jim was transported back even further, to his grandfather's house and the summer afternoons filled with this same sunshine and these same dust motes.

He smiled, then turned and made his way back toward the stairs, still opening doors. This set of rooms faced the fenced backyard, the alley, and the hill that rose behind the house to a copse, complete with the ruins of an ancient stone edifice. He would need to explore those ruins before much longer, to make sure they were safe to play in.

The middle room on this side was actually a bathroom. It was positioned over the powder room on the main floor, the one reserved for guests, so the water would have a straight fall and there should be fewer plumbing issues. Everything worked at present. That had been assured before they moved in, and Jim had been promised any help he needed in the house maintenance department—one of the perks of being his grandfather's heir. All the baths had been updated, too, which meant the fluorescent pink tile that had been in this room had been replaced with warm ivory and pale gold. Ginny had added yellow towels as accents. He moved on.

When Jim opened the last door in line he saw evidence of decorating. There were paint chips and swatches of fabric and samples of wallpaper. He picked them up and smiled. Ducks, pirates, dinosaurs, and one he decided was his favorite, a wallpaper border that showed a child having adventure after adventure as the images traveled around the room.

Jim set the materials down and left, closing the door behind him. In that room, even more than in her office, Ginny's absence was almost visceral. It should have been easy to fall into his before-he-met-her habits. He knew that, soon enough, he would relish these quiet moments by himself. But not today. Today he wanted her here.

He descended the stair and took himself off to his study, forced himself into his exceptionally comfortable leather chair, and faced the computer. His current work-in-progress came up sweetly and he read what he'd done so far, then read it again, then a third time, then gave up, realizing his attention was elsewhere. He leaned back in the chair and let his mind wander.

The reporter had said something last night that had started an idea in the back of his mind. He opened a blank document and began jotting down notes. *A single fact can lead to a full scale investigation.* That had relevance for medicine, too.

What usually happened when physicians were faced with a symptom they couldn't explain, was to set it aside. After all, medicine was mostly guesswork and playing the percentages. It would make an interesting article—the diagnosis that got away because the critical clue was missing.

He worked on the idea for an hour, then took a break. There were plates of sliced beef and containers of chopped vegetables in the refrigerator. Jim collected some of each, and salad dressing to dip them in, then sat down at the kitchen table.

"The problem with you," he said out loud, "is that you actually *like* your wife, and you would like to be able to impress her with your perception and incisive thinking." He took a bite, chewing thoughtfully on a carrot. What could he offer her, to help her solve the mystery of the dead child? What had he seen or heard that she might have overlooked? Because, although this wasn't a competition, he'd like to feel useful.

Jim chewed on the problem while he chewed on the food. There was a school of thought in the medical field that suggested chewing stimulated the flow of blood to the brain. There was also, of course, an equally erudite school of experts who denied the whole thing.

Well, true or not, the trick wasn't working. If he knew something, he was going to have to wait for it to surface. In the meantime, he now had two articles to finish. He cleaned up the kitchen and went back to work.

* * *

Wednesday afternoon
Various

When Jim heard Ginny come in, he abandoned his writing, ushered her into the kitchen, and fed her on roast beef sandwiches and iced tea. While she ate, he summarized his visit to the lake, and listened to her report of the morning's session with Patsy. When the conversation petered out, she set aside her plate and eyed him across the table.

"Well?"

"Well what?"

"You're holding something back. What is it?"

Jim took a breath and plunged in. "Darling, sweet, kind, understanding Ginny, I have something I want to ask you."

Her eyes widened. "Oh?"

"I've bought a boat."

The corner of her mouth twitched. "I'd noticed."

"And it's going to be great. You're going to love it." He watched her struggle to keep a straight face. "But there are some things we're going to need."

She had managed to control her mouth, but her eyes were laughing. "Such as?"

"I need a trailer, and a car capable of towing that much weight."

She blinked. "What kind of a car?"

"One designed for recreation, which means we can use it to go camping, or skiing, or antiquing, or hauling kids to soccer practice. Lots of things that I hope will be part of our life. And I want you to help me pick it out."

She was staring at him. "Now?"

He nodded. "We have just enough time if we leave right now. I know what I want and where to find it and we can be back in time for me to get ready for work."

"This is part of owning a boat, right?"

"Yes." Jim held his breath.

She smiled, then shrugged. "Well then, let's go."

He grinned. "Remind me later to tell you how much I love you." He escorted her back to the garage and into the passenger side of his car, and climbed behind the wheel. Twenty minutes later they were walking around the car lot, listening to the salesman.

"Four wheel drive, 6.4-liter V8 engine that'll give you 475 horsepower and 470 lb-ft of torque. Twenty-three mpg on the highway, twenty-four gallon tank, regular gasoline. 8,700-lb towing capacity. The tow hitch is standard and integrated into the frame for added strength. With the trailer-tow package you get a computer assist trailer brake, light hookups, and 360 degree camera coverage. We've added an integrated trailer brake controller to this model. You just rotate the control knob in the direction you want your trailer to go, and the system automatically steers the vehicle to turn the trailer for you."

Jim felt his eyebrows rise. That could be useful. The salesman smiled, then continued. "In Tow Mode the transmission modifies shift points for maximum engine efficiency and adjusts the suspension to combat pitch and yaw, which means better sway control and optimum vehicle stability."

The man eyed Jim. "This one's got more interior space than most, more head and leg room, which you might appreciate. You want to try it?"

Jim nodded, then climbed behind the steering wheel and adjusted the seat. Perfect. As if it had been made for him. "Can we test drive it?"

"Absolutely." He handed Jim the key, then got into the back. Ginny took her seat beside Jim. "Out the gate there and turn right."

Jim followed instructions, taking the SUV up onto the highway, testing the acceleration, then exiting and circling back to a large parking lot where he could put the vehicle through tight turns, rapid braking, and blind spot testing.

"The cameras eliminate the need for extended mirrors. Just touch here." The salesman demonstrated. "And the viewscreen will show you whatever you need."

Jim drove back to the dealership, silently consulted Ginny, then completed the paperwork.

"You'll have to drive the BMW home," he told Ginny.

"I can handle it."

Jim drove off the lot with a feeling that was half trepidation and half exhilaration. He'd left his Jeep behind him in Virginia, and with it his youth, but this new toy might make up for having to settle down and become a responsible adult. He found himself grinning as he followed Ginny back to the house.

As they turned in between the massive gates that marked the eastern perimeter of the Loch Lonach community, Jim could see something was wrong. There were police cars and people milling about on the sidewalks. He followed Ginny around the edge of the lake, then up the alley to the back of their house. They had both been driving "dead slow," partly because of the irresistible impulse to gawk and partly because the streets were littered with debris. Someone had seized the trash bins and dumped them where they would cause the most disruption to traffic. Many of the bags had been torn open. Some had animals rooting around in the mess, others had the owners trying to corral their refuse. In addition, someone had launched paint bombs onto the lawns. The normally placid green of the St. Augustine was now adorned with splashes of color in every shade of the rainbow.

Ginny pulled into the garage and parked the BMW next to her VW. Jim was left to park the SUV on the apron. He locked it carefully, reminding himself that the alley had restricted access, and resolving to get a proper garage built ASAP.

He let himself in the back and hurried to look out the front door. Yellow, with a hint of puce. He was still standing there when he felt Ginny's arm circle his waist.

"What happened here, Jim?"

He shook his head. "Vandalism."

"Do we call Angus?"

"I expect he knows, but I think so." Jim pulled out his phone and dialed his grandfather's number.

"Och! Ye should see th' Cooperative Hall! Graffiti on th' walls and language tae make a sailor blush."

"Did they leave a message?"

"Aye, they did. We're *persona non grata* and free tae leave afore th' real trouble starts."

Jim had shifted position so he could put his arm around Ginny. He tightened his grip. "Sounds like we have a problem."

"Aye, but 'twas only paint and th' trash bins. Th' worst'll be gone by morning."

"I have to work tonight." Jim felt his throat constrict. "Ginny'll be home alone."

"I'll keep an eye on her, lad. Dinna worry."

"Thank you." Jim hung up, took another hard look at his lawn, then turned and guided Ginny inside, locking the door behind him.

"Angus has the clean-up in hand."

"Jim."

He dragged his mind away from the implications and looked down at his wife. She was gazing up at him, her eyes calm.

"I'll be all right. I'll take my pistol to bed with me tonight."

Jim found the assurance terrifying. "Just don't shoot me when I come in tomorrow morning."

"I have to be at the hospital before you get off work."

"Even better. We can have breakfast together."

"Deal. Now, let's get you ready." She started to pull out of his embrace, but he didn't want to let her go.

She smiled at him, then reached up and stroked his cheek. "It's all right, Jim. The house is a fortress with the alarms on."

"I know."

"And I have sworn an oath to take care of the heir of Loch Lonach, meaning you, which I can't do if I get careless. I will stay quietly at home this evening and bake. That should give you something to look forward to."

He smiled at the thought. Bread and circuses. What more could a man want? A ghost of a memory nudged the back of his brain and his smile faded. Now why did he use that phrase? He'd heard it recently. Someone else had used it, but he couldn't remember who, or in what context. His brow furrowed. Just like earlier, something was niggling at his memory and he couldn't pull it out. He shook his head. Well, he had a lot on his mind. He'd remember eventually. In the meantime, he, too, had preparations to make. He let Ginny go, and went off to get dressed for work.

* * *

CHAPTER 15

Thursday morning
Hospital cafeteria

On Thursday Ginny rose early, found that the paint had been washed off her lawn, drove to the hospital, and met Jim for breakfast in the cafeteria. She studied his face over the scrambled eggs. He looked tired.

"How was your night?"

"Nothing interesting and nothing lethal, thank goodness."

"I'm happy to hear it. So nothing to disturb your sleep."

He snorted. "Guess again. I had planned to go buy the trailer and pick up the boat at the lake over the weekend, but there's been a change. The dry dock sent me an email saying they'd had a cancellation and I could have it, but I'd have to get the boat to them by noon tomorrow, or wait at least a month for another opening. Which means I have to get the boat out of the water and haul it home today."

"Oh, Jim! Will you get any sleep?"

He rubbed his hands over his face. "Have to, but it won't be as much as I need. Will you forgive me if I'm a bit grumpy tonight?"

"Of course." She gave him a crooked smile. She understood how working the night shift could produce sleep deprivation. "You're off for the next two nights. You can catch up before you have to come back."

He nodded, reaching for his coffee. "Only two and a half more months. I move to day shift on August first."

"Is that guaranteed?"

"According to Grandfather, yes, and I'm getting some dirty looks over it, but I don't care. My contract called for a full year of nights and I will have fulfilled that obligation. I've earned the promotion."

"And the cut in pay." Ginny grinned at him.

"That, too. No more night differential. But I can work extras and there will still be the weekend and holiday bonuses."

"I'm not worried." She reached over and took his hand. "If I have to, I'll take in washing."

He leaned toward her, smiling. "You will do no such thing. It would be beneath my dignity. You'll have to stick with nursing or sign on as Jean's helper. Your choice."

Ginny laughed. "Both! And I promise to uphold your dignity, at least in front of the clan. I have a reputation to consider, too."

She saw him to his car, then went back to her office and settled down to work. With any luck the preceptor program would be up and running in another month, but it wouldn't run itself. She had a job here as long as she wanted it. She sighed at the stack of files that had materialized on her desk, then picked up her pen and began reading.

* * *

Thursday afternoon
Mackenzie residence

Ginny spent eight long, hard hours at work, trying to coordinate staffing and classroom time for the seven Hillcrest

Regional Medical Center ICUs, then drove home to find a sailboat, trailer, and SUV parked on the grass along the edge of her backyard. She pulled her car into the garage, got out, and stared at the sight. The car and trailer were both new. The boat, by comparison, looked derelict. She heard the back door open, and glanced over to see Jim coming to stand beside her.

"I have an appointment to meet with the restorer at eleven tomorrow morning."

Ginny nodded. She had known the boat would need professional attention to make sure every inch of her was safe and in good repair.

Jim shifted his weight and Ginny turned to look at him. "And?"

"And we have to strip it tonight of anything we don't want thrown away by the shop."

"Tonight?" Ginny's voice rose on the word. "Have you forgotten? Your grandfather will be here in an hour." They had agreed to let Larry Scala pitch his story to the Laird, and offered the house as neutral ground.

"I know. We'll have to do the boat after they leave. It won't take long, not with both of us working on it. We can order take-out, and have them deliver, and I'll clean up afterwards."

Ginny's brow furrowed. "Don't take this wrong, Jim, but why weren't you working on this when I got home?"

He gave her a sheepish smile. "I wanted to include you. It's *our* boat, not just mine."

Ginny sighed, then nodded. "Okay, but you're going to owe me a back rub." She threw her bag in the closet, tucked her computer into its cradle, stripped off her credentials, and replaced her nurse shoes with old sneakers, then headed for the kitchen. She was almost ready when the doorbell sounded.

"I'll get it." He was early. She frowned. It was bad manners to arrive thirty minutes early. Signor Scala must be feeling especially uneasy about his reception. She opened the door and found Maury Patterson on her doorstep.

Her eyes widened. "Oh!"

"Good evening." The Senator from Illinois tipped his hat and smiled at her and Ginny recovered her manners.

"Good evening, Senator. To what do we owe the honor of this visit?" She did not invite him in.

"I am sorry to disturb you and perhaps this is not a good time—" He let the question hang in the air.

Ginny stood her ground. "I'm sorry, no. What can I do for you?"

"I find I need an escort to visit Patsy, and that you or someone else in authority will need to arrange the visit. So I am here to throw myself on your mercy and beg for an audience with my cousin."

Ginny bit her lip. This, too, would have to be faced. "If you will leave a way for me to get in touch with you, I'll see what I can do."

The Senator was ready for her. He pulled a card from his pocket and held it out to her. "Your servant, Ma'am, and thank you."

Ginny looked down at the card, noticing scratches on his hand. Scratches. "Did you hurt yourself?" On Tuesday, maybe?

"Just a minor disagreement with a holly bush." He lifted his hat again and, as he walked down the path toward the street, Ginny was suddenly aware of the rubber-tipped cane he used to steady his gait.

She watched him climb into a car and be driven off, then closed her door, but didn't make it back to the kitchen before the bell rang again. This time it was the expected guest.

Scala greeted her politely and accepted her invitation to come in, his manner somewhat subdued. Jim met them in the hall and escorted their guest into the living room, offering him a drink. Ginny excused herself and headed for the kitchen to fetch the snacks, but she heard Scala's first words to Jim.

"Was that Senator Patterson I saw leaving?"

Angus arrived on his heels and the four of them settled down to listen to Larry's story. He addressed himself first to the Laird.

"I am very grateful for this opportunity and I want you to know that I appreciate it."

Angus nodded. "If there's truth in what you suggest, the clan needs tae know o' it."

Larry nodded. It had taken two double scotches to loosen his tongue. Whatever he planned to say appeared to be weighing heavily on his soul. He rolled his head, settled deeper into his chair, then dropped his eyes to his drink and began.

"You have to understand that I didn't know then what I know now. I've been piecing this together for almost thirty years." He set the glass down, then pulled a sheaf of papers from the bag he'd brought with him and placed them on the coffee table. "This is an outline, a summary, of what I've found. Names, dates, places. Read it. Draw your own conclusions."

He sucked in a breath. "After that girl was found, the one I told you about, I did some serious digging. The Patterson family owned that cabin on the edge of the Hiawatha National Forest, and a half-dozen more scattered about the state.

"They have a lake house in southern Illinois near Carbondale, and there had been a cabin right outside the town where I grew up, Clifton, Illinois. That's where my story starts." He took a sip of his drink.

"There's a stream that runs along there, a branch of the Iroquois River. Most of the surrounding land is farms, but they left woods on either side of the creek. It's nice, cool most days, even in summer, and good fishing. It was a great place to be a kid."

Ginny smiled. Her mother called it *calf country*—the woods and fields and backyards where a child could roam free.

Scala continued. "I spent a lot of time fishing in that creek. I'd walk miles, find myself a quiet spot, then walk home. Lots of time to think, to dream."

Ginny watched as a smile played at the corner of his mouth, then faded. She was aware of how often reality falls short of youthful dreams.

He took a breath. "I suppose you'd call what I did trespassing, but no one seemed to mind. I took a different route each time, just so I could see what was out there. One day, when I was fourteen, I found a cabin tucked away in a little clearing, trees all around it. There was a man, a young man, talking to a young woman on the porch. Neither was smiling. I thought she was mad at him, but he said something to her and they both went inside." Larry shook his head. "Did I mention I was fourteen?"

Jim nodded. "You did."

"Well, I was male, and a country boy, and I hadn't had a lot of experience with girls, so I thought I'd see if I could watch them."

Ginny smothered a smile. Jim had his clinical face on, sympathetic and nonjudgmental. Angus' expression didn't change.

Larry lifted an eyebrow. "I crept up to the cabin and peeked in at the window, but couldn't see them. I was looking at a living room, complete with fireplace. It wasn't lit, of course. It was summer and too hot for a fire. So I snuck around to the back of the cabin and peeked into the bedroom."

His eyes grew troubled. "The woman was lying on the bed, alone, still wearing all her clothes. I heard the front door open and shut, and the car drive off. I'd only seen one car so I assumed they came together. She didn't move, didn't respond to the noise, or to being abandoned. I didn't know what to do, but it didn't seem right somehow. She was so still."

His frown deepened. "I stared at her for a few minutes, then decided I should go in and check it out. I tried the window. It was shut tight. I went around to the door and it was locked. I tried the other windows, but I couldn't budge them. About that time I started to smell something burning. I looked up at the roof and saw a thin trickle of smoke rising. I ran around to the back again and looked in the window at the girl. The bed was on fire."

Scala sucked in a deep breath. "I went looking for something to break the glass. There was a barn on the other side of the trees. I ran as fast as I could, shouting for help. I found a farmer, and told him what I'd seen. He pointed at an ax hanging on the wall and told me he'd catch up with me as soon as he called the fire department. I grabbed the ax and ran back.

"By now the flames had spread. All the linens in the bedroom were on fire and the smoke was heavy. I could see the girl hadn't moved. She was probably already dead, but I was still hoping I could rescue her. The ax was heavy, but I was determined, so I heaved that thing up and swung at the window. The glass shattered and there was a sucking sound, then the fire exploded.

"I was knocked backwards. When I got to my feet, the walls were burning, and the ceiling, and flames were shooting out of the window. I ran around to the front and smashed in the window there, thinking I could climb through and open the door from the inside, but all it did was feed more oxygen to the flames. You have to understand, this all happened really fast. The cabin was old and dry and made of wood. I'd managed to break out most of the window in the front room, but I couldn't climb through, the heat was too intense. I couldn't breathe, and the window frame was on fire. I burned my hands."

Scala paused and Ginny half expected him to look down at his palms.

He was staring off into space, his cheeks pale. "The farmer came, and pulled me away from the cabin. The fire department came, and the police, and the EMTs, but there was no hope. The station was a long way off and the place was a tinderbox. It was almost burned out before they got there. They had to fight the grass fires it started. And they had to interview me, of course.

"I told them everything I knew, everything I suspected, but I didn't know the man. I described him and the car, and looked at photos, but they never arrested anyone. The investigation took months." Scala looked up and met Ginny's eyes. "It was ruled an accident. The young woman was smoking in bed, and fell asleep. Just an accident."

"But?"

"Her death made the news. If he'd hoped the fire would destroy the evidence, it didn't work. They were able to identify her from dental records."

Scala shifted in his seat. "I didn't even start to look into that death until almost twenty years after it happened, then it took me another five years and a lot of arm twisting to get the reports. She was dead before the fire started."

Ginny swallowed. "What killed her?"

"He did. He strangled her."

Jim cut in, his voice low. "You're sure about that?"

Scala looked over at him and nodded. "The dead woman was Charlotte Patterson."

Ginny caught her breath. "Maury's sister?"

"There's more, I'm afraid," Scala said. He looked at Angus. "The reports were altered, sir. The official version of the autopsy said she was a heavy smoker and under the influence of alcohol. It left off the broken hyoid bone."

Jim scowled. "There's no way to measure blood alcohol levels in a charred body."

"Maybe they got the reports mixed up," Ginny said. She had a friend in the local Medical Examiner's office and knew how careful they were, but human beings could be tired or distracted, and could make mistakes.

"I went to the sources, interviewed everyone. In each case, the person responsible for the official report was 'unavailable for comment.' But I was able to talk to the techs. What they told me didn't match the record. So I called in a few chips and got my hands on the archived electronic files: pictures, x-rays, dictated transcripts—and the scribbled notes." He sighed. "It got me banned from the police beat. I also interviewed the girl's friends. She had never been seen to smoke anything and rarely drank."

Ginny blinked. "Someone made up a cover story."

Scala nodded. "Someone with enough clout to make it stick."

"Who would have the kind of power necessary to corrupt a police investigation?" Jim asked.

"The only person I could think of was her father. The elder Patterson was still alive at that point, but, as near as I can tell, he wasn't involved in his daughter's death. It was his wife who made all the arrangements."

"Maury's mother." Ginny said.

Scala nodded. "Which means his mother probably knew exactly what happened, and chose to sacrifice her dead daughter to save her living son."

* * *

CHAPTER 16

Thursday evening
Jim & Ginny's backyard

Ginny shut the door on her departing guests, then turned to Jim. "If we order now, the food will be here when we're finished, right?"

"Right." He took off in the direction of the kitchen. "I'll get the flashlights. We'll need them to make sure we haven't missed anything."

Ginny hauled out her long-sleeved scrub jacket and a pair of gardening gloves. "In case of spiders," she told herself, then tucked up her hair and covered it with a bandana. When she opened the backdoor, she found Jim dragging the big trashcan across the lawn and setting it up beside the boat.

"I don't have to do anything with the sails and lines," he told her. "And that includes the bags and covers. Those will all have to be ordered. It's the small stuff we need to examine and make a decision on." He helped her climb up onto the trailer, then across the rails and into the boat.

It was eight p.m. on a summer's eve in Texas. The sun was sinking below the horizon, the light lingering in the tops of the trees, long shafts of burnished gold sweeping the parkways before fading into dusk. The insects were rising: mosquitoes and fireflies and cicadas. Ginny thanked her lucky stars she didn't suffer from mosquitoes the way her mother did. She took a flashlight from Jim and moved forward.

"There are lockers in the bow that I can't reach. Will you check them out, please?"

Ginny was on her knees in the cabin, flashing the light around. She looked back at him. "Because of your shoulders. I understand now. You wanted me here because I'm smaller."

"Well, that's partially true, but I also like to watch you crawl around in tight spaces. It's a view I don't get to admire that often."

Ginny grabbed a cushion off the bench and threw it at him.

"Hey!" He caught it and grinned at her. "Keep or toss?"

"Are you referring to the cushion or yourself?"

"You made a promise. You're stuck with me, but the cushion can go."

"Humph." He was right. She made that promise in front of five hundred witnesses. Boat or no boat, she was going to have to make the best of it.

"I'll clear out these storage spaces for you, but if I get bitten by a brown recluse you're never going to hear the end of it!"

"I thought of that and sprayed the whole boat with insecticide earlier. The fumes should be bearable, but let me know if you can't breathe."

"Gee, thanks." Ginny shined the flashlight into each of the storage compartments in turn. Space on a boat was always at a premium and her talent for packing efficiently was going to come in handy when they were ready to put the boat back together.

In the first locker she found a lantern and a small camp stove. No fuel, but she did find a hook in the overhead from which to hang the lantern. She handed them back to Jim who was making a pile of the items left behind by Mr. Bryant.

The cushions would be replaced, but in the meantime Ginny

was using them to lie on as she reached into the cupboards. She was really going to need a shower tonight. And she should wash her hair. Because there were spider webs. She suppressed a shudder and moved to the next locker.

Jim was working on the benches. He had the seats up on all of them, pulling out extra rope, charts, an empty cooler, jackets, life preservers, a tool kit, and assorted fishing tackle. "Some of this may turn out to be useful," he said.

Ginny had worked her way around the cabin and had emptied all but one of the lockers, finding not much of interest. This one looked different, though. Darker. Deeper, maybe?

She flashed the light into the space and saw what looked like black plastic. She took a grip on the shiny material and tugged, finding that some of it came away easily while other parts seemed to adhere to the inside of the hull. Was it part of the boat? If that was the case, the restorers would fix it up like new so she didn't have to worry about cosmetic damage.

"I'm done." Jim loomed large in the entrance to the cabin, blocking the last of the gloaming, but adding his flashlight to her efforts. "What have you got there?"

She glanced at him. "Will you take the rest of this junk out of my way, please?" The latest pile included a port-a-potty that had seen much better days and was doing nothing to dispel her general discomfort. He nodded, removing the offending items and returning just as Ginny felt something give under her fingers. "Oops!"

"What? What do you mean, 'Oops?'"

"Nothing! I mean, I don't know. There's something here, but it seems to be wrapped in plastic. I didn't find anything like it in any of the other lockers."

"Maybe it's ballast, or trash, or something of that sort."

"Maybe." Ginny reached in and felt along the length of the black plastic. "I think it's one of those heavy-duty garbage bags.

Or used to be. Parts of it have deteriorated. Wait a minute, there's something inside." She gripped the plastic again and tugged. It tore again, revealing another plastic bag, smaller, but sturdier than the trash bag. She took hold of the second plastic bag, the hair on the back of her neck rising. The second bag was wrapped tightly inside the black trash bag and it took her several minutes to free it. When she had a firm grip on whatever it was, she took a final look around the interior of the locker, decided there was nothing else in it, then squirmed backwards until she could sit up on the cabin floor.

"What is that?"

"A plastic bag with what looks like a towel inside. But there must be more to it. This thing is heavy."

"Are you through in here?"

Ginny nodded. "Help me up, please." Jim hauled her to her feet, then collected the remaining cushions and jettisoned them.

"Watch your step." He guided her into the cockpit, then lent a hand to get her over the side. She was still clutching the plastic bag and was glad of his help to get her safely onto the grass.

"I've moved everything into the garage so we can examine it tomorrow, the ones that weren't obviously junk. Do you want to put whatever that is with them?"

She shook her head. "No, I want to unwrap this thing and find out what was hidden on that boat." Because hidden it had been. She took the package into the kitchen and set it on the counter, waiting until Jim finished closing up the garage before she touched it again. When he had stripped off his own gloves and washed his hands, he turned and met her eye.

"Okay. Let's see what treasure the previous owners left for us."

Ginny nodded. Still wearing her gloves, she pulled the

plastic bag open. She retrieved the contents, then, very carefully, unrolled the fabric, folding the edges back to show Jim. It was a candlestick.

* * *

Thursday evening
Mackenzie residence

Ginny refused to talk about their find until after both of them had a shower and something to eat. As a result, it was almost ten p.m. before they returned to examine the candlestick.

"Don't touch it," Jim said.

"I won't. I don't need to." She had brought her camera and was taking pictures. When she was done, she pulled out the portable computer she used for work. She set it up on the kitchen table, sat down in front of it, and uploaded the images.

"These are the new ones. And these are the ones I took of the murder weapon." She displayed them side by side.

"I don't see any difference, except for the blood."

She nodded. "It's the twin of the one Patsy sent me."

"Hidden on my boat."

Ginny turned to face him. "Hidden on Wade Bryant's boat. And I refuse to believe there's no connection."

Jim's brow wrinkled. "What do you mean?"

"Wade Bryant is Patsy's uncle."

"Oh!" Jim sat down. "So it's possible Patsy was on that boat."

Ginny nodded. "We can ask her about it, and Detective Tran can dust for fingerprints." She rose, donned a pair of kitchen gloves, crossed to the counter, carefully rolled the silver candlestick in the anti-tarnish cloth she had mistaken for a towel, and put it back in the plastic bag. "I'll drop this off at the police station on my way home from work tomorrow."

Ginny turned her back on the candlestick, studied her husband for a moment, then sugared her voice. "Jim?" He looked over and caught her eye. "Jim, sweetheart."

He grinned at that. "Yes, my love?"

"Where are you going to park the SUV, and the trailer? They won't fit in the garage."

"Figured that out, have you?"

"If we park them on the apron, we can't get the cars out. If we park them on the street they'll get ticketed, towed, vandalized, or stolen. If we leave them on the grass, we'll need a tow truck to pull them out of the mud. And without a roof over its head your pretty new toy is defenseless against hail stones."

He nodded, still smiling. "I've been giving that some thought. What we need is another garage."

"Another *garage*?"

"Across the alley, on the old section of the property."

Understanding dawned. "Behind us." Their lot included the section where the original house had stood.

"Yes, with access from the alley, and a better fence."

Ginny nodded. "Okay. That makes sense. You'll let me know if I need to park out front while the construction is going on."

"I will. And now, my darling wife," he rose and faced her, "it's been a long day. Time we went to bed."

She nodded. "Okay. I've had enough fun for one day." She turned back to look at the plastic bag lying on the kitchen counter, frowning to herself. There was something niggling at the back of her brain, something about that candlestick— something she had seen, or not seen, or something. She sighed, then turned and headed for the bedroom. "Close up the house, will you, dear?"

"I will, and Ginny—"

She turned back to face him.

"I'm sorry my boat is causing trouble."

She crossed the room and put her arms around him. "It's all right, Jim. It's a clue, another piece of the puzzle. I'm dying to hear what Patsy has to say about a candlestick hidden in her uncle's sailboat."

"Patsy doesn't remember a thing."

"Not yet, but she will. I have high hopes of Chris Urquhart."

Jim smiled, then bent down to kiss her. "I hope you're right." He turned her toward their bedroom, flipping the lights out as he went.

The ensuing darkness reminded Ginny of the black depths of the boat locker, and the effort someone had taken to make sure that candlestick never saw the light of day again. Her smile faded.

Patsy might be able to tell Ginny everything she wanted to know, but maybe they'd both be better off not knowing. *Be careful what you wish for, lassie*, she reminded herself. *You might get it.*

* * *

CHAPTER 17

Friday afternoon
Mackenzie residence

On Friday, Jim delivered the boat to the dry dock, signed it in, and was told the restorer would call him as soon as possible. Once home, he turned his attention to the garage construction.

He'd like to get the SUV under cover quickly as they were past the April showers portion of the year and approaching hurricane season. He made an appointment with the contractor to meet the following Tuesday, then settled down in his office to wait for Ginny to get home.

He didn't hear her come in. When he noticed the time, he went looking for her and found her upstairs.

She was settled in her desk chair, frowning at the window. He dropped into the only other chair in the room, a large, overstuffed recliner, made himself comfortable, and studied her for a few minutes. When it was clear she hadn't noticed his arrival, he spoke.

"A penny for your thoughts."

She started, then turned to look at him. "Jim! How long have you been sitting there?"

"Ten minutes. And I have to say my feelings are hurt. I would expect a new-made wife, such as yourself, to be unable to ignore her husband's presence. That comes later. Are you bored with me already?"

"Not a chance." She rose from her chair, came over, and settled down on his lap. He wrapped his arms around her, and proceeded to give her an appropriate newlywed-style kiss.

"That level of concentration could be dangerous," he said. "What if there was a tornado approaching?"

"You would have to climb the stairs three at a time, throw me over your shoulder, and head for the nearest shelter." She twined her arms around his neck. "Or we could do what we normally do when the sirens go off, ignore them until the power fails."

He started laughing. "At which point, we won't be able to work any longer, so we'll have to fall back on other amusements."

A smile spread across her face. "Watching the storm by candlelight. Sounds lovely."

Jim was fully aware of how often the tornado sirens went off with no actual threat looming. The weather service tended to cry wolf a lot during the Texas summer, but they weren't always wrong. "I could call you on the phone."

"Or send me a text message."

"Both of which you would ignore."

She broke into a grin. "Of course. My goal is to get you to come for me, to prove how much you love me."

She was teasing him and at the moment Jim was perfectly willing to come to her whenever, wherever. He kissed her again.

"Just remember, woman, that the knight in shining armor gets to keep the damsel in distress after he's rescued her. It's in his contract."

"Suits me."

"Now that we've got that settled, what were you thinking about?"

Her smile faded. "Do you believe him, Scala, I mean?"

"I don't know. I've met obsessed people before. Not all of them were crazy."

She caught his eye. "Which is he—just obsessed, or over the line?"

"Teetering. Another patient for our new psychiatrist."

"I'll bet Chris didn't expect to be dumped in the middle of something like this."

Jim shrugged. "It's his job, and you'd have to get Larry to agree to talk to him, so it probably won't happen."

"He was willing to talk to *us*."

"He's trying to persuade us to let him have access to Patsy, and I think he's happy to have an audience, however skeptical. I read that dossier."

"And?"

Jim's brow furrowed. "It's disturbing. According to Scala, Patterson had a habit of meeting privately with women who were never seen again. They just vanished. And the timing is interesting. Patterson was running for office each time, and each time, his opponent withdrew."

Ginny's brows drew together. "Why would they do that?"

"Scala's theory is that the women were prostitutes who were assigned to get close to the challenger, discover something disreputable, then pass the information to Patterson so he could use it to blackmail his opponent."

Ginny raised an eyebrow. "Were you aware that blackmail is a Scottish invention?"

Jim's lips twitched. "I was not." He could see mischief in her eyes and his heart soared.

She nodded. "A legacy from the Border Reivers. *Black* you understand. The derivation of *mail* is either *meal* which meant 'payment in money or kind,' or *mal*, Gaelic for 'tribute or payment.' It was well known by the 1770s and probably started earlier."

"You are a fount of esoteric knowledge."

She sniffed. "My mother teaches history, remember?"

"I remember."

Ginny's smile faded again and Jim saw it go with regret.

"I suppose the women had to disappear to cover up the election tampering," she said.

"It seems likely. If Patterson was caught strong-arming his opponents, his career would be over."

"If Scala was tailing Patterson and suspected foul play, why didn't the police catch Patterson in the act? They could have set a trap for him."

"Scala thinks the police were paid hush money."

Ginny frowned. "Assuming every man has his price, who would be able to corrupt that many police officers?"

Jim shrugged. "According to Scala, all the meetings took place at the lake house, so it was just one jurisdiction over a span of fifteen years. Which makes one missing woman approximately every three years. I'd be willing to bet that's just a drop in the bucket for women in that profession. And only one of them was ever reported missing. In Chicago, more than three hundred miles north of the lake house."

"What about his own evidence? Wasn't Scala taking pictures?"

Jim nodded. "He was, but he couldn't get close enough to investigate. Patterson had a driver with him every time. The driver, who was probably a bodyguard as well as a chauffeur, stayed in the car. As soon as Patterson left, Scala would run up to the house and look around, but he never found anything. No body, no blood, nothing."

Ginny climbed off Jim's lap and went back over to the desk. He watched her pull up a file and start making notes.

"Okay, correct me if I get it wrong. According to Scala, the first young woman Patterson killed was his sister and he burned the cabin in an effort to destroy the evidence, but it didn't work."

"Right."

"Then the second young woman looked like a sex-for-hire scandal. She was found strangled in the woods beyond the cabin."

"Not the same cabin."

"I remember. The cabin in the Upper Peninsula of Michigan. The first one, the one he burned, was near Clifton, Illinois." Ginny glanced at him. "Patterson didn't use the Michigan cabin again?"

Jim shrugged. "Not that Scala knows of. Maybe he did and there are more bodies to be found in the woods."

Ginny made a face. "Nasty thought." She went back to her typing. "Who's next?"

Jim recited from memory. It wasn't hard. The bare facts were memorable enough. "The third time, Scala was tailing Patterson, which he did any time Patterson left Springfield and headed to the country. It was two years after the Michigan cabin incident.

"They ended up at the Patterson's lake house. There was a second car parked in front when Scala got there, and Patterson's car, with the driver behind the wheel, but he was too late to see who had gone inside."

Ginny nodded. "Okay. What *did* Scala see?"

"Patterson comes out, gets in his car, and is driven away. Scala waits long enough to be sure no one is watching, then goes in. He didn't say so, but I gather he had acquired lock-picking skills in the interim."

"That could be useful."

"He looks around and finds nothing. No girl, no body, no sign of a struggle. He locks up and leaves, but not before he photographs the car and license plate, still parked out in front of the house."

"License plate. Something that can be traced to an owner. Got it. And the police did what?"

"He doesn't know. They wouldn't talk to him. His own sources identified the owner of the car, but he was never able to track her down. She had vanished."

Ginny's brow furrowed. "Missing girl number one. What does he do next?"

"At this point, he is also dabbling in the spy business. He bought a tracking device and managed to attach it to Patterson's car. He said he had a computer program that let him follow the movements of the car, and when it headed to Carbondale again, he got there before the Senator, in time to see a happy family party just setting out for the docks. Not a working girl. His wife."

"Ha!"

"But he is nothing if not persistent. Each time Patterson heads out, Scala is on his tail. It's a wonder he wasn't spotted."

"He probably was. I wonder why he wasn't detained."

"Maybe Patterson was enjoying the cat-and-mouse game. Anyway, the next girl that goes missing is four years later."

"You'd think Scala would give up."

"I'm worried about him, really I am, but I know someone who is just as stubborn." Jim smiled at his wife. She gave him a sidelong look, then turned back to her computer.

"Please continue."

"Scala gets to the lake house first, hides his car, and finds a good spot in the bushes in which to set up his camera. Patterson arrives in time to meet the woman, and get his photograph taken with her. They go in. Scala can see them through the front window. They talk, they walk to the back of the house, out of sight of the camera. Patterson comes out, the woman doesn't."

"Ah. I see where this is going."

"Do you? I didn't."

"Oh!" Ginny flashed him a contrite look. "I apologize for interrupting. Please continue."

Jim took a breath. "This time Scala searches the house. It's not that big. Every door, window, cabinet, etc. What he finds is a hidden entrance to a below-ground shelter. A tornado shelter."

Ginny turned on him. "That's why you had tornados on your mind."

Jim nodded. "It's possible. Anyway, he finds the shelter and pulls on the hatch, but it's locked. He can't get in. Well, if there's a dead body in the shelter, it's either been stashed there or the murderer is in there with her."

"I thought you said Patterson had driven off?"

"The hired killer, *if* that's how it was done."

"Okay."

"If the latter, Scala decides he doesn't *want* to open the hatch. If she's still alive, and the murderer has her, Scala carefully explains that he is not going to be able to overcome the villain. He is unarmed, not that strong, and cannot do any good if he's dead, too. There is also the outside chance she's alive and hiding in there, in which case she'll come out on her own, eventually."

Ginny's fingers were flying over the keyboard. "Missing girl number two. If Patterson killed her and dumped her body in the tornado shelter, he's going to have to wear a gas mask the next time the hatch is opened."

"True, but if it was solidly built, there will be no bugs and no animals and no water. If it also has an air conditioning system, there may even be a mild form of refrigeration in play."

Ginny looked over and caught his eye. "Patterson can't

leave a body in a tornado shelter. It's too likely someone would notice. He'll have to move her."

Jim's smile widened. "*Someone* will have to move her, I agree."

Ginny leaned back in her chair. "With Scala on his tail, Patterson can't go back for her. He *must* have hired someone."

Jim nodded. "Scala hangs around for hours that time, waiting for the woman to appear. She doesn't, but someone else does. Two someone elses. The first is a man who comes out of the house, opens the woman's car—with keys—gets in and drives off. Scala took lots of photos of him—a small time felon with an interesting connection to the Patterson family."

"Umm hmm?" Ginny didn't even look up from her typing.

"He was rescued by a special program designed to rehabilitate miscreants and return them to polite society. It was one of Mrs. Patterson's pet charities."

"And the other someone else?"

"The caretaker, complete with shotgun and dogs. Scala barely got away with his skin and camera intact."

"So he never found out if there was a body in the shelter."

Jim shook his head. "But he notes that the lake house was used almost every week between that day and the next incident, which was four years later. Again."

"I sense a pattern developing."

"Indeed." Jim smiled then continued. "You couldn't just ignore a body for four years. Nor could you leave the entrance to a tornado shelter barred from use by the people who might need it."

"Interesting point."

"As a matter of fact, the lake house was a meeting place for all sorts of political parties, family gatherings, and weekend getaways. It's hard to believe Patterson would choose that place for a murder."

"If it was family property and he had control over both access and the police, it seems safe enough."

Jim wrinkled his nose. "Well, perhaps you're right. So, four years later—"

"This is body number five, right?"

"Well, two bodies and three missing women. We see the same setup. The woman's car is parked out front, both enter, only Patterson exits. Scala is lurking around the corner and lets himself in as fast as he can. This time the tornado shelter isn't locked. It's just closed. He pulls the hatch up and sees stairs. The corridor is lit so he goes down to see what he can see. Quietly, because he still expects to find a woman, or her remains."

Ginny's eyes widened. "Did he?"

"What he found was a tunnel with an exit that came up in the woods. When he looked around, there were tire tracks, but nothing else."

Ginny sucked in a breath. "The plot thickens! Missing girl number three."

Jim couldn't help smiling at her enthusiasm. "Scala has come prepared this time. He brought sticky paper for lifting fingerprints, skin cells, and hairs from inside surfaces and he does so, rapidly, since he's in danger of being caught. He collects his photos and hightails it out of there, ahead of the dogs. When he gets his evidence home, he catalogues and stores it against future need."

"And all of this is in the dossier?"

"It is. Our boy, Scala, who is no fool, whatever you may think of his career choices, puts pencil to paper and discovers something. There is an odd coincidence attached to the disappearances. The first thing he notices is the timing. Each happens just before Patterson is due to be either confirmed in office, being the incumbent, or ousted by an enraged populace.

The second is that Patterson's opponent withdraws in the days between Patterson's visit to the lake house and voting day, leaving him in possession of the field and with an easy victory."

"Really!" Ginny was listening avidly, her eyes wide.

He smiled at her. "You're forgetting your notes."

"Oh!" She swung around and typed furiously until she had caught up with him. "Okay. Proceed."

"You should probably also note that the same thing happened between the visit to the cabin in Michigan and election day."

Ginny added this detail to her file.

"Scala spends the time waiting for his next chance to catch Patterson in the act seeing if he can catch him out in some other sort of illegal activity, all of it having to do with election fixing. His notes are full of suspicions, but no proofs."

"Poor Larry."

Jim nodded. "One can almost feel sorry for him—almost. So along comes the election season, which is a mere two years later this time, and that's an important detail. Take note of it."

"Yes, sir."

"Scala is determined to get proof of the disappearances. He knows the pattern by now. He stakes out the exit and catches two men hauling a limp woman out of the shelter tunnel, putting her in the back of a black van, and driving off. Scala gets good photos of the whole thing, cars and license plates included. The girl looks dead and Scala decides the best thing to do is go straight to the police. They ignore him."

"On what grounds? That's the fourth missing girl!"

"He's a known trespasser and troublemaker. I should also mention that he'd tried setting up camera traps in the woods, but the caretaker kept taking them down. Patterson responds by getting a restraining order against Scala.

"Larry's had no luck interviewing the political opponents,

none of whom will talk. He has no solid proof. No bodies. No witnesses. No one is willing to testify to being blackmailed. He's become a laughingstock. The people around Carbondale are now calling the police if he shows up at the local gas station.

"When the election cycle rolls around again, four years later, he positions himself on a ridge overlooking the Patterson property. The police catch him and haul him off to jail. They confiscate his camera and impound his car. It takes a week to prove he wasn't in violation of his restraining order and by then the next woman in line has come and gone."

"Missing woman number five. If it happened, which he can't prove because he wasn't there." Ginny blew out a breath. "This is a saga."

"There's an additional note that a cleaning crew was in the lake house later the same day on each of the occasions when a woman disappeared. We have to assume Patterson arranged the meetings to coincide with the routine cleaning. It would be one more reason why no trace evidence was ever found."

"Smart."

Jim nodded. "Two years later, Mrs. Patterson dies and Senator Patterson inherits. He resigns his seat in the Illinois senate and heads for Texas."

"Followed by Larry Scala, who wants access to Patsy in a last ditch effort to find a way to pull Patterson down off his pedestal. What happened to the women's cars? He had license plate numbers, didn't he?"

"Two of the plates showed up in northern Illinois attached to cars that didn't match the photographs. Larry suggests all five were driven to Chicago, abandoned in a bad neighborhood and left to be stripped and stolen. He was unable to trace the black van's plates."

Ginny swung around to face Jim. "I have the same problem

Larry does. There isn't any proof."

"You think he made it up?"

"I think it sounds like a rip-snorter of a movie script, but have you noticed he hasn't mentioned the candlestick?"

"I've noticed."

Ginny screwed up her face. "He's been telling us no one will take him seriously. Do you suppose he'd let Detective Tran look at his evidence?"

Jim looked at his soulmate, his partner in crime as it were, and smiled. "I've been wondering the same thing myself."

* * *

CHAPTER 18

Friday evening
Cooperative Hall

The ceilidh was in full swing before Larry Scala made his appearance. He stood on the edge of the room, scanning the crowd. Ginny started to go collect him, but Jean had seen him first.

Jean Pollack was the current Matron for the Homestead, and one of her duties was to greet visitors and make them feel at home. She was well up to the task, her spiel oiled and polished to perfection. She was therefore astonished when halfway through her opening remarks she lost her guest's attention. Ginny saw the change and followed Scala's stare. When she turned to see what had brought about this transformation, she found Senator Patterson staring back.

Ginny nudged Jim. "Look at Senator Patterson. Now look at Lorenzo Scala."

Jim turned to follow her gaze. "Brrrr. Do you get the impression they know one another?"

"I guess I was being naïve. I assumed Scala would study Patterson from afar, but these two are sworn enemies."

"So it would seem." They watched as Scala asked Jean a question, nodded, then headed off into the crowd.

"I'll go see if I can help." Ginny crossed the floor and

greeted Larry. "Good evening. Will you join us in the dance?" Ginny motioned toward the floor.

He looked over her shoulder at the fifty-odd kilted and sashed Scots dancing their way through diagonal reels—at speed—and his eyes narrowed. "No, thank you. I'll just watch."

Ginny sat down beside him.

His eyes swept the room. "Do the plaids mean anything?"

"Yes and no. That one," she pointed at a lighter blue example, "is the Bluebonnet, the state tartan of Texas."

Larry's eyebrows rose. "Texas has a state tartan?"

Ginny nodded. "There are corporate tartans, military tartans, and commemorative tartans as well as the regional and family tartans. Do you see the kilt with the prominent white stripes?" Larry nodded. "That's a 'dress' tartan, for formal occasions. The brown and green is a 'hunting' tartan, intended as camouflage. The red version has been so widely used everyone recognizes it. All three are Clan Stewart."

"How do you keep them straight?"

Ginny laughed. "We don't. There are computer databases for that."

"The women wear kilts, too?"

"Technically, no. On a woman it's just a pleated tartan skirt, even if it's made to look like a kilt."

"Do you have to wear a specific design?"

"No. We can wear any tartan we wish, unless it's protected by law. Are you thinking about getting a kilt?"

Larry turned to her and grinned. "I might just do that, if I can find a Scottish ancestor in my family tree."

Ginny lifted an eyebrow. "I should warn you that women are drawn to a man in a kilt, like bees to honey."

"Now *that* is a serious selling point!" He watched for a minute longer, then pulled his eyes off the dancers and looked at Ginny. "You said you had something you wanted to talk to me about."

She nodded. "Jim and I went over that document you left with us yesterday. We were wondering just how badly you want to prove your theory."

The man in front of her, fully engaged a moment before in the motion and color and laughter filling the room, was suddenly still. They sat, the two of them, as if cut off from the rest of humanity, alone in a sea of strangers. Ginny waited for him to speak.

"Does this mean you're going to let me talk to Patsy Olafsson?"

Ginny nodded. "Eventually, after the doctor is sure it will be safe for her. In the meantime, we'd like to suggest a different approach."

He leaned back in his chair, his eyes on her face. "What do you have in mind?"

"I have a friend in the police department. If she had some genuine evidence linking Senator Patterson to a crime, we might be able to do something about him."

"You want me to turn my evidence over to the Dallas police?" He sounded skeptical. "It's the police who keep saying there's nothing there, or that it means nothing, or that it doesn't implicate Patterson."

"I understand." Ginny waited.

Scala was silent for a minute, then answered her question. "I have given up my career, my reputation, my hope for a home and family for the chance to prove I'm right. I'd like to do that before I die."

"My contact will need access to everything you've got, nothing held back."

He nodded. "The physical evidence is hidden in Illinois, and my Will has instructions on where to find it and what to do with it. The images are all date/time stamped, with locations added where they weren't included by the software. The rest is digital copies of reports, articles, interviews, none of which are in my possession, and some of which have since been destroyed."

"If you'd like, you and I can go to Detective Tran together, explain what's going on, and ask her to see whether the forensics lab can tell us anything we don't already know."

"You trust this woman?"

"I have reason to."

He blinked, then nodded slowly. "All right. Tell me where and when."

Ginny nodded in return. "I'll set up a meeting." She cocked her head to one side. "I'm still puzzled about one thing, and I'm not being naïve here. I know corruption can happen anywhere. But, in my experience, it's hard to believe Patterson could suppress five missing girls for more than twenty years."

"He had help."

"Same comment." Ginny spread her hands. "Who could manage to do that, not once, but over and over again?"

Scala's brow descended. "I can't prove it. I can't *prove* anything, but I believe he had someone cleaning up after him." He pulled in a deep breath. "I'm good at my job. I know how to interview the locals so they'll talk, and to spot something they may not know they know. I can surveille and I've got resources that can dig into computer files, so long as they're not government protected. I know a whole lot more than I've told you already."

Ginny's eyes narrowed. "You had a reason to follow Patterson to Texas."

"Two reasons."

Ginny sifted through all the things she'd learned about him. "Something changed. Something in Patterson's life." She frowned, pulling the threads together. "His mother died and left him the estate and he moved back to Texas. That was the trigger, wasn't it?"

"Yes."

Ginny could feel the ideas in her head clicking into place. "You said he had help. Someone with a lot of money, and a motive for protecting him."

"Yes."

There was only one explanation that fit what she knew so far. "His mother was covering up for him."

"Yes."

"And she can't do it anymore." Because she was dead and buried.

"There may be a few things she can control from the grave, but not the police." Larry shifted in his seat. "It's likely we won't be able to loosen the tongues of those involved in the earlier cover-ups, but at least he won't have her help from now on."

Ginny's eyes widened. "You think he's going to try again?"

Scala shrugged. "His system has been working and he has no reason to think it won't work in Texas as well as it did in Illinois."

Ginny shook her head. "Senator Hunter hasn't got any secrets that could be used to blackmail him."

"Are you sure?"

Ginny paused. The Scots were a tight-knit community, and the lack of privacy helped keep the inhabitants in line, but no man was above temptation. She made a mental note to ask Angus about Ian Hunter.

"What's the second reason?"

"I think he believes Cousin Patsy knows too much."

Ginny's brow furrowed. "She can't remember a thing."

"He's not stupid. He knows you've got a psychiatrist working with her."

"But why come after her now? In a matter of months she'll be dead of the—" Ginny caught herself.

"Of the cancer. I know."

"How do you know about that?"

He smiled. "The Matron told me. I asked her why I hadn't seen Patsy at any of the events."

Ginny sighed. "Okay, if he thinks she's a risk, why leave her alone until now?"

"Because he was in Illinois, out of sight and out of mind, until now."

Ginny sucked in a breath. "I'll pass that on to Himself. He'll know what steps to take to keep her safe."

"You've got it backwards."

"What?"

"The only way we're going to stop him is to catch him in the act. We need for him to try to silence her permanently."

Ginny felt her jaw drop and forced it back into place. "We cannot put Patsy in that kind of danger. She wouldn't survive an attack."

"She's dying anyway."

Ginny jumped to her feet, her cheeks burning. She stared at the reporter. "I will *not* let you use that sick old woman as bait!"

Scala stood up and shrugged. "Then we'll just have to wait until he decides to kill someone else. You, perhaps."

"I'm no threat to him!"

"No? He must know by now that you're investigating."

Ginny's brow descended. "Why hasn't he killed *you*, yet?"

"I think his mother wouldn't let him. The police knew all about me. It would look suspicious if I disappeared. Besides, as long as I was powerless against him, he could afford to let me live."

Ginny heard the bitterness in his tone, and frowned to

herself. A man can be pushed just so far before he cracks.

He shrugged. "It's your choice. Lay a trap, or wait for him to strike again in a place and time of his own choosing. Either way, this time he won't have help covering up. This is the break we've needed, the break I've been waiting for."

Ginny found herself shaking, with anger and fear and dismay, because he might be right.

"Think about it," he said. "But don't take too long."

* * *

Friday evening
Cooperative Hall

Ginny scanned the hall, found her husband, and swiftly cut him out from his conversation with one of the Loch Lonach council members.

"Excuse us, please. I have need of my husband."

Jim looked at her face, his brow descending. "What's wrong?" He steered her to a corner chair and sat down beside her. "Now take a breath and tell me."

Ginny explained Larry's plan to use Patsy as a staked goat, and his theory that Mrs. Patterson had been using her influence to cover Maury's crimes for decades.

Jim frowned, then shook his head. "The only son of a Southern Mother!"

"What?"

"Don't you know that prayer?" Jim recited it. "Dear Lord, when I die and am born again, I don't want to be rich or famous or handsome. Just make me the only son of a Southern Mother."

Ginny snorted. "Appropriate, but what are we going to do about this?"

"Grandfather will have to be told. I agree that we can't use Patsy Olafsson as bait, no matter how dangerous Patterson is."

"Do we tell Scala about the candlestick?"

"No, and we ask Detective Tran not to mention it as well."

"You think we should still go to her?"

Jim nodded. "Let the professionals look at his evidence. It will give Tran an opportunity to size him up. She may have a suggestion on how to handle him."

Ginny felt her blood pressure settling back toward normal. "Okay. You and I are having Mother and your grandfather over for dinner tomorrow. We can talk then."

"Sounds good. Now, I have a question for *you*."

Ginny looked up and met his eyes.

"Are you all right?" he asked.

She nodded, feeling foolish. "Of course. I was just upset. It was such a coldblooded suggestion, and I was beginning to like the man."

Jim put his arm around her shoulders and tucked her up under his chin. "He's obsessed, and that can make a man unstable, even if he has right on his side." He looked down at her. "Promise me you won't be alone with him. Don't open the door, and don't agree to meet with him unless there are others present. No chatting in the parking lot."

Ginny nodded firmly. "You have my word on it."

"Patterson, too."

Ginny shivered. "Patterson, too." She hadn't repeated Scala's threat, but apparently Jim had enough imagination to come up with it on his own. She caught a movement out of the corner of her eye and pushed herself out of his arms. "Look out! Someone's coming."

"Forgive me if I'm interrupting."

"Not at all." Ginny smiled at the interloper. "Won't you join us?"

"Just for a moment." Ian Hunter sat down on a nearby chair and faced them. "My wife and I would like to invite you to dinner one day next week, if you are free."

Ginny glanced at her husband, saw agreement in his eyes, and smiled. "We'd love that."

"You were so kind to Wally last April, about that caber."

"How's he doing?" Jim asked.

"Community service, and deserves every minute of it, but, doing well. I think he'll come out of this a wiser man."

"We should all be so lucky," Ginny said.

A look of distaste flashed across Senator Hunter's face and Ginny frowned in response. "I'm sorry. Did I say something wrong?"

Ian shook his head. "Not wrong, just an odd coincidence."

Ginny smiled. "I'm a big fan of odd coincidences. Can you share, or is it a secret?"

Ian relaxed. "It was just your choice of the word, 'lucky.' I heard someone else use it recently in a different context." He lifted an eyebrow. "It won't surprise you to find that the Scots are superstitious."

Ginny burst out laughing. "You are looking at a marriage made under the mistletoe. Old wives tales are my stock-in-trade!"

"I overheard someone saying he was born lucky and had been lucky his whole life. He seemed to think his luck would hold, no matter what he tried. I hope he's wrong." Ian's smile faded. "There's something else I want to ask you about. Do either of you know if there is a proper procedure for reporting an attempted seduction?"

Ginny had trouble controlling her face. "What do you mean?"

Ian frowned. "I mean there's been a young woman of loose morals trying to interest me in consorting with her for the past week. I've found her very hard to dissuade."

"Surely you've had other women try to buy your political favors with favors of their own?" Jim said.

"Of course, but they've all taken 'no' for an answer. This one won't."

"If you report her to the police, they can make sure she understands the law on prostitution in Dallas County. She might also get herself arrested."

"And there's always a restraining order," Ginny added.

Ian nodded. "She's been approaching me in public, where she's sure I won't make a scene, and sneaking in beside me during photo sessions. The press are beginning to ask questions."

"I would take it to the Laird," Jim said. "He knows a lot of people."

"And I will alert the ladies to be on the lookout for someone who needs to explain herself to the clan. You have no idea how intimidating that sort of pressure can be."

Ian started laughing. "Oh, but I do! I have one at home, remember?"

They all three laughed, then Senator Hunter rose to take his leave. "Lola and I will be looking forward to getting to know you better, very soon, I hope."

Ginny and Jim rose as well, smiling and holding out their hands. Ginny held onto Senator Hunter's hand a shade too long, preventing his turning away. "Wait! You didn't tell us who this very lucky man was."

Ian Hunter smiled at her. "Didn't I? It was Maury Patterson."

* * *

CHAPTER 19

Saturday morning
Police Substation

Ginny had arranged to meet with Detective Tran fifteen minutes before Larry Scala's arrival.

"He's trying to prove Patterson has gotten away with murder many times."

Detective Tran nodded and set the manuscript aside. "Do you believe him?"

Ginny shifted uneasily in her chair. "I want you to make up your own mind. He's bringing material he describes as evidence he says he collected himself."

"Before or after the police cleared the scene?"

"Both."

"*That* is tampering with a police investigation."

"Yes." Ginny frowned. "I don't want to act—or fail to act—based on my own instincts. I want your opinion."

Detective Tran's lips twitched. "My opinion is that your instincts can be relied upon." She leaned forward. "I will withhold judgment until after I meet this man. Then we will see." The phone rang and Detective Tran answered it. She nodded to Ginny. "He is here."

* * *

Ginny sat through a second rendition of Scala's tale, thinking that the wording was almost identical, as if he'd rehearsed what he was going to say. Detective Tran also sat listening, taking notes. When he came to a halt, she waited a moment, then began asking questions.

"Please correct me if I go astray. You met Senator Patterson through the college you both attended, ten years apart."

"Yes, at an alumni dinner."

Tran glanced down at her notes. "You decided you did not like the man and set out to see if you could 'bring him down a peg or two' using your journalism outlets."

Larry nodded. "He struck me as pompous and condescending."

"You began stalking him."

"It's not stalking when you're a reporter. It's using your training to follow a potential story."

"You followed this potential story many times and found nothing to write about."

Larry sighed. "I was going to give it up, but my thumbs kept pricking."

Detective Tran looked at Scala, her face unreadable. "Why did you persist? What did you hope to gain by it?"

Larry licked his lips. "A scoop. The kind of story that can make a reporter's career. I just knew there was something there, and that I had to keep digging."

Detective Tran picked up Scala's summary. "You came across Senator Patterson in a compromising situation with a young woman. You saw him leave. She did not follow. There was a fire and you tried to rescue her."

Larry nodded.

Detective Tran turned over a page. "The investigating detective and the forensics team decided the death was an accident, that the young woman fell asleep while smoking in bed." She looked up at Scala. "But you did not believe it. Why not?"

"Because she didn't smoke."

"How do you know this?"

Larry squirmed in his chair. "I have to protect my sources."

Detective Tran lifted an eloquent eyebrow. "What did your sources tell you?"

"That there were no charges on her credit cards for tobacco. That her medical records listed her as having never smoked. That when she traveled, she always requested a non-smoking room and a non-smoking rental car."

Detective Tran's brows drew together a tiny bit. Ginny saw it, but doubted whether Scala did.

"You told the investigating officer?"

"By the time I got around to looking into that fire, the case had been closed for a long time. The original investigating officer was dead and the guy they assigned to talk to me wasn't interested."

"And these other cases? You have similar concerns about them?"

Ginny listened carefully as Scala laid out the discrepancies in the cases of the body abandoned in the woods and the five missing girls.

Tran's eyes flicked from Scala to her desk. Ginny could see the pocket-sized notebook Tran always carried. Ginny had gotten a close look at it earlier in the year, but she'd been unable to read it. The notes were in Vietnamese.

"I believe you said you removed evidence from one of the crime scenes."

Scala swallowed, then nodded. "I did."

"And you have it with you?"

He nodded again. "Here. It's all in the bag. All numbered

and labeled. And they're cross-referenced with the photographs I took at the scene."

Scala caught Ginny's start. "I flew home last night to get it."

Detective Tran rose from her chair, opened the bag and peered inside. She then took gloves from her desk drawer, put them on, and proceeded to remove the items one by one. Scala helped her match the baggies to his photographs and notes. When they were done, Detective Tran looked at him. "Do you have anything to add?"

He shook his head. "That's the lot. My life's work."

"I can see you have put a great deal of thought and effort into this. It will take some time to examine it thoroughly."

Scala gave her a tight little smile. "Take as long as you want. I'm just grateful you're willing to look at it."

"There is one more thing. We will need a set of your fingerprints, for exclusionary purposes."

"Of course."

Detective Tran put in a call to one of her colleagues. When Scala had been led away to be fingerprinted, Tran sat down again, removed her gloves, and rested her hands on the desk. She met Ginny's eye.

"I have no idea what the forensics team may find, but I can tell you already that none of this will be admissible in court."

Ginny nodded. "I know. No chain of custody."

"Nevertheless, we will look."

"Thank you."

"On the subject of the other item you brought to my attention, I have a new puzzle for you."

"Oh?"

"Based on your analysis of opportunity and consanguinity, I had the Illinois Department of Motor Vehicles send over a copy of both Maury and Charlotte Patterson's fingerprints. Neither matched the set on the candlestick."

Ginny frowned. Was she wrong? Was there another child involved and Maury Patterson completely innocent of Tommy's death? And if another child had swung that candlestick, how was she to prove it?

"You will let me know if you find any additional clues."

"Of course." Ginny rose. She hesitated for a moment. "What about Scala? Is he a danger to Patsy?"

Detective Tran's brow furrowed. "I would like to think about that before I give you an answer."

Ginny nodded. "Thank you."

She made her way back to the car, and sent a message to Larry Scala to the effect that they would all have to wait on Detective Tran before making any further decisions. She hoped that would satisfy him.

She was glad Angus was coming to dinner. He would probably toss the ball back into her corner, but at least she'd get a chance to pick his brain first.

* * *

Saturday afternoon
Mackenzie residence

The conversation around Ginny's dining room table had been mostly light and pleasant, though it had been a revelation to see the Laird instruct Sinia Forbes on her duty to the clan. Apparently Angus had assigned Ginny's mother to the task of evaluating Chris Urquhart. Ginny's curiosity went into overdrive, but she made no comment. In any case it would have to wait. She had her own puzzle to solve.

"Mackenzie."

"Aye, lass?"

"I would like your feedback on the candlestick mystery."

Jim burst out laughing. "That would make a good title for a novel!" His grandfather gave him a stern look and he subsided.

"Go on, lass."

"We suspect Patsy was a witness to her brother's death. Dr. Urquhart thinks she'll be able to remember, if she wants to. Which brings me to the first of my questions. Should we help her recover her memory, or should we leave her in blissful ignorance?"

Angus frowned down at the table for a moment, then looked up and met Ginny's eye. "Will it do aught o' good, tae force her tae face th' memory?"

Jim answered that one. "It won't hurt her physically, but it's bound to distress her. So this is an ethical question. Will she be better off knowing the truth?"

"Wha' does she say?"

Ginny sighed. "She's been asking all of us what happened to her little brother and why she can't remember him. She says she feels guilty for forgetting. It's preying on her mind."

Angus nodded. "Then help her tae th' truth. She's a strong woman. She'll be able tae handle it."

Ginny nodded. "Okay. One down." She saw the corner of Angus' mouth twitch. "The second question is about Maury Patterson."

"Patsy and th' senator are cousins, aye?"

"Yes, and he wants to visit her, to say goodbye."

Angus frowned slightly. "Is he no th' Peeping Tom?"

"We think so, and making Patsy face him could upset her rather badly. She saw a face peering in her window and was terrified. It's our theory—Jim's, and Dr. Urquhart's, and mine— that she recognized him from the killing."

"Then whitfor ar' ye suggestin' it?"

"Because Larry Scala told me Patterson may try to kill Patsy, to prevent her from remembering and telling on him. I was hoping, if we show him that she can't remember a thing, he might leave her alone."

"Wha' does Chris say?"

"He's against it, until she knows what she saw."

Angus shook his head. "We asked him tae come tae us in his professional capacity. I think we mus' listen tae him."

Ginny lowered her head in obedience to the decree. "Aye, Mackenzie. That's two."

"Ye hae another?"

"This one is about the reporter."

"Go on, then."

"The man is obsessed. He's made proving Senator Patterson is a serial killer his life's work. It's cost him his job, his reputation, even his freedom, at times. I arranged for him to meet Detective Tran this morning, so he could tell her his story, and hand over what he claims is evidence that can prove Patterson is guilty."

Angus' eyebrows rose. "And th' detective listened tae him?"

Ginny nodded. "As a favor to me. After he'd gone she pointed out that none of what he brought in could be used in a court of law. Which he already knew."

The Laird's eyebrows drew together. "Go on."

Ginny sucked in a breath. "Larry told me the only way we were going to stop Patterson was to catch him in the act, that we needed another body."

Angus frowned. "We dinna want tha'."

"No, but he may be right. There are cases on record that were solved only when there were enough victims to establish a pattern." Ginny repeated what Scala had said to her at the ceilidh.

"Sae wha' are ye askin', lass?"

"I want to know if you think we should put a tail on Scala, to find out where he goes, and what he does."

Angus' frown deepened. "We can put extra guards on Patsy, but we canna follow the man. 'Tis a violation o' his civil rights."

"He's been doing that to Senator Patterson for years."

"Aye, but tha' doesnae gie us th' right tae do th' same. If we follow th' man, it mus' be wi' his permission."

"Then we'll only see what he wants us to see."

Angus nodded. "We canna follow him in secret, but we can assign him a helper tae be there fer him."

Jim lifted an eyebrow. "And if he shakes off his helper?"

"Then we may ha'e tae drop a wee word in Detective Tran's ear, and let her tak' it from there."

Ginny nodded, tucking a small reservation into the corner of her mind. She might not be allowed to follow Scala, but there were other ways to discover where a man went on the Homestead.

* * *

CHAPTER 20

Saturday evening
Mackenzie residence

When the guests had gone, Ginny finished cleaning up, kissed her husband, and sent him off to work, then retired to her office to think. It had been twelve days since the blood-stained candlestick had started her on the latest investigation. She sniffed. So much for her promise to Jim. And what of her promise to herself?

Ginny frowned. She had been *hoping* to turn over a new leaf, *hoping* the wild days of her youth were behind her, *hoping* she could settle down to domestic life with her husband. As a result, she'd been dragging her feet. She had to admit, at least to herself, that the fastest way to get the promise she'd made to Patsy off her conscience was to solve the puzzle.

She opened her computer and pulled up her spreadsheet, making notes as she reviewed the events of the past two weeks. She'd been extraordinarily lucky. A large portion of the investigative work had been done for her.

In addition to the forensic evidence found on the first candlestick (done by the police), there were the assertions made by Scala (carefully laid out by him), Patsy's genealogy files with related family connections (online), Chris' attempts to restore Patsy's memory (no real responsibility on Ginny's part), and the face in the window, which she suspected was Patterson's because of his thwarted attempts to visit his cousin (yet to be confirmed) and the scratches on his hands (circumstantial, but suggestive). There was also the violence that had been going on in south Dallas and the attack on Loch Lonach (though she couldn't see a connection), and Patterson's intention to replace Ian Hunter in the state senate (same comment).

The discovery of the second candlestick was not to be believed and if she hadn't hauled it out of that dark hole herself, she wouldn't. *What* were the odds Jim would buy the one boat on the lake that had a clue hidden in it? That only happened in fiction. Badly written fiction. Except—

Jim's new toy was among the oldest sailboats on the lake. It had actually been here at the time the candlestick went missing. What's more there was the connection between the Bryant family and the Patterson family. It was chance, yes, that Wade Bryant had decided to sell his boat at this time, but he had been a holdout. Most of the older boats had changed hands long before this.

And there weren't that many choices among the boats for sale. The lake was almost private, small by comparison with the municipal lakes that had been constructed since. It had limited boat ramps and gated access to the docks, a restriction on motors (no speedboats allowed), and was located inside the Loch Lonach boundaries, though the community allowed access to the picnic grounds to anyone who would use the park gently and leave it clean.

Among the Homesteaders, a sailboat was a hobby, not a livelihood. People who could afford sailboats could also afford silver candlesticks, and Jim's choice of a Corinthian also narrowed the options. Roomier than most of the other sailboat models, it had spaces inside that could hide a medium-sized object of the home décor variety. Taken altogether, maybe it wasn't such an outrageous coincidence.

Even so, for Ginny to *find* the second candlestick was astonishing. Suppose, just for the sake of argument, that the boat had been on the lake at the time, and the person who wanted to hide a candlestick had had access to the boat. What were the odds the candlestick would still be there all these years later? Had no one cleaned that locker out in all that time? What if it had been Jim doing the cleaning, in daylight, and without waiting for her? Would he have tossed the package in the trash? What if the boat had sunk? What if someone else had bought it? What if the person who put the candlestick there had come back for it?

Ginny paused. Why hadn't she? Those candlesticks were valuable. She would want to wait until the incident was forgotten, then stealthily put them back into circulation. Except, she couldn't. The first candlestick, the one with the blood on it, had never surfaced. It was not safe to resurrect one without the other. Someone might ask questions. And there may have been reasons why she couldn't return to the boat and slide her treasure into her handbag. Maybe there'd been too many witnesses. Maybe she'd given up sailing. Maybe she had died.

Ginny sucked in a breath. If Scala was right, and Letitia Patterson had been covering up for her son all these years, when did it start? When he was eight? Did Mrs. Patterson find a disaster lying on her oriental carpet when she investigated the noises coming from the library?

Ginny's imagination produced a mental image of Tommy lying on the rug, blood everywhere, Maury standing over him clutching the candlestick, Patsy screaming. No, that wouldn't work. If Maury'd had possession of the bloody candlestick, Mrs. Patterson could have taken it, cleaned it, and never had to do without it. Okay, the candlestick left the room before Mrs. P. entered. Patsy must have taken the candlestick home and hidden it. Yes. That explained why there was blood on the bottom of her grandfather's sea chest and the guilty candlestick on a bookcase in her attic years later.

And as for access, Mrs. Patterson, along with her husband and family, had left Loch Lonach and moved to Illinois very soon after Tommy's death. The boat had stayed behind. When Mrs. P. returned to Chancie Mor, she may have considered taking back the candlestick, but the mate to the pair was still missing. Ginny's eyes narrowed. Had Letitia ever figured out what happened? That Patsy must have taken the bloody candlestick away? Or had her son never told her the truth? Perhaps she hadn't asked.

One thing was sure, Mrs. P. was dead and buried and could not tell them what she had done. If Ginny was going to find the truth, she would have to look for it elsewhere.

Which led to another sure and certain truth. If a pair of valuable silver candlesticks that normally lived on the Patterson mantel disappeared, an explanation would have to be offered. Someone would notice they had gone, even if it was only the person who did the household inventory once a year for tax purposes. Bad news for someone. Very bad news for the someone responsible for cleaning that room.

Ginny had no proof and no evidence, just a blossoming conviction that some poor soul in that house at that time, had taken the fall for those missing candlesticks. They would have to be accounted for. Broken and thrown away? Put away in the wrong place and never found? Or stolen during the chaos? Theft was much the more likely. If Mrs. P. had reported those candlesticks stolen, there would be a police report. Ginny turned to her machine and got to work.

An hour later, she had documentation to fit her scenario.

Right house, roughly the right dates, right owner, and a description of a pair of silver candlesticks. No photographs. The newspaper report said a housemaid had been blamed for the disappearance, and she had been dismissed from service, but released from jail for lack of proof, so she never paid for her crime. The girl was watched for years afterwards, in the hope that she had stashed the silver somewhere and would retrieve it when she felt it was safe to do so. But the candlesticks had never been recovered.

Ginny checked the date. There was a chance the housemaid, who was named in the article, was dead. She would be at least ten years older than Patsy. She might have moved away. She might have married or changed her name. Even if Ginny could find her, she might refuse to speak, or be unable to remember anything, or have nothing useful to contribute.

But at least it was a place to start.

* * *

Saturday evening
The Elysium Hotel

Maury Patterson walked through the lobby of the posh Elysium hotel in downtown Dallas, rode the elevator to the top floor, walked to the end of the hall, and let himself into his suite. He dropped his briefcase and tie on the table, then walked over to the window and gazed out at the city. It was almost midnight. He'd been meeting with his campaign manager and there'd been a lot to go over.

The night lights outshone the stars. From his perch he could see both the Flying Red Horse and the Electric Moon.

Pegasus made him feel young again. The eleven foot tall,

two-sided, revolving neon marvel had been created in 1934 and placed atop the Magnolia Hotel, the tallest building in north Texas at the time. It could be seen from every direction and from seventy-five miles away. You knew you were part of something big when you could look up and see Pegasus in the night sky over your head.

The Electric Moon was modern, and computer driven, and kind of fun to watch, but it just didn't have the emotional charge that big red horse did. Maury heard a quiet *clink* behind him. He identified it as the sound of ice in a glass. He turned his back on the window and faced his wife.

"Good evening, Maury. How was your day?"

Rita was the whole package. She had a mind like a steel trap, worked hard to keep her figure, and had some sort of magic wand that made her makeup look as if she wore none at all, though Maury knew better. Her clothes were tailored and of the finest material money could buy. She looked every inch the aristocrat her father hadn't been. Her mother's work, of course. But the connections all came through him.

Maury'd had to work up to Rita's station in life. She was third generation Chicago royalty, thirty years younger than he, and ambitious. There was nothing she wouldn't do for her high-profile husband, nothing she couldn't arrange, nothing too big or too small to escape her attention. She rose to greet him.

Maury stood where he was and waited for her to come to him. It was a ritual. He smiled and returned her peck on the cheek. "Rita, my dear! What a pleasant surprise. I didn't expect you until the end of the month."

"I decided I could do more good here then I could in Springfield."

"And the children?"

"With their grandparents." She took a sip of her drink and

Maury could smell the bouquet of oranges and rum. Rita liked her drinks sweet. She caught his eye. "You're not staying at that big white house on the edge of the lake?"

"It needs a serious cleaning before we can move in, and I've had more urgent things to attend to."

She perched on the arm of the sofa, tucking one slender leg behind the other, and let her eyelids droop just a bit. "Tell me."

Maury got himself a drink from the bar, a single malt whisky of an excellent brand and vintage, then settled into a leather chair facing her. He told her who he'd managed to hire to run the campaign, outlined the strategies they had come up with; summarized the expenses, including headquarters, staff, and advertising budget; mentioned public appearances she would be expected to make, at his side and with the children; and suggested she might enjoy shopping while he was tied up with work. He'd learned in prior campaigns, if he wanted her full cooperation, it was necessary to keep her sweet.

"Have I forgotten anything, my love?"

She eyed him over the rim of her glass. "I'll let you know."

Maury fought the urge to fidget, wishing again that he could read her mind. Fat chance of that. She was always one step ahead of him.

"What is it, Rita? Why did you come down early?"

Her eyes narrowed until they resembled a cat's. "I heard a rumor, about a silver candlestick that used to stand on the mantle at Chancie Mor."

Maury felt the blood drain from his face. Only two people beside himself were supposed to know about that candlestick. One was dying and the other was dead. "How did you—?"

"Daddy's intelligence network is very efficient, and you are at the top of their list." She took another sip of her drink, a twinkle appearing in her eye. "Oh, don't worry, darling. I'm impressed you could have done something of that sort at such a young age."

"But how—?"

"The Dallas police asked for a set of your fingerprints."

"The police? They have them already. I had to be fingerprinted for my Texas driver's license."

"I know, darling. But they wanted an earlier example. Something about scar tissue."

Maury took a breath. In his youth he'd done some rock climbing and it had left its mark. "I've had those scars since college. They're on every set of prints."

"Not the ones they did of you when you were in elementary school. Remember? They collected all the kiddies' prints and sent them to the National Center for Missing & Exploited Children." Her lips twitched. "Daddy's informant found out about it and passed it on to Daddy, just in case. Turns out those adorable little fingerprints of yours are on a seventeenth century silver candlestick currently in the possession of the Dallas Crimes Against Persons Division."

Maury was feeling sick. The last thing he needed was another thing for Rita to hold over his head. "It was an accident."

"That's what the official report says, I know." She downed the remainder of her drink, stood up and smiled at him. "I don't care what happened at Chancie Mor that night. I'm here to make sure you get the senate seat and that very collectable silver your mother left you." Her smile widened. "It's sure to be in the inventory somewhere. You won't mind if I do a bit of looking around, will you? Provenance, you know. And I can't help thinking there must be another tucked away somewhere. Maybe I can find the mate to the one at the police station."

Maury could feel the sweat trickling down his back. Rita would never give him away. She wanted him to win this election. But if that incident made it to the media's attention, his chances were gone.

"I don't suppose you'd be willing to wait until I've won this election before looking for those candlesticks?"

Her lower lip slid out into a very attractive pout. "Don't you trust me, darling?"

"Of course I do." He hesitated. "You'll be sure to be discreet. I wouldn't want you to have to return them as looted art treasures."

Her smile brightened. "*Are* they looted art treasures?"

"I don't know, but the insurance paperwork should tell us who Mother got them from."

Rita nodded. "I'll get on it first thing Monday. Goodnight, darling."

"Goodnight, my dear."

She disappeared into the bathroom, emerging in her nightclothes, and slipping into the unclaimed bed in the private section of the suite.

Maury Patterson went through two more drinks, thinking long into the night. If there was any way he could get Rita what she wanted, without publicity, she was welcome to it. If he could prove his mother owned the candlesticks and he was his mother's heir, there should be no problem handing them over to Rita. But there was a complication. Two, actually.

The first was that he had no idea where the other candlestick was. It had disappeared the night of Tommy's death and he'd never seen it again.

The second was that the family connections that made it possible for Rita to find out about that night were the same connections that might not understand the need for secrecy, though they should all know how to keep their mouths shut. On the Chicago end, anyway.

He'd been a child. Kids hit each other all the time, and the candlestick had been handy. The fact that there had been no police follow-up implied they had no case. So even if the candlestick he'd given to Patsy to hide all those years ago had somehow ended up in Dallas police hands, and they were able to match his youthful fingerprints to it, they still had no case. It was just two kids rough-housing.

As long as the media didn't get hold of the story. Because even the most cynical among his constituency was not going to want a child killer as their new senator.

* * *

CHAPTER 21

Sunday morning
St. Columba Kirk

It was approaching noon and Divine Service was behind them. Ginny sat with her mother and the Laird at a table in the Parish Hall and listened to the discussion going on between them. She had never been much interested in politics, and the historical aspects of founding a nation had barely made a dent in her consciousness. But this was different. She was being allowed to see why it would be undesirable to elect Maury Patterson to the Texas District 17A state senate seat.

"He would ha'e us gie up our sovereignty and be just anither herd o' spineless sheep!" Angus was a bit red in the face and Ginny hoped his blood pressure was well under control.

"What will happen if he succeeds?" Ginny asked.

"'Twill be th' end o' Home Rule."

Her brow furrowed. "What does that mean?"

"Th' Homestead will cease tae exist, 'twill be absorbed inta Dallas proper, and subject tae General Rule. We'll ha'e nae clan, nae laird, nothing o' wha' makes us wha' we are."

Ginny stared. "He can't do that! We've put a hundred and fifty years of work into this Homestead!"

"Aye, 'twill be a great loss."

Ginny frowned. "What makes him think he can get away with it?"

"He's arguin' th' original charter was drawn up improperly. We mus' prove he's wrong, that th' vote establishing Home Rule was valid."

"That will require legal and historical research."

"Aye. Th' documents are here." He patted the dossier beside him. "Th' problem is they dinna support our claim."

Ginny stared. "Why not?"

"He's arguing we didnae ha'e th' necessary five thousand and one in population at th' time. We did, o' course, but some o' the men were missed by th' census 'cause they were awa, preparing fer World War One."

"This sounds like the Glencoe debacle, except without the snow."

The Laird smiled at her. "Aye, bureaucracy ne'er changes." He sighed. "Worst case scenario, we hold a vote, right now, tae establish Home Rule from today forward."

"Would it be upheld?"

"Aye, if we follow th' procedures."

"Would it change anything?" Sinia asked.

"'Tis possible. We've a provision tha' says th' laird is fer life, unless voted oot. Th' general rule is tha' th' mayor must be re-elected every four years."

"We could do that, if we had to."

Angus nodded. "We've a more traditional method o' selection, but it's still up tae th' clan." He caught Ginny's eye. "Ye and Jim, fer instance, ha'e been confirmed by a vote o' the Council and th' Clansmen and women. But it's conditional. Ye need tae earn th' clan's trust and respect."

Ginny blanched, then nodded her head. "Aye, Mackenzie. Is there anything we can do to help?"

"Keep yer ears open, lass. I'll need tae know it, if th' wind changes."

As if in response to his words, the opening notes of "Largo al factotum" from *The Barber of Seville* wafted through the Hall, followed promptly by a rich baritone. Everyone in the room stopped what they were doing, turned to the source of the sound, and listened.

Even those not especially fond of opera were listening, and those that were, were smiling, then clapping, then laughing. The performer knew what he was doing. The light, cheerful number was studded with vocal wit, making fun of itself, and sharing the fun with the audience. Ginny was enchanted.

When Scala rose from the piano, it was to thunderous applause, whistles, and entreaties to continue. He turned and looked at her, then resumed his seat, choosing *Finnegan's Wake* next. This was followed by *The Bricklayer's Song, Wild Rover, Drunken Sailor,* and *The Irish Washerwoman,* by which time he had them eating out of his hand. The bolder among the audience had gathered around the piano, shouting requests. The more sedate sang along from their seats or tapped their toes in time to the music.

Again, he seemed to know his audience. He moved from the humorous and dance tunes to more traditional songs including *The Shoals of Herring*, and *Loch Lomond*, working up to and finishing with *Scotland the Brave*.

With a twinge of regret, Ginny watched him accept his accolades and depart. When he was done here, he would go home, back to Illinois and the Muni. But perhaps he could be persuaded to come visit and sing for them again. That would be something to look forward to.

* * *

With Scala's performance over and the man gone, Ginny addressed the task she had set herself for this morning. She went looking for the Matron. If anyone could help her locate the hypothetical, much-maligned, Chancie Mor housemaid of fifty years ago, it would be Jean.

"Can you point someone out to me, please?"

Jean looked up from her ladle, studied Ginny's face for a half a moment, then delegated her task to another woman and steered Ginny off into a corner. "I know that look. You've had an idea."

Ginny admitted it was so.

"Well?" Jean expected payment in the coin of the realm—gossip—and to be well paid, too.

Ginny outlined her theory. "She may be dead, or have moved away, or kept her secret to herself all these years."

"Hannah McLachlan?" Jean snorted. "On the contrary. The old dear is hale and hearty and just as angry as she was when it happened. Everyone knows the story! Her family doesn't listen anymore. They know it all by heart. She married Hugh McLachlan, the grocer, and they had seven children. When he died, her eldest took her in."

"Is there any chance I can visit her?"

Jean grinned. "How much time have you got?"

"Why?"

"She's sitting over there. You don't even need to bring her a cookie. She'll chew your ear off for free, but it'll take some time."

Mrs. McLachlan was approximately eighty years old, though she wasn't really sure whether 'twas this side or that. She had fudged a bit o'er the years. First down, then up, as it suited her. She winked at Ginny. She recollected the incident as if it were yesterday. "Could hardly do otherwise. 'Specially with the sinful old woman so recently deid, good riddance tae her. The

De'il ha' taken his ain at last, I say, but left th' boy tae plague the clan, what had been shed of him after th' poor little lad deid, and 'twas a guid thing."

Ginny interrupted. "I'm so sorry, but would you let me ask you a few questions, just so I can keep it all straight?"

"Sure, lass, I mean Mrs. Mackenzie." The older woman bobbed her head.

Ginny smiled at the courtesy. Being Jim's wife might have its uses. "Thank you. Now, the lad that died, that was Tommy Bryant?"

"Aye and a precious bairn he was, 'ceptin' he was a boy, o' course."

It took the better part of an hour to extract the background information she needed from Mrs. McLachlan, but in the end Ginny had the gist: The four parents had dined in civilized state, while the four children had eaten in the kitchen, along with two children belonging to the staff. After which little Charlotte had been called for and taken off to a sleep-over at a friend's house. The children of the staff stayed with their parents, helping where possible, staying out from under foot when no help could be given. Mr. and Mrs. Bryant, and Mr. and Mrs. Patterson moved to the veranda where they could play bridge, sip on adult beverages, and watch the sails on the lake. It was not Mrs. McLachlan's responsibility to watch the remaining three children. There was a nursemaid, but she was apparently unwell and told the police she was lying down in her room when the accident occurred.

Ginny wrote down all the names of the staff and the who-was-where-when information. "All right. What happened then?"

"No one knows fer sure, as there were no one wi' th' bairns. I was in the kitchen when th' mistress, old Mrs. Patterson, come tae us and tells us tae refill th' drinks tray. That were th' butler's job, sae I went on doin' what I was, which was washin' dishes. Th' next thing ye ken, Mrs. Bryant was screechin' and howlin' and it was seech a noise I dropt ane o' the good plates and it smashed tae pieces!"

"Did you go find out what all the noise was about?"

"I was told tae stay where I was until called fer."

Here followed a detailed description of the arrival of the ambulance, accompanied by a policeman. Tommy was taken to the emergency room and the policeman stayed behind to interrogate the staff. But no one knew anything and they were allowed to finish their duties and go home.

It was clear Mrs. McLachlan had gotten all of her information second, and sometimes third-hand, from the other staff members, distorted by shock and ignorance. Ginny sighed, wondering if it was worth her time to continue listening, but she was here and Jim was asleep so she might as well do the job properly.

"After the policeman left, what happened?"

"We were sent in tae clean up." Mrs. McLachlan shook her head. "Th' carpet were a mess. The men rolled it up and carried it oot, tae be taken tae th' cleaners th' next day. That left me and Dot tae wipe doon all th' surfaces." She shook her head again. "We'd seen blood, th' both o' us, what wi' th' animals and seech. There weren't even much o' it left, once th' rug had gone. We got down on our hands and knees and went inch by inch 'cross th' floor. We used our eyes and followed the drops o' blood." She stopped and looked Ginny in the face.

"I didnae understand at th' time wha' I were seeing, ye ken. Tha' came later. I cleaned th' floor, and th' legs o' a chair tha' stood aside th' hairth, and up the side o' the mantle, and that's when I noticed."

"What did you notice?"

"Tha' they were no' there, th' candlesticks."

"There were supposed to be candlesticks on the mantle?"

"Aye."

"How did you know?"

"I put th' tapers in them myself that mornin'. Dark green tae go wi' th' drapes."

Ginny blinked. If Mrs. McLachlan handled the candlesticks that morning, her fingerprints should have been on the one Patsy had hidden.

"Did you touch the silver when you put the tapers in, or just stick the wax in the top?"

Mrs. McLachlan gave her a sharp look. "I know my business. The butler cleans and if I mus' touch the sticks themselves 'twill be w' cotton gloves, which I did on the day as they'd jest been cleaned and were as shiny bright as ye could wish fer, and wiped them doon when I finished, fer guid measure. Th' point bein' they should 'ave been there."

"Can you describe them?"

"Aye!" The old woman made a face. "I've done so a hundred times since then."

Ginny listened for a moment, then pulled out her phone. It was a long shot—a lot can get muddled in a woman's mind over fifty years—but worth a try. She located the photo of the candlestick that had been hidden in the boat, the one without the blood, and showed it to the old woman. "Is this one of them?"

She took the phone from Ginny, peered at it, then nodded. "Aye, except it should ha'e blood on't."

Ginny started, then took back the phone, thinking fast. If the old woman had not seen the blow, and the guilty candlestick was not on the mantle when she was sent in to clean, how could she know there should be blood on it?

"Why do you say that?"

The old woman's brow furrowed. "She accused me o'

stealing th' silver, but she couldnae make it stick because I hadnae done it. It took me years tae figure out why she would do seech a thing, accuse me o' seech a thing. Me! As honest as th' day is long. My faither saw tae that. And she knew it. I couldnae understand her." She shook her head.

"Hugh believed me, and took me in, and ne'er regretted it. But I couldnae let it go. I went over and over tha' room in my mind's eye, and I watched all th' crime shows on th' TV, hopin' fer an answer." She paused for a moment to draw breath. "One day th' box had a special about blood splatter." Mrs. McLachlan's frown deepened. "I dinna know wha' they called it in th' yard, but I'd seen it. When they butcher a hog, or a sheep. Ye have tae stand back 'cause th' blood spurts."

Ginny nodded.

"I hadnae put two and two together afore that show, but blood comes off th' knife, too. And th' men aren't always careful. I've gotten blood on my apron tha' way." The old woman nodded her head several times. "At last, I understood, but I couldnae forget. I wanted the woman tae apologize, publicly. Then she went an' died on me."

Mrs. McLachlan looked straight at Ginny. "But the Lord is just. He showed me th' way." She reached over and tapped her finger on the table. "Tha's my plan tae pay her back. Wi' th' blood off th' knife, except in this case it's a candlestick."

Ginny was fascinated. "Your plan?"

"That no-good spawn o' hers. Thinks he can be senator here, in the place of our good Senator Hunter. Over my deid body! Once everyone knows th' truth, no one amang us will vote fer him and I'll ha'e my revenge."

Ginny waited a moment then asked the question. "What is the truth?"

"Why, what else? That boy of hers snatched up one o' th' candlesticks and killed his little cousin wi' it!"

Ginny counted to five, to give her brain a chance to catch up. "Why would he do that?"

The old woman shrugged. "Boys. They're all bad until civilized. But I heard there were a fight o'er a rubber sword the smaller boy was plaguing his cousin with. Tempers flared. That part was in th' newspapers. Rough-housing, they called it." She leaned toward Ginny. "Wha' ne'er appeared was th' blood splatter, off th' candlestick. The blood splatter that climbed th' side o' th' mantle and couldnae have come from Master Tommy Bryant hittin' th' back o' his head on th' corner o' the coffee table. Th' blood splatter I cleaned off myself, ne'er realizing until it was too late wha' it meant."

She emphasized the last three words by stabbing her finger down on the table. The motion caught the eye of her daughter, who rose and came over to help. "Now, Mother, there's no need to upset yourself. Time to go home." She gave Ginny an apologetic smile, guiding her mother to her feet.

Ginny rose, too, half in shock. She took the old woman's other arm and helped steer her to where her male kinfolk waited. When she had handed Mrs. McLachlan off, she plucked at the daughter's sleeve. The woman turned back, chagrin on her face.

"Forgive, her, please. She's an old woman with a grievance. She means no harm."

"Of course not, but I'd feel better if you kept her at home for a while. What she told me could be taken as a threat."

"So it was." The daughter made a face. "If she could get back at Mrs. Patterson, she would, in spite of coming to church every week and promising to forgive her enemies."

"Maury Patterson is a powerful man, with powerful connections. Your mother may not realize it, but she could get into serious trouble by accusing him."

The daughter nodded, then sighed. "It's the Scottish blood,

ye ken. A feud gives her life meaning and she'll relish every minute of it."

"I understand. Just take care of her."

"We will, and thank you!"

Ginny watched them out the door, then gathered up her things and followed, the sexton locking the door behind her. The interview had taken more than two hours. She hurried toward her car.

Her phone went off as she opened the door. She glanced at it and saw a text message from Himself. Senator Patterson was insisting on seeing Patsy. Go, now, and let him know what she finds.

She read it twice, swore fluently in a specialized, medical version of Anglo-Saxon that she'd learned at the hospital, then turned the engine on and headed in the opposite direction from home. When the Laird gives you an assignment, you go, no matter what. Besides, after what she'd just heard, there was no way she wanted Senator Patterson to have access to Patsy Olafsson. *Everyone has heard the story*, Jean had said. *Everyone*. But it would be so much better if Maury Patterson didn't. Ginny pushed the accelerator to the floor.

* * *

CHAPTER 22

Sunday afternoon
Olafsson residence

Ginny made all possible haste to Patsy Olafsson's house, hurried up the walk, and was met at the door by an agitated caregiver.

"He pushed past me when I said he couldn't come in. I tried to tell him she wasn't receiving visitors, but he just insisted she'd want to see him. I'm sorry. The officer is keeping an eye on him."

"It's all right, Violet. I'll take it from here."

Ginny strode down the hall and into Patsy's room to find her awake, sitting up against her pillows, and smiling at Maury Patterson. She looked up when Ginny appeared.

"Look, dear! A visitor from my past. Do you remember my cousin? No, of course not, you're too young, but I remember him. We were children together." Patsy beamed at Ginny, who felt her heart rise into her throat. *Did* she remember him? And, if so, did this mean she wasn't afraid of him, that he *wasn't* the face in the window that had triggered those night terrors?

Ginny nodded at the Senator, her manners at their most gracious. "I'm delighted the two of you have had this chance to meet again after so many years, but I'm afraid we're all under doctor's orders, and I must ask you to say goodbye."

Patterson looked from her to Patsy, and Ginny felt her skin crawl. His smile stayed in place, but his eyes lost all vestige of warmth. There was an expression in them Ginny had seen before.

She'd been assigned to the ethics committee at the hospital, to help decide how to allocate a very limited resource. Each candidate had been allowed to make a statement, then the room had been cleared for the final debate. Up until that moment, Ginny had seen compassion, even distress on the faces of all involved. Such decisions could haunt the committee for the rest of their lives. But in that moment, she saw the issue crystalize. In the eyes of the swing vote, the tie-breaker, all compassion died, replaced by a stony calm. His decision had been made.

Patterson took Patsy's hand and patted it. "I will come to see you again, Cousin, if they will let me. In the meantime, take good care of yourself. Do everything the doctor tells you to."

"I always do," she replied.

He rose and bent over Patsy's hand, brushing the knuckles with his lips, then turned, took his leave of Ginny, ignored the security officer, and followed the nurse to the door.

Ginny gestured with her head to the officer, silently instructing him to make sure Patterson actually left the premises, then turned her attention to Patsy. She seemed unharmed by the encounter. Ginny settled into the vacated chair.

"Do you know who that man was?"

"My cousin, Maury Patterson."

"Did you recognize him, when he first came in?"

Patsy's expression clouded momentarily. "No, not really, though he did seem familiar. And he told me who he was, so I knew we were related. His mother and mine were sisters. That makes us first cousins."

"Yes, it does." Ginny searched for a way to ask what she needed to know, without either putting words in Patsy's mouth or scaring her. "Did he ask you if you remembered him?"

"Yes, of course. It's been a long time and we've both changed."

Ginny nodded. "What did you tell him?"

Patsy smiled. "You know how it's done, dear. Never let a man think he isn't the most important thing in the world. It's how we keep them in line. I looked him in the eye and told him I remembered playing together when we were children, but I don't really. I believe him when he says we did. I just don't remember."

Ginny breathed an inward sigh of relief. Whatever Patterson thought, at least he hadn't triggered a crisis. Chris would be glad to hear that Patsy's defenses had held.

But what Angus would make of it Ginny didn't know. "I don't suppose he was here very long. What did you talk about? Tell me everything."

A half-hour later Patsy was winding down, her voice and eyelids drooping. Ginny called the nurse in and between them they got Patsy settled for a nap.

When that was done, Ginny retired to the kitchen, made herself a cup of tea, and found a pad of paper and a pen. She made a note of everything she'd heard, then studied it, considering what it might mean—assuming Patterson had come on a mission, and assuming also that he actually was the killer of little Tommy Bryant.

He hadn't asked about the candlestick, even though he might be wondering what had happened to it. What he *had* asked, according to Patsy, was whether there were any chests or trunks or cabinets that held memorabilia from those long ago days of childhood. He had been feeling nostalgic, she'd said, and looking wistful. He had come home, to the home he'd grown up in, and it was raising all sorts of ghosts. He and she were the last survivors in the family, just the two of them. Maybe she could come to Chancie Mor for a visit, he'd suggested. For *auld lang syne*.

Ginny stared at her notes. For *auld lang syne*. Not likely. To find out where she'd hidden the candlestick all those years ago! To find the candlestick, if he could.

Patterson could not know that Patsy had sent the candlestick to Ginny or that Ginny had given it to Detective Tran. Patsy barely knew it herself. So what would Patterson do next? Search the house? He must have already searched Chancie Mor and found nothing. The next most obvious place to look was Patsy's childhood home, but that had been stripped and sold and re-decorated, and the odds were poor that the candlestick was hidden in the walls. Not impossible though. Ginny made a note to pass the idea along to Angus.

Patterson would want to look here, of course, in the house Patsy had occupied for forty years. Ginny's brow furrowed. If Detective Tran wanted to gather evidence, she needed to get herself over here. Tomorrow, if possible. And, if there was anything Ginny wanted to know about this house, she should look for it today. And take pictures, just like Scala. Ginny squirmed at the similarity, then rose from her chair, cleaned up the tea things, tucked her notes in her bag, and headed for the attic.

She climbed the stair, turned on the light, and looked around. The candlesticks were not here. They were both at the police station. But Patterson didn't know that. He might believe the evidence of his childhood crime was still here, tucked away in a box in this attic, just as the knowledge of that crime was tucked away in Patsy's brain.

Ginny felt goosebumps rise on her arms. She returned to the kitchen and pulled out her phone, tapping a note to Angus.

Patterson is looking for objects from his childhood. Patsy has lied to him, telling him she remembers. He has been denied an opportunity to search here. I think he may try to destroy this house, with her in it.

She sent it, then dropped a word of caution in the ears of the caregiver and guard. Because she had seen the Senator's face as he took his leave. Senator Patterson wasn't just satisfied. He was in motion.

* * *

Sunday afternoon
Mackenzie residence

On the way home, Ginny popped into the office supply store and bought one of the over-sized planning calendars that really don't fit anywhere. At the moment it was taking up half of her kitchen table. She had also invested in two sets of colored markers, one bold and broad tipped, the other fine tipped, suitable for making small additions to the larger entries. She had also purchased an array of sticky notes in all the colors of the rainbow, perfect for flagging and prioritizing.

Before settling down to work on the calendar, Ginny made three phone calls. The first was to Detective Tran, reporting the invasion of Patsy's house and Hannah McLachlan's blood splatter theory. The second was to Himself, explaining about the threat to Patsy's childhood home, which Angus had taken seriously and promised to follow up on. The third was to Chris Urquhart. Here Ginny found herself thwarted. He was not answering his phone. She had to leave a message asking him to call her.

She turned to the calendar, laying out the remainder of May in pencil, to make sure she knew when and where she and Jim were expected to be, before inking them in, using the appropriate color coding. She was working her way through the promises she found on her phone, in her day book, on computer print-outs, and scraps of paper with notes to herself scribbled in every possible manner, when Jim appeared, tousled from sleep and blinking in the afternoon sun. She looked up and smiled at him.

"Hello, darling. Did you sleep well?"

He nodded, then drew her away from the table to kiss her. "What's this?"

"Our calendar and it's going to be a life-saver, as soon as I get organized." She slipped her arms around his waist. "Do you want to eat first or get dressed first?"

He hugged her tightly, then released her, rubbing the back of his neck. "Get dressed, I think."

"Dinner will be on the table in fifteen minutes."

He nodded, then disappeared into the shower and emerged just as Ginny was taking the casserole out of the oven. It was one of her favorites, a rice-based dish with black olives and garlic and the finest ground beef in the country under a layer of sauce that set one's taste buds watering.

"Ummm! Smells good."

"Get yourself something to drink while I finish serving."

The two of them ate in peace, Ginny making sure Jim had samples of all four food groups, at least in small portions, to round out the menu.

He finished his meal then smiled at her. "So, what have you been up to today, in addition to the calendar?"

"I've had a very interesting day. First, your grandfather gave me a lesson on Home Rule, then Larry Scala sang for us. He's very good."

Jim lifted an eyebrow. "I'm sorry I missed that. Anything else?"

"Yes. I spent quite a lot of time with Hannah McLachlan."

"Who?"

"She's the housemaid who got blamed when the candlesticks went missing. But it's going to take me too long to tell you all about it tonight. It'll have to wait until tomorrow."

Jim glanced at his watch. "All right. Anything else?"

"Yes." Ginny sighed, then told him about Senator Patterson's visit to Patsy.

"You think he's looking for the candlestick?"

"Only if he's guilty and thinks Patsy still has it."

Jim's brow furrowed. "I see your point. But what other reason could he have for visiting her?"

"Well, he may be wondering if she remembers how her brother died and has told anyone."

Jim raised an eyebrow. "I would, in his place." He leaned back in his chair, his eyes narrowing. "You think that's what he wanted?"

"I've been trying to sort out what I think. Patsy hasn't turned him in, so he may believe she never will. Whatever hold he has on her is still strong enough to keep her quiet."

"Did you tell him she couldn't remember?"

"No."

Jim nodded slowly. "So Cousin Maury must visit Patsy to find out where he stands. What did he learn?"

"That there are lots of hiding places for a murder weapon in her house."

"Okay, not really news. What about the wedding present? Did she mention that?"

"I asked and she told me the candlestick didn't come up. But I have to wonder what she *did* say."

"What do you mean?"

Ginny frowned, remembering the disconnect between the smile on Patterson's face and the coldness of his eyes.

"He didn't look worried when he left. He looked satisfied, as if she'd already told him what he wanted to know. It scared me."

Jim frowned. "You said she hadn't told him anything."

"What she told him was what she thought he wanted to hear, that her memory of those early days was crystal clear because who could forget anyone as charming as Maury Patterson."

* * *

Sunday evening
Mackenzie residence

When Jim had taken himself off to work, Ginny went back to her calendar. She penciled in all of the scheduled appointments: shifts at the hospital, church services, Friday night ceilidhs, and Homestead duties—including training sessions with Jean and Angus. Next up were social obligations, after which she could pencil in personal time: exercise, working on the boat, relaxing with her husband, sleep.

Patsy Olafsson's birthday—the last one she would ever have—was a week from today. There was a large celebration planned at the church, with friends from all her numerous charities and volunteer jobs, her students, her remaining contemporaries, the clan, and outsiders who had come to know her through her medical treatments and support groups. It promised to be the event of the season.

Also coming up was the performance of *Macbeth* in two weeks. Ginny penciled in the date and made a note to remind Jim to make sure he had the night off. She was just finishing the entry when the phone rang.

"Dr. Urquhart," Ginny began.

"Chris, please."

She nodded, wondering if she actually heard a certain tightness in his voice or whether she was imagining it. "All right, Chris. I just wanted to let you know what happened today." She told the tale of Patsy's unauthorized visitor for the third time, then added, "but I don't think it hurt her."

"She was confronted with Patterson, close up, and didn't remember him?"

"That's what she said."

"Was it your impression she associated him with the face in the window?"

Ginny shook her head at the phone. "I really couldn't tell, but she was calm and smiling, so I'm guessing not."

"Okay. I've got another session planned for Tuesday morning. Can you be there?"

Ginny bent over her calendar. "Yes."

"Good. Same time. I want to use a mild hypnotic this time, to see if we can get past her conscious mind."

"I'll be there. Is there anything else you need?"

"Not at the moment. Thank you for letting me know."

"See you Tuesday." Ginny added the new appointment to her calendar wondering why she hadn't told the psychiatrist what she had told Jim, about Patsy's little white lie and Patterson's response to it, then decided she didn't want to prejudice him.

Ginny set the calendar aside and settled into a chair. She'd been thinking about Larry's threat and Angus' refusal to put a tail on him. She hadn't talked to Angus about it since the dinner yesterday, but she hadn't given up, either.

In a community this size, with as many connections as there were between families, very few things went unnoticed. The Cooperative Hall served as a meeting place for the retired and their caregivers. Porches had swings and wicker seating. The able bodied strolled along the park walkways with their eyes and ears open.

Coordinating all this information fell to the Matron. Which would be Ginny's job when the time came. No one should be surprised if she was helping out as she learned the ropes. She picked up the phone and called Jean.

"Are you busy or can I pick your brain for a bit?"

"You may pick my brain any time, even if I am busy. You have a question about what happened at church today?"

"Well, yes and no. I'm uncomfortable with letting Larry Scala wander around Loch Lonach unchaperoned."

"Why is that?"

Ginny explained about Larry's threat against Patsy. "I told Angus yesterday, but he said we couldn't spy on Scala. It would be a violation of his civil rights."

"I see."

"So, I've been thinking. If he appears in public, it's his choice and anything he says or does becomes common knowledge. Right?"

Jean laughed. "He certainly made sure every eye was on him today. That man can sing!"

"And a lot of people who didn't know him before, know who he is now."

"He's been the talk of the town all afternoon. I've gotten a dozen phone calls asking for additional information."

"What did you say?"

"That he's from Illinois and has some connection with the Patterson family."

"Both true."

"How can I help you, Ginny?"

"I want to activate the surveillance network. Anyone who sees Scala, or Patterson, is asked to call in the details. I'll coordinate what we find, but we need the eyes and ears of the clan to gather data for us."

Ginny heard a chuckle on the other end of the line. "You are going to be a very busy woman!"

"I know, but I think if he realizes people are watching, Scala won't do anything drastic."

"Why Patterson?"

"Because the trouble started when he showed up."

"Well, there's bound to be some disruption when a new broom arrives."

"New broom? You mean Maury?"

"I mean the new Mrs. Patterson, Rita. She was over at Chancie Mor today turning out every cupboard and closet, looking for something. Made the most awful mess and not a few enemies. I was called in to mediate."

"Okay, include the new wife. Maury and Rita Patterson, and Larry Scala, their biographer."

"Is that what he's doing? Writing a biography?"

Ginny hedged. "He's been collecting data on the family for years."

"Well, that fits. When he left church today, he went to the Cooperative Hall. Brought food and drinks and a recorder. He spent the rest of the day asking questions and there were a lot of loose tongues, you can imagine. He's not bad to look at, when he smiles. And he sang some more, which put him on the right side of the auld folk. They like hearing the familiar tunes. He's planning to come again tomorrow and let them talk some more."

Ginny filed the information away. "Perfect. Just get the word out that we'd like to know where those three are. They're strangers in town. You know what to say."

"I do. All right, I'll take care of it. 'Bye."

"Thank you! 'Bye."

Ginny hung up the phone, well satisfied that the network of

not-spies would be in full blow by mid-day. Gossip might be a sin, but keeping a friendly eye on possible threats to your family was not. It was a duty.

* * *

CHAPTER 23

Monday morning
Insurance agent's office

The man rose as Rita entered the inner office. "Good morning, Mrs. Patterson. How nice to meet you."

Rita extended her hand to Mr. Uriah Hoffman of Cayman, Marker, and Hoffman. "Good morning. Thank you for seeing me."

"Please take a seat."

Rita did so, aware that her carefully chosen wardrobe was having the desired effect. Mr. Hoffman was wearing a wedding band, but his eyes raked her body before settling on her face. She smiled.

"I'm very sorry," he said, "but I'm afraid I have bad news for you. The candlesticks you're looking for are no longer part of the Patterson estate."

Rita paused for a moment, then looked puzzled, then pouted ever so slightly. "But I found the bill of sale among the inventory papers."

He nodded. "They were in the Patterson family collection, and quite fine pieces, as I understand. But they were reported stolen almost fifty years ago."

"Stolen!" Rita expressed surprise rather well. It was one of her more useful emotions.

"I'm afraid so. They were never found."

"What a shame!" Rita uncrossed her legs, then crossed them in the other direction. She leaned toward Mr. Hoffman, her eyes on his. "But if they were recovered, they'd go back into the estate inventory?"

He shook his head. "No. The company paid out on the insurance claim and took the loss. If the items surfaced, they would revert to the company as assets recovered."

Rita thought for a moment. "What would happen then?"

Mr. Hoffman shrugged. "They'd be put up for auction." He eyed her shrewdly. "Do you know where they are?"

Rita's gaze never wavered. "No." It was not a lie. She only suspected where one was and the other was still missing. "I saw a picture of them on the mantelpiece at Chancie Mor and went looking. Someone mentioned the theft and I contacted the company in the hopes you could tell me what became of them. And you have." She rose. "Thank you for your time."

He escorted her to the door. "I'm sorry I couldn't help. You'll let me know if you find them, won't you?"

Rita smiled. "Of course."

She climbed into the taxi and gave the driver the hotel's address, then sat back and considered her options.

There was no way the Dallas police were going to give her that piece of evidence. Even if they decided not to prosecute, because Maury had been a child at the time and lacked the emotional maturity to form intent, the candlestick would not be released to her.

Rita understood auction houses. They might run the blood-stained candlestick under a tap and give it a once-over-lightly with a silver polishing cloth, but they would not do the kind of forensic cleaning necessary to remove the DNA.

She could buy it and do the cleaning herself. Maybe. It was unlikely to command a price she could not afford. But someone might decide to outbid her, and neither Maury nor her father would approve of her exceeding her budget for household goods. What's more, if she went seriously over budget, someone might wonder why.

And there was the timing to consider. The police could decide to close the case at any moment. What would they do with the bloody candlestick? Send it to the owner of record, or give it back to whoever had brought it in and let them explain to the insurance company how they came to be in possession?

Rita paused.

Who had been in possession of that piece of silver all these years? Who had taken it to the police? Did that person know what Maury had done with it?

Fool! He should have told her. Rita felt a flash of anger. Letitia should have told her! If that story got loose, even if the police didn't care what Maury had done, the voters would!

This was going to call for some serious damage control. She needed to "liberate" that candlestick from the police evidence locker and erase all traces of it ever having been there. Do-able, with the right sort of help. She paid off the driver, crossed the hotel lobby, found the suite empty, picked up the phone, and dialed home.

"Daddy? I need a favor."

* * *

Monday evening
Mackenzie residence

On Monday, Ginny came home from work to find Jim still asleep. She moved quietly about the kitchen, laying plates, chilling wine, and locating a tablecloth and napkins. Tonight she would host the first of many ceremonial social events. As

Jim's wife her responsibilities included entertaining, but Angus had been apologetic. Patterson would have to be properly received, since he was now officially a member of the community, and his wife had joined him on Saturday, from Illinois. It was short notice, aye, and if she wasnae up to it, he'd understand.

Ginny had put her foot firmly down on that idea. She would be happy to have the couple to dinner. She and Jim and Angus, with the Pattersons, made five. Angus would bring Sinia, so that made an even number of men and women at the table. No problem.

When Jim woke, she explained the change of plans. He sighed.

"I will do all that is required of me as long as you promise to have them out of the house by midnight."

"Why midnight?"

"Because that's when I plan to turn into a pumpkin, a sight only my wife should be forced to see."

Ginny laughed. "I think I can promise you that. If either of them has an ounce of breeding, they'll be making exit noises long before ten."

"One can only hope." Jim rubbed his face with his hands. "Can you talk and cook at the same time?"

"I can."

"Then tell me what else happened yesterday at church."

She nodded, then explained about the candlesticks, pausing only long enough to baste the roast, and press Jim into service to help her set the table. He listened in silence, then started asking questions.

"You came up with this theory all on your own?"

"That Mrs. Patterson would have to account for the missing candlesticks? Yes."

"But everyone in Loch Lonach, except you, already knew

about it."

"Apparently so."

Jim smothered a smile and Ginny gave him full marks for tact. "Did the housemaid, Mrs. McLachlan, approach Mrs. Patterson and ask what had happened to the candlesticks?"

"I don't think so. It wouldn't have been that kind of relationship. The girl would have asked the senior staff members to find out for her. The butler, for instance."

"Why the butler?"

"Because it was his responsibility to clean the silver and make sure it stayed in good repair. If one of the candlesticks had been knocked off the mantle, for instance, it would have been his job to have it fixed, keep track of the uninjured mate, maybe even find temporary replacements, then report to the lady of the house."

Jim's brow furrowed. "Why pin the theft on the girl then? Why not accuse the butler?"

Ginny shrugged. "I think Mrs. Patterson heard Mrs. McLachlan—Hannah Jordan, as she was then—asking around and decided she was too inquisitive. I also think Mrs. Patterson decided the best defense was a strong offense. The sooner she noticed the candlesticks were missing and the bigger the stink she made about it, the less likely it would be that someone else would start asking awkward questions."

Jim nodded. "So the police investigated and found no evidence against the girl. Did Mrs. Patterson change her story?"

"No. A lot of people had access to the room that night— police, EMTs, the laird, clergy, staff, family—and no one was paying any attention to candlesticks, so it could have been someone else, but no one else was ever accused and no one was ever charged."

"Angus was there?"

"His uncle, James."

"Oh. This business about Maury Patterson using the candlestick as a weapon, did our little housemaid see the blow?"

"No, she deduced it from the location of the blood splatter."

Jim smiled. "Did she now? Clever girl, but she's just guessing, and it was fifty years ago. That makes her threat to expose Patterson pretty weak."

Ginny lifted an eyebrow. "The press are voracious and not always scrupulous in checking their facts before publication. I can see them prefacing the news item with, 'It has been suggested that. . .' and letting the voting public draw its own conclusions."

"True. Did she take pictures, the housemaid, I mean?"

"No, but I've got *ask Detective Tran if there are any crime scene photographs in the archives* on my To Do list."

"Has she told anyone about her theory, about blood coming off the guilty candlestick and landing on the woodwork?"

"Her family, I think, but no one else. For one thing, Maury Patterson has only recently come back to Chancie Mor, and then only after his mother died. Hannah's venom has been directed at Letitia Patterson for fifty years. It would take time for her to switch her focus. She'd have to realize that destroying the son was as good as destroying the mother, and that sharing her blood splatter theory would be enough to bring him down."

Jim fell silent and Ginny waited for him to process the information.

"If Hannah McLachlan is determined to ruin Patterson's reputation, he may try to stop her."

Ginny nodded. "If he finds out about it. I've suggested to her daughter that it would be wise to keep her out of the

Incarnadine

public eye, without telling her why. If we can do that, there's a good chance Patterson won't hear about her or her story. They don't move in the same circles."

Jim's eyes clouded. "And what about you, my love? When is Patterson going to find out how much *you* know?"

Ginny's brow furrowed. "Hopefully never. Detective Tran can be trusted to keep her mouth shut, and the same should be true of all the police. Larry probably can't, but Angus has assigned a hulking high school senior, Tor McLeish, to stay with Larry as much as possible. The boy wants to be a detective and Angus has given him enough details to whet his appetite. He has also given him instructions to prevent a meeting between Scala and Patterson, explaining that this will interfere with the Laird's plans for them.

"The young man hero-worships Angus, as well he might, and has accepted the assignment. He has instructions to keep us posted via email, text-messaging, and phone calls, as needed. The whole thing is hush-hush and Angus has promised him school credit if he pulls it off."

Jim laughed. "I'll have to remember that one, when I'm a laird. What about Patsy?"

"Patsy's a problem. I really don't know who she's talked to, and she might tell someone what we've told her—that she sent the candlestick to me while under the influence of the sleeping pill. But I asked and she said she hadn't, so let's hope it's true."

"Is there anyone else who knows?"

Ginny shrugged. "I'm assuming Patterson knows, and his mother must have known, because she covered up for him."

Jim's brow furrowed. "You're sure about that?"

"As sure as I can be without actual proof."

"Well, Detective Tran has both candlesticks, and Scala's suspicions." Jim rose to his feet. "I can't see what else we can do at the moment. So, what can I do to help you get ready for the feast?"

"Go get cleaned up."

"I hear and obey! But first—" He caught her in his arms and began to kiss her repeatedly. Ginny cooperated for a few minutes, then duty reasserted itself. She reluctantly sent him on his way and turned back to the vegetables. One of the nicer things in this new kitchen of hers was a warming oven, a place to store bread and side dishes while the main dish finished cooking. She tucked the caramelized carrots in beside the sourdough loaf, checked the roast, then hurried off to get into her hostess clothes.

Ginny's braid was long enough for her to sit on. This was both a blessing and a curse. Everyone loved it, but it limited the hairstyles she could adopt. She pulled out the heavy-duty hairpins, arranged the braid in a crown on the top of her head, anchored it to keep the weight from shifting, and added a small faux-jeweled clip to the back.

Moving on, she touched up her makeup, then slipped into a dark red cocktail dress with a stand-up collar, three-quarter length sleeves, and a skirt that flared from her nipped-in waist to mid-calf. The dress code was kilt, so she would be wearing the Mackenzie sash draped from shoulder to hip. The effect was striking. With her lady-like pumps in place and her earrings on, she felt ready to face even the Pattersons.

It was disturbing to think that Maury Patterson might have killed his little cousin and, if Scala was right, his sister. Such a man should not be in a position of power. She frowned. With Hannah's testimony, Ginny had the means to prevent it. Which made her—potentially—judge, jury, and executioner. Was that her role, her destiny, to be the arbiter of justice among her people?

She studied herself in the mirror. The face that stared back didn't look like justice. It looked like mercy, or the hope for mercy—pale and tentative and sad. But the blood red stripe in the Mackenzie tartan was there for a reason—to remind them that peace comes at a price.

* * *

Monday evening
Elysium Hotel, downtown Dallas

Rita Patterson had been downstairs making good use of the beauty salon supplied by the management of the Elysium Hotel. They were invited to dinner at the Mackenzie's and she wanted to make a good impression.

She turned left out of the elevator and headed down the hall. Lost in thought, it took a minute for her to realize there was a women standing in the doorway of the corner suite, a thin, well-dressed woman, talking to Maury. Rita was too far away to hear what was said, but she saw money change hands, then the woman turned, let herself into the stairwell, and disappeared.

Rita was no stranger to the underbelly of life. She recognized the expression of disdain she'd seen on the other woman's face. A working girl. A bit higher class than average, but in it for the money. Well. It wasn't the first time. Maury drew ambitious women to him like bees to honeysuckle. They posed no threat to Rita. She knew how to handle such women.

She strode down the corridor and let herself in.

"Ready, dear?"

"One moment. I'm just choosing a tie."

Rita walked over to stand in front of him as he showed her the choices. "Blue, definitely. It brings out your eyes." She smiled at him, then perched on the arm of the chair while she waited.

"Who was that at the door?"

Maury glanced over at her and shrugged. "The girl I hired to investigate Ian Hunter. She tells me he's sea-green incorruptible."

Rita pulled in a long breath. She had been unable to come to Texas for the old woman's funeral. She now saw she should have tried harder. It was a mistake to leave Maury to his own devices.

"I saw you pay her off."

Maury pointed to a photograph on the dresser. "She got one clear shot with her snuggled up beside him. She'd done her best, she said, so she'd earned her fee."

"You're getting soft. I would have cut the fee in half."

"It wasn't that much. I didn't see any reason to haggle, and that photo is useful. If the media aren't interested, we can approach the wife."

Rita walked over to the dresser, picked up the photo and examined it. Not bad. High resolution. It had possibilities. She'd send it to Kiki tonight and tell her what was wanted. Shouldn't take her long, no more than a day or two.

Rita tucked the envelope into her bag, then followed her husband out into the hall and into the elevator. They needed to have a long talk, just the two of them, but it would have to wait. Besides, tonight promised to be interesting.

Tonight she would meet Ginny Mackenzie, the woman whose name was on the police record. It was Mrs. Mackenzie who had brought the candlestick to the attention of the police. If she'd had possession of one of the candlesticks, one had to wonder where she'd gotten it—and if she also knew where to find the other.

* * *

Monday evening
Mackenzie residence

They made it through the meal with small talk about children, weather, and memories, the most entertaining of which belonged to Angus. The roast and cook were both admired, and Ginny was beginning to relax. She invited her guests into the living room for coffee. Rita toured the room, her eyes on the décor, though she refrained from overt discourtesy. When they were settled, she turned to Ginny.

"Do you like antiques? Because I do and I'm so hoping there will be an opportunity to do some shopping in Dallas."

Ginny smiled, shaking her head. "I don't like using things that belong in a museum, so I tend to choose sturdy modern substitutes."

Rita gave her a jaundiced look. "The linen fold motif on those cabinets is not modern."

"You have a good eye, but even those pieces are reproductions. If you crawl underneath, you'll find screws, not pegs."

"How disappointing!" She set her coffee cup down and crossed the room to a tea service nestled on a silver tray set on the dark wood sideboard. "Silver is harder to counterfeit."

Ginny joined her. "You know silver?"

Rita smiled, "I do."

"Feel free to look around. I have no really old pieces, but I've been collecting for a while. As a matter of fact, I usually find them in trash piles, sadly neglected." She pointed to the tray. "You can see where the silver has been worn away, revealing the copper that gives the tray its strength."

Rita nodded, looking around the room. "Georgian, Regency, Jacobean. Mostly English pieces."

"Correct."

"But you're Scottish?"

Ginny nodded. "The family has been in America since the 1600s, but our roots go back to Scotland."

"Do you have any silver that's authentically Scottish? As far as I know, I've never seen any."

Ginny hesitated. "They didn't make much. The Scots didn't see any reason to waste time and money on decorating household items. However, I do have two pieces, a quaich made out of cherry, banded in silver, and a stirrup cup in the shape of a stag's head."

Rita smiled. "I'd like to see them one day."

Ginny nodded and retrieved her coffee, aware that all four of the others had been listening to her conversation with Rita.

"Have you visited the Homestead? We have a museum on the grounds, and it has some fine old pieces."

Rita resumed her seat beside her husband. "That sounds like fun." She smiled at Maury. "You've been, I'm sure."

He nodded. "As a small boy, I had to work the Homestead Living History displays, just like the rest of the clan."

Rita wrinkled her nose. "I don't think I would have liked that. I'm an indoor girl. I much prefer watching sailboats from an air conditioned upstairs window."

Ginny's eyebrows rose. "You're staying at Chancie Mor?"

"No. We're staying downtown. I just remember how lovely it looked."

"So you've visited Loch Lonach before."

Rita nodded. "Before we were married, I came down to meet Mrs. Patterson." Rita winked at Maury. "I had to pass inspection, you see."

"She was a formidable personality."

"Indeed she was, but we hit it off immediately. We had many things in common."

"Love of antiques?"

"Yes, and believing children were our most important legacy."

Maury nodded. "They kept throwing me out of the room so they could talk privately. Girl stuff, you know."

"Oh, more than that, darling. Much more than that." Rita set her cup down and rose to her feet. She smiled at Ginny.

"Thank you so much for your hospitality. The dinner was delicious and I've had such fun meeting you all. You have a beautiful home and I do hope we can go antiquing together some day. I'm counting on you to show me all the little holes-in-the-wall where you find your treasures." She was maneuvering Patterson to his feet as she spoke, then herding him toward the front door.

"I'll be happy to," Ginny said. She and Jim saw the Pattersons out the door and waved goodbye, then returned to the family party that remained.

Ginny collapsed onto the sofa and turned to her mother. "Well! What do you think?"

Sinia lifted an eyebrow. "I think she's a shark in wolf's clothing and we'd better lock up the sheep."

Ginny threw her arms around her mother's neck and kissed her on the cheek. "If you need to circle the wagons, give me a call and I'll send Jim right over."

"If it comes to that, you'd better send a Highland Regiment. I don't think anything less could control her."

Ginny's smile faded, only to be forced back into place for the duration of the visit. Her mother had hit the nail on the head. Patterson had seemed formidable enough alone. What would he be able to do to the Homestead, now that reinforcements had landed?

* * *

CḩapⲧⲉⲢ 24

Tuesday morning
Dry dock, Lewisville

On Tuesday morning, Jim rose early, leaving his wife still asleep. He had an appointment.

He tip-toed to the car, grabbed a cup of coffee from the drive-thru, then joined the traffic headed north. He was outside the door when the Lewisville Marine Restoration shop opened.

He listened as the man he'd hired to help him update his sailboat explained what to expect. The man's name was Samuel Boatwright—yes, and yes, his ancestors built wooden boats—ships, actually—and he'd been doing this sort of thing for forty years. He knew what he was about and he came with good references. Of course, it was useful if the owner spent some time helping out. You couldn't know too much about your boat, especially since your life might depend on it. Here was a schedule of the repairs and the days he was planning to be working on Jim's boat. Jim would be welcome to come and watch at any time, and here was a list of things Mr. Boatwright suggested Jim learn how to do.

Here, too, were the inevitable regulations—federal, state, and local—that governed sailboats, including the restoration of an older vessel. He was advised to memorize them. Mr.

Boatwright had highlighted the ones Jim needed immediately, and emphasized the importance of not missing filing deadlines, which could be costly.

Jim took notes, accepted an itemized estimate, looked it over, and approved the plans and timetable. When they had settled as much as was possible at this first meeting, he thanked his new friend, exchanged contact information, and took his leave, scanning the lists as he walked back to the car. Some of the terms he knew. Others were unfamiliar. It was a specialized vocabulary, the sea and the ships that sailed on her. But one thing stood out from all the others. Whether he was ready or not, his little sailboat would be ready by September.

* * *

Tuesday morning
Olafsson residence

Ginny climbed the steps onto Patsy's porch, thinking they were in for a hot summer this year. She could smell it on the air. She rang the bell and was admitted by the caretaker, the armed guard behind her.

"Good morning, Mrs. Mackenzie."

"Good morning, Violet. Is Dr. Urquhart here yet?"

"He's in with Mrs. Olafsson."

Ginny took a moment to examine the guard. He looked rock solid and very intimidating. She did not know him.

"This way, please."

She was ushered into the solar, a comfortable room that caught the morning sun and boasted a variety of flora in pots. Patsy was on her feet, watering the plants.

"Good morning."

Patsy turned to greet her. "Oh, good. Now we can begin."

She set down the watering can, positioned herself on a cushioned wicker chair and waved Ginny to a seat.

Ginny sat where indicated, then looked up and found Chris smiling at her.

"As you can see," he said, "we are being honored with both sunshine and shrubbery this morning."

"It's a very pleasant room."

Patsy smiled. "Yes, and I was getting sick of the bedroom. I figure I can be psychoanalyzed as easily in here as in there."

Chris nodded. "A change of venue can often be very helpful." He rose, handed Patsy the low-dose sedative, then took her through the hypnosis protocol. Ginny pulled out her notepad and got ready.

Two hours later, the medication was wearing off and Chris called a halt. The session had been a success, in that Patsy had been able to recall the evening Tommy died, and reported all the same things Hannah McLachlan had recalled, about who was present and what they had been doing, with the added detail of what they had all eaten for dinner. But she had not been able to describe the attack. Nor could she remember, when awake, what she had said while under hypnosis.

"We're making progress," Chris told her. "Don't worry. It's all in there." When he took his leave, Ginny stayed behind.

"I have a question for you, if you feel up to it."

Patsy smiled. "Of course, dear. What may I do for you?"

"Your uncle had a sailboat."

"Why, yes. Uncle Wade, my father's brother."

Ginny nodded. "Were you ever on that boat?"

Patsy's brow wrinkled. "I must have been, as a child, but I wasn't a good sailor and I never wanted to learn. So I stayed home, or ashore, when the others went out."

"Do you remember who went out on the boat?"

"My cousins, the older ones, Uncle Wade, of course, and

Aunt Margaret. Aunt Letty and Uncle Maury."

"What about your parents, and Tommy?"

"Tommy was too small. My father went. His father was a sailor and he used to say it was in his blood, but not mine."

"And your mother?"

"She stayed with me."

Ginny nodded. "Thank you. That helps a lot. Is there anything I can do for you, today?"

Patsy stood up, walked over to an octagonal glass table, picked up a sheaf of white pages, and flapped it at Ginny. "Can you tell me how to memorize this nonsense when I can't remember why I left one room and went into another?"

Ginny started laughing. "Is that the *Macbeth* script?"

"Yes!" Patsy sat back down and settled the script on her lap. "My cue is 'Why, how now, Hecate! You look angerly.' To which Hecate replies." She closed her eyes and started reciting.

Have I not reason, beldams as you are,
Saucy and overbold? How did you dare
To trade and traffic with Macbeth
In riddles and affairs of death;
And I, the mistress of your charms,
The close contriver of all harms,
Was never call'd to bear my part,
Or show the glory of our art?

"And that's as far as I get. I can't remember the rest of it."

Ginny sat down in one of the easy chairs and smiled. "Sounds pretty good to me."

Patsy nodded. "Well, that's the part that makes sense. She's mad at them because they didn't wait for her. She feels left out."

Ginny nodded. "Is there more?"

"Oh, yes. It goes on forever."

"Well, what's the message in the next section?"

"The message?" Patsy peered at her handout, then read it out loud.

And, which is worse, all you have done
Hath been but for a wayward son,
Spiteful and wrathful, who, as others do,
Loves for his own ends, not for you.

"That means they have wasted their talents on an undeserving man."

Ginny nodded, unable to avoid thinking of a wayward son who was trying to upend their way of life for his own benefit.

Patsy continued to read.

But make amends now: get you gone,
And at the pit of Acheron
Meet me i' the morning: thither he
Will come to know his destiny:
Your vessels and your spells provide,
Your charms and every thing beside.

Patsy looked up and explained to Ginny. "Here she's saying they can redeem themselves if they will do as she tells them. They are to leave now, but meet her tomorrow morning at the—at the—" Patsy peeked at her paper. "Pit of Acheron and bring vessels, spells, and charms, and whatever else they might need. Macbeth has made an appointment to have his fortune read."

"Makes sense." Ginny nodded.

"Yes, it does. Hecate then tells us what she will be doing, but I don't understand this part." Patsy read on.

I am for the air; this night I'll spend
Unto a dismal and a fatal end:

Ginny nodded. "Okay. Somebody is going to die."

Great business must be wrought ere noon:

"And she's on the clock."

Upon the corner of the moon

There hangs a vaporous drop profound;
I'll catch it ere it come to ground:
Patsy's brow wrinkled. "Sounds like she's got a still set up in her backyard."
And that distill'd by magic sleights
"I knew it! She's making usige!"
Patsy's face was alight with excitement and Ginny could not remember ever having had so much fun studying Shakespeare before.
Patsy leaned forward, one hand making stirring motions in the air.
Shall raise such artificial sprites
She turned her hand palm up and lifted it slowly toward the ceiling.
As by the strength of their illusion
Shall draw him on to his confusion:
Her fist closed and smote her breast, then her face cleared. "You can understand why so many people believe in the supernatural. We've all been confused at some point in our lives."
"Yes, we have." Ginny was thinking that the whisky contributed strongly in a lot of the cases.
Patsy's brow descended as she spoke the folly of ambitious men.
He shall spurn fate, scorn death, and bear
He hopes 'bove wisdom, grace and fear:
"Which means he thinks he's unstoppable."
And you all know, security
Is mortals' chiefest enemy.
Patsy slid her bifocals down her nose and looked at Ginny over them. "I know Shakespearean actors don't nudge one another in the ribs, but that couplet seems to be begging for it."

Ginny chuckled. "It does, doesn't it?"

"Then she finishes with a comment that her taxi is waiting."

Hark! I am call'd; my little spirit, see,
Sits in a foggy cloud, and stays for me.

"Then she leaves, but it doesn't say in which direction."

"Alan will tell you, I'm sure."

Ginny rose and came over to sit beside Patsy. "I'm going to suggest you make note cards to help you memorize this speech. Put the translation—what's she's talking about—at the top, then just a few lines underneath, and memorize it in conceptual chunks. And be sure to number them, or you'll get confused about what comes first."

Patsy nodded. "What a good idea." She looked up and caught Ginny's eye. "I don't suppose you have time to come help me study?"

Ginny hesitated. "I'll have to look at my calendar, but, yes, I'm sure I can squeeze you in." She rose to her feet. "And when I'm not here Violet, or that hulking centurion can help."

Patsy laughed. "I'll bet he hasn't read any Shakespeare since high school and maybe not then." She held out her hand. "You would have made a good teacher, my dear."

"I'll tell my mother you said so."

"Take care and come again soon."

Ginny waved goodbye and headed for the car. She was running a little behind schedule, but it had been worth it. Seeing Patsy blossom like that had persuaded Ginny they weren't making a mistake. She'd had concerns about Patsy's involvement in *The Scottish Play*, given her prognosis, but art can heal souls, and Patsy's certainly deserved a helping hand.

* * *

Tuesday noon
Mackenzie residence

Ginny drove up the alley and paused to let a construction vehicle turn in front of her. Jim saw her and came over.

"Sorry about that. We've just started. I hope you don't mind parking on the apron, and giving me a ride to work tonight. That will save having to shuffle the cars to get mine out of the garage."

Ginny nodded, pulled up to the back of the house, locked her car, and let herself in via the kitchen. She took a moment to locate a number, then picked up her phone. The line rang five times before someone answered in what sounded like a child's voice.

"Hello," Ginny said. "I'm trying to reach Wade Bryant. He sold my husband a sailboat. Is he there?"

"Uh huh."

"May I speak to him, please?"

"Great-Grand-Pa!" The child's voice was loud enough in her ear for it to hurt. Ginny held the device away and waited for an adult to take over.

"Hello?"

Ginny repeated her request to the woman on the other end of the line.

"He's not available right now. May I take a message?"

"Yes, please. What I would like to know is whether or not Letitia Patterson was a good enough sailor to take your father's boat out by herself, and if so, did she ever do that, go out on her own? Will you ask him to call me with the answer, please?"

"I'll ask him, but I don't know if he'll remember. I'm afraid he's had a small stroke."

"Oh! I'm so sorry to hear that. Well, it's not urgent. Here's my name and number, if you get a chance and if he remembers. Thank you for your help!"

Ginny hung up the phone thinking about the nice man she'd gone sailing with, and wishing old age didn't have to happen to anyone. Death was all right, but that rotting stage between a healthy, happy life and no life at all she could do without.

She put together sandwiches and took one out to Jim.

"Look, love! They've unearthed red bricks." He accepted the sandwich, but continued to stare at the gash in the green hillside. "I've asked them to collect the bricks and use them as part of the driveway. That will be pretty, and a tribute to the old house, and it's recycling." He smiled at her and Ginny took comfort in the thought of creating something new, even if it was just a garage. Between Shakespeare, Patsy's cancer, and Wade Bryant's stroke, she'd had enough of approaching death for one day.

* * *

Tuesday afternoon
Mackenzie residence

The crash woke her. Ginny sat up, momentarily disoriented, then she was out of bed and running for the back of the house. She'd stretched out to relax for a few minutes after lunch, but she must have been more tired than she'd realized because the sun was now slanting across the hall floor.

She ran to the kitchen window and looked out to find Jim gesticulating in a manner that did not imply patience with the foreman on duty. There was a construction vehicle sitting on top of a section of her backyard fence and two workers pulling on rubber boots and heavy electrical gloves, and motioning to the driver to stay where he was, before killing the connection to the security perimeter. The enormous tires on the backhoe would protect him as long as he avoided closing the electrical circuit.

Ginny couldn't see any blood and Jim was being forced off the grass and onto a rubber mat that had materialized from one of the trucks. They hadn't cut the power to the fence before they started. There hadn't been any need. The construction was slated for the *other* side of the alley, not this one.

Ginny sighed. Someone would have to pay to have this repaired. They had insurance, of course, and she'd be willing to bet the construction company did, too. But they would need pictures. She found her camera, her real camera, not the cellphone version, opened the window, set the camera on the ledge and started snapping. When she'd done as much as she could from the safety of the house, she set it aside, and picked up the phone.

"Angus? We've a wee problem here." She explained what had happened and heard him sigh.

"I'll send Reggie tae ye. He'll know wha' tae do."

He was there before Jim had finished with the construction crew.

"Well! What moron decided it would be a good idea to flatten your fence, I wonder? Did he even consider that he might be driving into a live circuit? That's why we put up the signs, to ward off idiots, but maybe he can't read. It doesn't really matter, you know, about the fence, I mean, since the house is on a different circuit and I have the perimeter fence set up in sections for just this sort of emergency, and in any case it's not an electrified fence, not really. It's all sensors and they have an electrical supply of course, because they have to have power, but the signs are there to keep people from climbing, not running over the fence. We'll take this back section out of the loop and leave the rest in place, then put up temporary fencing and more signs and maybe some motion-controlled lights to scare off the raccoons." He was working as he talked. The main panel was in the pantry and Ginny could hear him as she threw together a meal for the three of them. Reggie declined the food, showed her the extra set of keys he had to the house and grounds, assured her it was safe to leave the repairs to him, then repeated himself to Jim when he came in.

Ginny fed her husband, helped him get cleaned up and dressed for work, and made soothing noises about the fence. On their way out the door, she grabbed her camera so he could look at the images while she drove them to the hospital.

"Well, it's a mess."

"But Reggie will take care of everything."

"Yes, and at least we got the digging done. I'm told they can layout the driveway and pour concrete on Friday." Jim sighed, then smiled at her. "Have I told you yet today that I love you?"

Ginny smiled. "No, and now would be a good time to mention it."

He reached over and captured one of her hands. "I adore you, my level-headed, practical, clever wife."

She laughed. "If you can keep your head when all around you are losing theirs, you just don't understand the situation."

He guffawed, kissed her knuckles and let her have her hand back. Ginny kept the conversation light for the remainder of the commute, sharing Patsy's analysis of Hecate's speech, and avoiding mention of candlesticks, bloody or otherwise. There would be plenty of time later to tell him about Wade Bryant's stroke.

* * *

CHAPTER 25

Wednesday morning
Hillcrest Regional Medical Center

Jim met Ginny as she was getting off the elevator. "Tough night?"

She nodded. "Three admissions to the Neuro ICU, all gunshot wounds to the head. Medically induced comas, vents, and drains. Another four to the Surgical ICU with chest wounds. They're all on bypass of one sort or another, but in better shape than the heads. Then two more in the Medical unit, both with fresh colostomies. The newbies are getting an education tonight!"

Jim nodded. "I took care of the chests, but the head wounds were shunted straight to the OR."

"Where did they come from? It looks like a gang fight!"

"All nine came off the highway."

"Our highway? The one that runs in front of the hospital?"

"That's the one."

"Dr. Mackenzie! Ginny!"

Both of them turned to see a harassed looking ICU Head Nurse hurrying to catch up with them. Margot had been one of the charge nurses in Ginny's ICU as recently as last December, but had been promoted to department head when the position had become available. She had accepted the challenge with her usual cool competence and had the Medical ICU fully staffed and back on its feet in record time.

Ginny noticed she was still wearing the blue scrubs that made her dark skin glow, especially when juxtaposed with the white lab coat. She also noticed a shorter hairdo, one that made Margot look more professional, and framed her face to perfection.

They both waited for her to reach them, then catch her breath.

"I have something you should hear. Well, Mr. Mackenzie should hear, but I don't want to call him at two a.m. if I don't have to."

Jim nodded. "What is it?"

"The first of the two belly wounds is out of anesthesia and he's talking." Margot sucked in a deep breath, her eyebrows rising to her hairline. "He says they were paid."

"Paid for what?" Jim asked.

"A man recruited them, eight total, and gave them gas money and—apparently—drugs so they would enjoy themselves, then sent them to 'Tartan Town to kill Scotties.' He was quite upset when he found out which hospital he'd landed in."

Ginny could feel her throat close, and Jim's voice sounded tight when he spoke.

"I take it he wasn't expecting the Scots to shoot back."

Margot's mouth twisted. "Apparently not. Anyway, I wanted to let someone know we've got an informant."

Jim nodded. "I'll make sure Grandfather is told first thing in the morning. And I'll send the police to talk to your patient tonight. Do you need anything else right now?"

"No, thank you." Margot turned to face Ginny. "If I have to, I'll ask your bride here to report back to her old job, but at the moment, we've got it under control."

Ginny smiled. "I have no doubt of that. I need to eat, but I can drop by afterwards so you can show me exactly how much better you are at being the Head Nurse than I would have been."

Margot's face split into a grin. "Don't give me any ideas. I might walk out and leave you holding the bag. See you later!" She turned and hurried back to the elevators.

Jim and Ginny made their way through the cafeteria lines, then settled down at a table in the corner. Ginny applied herself to her meal, knowing she would have to eat, talk, and get back to duty in half the time those three tasks would take. When she'd taken the edge off her hunger, she picked up her water and forced eight ounces down the hatch. It was far too easy to get dehydrated on a twelve-hour shift. That done, she went back to her meal, picking half-heartedly at the naked lettuce left behind when the vegetables and meats were gone. She frowned, trying to account for this evening's attack. "I don't understand it."

Jim paused, his fork halfway to his mouth. "Don't understand what?"

"All these things that are happening."

"Go on." Jim resumed his meal, but Ginny could see he was listening.

She pushed her plate aside and folded her arms on the table. "Well, the timing for one. We haven't had a lick of trouble in the neighborhood, outside of our own bar room brawls, in half a century. We've been good neighbors and we've gotten good friends back in return."

Jim nodded.

"Suddenly, we have Patsy and her candlestick and missing brother. Then, hot on the heels of that mystery we get Larry Scala. He's easier to explain because he followed Patterson and he admits to his obsession. But why is Patterson here? Why did he decide to give up his cushy job in Illinois to try for a senate seat in Texas? I know he was born here, but he's no spring chicken and he'll start as a Freshman Senator even if he wins. Illinois has been his home for most of his life. His wife's family is in Illinois, and the children are in school there. What possible reason could he have for uprooting everyone and starting over here?"

"He inherited the estate."

"But he doesn't have to live in Texas. He can run the business from anywhere."

"Maybe he's sentimentally attached to Chancie Mor."

Ginny shook her head. "If you want me to believe that, you'll have to explain why he and his three wives have refused every effort made by the Chicago and Springfield Homesteads to include them in the community."

Jim frowned. "My parents did something like that."

"Your parents made sure you grew up Homestead. That's why your grandfather was able to persuade the council to take you on. Maury Patterson did the opposite. He rejected everything we stand for. He hasn't come out and said so in his campaign speeches, but he's offering to oust the current administration and put in one that cares about the populace, the implication being that Ian Hunter is the problem, and we both know that's not the case."

Jim nodded. "According to Scala, Patterson is supposed to have used his vast wealth to turn the Illinois popular vote in his favor."

"Which is legal if you don't use coercion."

"Maybe he's been doing more than buying them chicken dinners."

Ginny was silent for a moment. Would someone born in Loch Lonach, whose mother's family had been here since the original settlement, be capable of such animosity against the clan?

"You're suggesting that Maury Patterson hired the people who vandalized our house."

He nodded. "And took potshots at people on the highway, under the mistaken assumption that they were all clansmen. There's something else. Remember that refinery fire? The company belongs to the clan. Ian is majority stockholder."

"So these are not accidents. We're being targeted."

Jim nodded. "Looks like it."

"And you think Maury Patterson is paying for it."

"He's rich enough."

Ginny frowned. "I suppose it's possible. Scala has accused Patterson of election tampering which I am willing to believe. But I'm less willing to believe he eliminated the witnesses."

"Why is that?"

It was a good question. Ginny fired up her little gray cells and tried to find an answer. "According to Scala's notes, the police exonerated Maury on each occasion. I do *not* believe every police officer between here and the Canadian border is corrupt. If they found no evidence of Maury's guilt, there must have been nothing to find."

"That doesn't mean he wasn't behind it." Jim's brow furrowed. "The shooting tonight took place just outside our jurisdiction, on a public highway. We can't argue that the Homestead was the target, not on those grounds. But we're a big part of District 17A and I'm really unhappy at the thought that someone hired those shooters and pointed them in our direction. I'm hoping Grandfather can call in some favors and find out what money changed hands."

"If Patterson plays dirty, there should be some evidence of it. What did Scala find?"

Jim shook his head. "Stonewalls. No access. No informers. No one willing to talk to him."

Ginny sat back in her chair. "How scared do you have to be to back out of a political race and refuse to give a reason?"

"Oh, they all had reasons, but none of them were sufficient to explain the actions." Jim's brow rose. "We have to remind ourselves that all our information is coming from Scala. It would be useful to corroborate it."

"Would Detective Tran be able to do that?"

Jim shook his head. "Not unless she sees a pretty strong case for prosecution."

"She's still got his manuscript, hasn't she?"

"Yes."

"I think I'll give her a call tomorrow and ask for her opinion."

Jim nodded. "Okay, and I can ask Grandfather to touch base with the Illinois Homesteads to see if they know anything."

"Good idea."

He rose, collected the trays, shepherded her to the hall and turned her in the direction of the main elevator banks. "And now, wee wifie, how about a moonlit stroll on the parking garage roof?"

Ginny shook her head. "I have to get back to work." She kissed her husband just as the elevator car arrived. "But I will see you later."

"I'll come get you."

"I'll be waiting!"

* * *

Wednesday morning
Mackenzie residence

Ginny pulled into the garage and lowered the door, pausing only a moment to glance at the construction nets blocking access to the side of the house where the security fence normally stood. She got out, opened the house door with her key and turned to cancel the alarm system. The little light was glowing green.

"That's odd. Jim come look at this." She pointed. "Did we forget to set the alarm when we left yesterday?"

"Wasn't Reggie still here when we left?"

"Yes. Would he forget to set the alarm?"

"I wouldn't think so. Does he know our code?"

Ginny snorted. "He knows everything there is to know about this system. Angus, too."

"So why is it off?"

"I guess we'd better call and ask." She headed for the phone, while Jim headed for the coffee pot. "Reggie, it's Ginny. Was the alarm set when you left last night?"

"Of course, no sense having an alarm system if you're not going to use it. I put everything back the way it should be except for the missing section of the fence and gate across the back but added motion detectors and remote sensors to cover that part of the yard for the interim."

"Was there an alarm last night?"

"None that I'm aware of. You're sure the system is off?"

"The little green light is glowing on the keypad. What about Angus? Was he over here? Or someone else who knows the code?"

"We spoke on the phone but he didn't come over and there was no one but me working on the repairs and no one else has the code unless your mother does which would make sense of course. I think I'd better come over and look around and you should too but if you see any reason to think someone's been inside the house get out and call the police. No sense confronting a burglar by yourself. I'll be there in twenty minutes."

Ginny hung up the phone feeling that she had underestimated the inconvenience of having the fence knocked down. Burglars! She found Jim making coffee and told him what Reggie had said.

"Well, we can't go to bed yet. Would you like something to eat?"

Ginny nodded, sat down at the table, fidgeted, got back up again, helped Jim find the makings for waffles, sat back down again, sipped her coffee, then got back up. "I'm going to go look around." Jim moved to stop her.

"I think we should wait until reinforcements arrive."

"You and I are the only ones who can spot if something is missing."

"All the more reason to have something to eat. Your brain will work better on a full stomach."

"It's just going to make me sleepier."

"Just a couple of bites, and some coffee."

"Jim!"

"It's decaf. It won't keep you up."

"Oh, all right." Ginny sat back down and addressed the waffles, which were delicious. By the time she'd finished, Angus had arrived, pulling up to the front of the house and bringing a pair of security guards with him. Ginny blinked when she saw them.

"Is that necessary? No offense, guys."

"None taken, ma'am, and we hope not."

She nodded, fed everyone coffee, and let Reggie in when he arrived. He went straight to the electrical panel. Ten minutes of testing later he turned to the group assembled in the kitchen, frowning heavily. "It's been bypassed. Nice job, too."

Ginny was standing beside Jim and heard him swear under his breath. "So what do we do?" he asked.

"Sweep for hazards first." Reggie nodded to the two security guards who pulled wands and digital interfaces off their belts and got to work. Ginny found out later that the sniffers could find explosive residue, the heat sensors could pinpoint hot electrical circuits (or a man hiding in a closet), and the laser could reveal hidden DNA or trace evidence invisible to the naked eye, without the need for powders or sprays.

Jim, Ginny, and Angus had all been shooed into the backyard during the sweep. Jim had ushered the other two across the alley and was showing them where the garage would be, and the red bricks that had paved the approach to the original house. Ginny held his hand and tried to assuage the guilt she saw in his eyes. She put an arm around him and whispered to him.

"This is not your fault, Jim. Someone else is behind this."

He nodded, then looked down into her face and smiled. "Whoever it is owes me a good night's sleep!"

Ginny was thinking the same thing. The security officers were done in fifteen minutes. One of them came out to report to them.

"No traces of anything that looks like a trap. There are some cabinets ajar. You'll need to check to see if anything's been taken."

They all three nodded and went back into the house.

"I'll take the upstairs," Ginny said.

Jim nodded. "And I'll start down here."

It took them an hour to finish the second sweep of the house. Again, they assembled in the kitchen.

"Nothing's been taken. No jewelry, no electronics, and most

suspicious of all, none of the silver wedding presents." Jim frowned heavily. "Who would break in and leave all the portable goodies behind?"

"Someone lookin' fer something specific, and wi' orders tae leave th' rest alone." Angus' brow furrowed heavily. "Pack yer toothbrushes. Ye'll stay wi' me fer th' present."

Ginny hurried to obey. She and Jim each took their own cars and followed Angus to Brochaber. They were both stumbling by the time they made it to Angus' guest bedroom.

Reggie had called in a crew to repair the security damage today, rather than tomorrow, and Angus had officers scouring the house and grounds for evidence. If they found anything, they would call in the police.

There would be no sleeping in their own bed until this crisis was resolved, but there was something infinitely comforting about being part of a system, a community, that took care of its people. Ginny didn't have to worry about what was happening at home right now. She collapsed onto the borrowed bed, curled up in her husband's arms, and was instantly asleep.

* * *

CHAPTER 26

Wednesday afternoon
Brochaber

It had been hard to drag herself out of bed and get dressed for work, but Ginny had managed. To her delight, Angus had provided the farmer's breakfast that would hold her and Jim until their two a.m. lunch in the hospital cafeteria.

Jim must have risen before her. He had finished his steak and was piling bacon and scrambled eggs on his plate. He smiled at her, but careful inspection showed he had dark circles under his eyes and a tightness at the edges of his mouth. Ginny grieved, wishing there was some way she could take his place at work, so he could go back to bed. She settled down with a smaller portion of the feast and a steaming cup of coffee. The minute the liquid hit her taste buds, she remembered. She almost choked.

"The shooting! Jim did you tell him about the shooting?"

"Yes, but it wasn't necessary."

Angus nodded. "Th' hospital called just afore you did this mornin'. I went o'er tae see aboot th' situation while ye slept."

"What about Detective Tran? Has anyone told her?"

Angus' brow furrowed. "'Twas Dallas police tha' responded."

"I mean, has anyone told her we think Patterson is behind

the attack? I want to talk to her. I'll be in the other room."

Jim reached over and caught her arm, preventing her from leaving the table. "Eat first."

Ginny sank back into her chair. As the adrenaline subsided, she recognized the purely physical need for fuel in the system. He was right, of course. She picked up her fork and ate. They were in his car and on the way to the hospital when she finally got through to Detective Tran.

"Mrs. Mackenzie! I thought I might hear from you today."

"I hope I'm not disturbing you, but I was wondering if you'd heard about the drive-by shooting."

"Yes. We have a gang violence unit assigned to the incident, and have already made arrests."

"That was quick! Do you know who was behind it?"

"Not yet, but we are working on a lead from one of the victims."

"Which one?"

"I am not at liberty to say more at this time."

Ginny nodded into the phone. "Of course not. It's just that Larry Scala has accused Maury Patterson of trying to manipulate elections in Illinois and I'm wondering if he's trying to do the same thing here."

"We are considering that possibility."

"I know you don't need my help, but please let me know if there's anything I can do for you on this end."

"I will. Was there anything else?"

"Yes. Have you had a chance to dust that second candlestick for prints? I ask only because I'm determined to be as much of a nuisance as I can possibly manage."

There was a laugh on the other end of the line. "The police are always grateful for any help they can get."

"Anytime. The prints?"

"None on the candlestick. It was wiped clean."

Ginny had expected this, but it was still a blow.

"However."

Ginny's ear pricked up again. "Yes?"

"There were prints found on the plastic bag in which the candlestick was stored. They belonged to Letitia Patterson."

Ginny caught her breath. "You had exemplars for her?"

"From the original police report about the theft. Everyone in the house had to be fingerprinted."

Of course. "Thank you! I also wanted to ask if you'd had a chance to evaluate Larry Scala's materials."

"I have. I have also had an opportunity to confer with the District Attorney's office. The alleged incidents were investigated by local authorities, with the cooperation of the family, and no evidence of violence was ever discovered. It is extremely difficult to prosecute a suspect when there is no evidence of a crime. As a result, the DA has declined to file charges on the missing women."

"I'm not surprised."

"Would you like for me to notify Mr. Scala of the decision?"

"No. I'll do it, but thank you for the offer." Ginny was still thinking about how uncomfortable that conversation was going to be when she realized Tran had changed the subject.

"I understand there was a break-in at your house last night."

"Yes."

"Shall I tell you what the forensics team found?"

"Yes, please, if you are allowed."

"I must in any case. We will need your cooperation to exclude you from the list of suspects."

"Suspects?" Ginny looked over at Jim. She had, as a matter of course and with the detective's permission, put the call on speaker so he could hear both sides of the conversation. She saw the corner of his mouth twitch. "Why would I break into my own home?"

"It seems unlikely."

"What did the team find that requires my cooperation to identify?"

"A woman's shoe print on the kitchen floor and again in various places where there is wood or tile rather than carpet. They begin at the kitchen door, the one that communicates with the backyard, not the one that opens into the garage." The prior owners had used a carport and concrete drive as the rear entrance to the house. The garage had been added later.

Ginny nodded. According to Reggie, that was the door that had been bypassed, along with the motion detectors and interior cameras.

"And you want to look at my shoes."

"Yes, please."

"Well it will have to wait until tomorrow. We've got shifts to work and sleep to catch up on."

"I understand. Please let me know when it will be convenient to continue this investigation."

"Are you heading it?"

"No. I am cooperating with the assigned detective, since I am the liaison to the clan."

"I'll call you tomorrow to set up a time. Thank you."

"Good day."

Ginny ended the call and slid the phone back into her pocket. A woman's shoe print. Well, there was no time to think about it now. Jim had pulled into the parking garage at the hospital and was holding her door open for her. Time to go to work.

* * *

Wednesday evening
Scala's motel room

Larry Scala hung up the phone, then stretched out on the bed, his hands clasped behind his head. He stared at the mirror on the opposite wall. Such a bad place for a mirror and all too common in the sort of rooms he spent far too much time in. It was hung over the dresser, to facilitate getting dressed, one supposed. But nine times out of ten both the lighting and the floor space were inadequate for the task and guests were forced to dress in the bathroom. Which left you lying on the bed staring at yourself. It was not a flattering angle.

With the reading lamp on, every wrinkle threw shadows across his face. Sagging jowls, bags under his eyes, even his hair drooping. He wondered briefly if anyone had ever been driven to suicide by the reflection they'd seen in that mirror.

He wasn't surprised. He'd expected Ginny's tame detective to fail, the same way all the others had. He wasn't even disappointed. The odds had been against him and he'd known it. It was more a feeling of coming to the end of the line and not knowing what to do next. Like walking all the way into a tunnel, following the twists and turns, hoping for light, and finding a solid, black wall instead.

But a tunnel was just a hole in the ground, and a man-made one at that. All he really needed was a shovel.

On Sunday, after he'd performed at the Parish Hall (and he'd had to admit that had been fun), a young man had come over and introduced himself. His name was Tor McLeish. He was seventeen, in the local high school, and interested in becoming an investigative reporter. He'd been told Mr. Scala might be willing to let him tag along to see how it worked. The boy had been exceedingly polite, but there had been lust in his eye. Larry had taken to him immediately. He recognized that look. The boy would make a reporter, if his luck held.

He had let the boy follow him around for a couple of days, starting with the senior citizen center in the Cooperative Hall. The time spent there was just note taking, and listening, trying to gain their trust. They'd been happy to help the boy write up the history of the Homestead. They'd drowned him in help, and Larry'd had to pull him out and give him some tips on what to keep and what to toss.

He had explained to the boy how to make a plan, do research, and in general gather the background needed to get to know a subject, and had selected the incumbent senator, Ian Hunter, as the target, figuring he was probably safe for an impressionable young man to teethe on. Tomorrow they would meet at the library to do some digging in the newspaper morgue and he would explain how to spot a lead.

All of this had been nothing more than marking time, waiting for what the detective would say. It had been fun showing a newbie the ropes, sharing his expertise. If he'd had a son, he might have been able to interest the boy in his work. Maybe not, though. He hadn't found any woman who understood his passion for investigating.

Scala's eyes narrowed. If Tor had caught the investigation bug, he might be able to use him. After all, the boy was a local. There was no telling how much dirt he could dig up, without even realizing it. People never noticed the things they grew up with.

Scala pulled out a pad and pen and began to make a list. It was well after midnight when he finally turned out the light.

* * *

Wednesday evening
Elysium Hotel Bar

Maury Patterson took the drinks from the server and handed his wife her selection. She looked especially lovely tonight, and pleased with herself. He smiled, lifted his glass in a small toast and took a sip.

"What did you do to amuse yourself today, my dear?" he asked.

"I went shopping, then did a bit of sightseeing. There's actually quite a lot going on in Dallas. I had no idea."

Maury nodded. The delights of his childhood would hold no interest for her, but there were a few things he might be able to offer her. "If you like, we can have the driver take us around to look at the nicer parts of town. You might want to see how the upper crust manage to survive here." He was teasing, but Rita's left eyebrow rose.

"Yes, I think I'd like that. We could use better neighbors than I've seen at the Scottish events."

Maury took a pull on his drink. "You realize," he said, "that I will need their support to be elected."

Rita brushed the comment off with a wave of her hand. "You won't have any trouble with them. You have roots and standing and a dead mother buried in the churchyard."

He nodded. "I also have a part in the local theatricals."

Rita almost choked on her drink. "You what?"

"I offered my services as one of the actors in the summer stock they are putting on."

"What on earth possessed you to do such a thing?"

"Politics, my dear. They are performing *Macbeth* and they needed an elder statesman. I am perfect for the role."

Her eyes narrowed. "Which role?"

"Banquo."

"The corpse?" She started to laugh.

"The ghost. The one whose progeny will sweep all of Macbeth's ambitions into the dustbin." Maury sniffed. "I have performed Shakespeare before. I know my way around the theater."

Rita had recovered her reserve and was now eyeing him with a calculating expression. "It would be a good publicity stunt. Lots of airtime and the implication that you are not afraid of the spotlight." She nodded to herself. "And the ghost who wins in spite of the odds is a good image for the have-nots you've been cultivating in the poorer sections of the District. I like it."

"I'm so happy you approve, my dear." Maury raised his glass in further salute. Rita downed hers and ordered another.

"I think I'll pass on the home tour. I need to talk to your publicity manager. You'll arrange that for tomorrow. Around noon. We can lunch together."

"Yes dear."

"And as for tonight, I think I'd better reread the play. There may be other angles we can exploit."

"Yes, dear." Maury ordered another drink, then addressed the menu. He could safely turn the strategizing over to Rita. As long as he did what she suggested, he was assured of another win. A useful wife for a politician to have. He smiled at her. "Would you prefer steak or lobster?"

* * *

CHAPTER 27

Thursday afternoon
Mackenzie residence

Ginny rose from sleep in the Laird's guestroom, ready to go home. She dressed, packed, and presented herself downstairs. Angus confirmed the "New Hoose" was free of wandering policemen and had been stripped of crime scene tape before they departed.

Again, Jim had risen before her, leaving her to sleep as long as she wished. Ginny kissed the Laird, thanking him for his hospitality, and took her leave. Fifteen minutes later, she was parked in her own garage.

She let herself in and went in search of Jim, finding him in the kitchen with Reggie. The tech wizard did not look happy. Jim whispered in Ginny's ear before she could say anything.

"He's trying to make sure it doesn't happen again and I gather this is not as easy as it sounds."

Ginny nodded, gave her husband a swift hug, then approached Reggie. "May I offer you something to drink? Or eat?"

He scowled up at her from his seat on the floor, then his face softened. "Aye, if Jim's willing, I'd be most grateful for a wee dram. I think my brain's stuck."

Jim hurried to oblige. Neither of them had ever heard

Reggie utter so few words at a time, or with such an air of frustration. He was universally cheerful, optimistic, and gregarious. By the time her husband returned, Ginny had Reggie seated at the kitchen table. She settled into a chair and waited for him to take a sip, then caught his eye. "What can you tell us, Reggie?"

He sighed, then shrugged, then took another pull on his drink. Jim had brought the bottle and made sure it was within reach. "First off, I need to admit that I'm not as smart as I thought I was what with all the thought we put into this system in the first place and it shouldn't have been possible for anyone to slip in as easily as that and I'm sorry and ashamed and I hope you'll forgive me."

Both Jim and Ginny hurried to assure him that neither blamed him.

He nodded, finished his drink and poured himself another. "I shouldn't have tied the house into the perimeter circuit, which seemed like a good idea at the time, but all it did was cut some of the backups out of the system when the fence came down and I won't make that mistake again. The second problem was putting the wiring on an exterior wall which meant it could be accessed from the outside of the house and just because it's never been done before is no excuse since I should have seen it was a possibility, even if I had no reason to think the two of you would be a target because, after all, Jim's the heir and I suspect you've got a few people looking at you sideways Miss Ginny, after that business in Louisiana."

Ginny lifted an eyebrow. "Looking is one thing. Breaking into our house is another."

Reggie nodded. "It was meant to be a secret – slip in, slip out, and no one the wiser, but something must have gone wrong because the panel was rigged to respond to a remote signal and the relay should have closed, which would have reset the system to the default, which in your case is armed, and if that had happened then you would never have noticed the alarm being off because of course it wouldn't have been, it would have been on and you would have come in and put your security code in and canceled the system as usual and the only way I would have known was if I'd done some fairly intense maintenance because the tampering was first rate and was done by a real professional."

"Wait a minute," Jim said. "Did you say someone has a remote that controls our security system?"

"Not anymore they don't because I've removed it, but that's what was inserted into the circuit and it's pretty simple in this case 'cause it was a power on/off set up. The elegant part was bypassing the alarms that are supposed to go off when that happens. Whoever it was understood how we handle power outages and the fact that the owner of the house might return unexpectedly and the system shouldn't blow a gasket if you or Ginny came home early from work."

"So you've taken the alien device out of the system."

Reggie nodded at Jim, and took another pull on his drink.

"What else do we need to do?" Jim asked.

"Well, what I'm going to advise is you let me rewire the whole system and put the controls in the interior of the house behind a shield that will stop remote signals like this one. It will take some time and while I'm working on getting it done we'll need to make other arrangements, unless you can find out who the intruder was and what he wanted so we can be sure he won't try again."

"She," Ginny inserted.

The two men looked at her. Ginny shrugged. "The one bit of evidence the intruder left behind, unless Reggie can give us something else to go on, is the female-sized footprint, which could, of course, be a teenager or a small male who likes women's footwear. I may find out more when Tran inspects my closet."

Jim nodded. "Okay. Reggie, do whatever you need to do. We'll cooperate and thank you for it."

Reggie nodded. "In that case, I need to go round up a crew and supplies because I'd like to start this afternoon, so that we can put up a temporary before you two go to bed tonight, unless you're still at Brochaber, which might be a good idea if you can stand it, but it will take more than a week to make the changes I have in mind so you may not want to be away from home that long which I can understand because I certainly wouldn't." He handed the bottle back to Jim. "You'd better lock the liquor cabinet. I can't swear we won't be wanting more before we finish here today."

Jim handed it back. "Take it home with you. You can have a nightcap."

Reggie nodded and rose from his chair tucking the bottle into the crook of his arm. "Just leave everything where it is. I'll be back as quick as I can." He nodded to the two of them, let himself out and was gone.

* * *

Thursday afternoon
Mackenzie residence

Ginny looked across the table at Jim. "All I wanted was a nice, quiet honeymoon."

Jim smiled at her. "Quiet lives are boring."

"Yes, but at least I wouldn't have to flee to my in-laws for a safe place to sleep."

Jim rose, came over to her side of the table, drew up a chair, and sat down, facing her. "Talk to me."

"Are you being therapeutic?"

"Maybe." Ginny saw his dimple flash.

"You know I'm not allowed to show weakness."

"Except to me." He held out his hand, palm up and she laid hers in it. "Talk to me."

Ginny looked up and found his eyes focused on hers, smiling into hers, radiating warmth. Her lips smiled, but her brow furrowed. "I'm willing to give up poking my nose into things that don't concern me, or even if they do, if that's what it takes to keep you safe."

"Me?"

She nodded. "Laugh at me if you dare. My father died young."

His smile faded. "I know, love."

"And you and I both know, because of our chosen professions, that every man and woman will die, some sooner, some later."

He nodded.

"Well, I want your death to be later."

His mouth twitched. "I think we can agree on that."

Ginny caught her breath. "I'm being irrational. I know I am, but I can't help feeling this is my fault somehow. That all of this is happening because of me."

"How do you figure that?"

"First it was Tommy, because I volunteered to help Patsy with her genealogy. Then that stupid candlestick shows up, and it turns out Patsy sent it to me. Then Larry appears on our doorstep. Then paint appears on our lawn, and now someone breaks into our house."

Jim rose and drew her to her feet, settling her against his chest, and wrapping his arms around her. Ginny buried her face in his shoulder.

"This is not what I want. I don't want excitement, not this

kind. I want peace and quiet and not to have to run from shadows in the hall." In spite of her best efforts, Ginny could feel tears leaking out from under her eyelids.

Jim held her close, hugging her. "This is temporary, my darling. There's something specific going on, and we're going to get to the bottom of it. After which, you and I can be as boring as we like."

She laughed. She couldn't help it. She looked up into his smile and suddenly felt safe. It was an illusion, she knew, but she'd take it and be glad of it. She twined her arms around his neck and drew him down to her, to kiss him properly.

"Have I told you yet today, husband, how much I love you?"

"You mumbled it in your sleep when I left this morning, but you can tell me again."

"I adore you, and I'm so grateful to you for loving me. You do love me, right?"

"More than life itself!"

"Oh, don't say that! I don't want to think about death." She kissed him again, then wiped the tears from her face. "I must be more tired than I realized." She slipped out of his arms and went over to the sink to splash some water on her face. He followed her over, handing her a towel. "Would this be a good time to have Tran come over and look at my shoes?"

He nodded. "Let's get that done, then I'm going to take you out to dinner."

Ginny smiled. "That sounds lovely." She called the police station and affirmed they would wait for the detective. "Fifteen minutes."

An hour later Detective Tran was replacing the last pair of Ginny's shoes, having inverted each in turn, compared it to the image collected by the crime scene investigators, and eliminated it as a potential source of the shoeprint in question.

"These are all of your shoes?"

"Yes." Ginny had even removed the pair she was wearing and handed them over for inspection.

The detective nodded, made a note in her little book, and turned to Ginny. "I will file my report and you will be asked to endorse it, signifying thereby that you have withheld no evidence from me or the other investigators. It will have the force of a sworn statement."

"I understand." Ginny knew the penalty for lying to an officer of the court.

"Thank you for your cooperation." Detective Tran slid her notebook into her pocket and gave Ginny a smile. "We will now look further. Good day."

Ginny blinked. Look further. When the detective had gone, Ginny made a beeline for her office, Jim following. He watched as she pulled up the investigation files on her computer and added the break in and shoe print to the evidence list.

"What are you thinking?" he asked.

"It suddenly occurred to me that the fence may not have been an accident."

"You think it was planned, to make it easier to enter the house?"

"I do. Hang on a minute." Ginny flew down the stairs and into the bedroom, grabbed her camera and headed back to her office. She found Jim reading the file.

"Have I overlooked anything?"

"I don't think so. What have you got there?"

"The insurance photographs." Ginny uploaded the images she'd taken of the damaged fence and looked at them one by one. "Here." She pointed to a man sitting at the controls of the excavator. "I assume you hired a reputable contractor and that any worker he hired came with references."

Jim nodded. "I'll see what I can find out about that man."

Ginny enlarged the image of the driver's face, then printed

out two copies, handing one to Jim and setting the other aside for her own use. She swiveled around to face him. "Is your offer to buy me dinner still on?"

"It is."

"Dress code?"

"Come as you are."

She nodded, then pulled out her phone. "I'll meet you in the garage. I just want to tell Reggie we'll be out of the house and ask him what he wants us to do about the alarm system."

Jim nodded. "And I think I'll check in with Grandfather, just in case."

"In case of what?"

Jim lifted an eyebrow. "With him, you never know. See you downstairs."

* * *

CHAPTER 28

Thursday evening
The Canny Coo Pub

Ginny was seated in one of the leather-bound chairs at The Canny Coo Pub, nursing a root beer, her mind wandering. They were there because Friday night was devoted to the ceilidhs, but a man might develop a thirst on any of the other six nights of the week and it would be useful to ken where tae find a drink. Also, because this was the oldest watering hole in the area and therefore a fixture in the minds of the locals, and Jim wanted to learn how to play darts and this was the place to do it.

Other than an occasional smile from Jim which Ginny dutifully returned, she felt free to spend the time as she wished.

The pub was an ancient establishment by Texas standards, on its fifth iteration, having been founded by the first wave of Scottish settlers. Situated at the corner of Thistle Lane and The Highgate, it was the place where everyone ended up, sooner or later. It had gotten its name from the shaggy, red-headed Highland cattle that had nosed out the fresh water needed to support the settlement. This clear and most welcome stream had proved to widen as it moved east. The early homesteaders had taken advantage of its gentle fall toward the Gulf of Mexico, built a dam, and created Loch Lonach.

The Coo was located on the eastern side of the loch. It was the second permanent structure built (the first being the Kirk on the Hill), was situated along the original Indian trail where it bridged the East Fork of the Trinity River, was surrounded by cottonwood trees, and looked exactly as it had a hundred years earlier, except for the addition of indoor plumbing and air conditioning.

The public highway, when it arrived, had been laid in an arrow-straight path from Terrell to Dallas and there was no exit for the pub. As a result, only the locals knew how to find it, which was just as well since it clearly did not belong on any Texas Highway Tourist brochure.

On arrival, Ginny had taken a moment to look around, half expecting to find Larry Scala, or the Pattersons, but they either didn't know about the Coo or preferred to drink elsewhere.

Ginny was known, of course, and greeted by all but a few of the evening's patrons. As a child, she had been sent into the pub to fetch individuals and carry messages.

Jim, too, was greeted and engaged in brief exchanges on the weather, the quality of the darts competition he was watching, and wishes for his health and happiness. The community was growing used to him. Ginny found a number of the customers eyeing him surreptitiously, their faces registering curiosity, but no malice.

At the edge of this comfortable throng sat a very old man weeping—literally—into his beer. He was being quiet about it, his grief personal and private. Ginny averted her eyes and considered whether or not she had a duty to check on him. It was the two-pronged responsibility of her profession and her position in the clan that goaded her.

Nurses helped people in pain. That was what they did. And she had married Jim and would be Matron when he became Laird. She decided to ask the bartender if he knew what was going on. She rose, using her almost empty glass as an excuse, and made her way to the bar.

"Miss Ginny." The bartender was almost as old as the weeping man and had known Ginny since her birth. To him, she would always be "Miss Ginny."

"Jed." She smiled at him, and accepted a fresh root beer and his hope that she was doing well this evening.

"Very well, thank you." The courtesies concluded, Ginny was able to introduce her question. She was known for being nosey. Jed would find nothing surprising in that.

"His name's Jock Brodie. He's one of the Big House staff. Retired now, but he started as chauffeur for the elder Mrs. Patterson, then did the same for the Senator until the job got to be too much for him."

Ginny nodded. "Did he attend Mrs. Patterson's funeral?"

"Aye. All the auld folk did, the ones that are still alive and able to get about." Jed looked over at the ancient retainer, his brows drawing together. "He has no family o' his own. He's got a cottage on the Patterson place, but there's no knowing wha' the Senator will do with him now he's back."

Ginny turned to look at the old man. "He seems very upset."

Jed nodded. "They do say as he was sweet on the old girl. Would do anything for her. And the housemaids used tae gossip, saying she'd have him in fer tea and scones. It could be true. In any case, I never heard of her taking up with another man after her husband died."

Ginny considered this. Devotion could be mistaken for love, could be a form of love, she supposed. She looked back at Jed. "Can he handle another round, or has he had enough?"

The barkeep hesitated, then poured another home-brewed Scottish ale, and handed it to Ginny. "One more, I think. After which, I'll have to cut him off."

"Thanks!" Ginny carried her root beer and the 'wee heavy' over to the table and addressed the old man.

"May I join you?"

He peered up at her, then at the glass in her hand, then nodded. Ginny set the ale down and settled into the other chair.

"I'm Ginny Mackenzie."

He nodded, then lifted the glass and took a swallow.

Ginny studied him, not without sympathy. He was unshaven, red-eyed, and his clothes needed cleaning, but he didn't smell and he seemed to be eating regularly.

"I understand you worked for the late Mrs. Patterson." She had his attention now.

"Aye. What's it tae you?"

"I was hoping you could tell me about her. Was she a good employer?"

The old man teared up. "Aye, tae me she were."

"You miss her."

He blinked hard, then set his drink down, fished a handkerchief out of his pocket, and blew his nose. "Aye. We were two o' a kind, her and me."

This seemed quite a claim from a ghillie of Chancie Mor, but Ginny seized the opening. "I expect she talked to you, while you drove her around."

He nodded. "Been driving her for close on sixty years. All the early years, then again when the Senator decided to retire me."

He frowned at his drink, then lifted his eyes and studied

her. "Yer th' young laird's wife."

"I'm Jim's wife, if that's what you mean."

He turned and looked at the darts players. "I heard his father was deid."

Ginny nodded.

The old man watched the darts players for a moment, then turned back to Ginny. "We used tae talk about family, Mrs. P. and me, about how ye had tae do yer best by them, no matter what. Even that no good son o' hers. Bad seed, if ye ask me. She deserved better."

Ginny longed to ask for details. She was racking her brain for the exact right phrase when he spoke again.

"After the Master passed on she had no one." He pulled in a breath. "We were kids together, Letty Killough and me. Friends. Then she had to go and marry Patterson. But she never forgot. When he died, she remembered how we used tae be." He lifted his glass to his lips, and his hand trembled. He set the glass down and pulled out the handkerchief again. When he'd blotted his eyes, he looked at Ginny, his expression urgent and sad and pleading.

"Dinna mistak' me. 'Twas proper feeling on her part, her only son, but I ne'er liked the boy. Too arrogant by half. Spoilt he was. He thought 'twas his own doing, his success, but it weren't. It were his mither, all o' it."

"She looked out for him?"

"Aye. Smoothed th' road fer him."

Ginny probed carefully. "In what way?"

The old man looked at her and shook his head. "Won't do ye no good tae ask. I'll no tell ye. She wouldnae like it. She buried her troubles at Chancie Mor, sae she could turn a braw face tae th' world. And noo she's buried hersel' and th' world doesnae care."

The old man dissolved into a Gaelic lament, his voice

cracking and the tears running unchecked down his face. It wasn't very loud, but it tore at the heartstrings and Ginny found herself grieving for a woman she'd never known.

Others in the pub heard the singing, Jim among them. He came over and put his arms around Ginny and gave her a kiss, whispering in her ear. "Let's take him home." She nodded and rose, then followed as Jim and another darts player hoisted the old man to his feet, settled his tab, and steered him out the door. Ginny smiled at a pair of men who had risen to help, holding the door open for them, then slipping away into the night.

They took him to Chancie Mor and handed him over to the housekeeper, making sure he got safely to his cottage.

"I'll take him from here," she said.

Ginny thanked the woman, handed over the keys to the old man's car, and let Jim take her home. He pulled into their garage and escorted her inside, then wrapped her in a hug.

"Who was that lachrymose old man you were drinking with?"

"Mrs. Patterson's driver." Ginny took Jim's hand and headed for the bedroom.

"She seems to have had devoted servants," Jim said.

Ginny kicked off her shoes. "Loyal, anyway. He told me he wasn't about to give away her secrets."

"What kind of secrets?"

"How her son was so successful in politics, maybe. He told me it would do me no good to ask, because he wasn't telling, and, anyway, she was dead and buried so that was an end of it. I paraphrase."

Jim dropped into the big chair in the corner of the room and sighed. "I have no doubt she pulled strings behind her son's back. That's the way the game is played."

Ginny nodded. "What he said was that she buried her troubles at Chancie Mor. It might be useful to look through her papers." Ginny pulled the clips out of her hair, letting the braid fall down her back.

"They belong to Senator Patterson now," Jim said.

"Would he allow that?"

"Probably not." Ginny sighed. "It wouldn't do me any good anyway. I know nothing about politics. I could be looking right at a smoking gun and I wouldn't recognize it."

She dropped her earrings in the brass tray on her dresser and turned to look at her husband.

By definition, the job of an emergency room physician was to figure out what was wrong with a patient, usually with incomplete information to go on. There was a chance he was just curious, but she was beginning to suspect he liked playing detective as much as she did.

"How about you? Would you be able to tell if there was evidence of malfeasance buried in her files?"

"Maybe. Chart review is one of my specialties. But it would take full access and a great deal of time."

Ginny sighed and turned back to her dressing table mirror. She wrinkled her nose at her reflection. "Oh, well. It was a good idea while it lasted."

He smiled, then rose and came over, lifting her braid aside and bending down to brush the nape of her neck with his lips. "I have a better one," he breathed. "Let's put the question away for the night."

Ginny smiled. "So my subconscious can chew on it while I sleep?"

"Something like that."

* * *

Thursday night
The banks of Loch Lonach

Just before midnight of the same night on which Ginny had taken pity on an old man, two fishermen pulled his body out of the waters of Loch Lonach. In accordance with clan custom, they called the Laird first.

"Where'd ye find him?"

"Floatin' just there." The man pointed toward a swirl of water on the surface of the lake. "Snagged on th' submerged tree, I think."

"Have ye any idea where he went in?"

The two fishers of men shook their heads.

Angus thanked them, then pulled out his phone and placed a call to the Loch Lonach police. When they arrived, he turned the scene over to them and went home.

Twelve hours later he received a copy of the preliminary autopsy explaining that the old man was drunk, well over the legal limit, and had drowned. There were bruises on his back and arms which might have been from hitting something along the edge of the water, or something submerged in the loch. He was ancient and his skin fragile so it might mean nothing. The full autopsy would follow when complete.

The Laird of Loch Lonach put the report away and headed for Chancie Mor. The funeral would be held on Sunday, but he would be expected to say a few words about their loss tonight at the ceilidh. He needed to talk to someone who knew the man.

* * *

CꞪAPCER 29

Friday morning
The Cooperative Hall

Larry Scala sat on the bench outside the Cooperative Hall sipping coffee and waiting for Tor. He had something special planned for today. Something fun. His eyes drifted over the blues and whites and greens of the lake and surrounding park. It was a very pretty place. No wonder the natives seemed content.

A pity about the graffiti. Scala had seen the likes before and sometimes it was hard to remove the paint. The real problem, of course, was to remove the malice behind it.

He'd spent most of the week talking to the community. He'd heard reams of stories from the auld folk, mostly about the War, but nothing about Patterson.

Even those who were old enough to remember the family had been reticent. Most pleaded faulty memory, and that might be true. A few expressed an inclination for forgiveness. Hoping for the same, he suspected. One or two were dead set against the Irish blood Patterson had introduced into the clan, but even they had to admit that his money was good and his estate well run.

He'd heard several versions of how a housemaid had been accused of stealing a pair of silver candlesticks, and how the police had let her go as there was no evidence she'd done it – with details about how Mrs. Patterson, Sr., may she rest in peace, crossed the line that time. They were only things, after all.

Larry had tried to steer the conversation in a new direction. What he wanted was personal information about Letitia and her husband, about why they left Texas to go to Illinois, what skeletons they had in their closets. That sort of thing. But it didn't work. His sources either dried up or reverted to talking about themselves.

Larry sighed. He understood the problem. He was an outsider. They would never talk openly to him. Good thing he'd acquired a helper who was born and bred in the briar patch. And here came the lad now.

Scala greeted Tor cordially, almost with affection, then handed him a painter's coverall and cap and showed him how to don the costume. He had props, too.

"Where are we going, sir?"

"To Chancie Mor. They've got cleaners and painters and repairmen all over the place today, probably tomorrow as well. We'll blend right in."

Tor followed him to his car, eagerly adding brushes and putty knife to the pockets. He watched as Larry threaded a paint-stained rag through the loop on his coveralls, then did the same. "What are we looking for?"

"Nothing in particular. Just looking around. I want you to get a taste for how to be inconspicuous. The best reporters look like they belong, wherever they are. We're not going to actually paint the walls, though I've done that. Today we just act nonchalant and wander through the building. Once we've done that, we're going back to the library to do some more digging."

"Yes sir!" Tor grinned, his enthusiasm palpable.

Larry smiled. He needed to make sure he didn't hurt the boy. Which meant he needed an excuse to get rid of him tomorrow morning. An errand to run. Something like that. Because he definitely did not want that lad underfoot tomorrow. He had work to do and wanted no witnesses.

* * *

Friday morning
Mackenzie residence

Ginny grabbed breakfast and headed for the back door. She stepped up beside Jim and gave him a quick hug.

"Good morning," he said. "Where are you off to?"

"Patsy again. What are you going to do with your morning?"

He waved his hand at the construction. "Supervise. I want no more surprises."

"Is Reggie still working on the wiring?"

"Yes, and he's asked me, very politely, to stay out from underfoot. Will you be back for lunch?"

"Yes, but I may be late. One or two o'clock. Fix yourself something if you get hungry."

"Okay." Jim's eyes had hardly left the construction crew.

Ginny followed his gaze, seeing the workers running string and pounding boards into the dirt.

Jim explained. "They're framing the foundation. They're going to sink the equivalent of metal fence posts into the dirt at each of the corners, for stability. They'll add drains in the floor and channels around the sides. The goal is to have a foundation that won't move when the heavens open up."

"Good luck with that one!" The land under most of Dallas had a very high concentration of clay which expanded and contracted with the weather. Every house had cracks. It was expected.

"The contractor and I had a long discussion about it. He guarantees that the foundation will last and that it will be suitable for the purpose intended. He's going to slope both approaches so the whole area should drain into the alley. I'll probably get a landscaper to look at the site to see if we can recycle the runoff."

"Good idea."

"He has to set the anchors into the concrete. That's what we're going to attach the garage walls to, and he'll have to sink tie downs tomorrow, while the concrete is still wet, to make the structure hurricane proof."

Ginny nodded. "How long will it take to dry?"

"Thirty days, but we can park the SUV and trailer on it in seven."

Ginny had been looking at the crew as Jim talked. "I don't see him. The guy who knocked down our fence."

Jim turned and looked at her. "They finished the excavations on Tuesday. He hasn't been back. I showed the photo to the foreman and he promised to give me whatever information he had on the man."

"We'll just have to wait, then." Ginny gave her husband a goodbye kiss, maneuvered her car around the construction site, and headed off to her appointment.

She could be wrong, of course, but she was still sure she'd seen that man somewhere before. And she'd feel a lot better when she figured out when and where.

* * *

Incarnadine

Friday morning
Olafsson residence

The session with Patsy Olafsson had gone as well as could be expected. Chris expressed himself satisfied, explaining that it had taken him less effort to reach the same place in her memory this time. He bid them good day and left Ginny in possession of the *Macbeth* script and a restless patient.

"Would you please explain to me what he wants? I can't figure out what I'm supposed to do!"

Ginny made soothing noises. "He's removing barriers in your mind, the barriers that have kept you from remembering what happened all those years ago."

Patsy turned and paced back across the room. "Now that I'm off the chemo and radiation treatments, I feel better than I have in months, but I know the clock is ticking. I'd like to see some progress."

Ginny hesitated. She did not have permission to share her notes with Patsy, and had no idea whether it would help or hurt if she did. "Tell me what you do remember."

"About the night Tommy died? Nothing." Patsy settled down on the bench beside Ginny. "I'm getting flashes, though. Pictures in my head of a little boy in a Cub Scout uniform."

Ginny smiled. She hadn't shared her attic discoveries with Patsy. "He was in the Cub Scouts. What else do you remember?"

"Well, a baseball game, maybe, but it was so long ago. Are these memories or did I dream them?"

"There's a picture of you and Tommy and your parents at a baseball game. That's probably a memory." She smiled. "It's working. Slowly, but steadily."

"So I just have to be patient."

"I think memorizing your lines for the play may be helping.

You're using muscles you haven't needed for a long time."

"You mean the ones between my ears?"

"I do. Would you like to rehearse for a bit?"

"Yes." She patted Ginny's knee, then rose and walked a few paces away, turned and faced her audience. *"To be, or not to be.* Oops. Wrong play."

* * *

Friday noon
Chancie Mor

Larry parked behind the Patterson estate, in a neglected turn-around at the end of the lane. The only traffic in this location would be the vehicles making pick-ups and deliveries to the mansion. He loaded Tor down with a drop cloth and handed him a small bucket of paint that had originally been white, then tucked a paint tray under his own arm and picked up a pair of brushes.

None of the items in the costume was new. The coveralls had spots of paint, including a few decorative hand prints that looked smeared and accidental. The brushes had paint along the edge of the handle, though the bristles were clean. One of the pockets had painters tape and another a key that opened paint cans, and the rags smelled faintly of turpentine. They were genuine, even if the wearers were not.

Scala led the way through the back door. "It's okay to look around, as if you're unsure where you should be. If anyone challenges you, say you got separated and would be grateful for help finding the right room, then wander off. You go that way, toward the front of the house. I'll see what's to be seen back here. We'll meet at the back door in thirty minutes. Got that?"

Tor grinned. "Yes, sir!" He strode off, then paused, slacked his stride and his posture and twisted his head around, looking at the house as if he'd never seen such a place before in his life. Larry was proud of him.

He let the boy move out of sight, then headed for the bedrooms. There weren't many places in this vintage house where you could put an old lady who had needed a wheelchair at the end of her life. He followed the ramps.

He met no one. There were voices in the distance, workmen calling to one another, women, too, but none in his vicinity. He located the old dame's suite and looked around. The room reeked of decay and neglect. Personal items had been abandoned on the bed and in the chairs. Laundry lay on the floor. No one had disturbed the dust in weeks.

He knew what he was after. Medical records were privileged information, but bills for pharmaceuticals were not. He slipped into the bathroom pulling on nitrile gloves, opened the medicine cabinet, and extracted the digoxin bottle, slipping it into his pocket. He took a couple of the insulin syringes as well, and a pill crusher he found in a drawer under the sink. He closed the drawer and the cabinet, then retraced his steps. Tor was there ahead of him.

"Okay, let's go."

He led the way off the property and headed for the cul-de-sac. When they were out of sight, he stripped off his disguise and tucked it and the props into the trunk of his car. Tor did the same. When they were safely back on the road, he glanced at his protégé.

"Well?"

Tor broke into a huge grin. "That was great! No one took any notice of me. Not even the painters. They just glanced over, then went back to work. I had no idea people were so clueless."

Larry nodded. "That's mostly true, but you need to be ready to play the part if you go undercover. I assume you could lay a drop cloth and open a can of paint, if you needed to."

"I can." Tor's brow furrowed. "What if I'd had to do that? I couldn't refuse and I couldn't pick it up again."

"The props are expendable."

Tor nodded. "What if I'd met someone I know?"

"There's always a chance, but the only danger would be someone who knew you really well. There are ways to alter a face so it looks similar, but not identical. And people don't recognize those they know when they run into them out of context. They just assume they're mistaken."

"I see. I suppose it would help to study acting?"

"Couldn't hurt, as long as you realize real actors want everyone to look at them. We want the opposite."

They drove down to the public library with Tor sharing every detail of his adventure. Larry felt a stirring of conscience as they approached the parking garage. He needed this boy's help too much to dismiss him, but he also didn't want to spoil his excitement. It was like tonic to Larry's cynical soul. He was enjoying his time with Tor as much as the boy was enjoying learning the ropes.

Larry was under no illusions. He knew the boy had been assigned to him by the old fox who ran this place. Tor had let something slip to that effect. But, unlike the jaded policemen he was used to, here was a fresh-faced kid taking delight in something Larry loved. It was seductive. He just needed to remember that, like any seduction, when it was all over, at least one of the parties was going to end up irretrievably wiser.

* * *

CHAPTER 30

Friday afternoon
Hunter residence

Ginny was sipping tea and consuming scones in the comfort of Lola Hunter's living room when the sound of the doorbell, followed by a knock, interrupted them. The two women had been discussing the arrangements for Patsy's birthday party.

Lola rose and headed for her front door. She returned with a large manila envelope in her hands and a puzzled expression on her face. "I found this leaning up against the front door, but I didn't see anyone who could have delivered it. There wasn't a soul in sight." She turned it over, then looked at the front again. "There's no return address. And no postage."

Ginny took another sip of her tea, politely not showing too much interest, then frowned, remembering the recent attacks on the community. "Who is it addressed to?"

"Me."

Ginny rose swiftly and held up her hand, palm forward. "Don't open it!"

Lola paused with a finger under the seal of the package. "What?"

"Don't open it! It might be a bomb, or a biologic weapon. Anthrax. Something like that."

Lola paled. "What should I do?"

"Don't move. I'll be right back." Ginny hurried into the kitchen, located a plastic trash bag and hurried back into the living room. She held it open. "Lower the envelope into the bag, then go wash your hands."

Lola hurried to obey. While she was gone, Ginny set the trash bag on the rug, backed away, and dialed Detective Tran, asking if it was safe to bring the suspicious package to the police station. Her response made Ginny's skin crawl.

"Put the envelope down gently and move out of the room. The police are on their way."

Ginny caught Lola before she could re-enter the living room and explained what was going on.

Lola nodded. "I'll meet them out front and let them in."

They circled the house and were outside the front door in time to meet the bomb squad. The officer listened carefully to their description, then sent them to sit in the squad car and write witness statements while he took the house keys, organized his team, and entered the home.

Twenty minutes later, the officer approached the squad car and addressed Lola. "It's all right, ma'am. There's no explosive and no evidence of biologic contaminant. We've swabbed the envelope and the contents. But you should probably turn the thing over to the police anyway."

"Why?"

"Because people who try to blackmail a public official, like your husband, sometimes escalate to physical violence if they don't get what they want." He placed the envelope in Lola's hand. "Let us know if any other suspicious packages arrive." He touched his cap. "Ma'am."

Lola stared at the envelope, then looked at Ginny. "I have a feeling I'm not going to like what I see. We'd better take it inside."

Ginny nodded, and followed Lola back to the living room.

Lola sat down on the sofa, then took a breath, and pulled the contents out of the envelope. She looked at each one, then dropped the collection on the coffee table and rubbed her face with both hands.

Ginny picked up the photographs. There were five eight-by-ten glossies, each showing Ian Hunter in a compromising situation with a woman.

"I guess I should be glad there's only one," Lola said. The images all featured the same woman, her face turned to the camera, smiling, almost as if she knew she was being photographed.

Ginny's brow furrowed. "The officer mentioned blackmail. Were there instructions?"

"I didn't notice."

Ginny picked up the envelope and looked inside, then reached in and pulled out a folded sheet of paper. She opened it and read aloud. "Tell your husband to drop out of the senate race or everyone in Texas will see these, and more."

Ginny frowned, picked up the images and the note, and stuffed them back into the envelope. "He's not guilty."

Lola's brow furrowed. "Pictures don't lie."

"Oh, yes, they do. Come on." She hauled Lola to her feet, then herded her out the door and into Ginny's car.

"Where are we going?" Lola asked.

"To see Reggie." Ginny pulled out her phone and called Jim, asking him to confirm that Reggie was still working on the security system.

"He's here. What's up?"

"I'll tell you when I get home. Don't let him leave."

* * *

Friday afternoon
Mackenzie residence

Ginny let herself in the back door and escorted Lola into the kitchen. She set out a variety of snacks and drinks, then went in search of her husband. She found him watching Reggie label a series of switches on a shiny new electrical panel. He slapped the last one in place, then closed the panel door.

"There! Done. You should have no more problem with remote devices. The shielding will stop anything that doesn't come from me which includes you as I'll give you the codes so you can access the control panel and instructions on when you should call me so that should stop attempts to override the security system." He glanced up at Ginny and smiled. "I'll take that wee dram, now."

"And welcome to it." Ginny smiled as Jim pulled Reggie to his feet and the three of them went back to the kitchen.

"A neat job, though I say it myself, especially because the tampering was a very neat job and I wouldn't have spotted it on a routine check, so in a way I'm glad this happened, because now I can be sure it can't happen again, and that's highly satisfactory. What have we here?"

Ginny made the introductions, but found that Reggie and Lola already knew one another. She set the envelope down in front of Reggie, but left her hand on it until she'd had a chance to introduce it as well. "This arrived today, hand delivered, and addressed to Lola. The police—"

"The police!" Jim interrupted.

Ginny met his eyes. "—have already tested for explosives and biologic weapons and found nothing."

"Then what is it?" Jim asked.

"A blackmail attempt." Ginny saw comprehension in Jim's eyes. "We've brought it to Reggie to see if he can prove these images have been modified."

Reggie's mouth twitched. "Modified? Let's see them."

Ginny took her hand away and let him draw out the pictures and the blackmail note. Reggie studied each item, then handed them to Jim.

Ginny addressed Reggie. "There are actually two things I'd like from you." She pointed to the female figure in the image. "Prove these are fakes and identify this woman."

Reggie's eyebrows drew together. "Without the original, it'll be hard to actually prove they're not genuine, but we can do some analysis on the color gradients, borders, lighting, things like that to give us an idea of how good the person who produced these really was, though I'm sure I'm better. Why do you want to know who the woman is?"

"Because," Jim answered, "she's the next prostitute in line."

"What?" Lola and Reggie had produced the query in chorus. They looked at each other, then back at Jim. He nodded, then told them Scala's story about the missing prostitutes.

"And, if we can find her before Patterson does, she may not disappear the way the others did," Ginny said.

"And she might be able to explain what she was doing with my husband!" Lola sniffed.

Ginny nodded. "Which she won't be able to do if she's not alive. So, forgive me for being pushy, but can we put that at the top of our to-do list?"

Reggie nodded. "Where's your computer?"

Ginny led Reggie to her office. He scanned the images and sent digital copies to himself, then handed them back to her, headed downstairs, and climbed into his car. "I've got some special software on the system in my office which may be able to answer some of our questions, but it will take me a couple of hours so don't hold your breath, and I promise I'll send anything I find to you ASAP."

Ginny waved goodbye and returned to the kitchen. Jim was calling Angus, to let him know what had happened. Lola was calling her husband, to do the same, and ask him to pick her up. Ginny pulled out her phone and dialed the police.

Detective Tran picked up on the third ring. It was one of her charms that she answered her own phone, worked in her own office, and was willing to interrupt what she was doing to listen to callers with her full attention.

"Mrs. Mackenzie! I am happy to hear that you have been neither blown up nor poisoned. How can I help you?"

Ginny explained about the blackmail pictures and the need to locate the woman in them. "I was wondering if you could use facial recognition software, or something of that sort."

"I can ask the Special Investigations Division to look at the photograph. They may be able to identify her, if the picture is clear enough. You think she is in danger."

"I do. If she's the latest in Patterson's attempts to manipulate the election, she knows too much."

"Please forward the images to me, all of them. I will see they get into the right hands."

"Hang on." Ginny climbed the stairs to her office again, sat down in the chair vacated by Reggie, and queued up the scanned images to send to the detective. "Can you do it today? I would really hate it if she disappeared like the others."

There was a pause on the line, then a sigh. "I understand your wish to prevent a death, but I cannot hurry the system, and there is another angle I would like you to consider. To prosecute, we need a crime and a criminal, with evidence to prove the connection. You already know we do not have either in the cases cited by Mr. Scala."

Ginny nodded. They needed facts. Ginny took a breath, wondering if it was ever right to use a human being as bait to catch a rat. "If we can find her, we can ask her if she's willing to help."

"I will do what I can."

"I have another favor to ask. I would like to see the pictures that were taken by the coroner's staff when Tommy Bryant was killed. There must be some, if the police responded to the scene."

Ginny could hear the regret in Detective Tran's voice. "I am sorry. There were none made. The child was taken by ambulance to the hospital and pronounced dead there, so no coroner examined the scene."

Ginny felt her spirits sagging. How was she going to prove or disprove Hannah's theory without evidence?

"There are, however, a series of images made by the officer who determined the incident was an accident."

Ginny perked back up. "You've been looking at them! Can you tell me what they show?" Ginny knew she was treading on thin ice because it really was an ongoing investigation, and she had no standing to have access to information like that.

There was a moment's hesitation. "I am going to show you what I found and ask you if you recognize any part of the image. Please check your email."

Ginny did so, impatiently waiting for the image to appear. When it did, she enlarged it and examined it closely. "There are no candlesticks on the mantle, which is filled with family photographs instead. I see spots on the white paint on the left hand side of the surround, as you face the fireplace. Hold on a moment." Ginny peered closer. One of the photographs looked familiar.

"There is a picture in a frame on the mantelpiece over on the right hand side. It shows a man, a woman and two children standing in front of a Christmas tree. I've seen that image before."

"Where did you see it?"

"In Patsy Olafsson's scrapbook."

"Is it your opinion that the people in the photo are Patsy, her brother, and her parents?"

"I think it's possible, even likely. I would need to see the images side by side to go further."

"Thank you for your help in this investigation. I will let you know about the other as soon as I have any information."

Ginny hung up and went back to examining the photo, smiling to herself. By asking for her help in identifying the image, Detective Tran had legitimized sending her a copy of it. Sneaky, but legal.

Ginny ran the picture through a variety of filters, to enhance the quality, then enlarged it again. It wasn't really possible to say for sure, but there certainly *appeared* to be blood drops splattered on the white paint.

Ginny stared at the image, her smile fading. Detective Tran had been looking at these pictures. She had been ready when Ginny asked for them. The police had better digital image analysis resources than Ginny did. She would have to ask, but she was pretty sure she already knew where this was headed. The District Attorney had also seen the images. If the DA had felt there was a provable case supported by the physical evidence of that candlestick, she would have filed charges. She hadn't, which meant she didn't. Which meant that Patterson would likely get away with this murder, too.

Ginny gritted her teeth. There had to be proof somewhere. She just wasn't looking in the right place. And she had to hope she could figure out where she *should* be looking, before someone else got killed.

* * *

CHAPTER 31

Friday evening
Mackenzie residence

Ginny was finishing up in the kitchen. Jim had helped clean, but there comes a point when the chief cook and bottle washer wants elbow room, so she had shooed him into the den. She could hear the television starting the early news. She tucked the towel on the rack, then went to join him, snuggling up and letting his arm settle around her shoulders.

"What have I missed?" she asked.

"Not much. The weather is not predicted to change for the next week. The traffic is snarled, and that won't change, either. World leaders are debating who should be allowed to save the planet. The usual. What did you and Tran talk about?"

Ginny summarized her conversation. "So, unless we're either very smart or very lucky, he's going to get away with it."

Jim gave her a squeeze. "He didn't get away with the blackmail attempt. I spoke to Ian when he came to pick up his wife. There's no way he's going to give in to that threat." Jim smiled down at her. "And neither is Lola."

Ginny nodded. "She may look delicate, but there's steel in her soul."

"What about Patsy?" Jim asked. "How is she doing?"

"She's amazing. To look at her, you wouldn't know she was

sick."

"Will she be able to be in the play?"

Ginny nodded. "Unless something goes wrong. I'm glad she's getting this respite before the end." Ginny was silent for a moment. "I'm going to miss her."

Jim pulled her closer, and planted a kiss on the top of her head. Ginny was grateful to him for not spouting platitudes. The result of dealing with death in his professional capacity, no doubt. Still, it took a smart man to recognize that grief couldn't be dismissed with shallow words.

She was staring at the television, not really paying any attention, just letting her mind wander, when she saw someone who looked familiar. "Is that Patterson?"

Jim nodded. "He and Rita are in Austin for a political do."

Ginny's eyes narrowed, then she broke out of Jim's arms. "Freeze that picture!"

Jim started, then grabbed the controller. "This one?"

"No, go back." Ginny was staring at the images. "There! That one!" She turned to look at Jim. "Do you see what I see?"

His forehead creased. "It's the Pattersons getting out of the limo."

"Take a look at the man holding the door."

Jim squinted at the screen, then turned to face her. "Is that the guy who knocked down our fence?"

Ginny nodded. "Patterson's driver. I knew I'd seen him somewhere before."

The image righted itself and moved on, showing no more of the car or the driver, but Ginny'd gotten a good look at him. She turned to face Jim. "Did you get his name, from the foreman?"

Jim nodded and rose to go fetch the information. Ginny had also risen. She took the note and headed for her office.

"Don't forget the ceilidh," Jim called.

"I'll be ready. I just have to look something up first." She settled into her chair, located as many images of Senator Patterson's driver as she could find, and compared them to the photos she'd taken of the excavator operator. Different names, of course. But the two men could have been twins.

Ginny sat back in her chair. She would have to ask for more help, to see if she could confirm that the two men were one and the same. On the supposition that they were, it implied the accident had been planned.

It was no trouble at all for Ginny to leap to the obvious conclusion. Someone from the Patterson household had sent the driver to do a little job for them. And, since the intruder inside Ginny's house had been (presumptively) female, the most likely place to look for a match to those shoe prints would be in Rita Patterson's closet. Which put a whole new complexion on the break-in.

Ginny took a moment to send an email to Detective Tran, explaining about the driver and including images of the man for comparison. That done, Ginny went back to Rita. Why break in and take nothing? Why not make it look like a robbery? What was she looking *for*?

Ginny was still staring off into the distance when Jim called up the stairs.

"Ceilidh express leaving in ten minutes."

Ginny tumbled out of her chair, flew down to her bedroom and scrambled into her dancing clothes.

Rita Patterson had broken into her house looking for something. Why? What could be worth the risk?

Ginny filed the puzzle away in the back of her mind to let her subconscious chew on it. The answer was there, somewhere. It had to be.

* * *

Friday evening
Cooperative Hall

At the first break in the dancing, Angus Mackenzie, the Laird of Loch Lonach, climbed the steps to the stage and took the microphone. The room instantly quieted and came closer, to hear what he had to say, Ginny among them.

"Clansmen. An evil hae come amang us. Ye know this fra th' attacks on yer lawns and property. Ye will hae heard o' th' shooting in th' street outside our walls. An' there hae been other things. In th' comin' days, I expect there may be more." Angus took a breath. "Throughout our history, the Scots hae had one thing their enemies did not, a single loyalty tae th' clan, tae their family. 'Tis th' glue that binds us and th' strength that sustains us. Th' evil would break us apart, set us kin against kin. It would hae us question our way o' life, our values, our beliefs."

Ginny slipped her hand into her husband's. The room was so quiet you could have heard the proverbial pin drop.

"'Tis hard, I ken, tae keep fear at bay. 'Tis hard tae face an enemy that wants us gone. But worse is an enemy that wants us slaves. Slaves tae fear, tae power misused, tae cruelty." The Laird paused, taking a moment to look at them, to make eye contact with them.

"Th' council and I are workin' tae identify th' source and tae deal with it, but th' peace has been broken, and it will take some time tae restore. As we do so, I call on each ane o' ye tae stand, shoulder tae shoulder, wi' his neighbor, friend, family. Take oot yer courage and gie it a shake. Check yer defenses, and yer weapons. Make sure ye know wha' ye can do, and wha' ye'll need help with.

"We'll be strengthening the physical defenses, and running drills, tae make sure ye all know how tae respond. But it's no th' physical attacks ye'll need tae be wary of. 'Tis th' worm. Th' subtle, insidious lies. Th' suggestion that yer neighbor is no who ye thought he was. Th' remark that our way o' life is outdated. Th' seductive lure o' idleness.

"Yer educated people. Ye may recall that, when Rome allowed its citizens tae vote themselves inta gluttony and sloth, the civilization fell. I hae no intention o' lettin' that happen here.

"We are an island community. The larger world hae grown up aroond us, engulfed us, and would obliterate us. Tae keep our property and our lives, we must understand that threat."

Angus' brow furrowed. "I would spare ye th' examples, but tonight I must show ye one, at least. Jock Brodie was an auld man wi' a lifetime o' service tae his credit. Born here, raised here, attached tae a powerful family. His body was found in the loch last nicht. Drowned, by others."

There were exclamations all over the room, and movement. Ginny followed Angus' eyes and saw people drawing closer— and further apart. When she looked back at Angus, his expression was grim.

"Until we find those as hae done this deed, 'twill be even harder tae trust one anither, but I call on ye tae do just that. Keep yer eyes and ears open, but yer mind as well. Watch fer th' worm. Tell it ye'll no let it destroy what we've built here. We're Scots tae the core and will fight fer what's ours. Services fer Jock will be held tomorrow at two p.m. at the Auld Kirk."

Angus descended the steps and was instantly surrounded by questioners. Ginny turned to her husband and slipped her arms around him, hugging him tightly. He did the same to her. She looked up at him. "This has got to stop."

* * *

Friday evening
Scala's motel room

Scala locked the motel door, threw his purchases on the bed then extracted the stolen items from the painter's coverall pocket. He spread paper towels on the bathroom counter, then laid out his project.

He pulled on gloves, dumped the contents of the digoxin bottle onto the counter, and counted how many pills remained. One per chocolate meant he could dose twelve of the candies, with two tablets left over to set the scene tomorrow.

He went to work crushing the pills, one at a time, then mixing the powder in two milliliters of one-hundred-and-twenty proof vodka, and setting them aside to dissolve. When the contents of the syringe was as liquefied as it would get, he added a large bore needle, carefully peeled back the foil wrapper on the individually wrapped chocolates, injected the drug/alcohol combination, smoothed the wrapper back into positon and set the dosed dainty aside.

It had taken him three hours, working steadily, to prepare the candies; half crush another pill, then slide it and the undamaged tablet into the pill bottle; to wipe the bottle clean, using the vodka and a lint-free fabric square; to put the cap back on the bottle, making sure it, too, was free of trace evidence; and to clean the outside of the pill crusher in the same manner. One of the syringes would be included in the set dressing, with a large bore needle attached, also wiped clean on the outside.

It was necessary that the police find the drug inside the syringe and needle, but there was almost no chance they would find Scala's DNA inside as well. The vodka would see to that.

He inspected the wrapping of each chocolate as he stowed them in a plastic baggie. He wouldn't put them in the gift box until after he and Tor had added the listening device, then the chocolates could go on top. The final step, for tonight, was to hide the evidence in the painters' coveralls, and the chocolates in a special compartment of his luggage, zipped tight, and secured with a lock.

He didn't have access to Patterson's fingerprints, and would probably not have been able to successfully transfer them to the crime scene even if he had. The best he could do was make sure the whole area had been wiped clean, to remove all trace of who had done the deed. Without DNA, the police would suspect the person with access to both the drug and to Patsy. That would be Maury Patterson.

Scala cleaned his teeth, then crawled into bed, tucking his hands behind his head. Sleep would be hard to come by tonight.

He wasn't happy about the chance that the drug would actually kill Patsy Olafsson. He hadn't even met her—and wouldn't until the birthday party on Sunday—but he bore her no ill will. He just needed a way to get to Patterson and she happened to be it.

What would happen on Sunday? Would she open the chocolates at the party? Not likely. There weren't enough to share with the expected crowds. She would take them back to her house to nibble on them when she got around to it.

Her keeper would be paying attention, fussing like an old hen with one chick. She'd yell for help at the first symptom. And there was an antidote available.

The sooner she ate that first candy, the sooner the police would start looking for an explanation. And every passing day increased the chance of someone cleaning Letitia's room. He should point the police to the scene, if he could figure out some way that wouldn't incriminate himself.

The main thing, he told himself, was to get Patterson off the streets. The greater good. An ethical question in which sometimes someone had to die to save others. And she was dying anyway.

He closed his eyes, but the problem kept circling his mind. He wasn't a killer. He didn't want Patsy to die. He just wanted Patterson to be blamed for the attempt.

It was the wee small hours of the morning when his conscience finally allowed him to drift off, after promising himself he would make sure Patsy wasn't harmed. Because, if he didn't, he was no better than Patterson, and that wasn't at all how he wanted to see himself. A knight in shining armor, slaying a dragon, that was his goal, to save, not to kill. That was always his goal, to expose corruption and take down the crooks.

He slept badly and woke the next morning feeling as if he hadn't slept at all.

* * *

CHAPTER 32

Saturday morning
Prostitute's apartment

The plan was to have Jim persuade the prostitute she was in enough danger that she needed to flee. Not an easy task. The neighborhood was suburban, sporting three miles of aging apartment houses fronting a side street. Jim checked the address, pulled his car into the lot, and studied the layout.

The buildings were well labeled, but he would have to walk past the office and the pool to get to the right one. He looked around. No people. There were birds singing, green grass, and a pool sweeper losing the battle against tree litter. It was quiet, restful even. Jim walked on.

The detective from Vice had cooked up this scheme, hoping the woman would lead him to her handler, or something else of equal value. Angus had agreed and Jim had been assigned the task. He found the building, climbed the stair to the second floor, walked along the balcony, and stopped in front of a door with no distinguishing marks. Some of the residents had personalized their space. Apparently this one hadn't felt the need.

He double-checked the number, then tucked the slip of paper into his pocket, and knocked. The door was opened by a slim, not-quite-young woman in sweats. Her hair was pulled back in a ponytail, and her face was devoid of makeup, but Jim could see she matched the picture.

Her eyes raked his body, clearly assessing his potential, then smiled. "Howdy handsome. What can I do for you?"

"I'm Jim Mackenzie and I'm looking for Marilee Broussard."

"That's me."

"May I come in?"

She smirked. "You're in luck. I'm alone." She stepped back and let him into the apartment.

Jim looked around, taking in the leather sofa, wall-mounted TV, built-in bar, and picture window looking out on a pocket park.

She stepped over to the bar. "Can I get you something to drink?" She was smiling at him, her natural charm showing. Jim smiled back.

"No, thank you. I apologize for breaking in on your morning, but I need to talk to you."

She put ice in a glass, poured three fingers of bourbon over it, and stirred it with her finger. Her face took on a puzzled expression. "Funny, I wouldn't have pegged you for an official visit, and I'm good at reading men."

Jim nodded. "I'm sure you are." He hesitated, then decided to level with her. "I'm an Emergency Room physician."

She frowned. "Health department! Someone lied and now I gotta be tested, right?"

"No. It's nothing like that."

She relaxed. "Oh? You got a friend that recommended me?"

"I'm afraid not. May we sit down?"

"Sure, sugar, come sit here." She patted the sofa.

Jim nodded and settled down beside her, pulling the pictures out of his back pocket and unfolding them so she could see. "Can you tell me anything about these?" He handed them over.

At first she looked amused, but as she studied the images her smile faded. "What is this? Some kind of a joke?"

"I'm afraid not. Do you know the man in the picture?"

"What if I do?"

"Did you pose with him for those pictures?"

"Are you kidding? He's the only man in my whole life I couldn't get a rise out of! Spoiled my record."

The corner of Jim's mouth twitched. "So the pictures are faked?"

She frowned. "Of course they are. That man never gave me a chance. I mean, he bought me a drink, and told me I should vote for him, but that was it." She paused for a moment, her face softening. "He was nice, though. Not like the others. Guess that's what happens when you're in love with your wife."

"Was the plan to get him into bed?"

"Of course! Pillow talk. See if I could find out what he was hiding. They've all got secrets. Even him. I could tell. But no soap. I couldn't get past first base."

"Who hired you?"

She leaned back into the cushions, playing with the drink. "You want information, you gotta pay. One way or another."

"Ms. Broussard—"

"Call me Marilee."

"All right. Marilee."

"And I'll call you Jim."

"Marilee, your life is in danger."

Jim saw the skin at the corners of her mouth tighten. She knew what that word meant.

"Nice of you to warn me. Kinda goes with the territory, though."

"Maury Patterson has a history of hiring girls like you, then making them disappear when he's done with them."

The ice in her glass betrayed the shock he'd given her, but

she covered it well. "Who?"

"Ian Hunter and Maury Patterson are rivals for the District 17A Texas state senatorial race. But you already knew that."

She took a pull on her drink. "What if I did?"

"We would like to make sure you don't become his next victim."

She shrugged. "I can take care of myself."

Jim sighed, then leaned forward, using his most persuasive bedside manner. "We know of two dead girls and five more are missing. We don't want you to be number eight."

She put the drink down and stared at him. "Who's *we*?"

"Both Senator Hunter and Maury Patterson have connections to the Loch Lonach Homestead. I'm here on behalf of the Laird."

Her brow furrowed. "I've heard of that place. Celts. Irish. Something like that."

"Scots. We're descended from the Scottish immigrants who settled in the Dallas area."

"Yeah, that's right. You've got a farm."

"Sort of. It's a Living History exhibit."

"I was there once. It was fun."

Jim smiled. "*We* also includes the police. We've been working with them to try to get to the bottom of these disappearances."

Her face took on a hard expression, her eyes suddenly cold. "You think they're dead."

Jim nodded. "It seems likely."

"How?"

"We don't know." Not for sure, anyway.

"Why?"

"Because they knew too much."

"I didn't learn a thing."

"You know who paid you, and who you were supposed to

pry secrets out of, and why."

She was silent for a long moment. "You're serious? About the danger?"

"I'm afraid so."

Her face grew troubled. "How do I know I can trust you?"

"You don't have to. All we want is for you to leave town for a few weeks. Go visit a friend. Tell no one, and don't leave a forwarding address."

"What if someone follows me? The police think I know something. Or someone."

"All you're doing is going on vacation. If you don't break any laws, it doesn't matter if the police follow you. I would suggest you avoid hanging out with known criminals, though. You don't want to draw attention to yourself."

"When would I have to leave?"

"Now would be best."

She rose from her seat, tossed back the remains of the drink and headed for the bedroom. "I've been promising myself some time off." She paused in the doorway. "Sure you don't want to give me a going away party?"

Jim rose and shook his head. "Pack your bag. I'll see myself out."

"Wait!" She came over and stood in front of him, placing a hand on his chest and smiling up into his face. "When this is over, can I come visit you?"

"My wife and I would be happy to have you come for dinner."

She snorted. "Wife! I should have known." She turned and stalked toward the bedroom.

Jim put his hand on the doorknob, then paused. "Good luck."

"Yeah, yeah."

Jim let himself out and retraced his steps, feeling vaguely

dissatisfied by the whole encounter. He strode back to the parking lot, approached the unmarked police car parked beside his BMW and rapped on the glass. The detective inside rolled down the window.

"Well?"

"She's packing. I think she took me seriously."

"Good. I'll wait here and follow her to the airport, just to make sure she actually goes in. After that, we don't really have jurisdiction."

"Just as well. She's safer if no one can find her."

"Hey, look at that." The detective pointed to Marilee, dragging a suitcase and hurrying across the lawn toward a yellow car. "She didn't waste any time."

Jim turned to watch. He had just caught sight of her, putting the suitcase into the trunk of her car when a white van blocked his view. The side door opened and two men jumped out. They grabbed Marilee, hoisted her into the van, and drove off, all in less than sixty seconds.

The detective swore and started his car. "Get in."

Jim grabbed the passenger side door and jumped inside, closing the door and putting on his seatbelt as the car accelerated. When they were on the street, with the van in sight, the detective called it in. "We've got a witnessed abduction. In pursuit. Need backup."

Jim listened as he gave further details on location, direction of travel, and license and markings on the van. When he caught his breath, he did the same, calling Angus and reporting where he was and what he was doing. Angus took it in stride.

"Stay safe, lad."

Jim hung up, then grabbed for a handhold as the car swung abruptly to the right.

"They've seen us."

The van accelerated, weaving in and out of traffic and

running stop lights. The detective turned on his lights and sirens, and gave chase. Jim was beginning to regret his decision to ride along.

They were pushing eighty as they approached the river, squealing tires announcing the traffic yielding to the high speed chase. They had been joined by two more police cars, marked this time, and Jim could hear an approaching helicopter.

The van was still weaving, cutting off other drivers and causing near-wrecks as it sped toward the bridge. Jim had his eyes glued to the windscreen. There was construction on the bridge. There was always construction going on in Dallas. In this case, there was damage to the railing.

The workers heard the sirens and dove for cover as the van plowed into the utility vehicles. It side-swiped something that must have been heavier than it was, went up on two wheels, struck a utility pole, was deflected sideways, and left the deck of the bridge through the hole in the rail, rotating gracefully along its longitudinal axis as it fell toward the river. Jim heard the impact as it hit the bridge's foundation.

The detective pulled the car over and they both got out, joining the construction workers who were already leaning over the side of the bridge to survey the damage. There was no movement around the van, which was not surprising. It had landed roof down on the concrete and crumpled like a beer can. Jim stepped aside and was promptly sick.

It took the EMS and rescue crews more than an hour to establish all four occupants had died on impact. Jim was sitting in Angus' car, waiting for him to finish conferring with the police, trying to focus. He had already given his witness statement to the investigating officer. He needed to go back to the apartment complex and pick up his own car, then go home. He would have to tell Ginny. He wiped cold sweat from his forehead.

The driver side door opened and Angus climbed in. "How are ye, lad?"

Jim grimaced. "Embarrassed." It had been a very long time since he'd been shocked by violent death.

Angus nodded. "I've asked th' police tae see if they can trace th' money. 'Twould be useful if we could prove Patterson hired them."

Someone had given Jim a bottle of water. He had used it to wash his mouth out, then to settle his stomach. He finished it off, put the cap back on and carefully tucked it down next to his legs, so he could dispose of it later. It was a small thing, but it gave him the illusion of control.

"Are ye ready tae go?"

"Yes, please."

Angus put the car in gear and headed back toward the east side of town. Jim gave him directions to the dead girl's apartment complex, then to the lot where he'd left his car.

"When ye feel up tae it, I'll be interested tae hear wha' th' girl had tae say."

Jim met his grandfather's eyes and forced a smile. "Thank you for coming to get me."

"Any time, lad." He paused. "We'll talk later."

* * *

CHAPTER 33

Saturday morning
Chancie Mor

Larry Scala sat on the bench outside the Cooperative Hall, sipping coffee and waiting for Tor to arrive. He had given up on sleep and risen early, eaten breakfast at a nearby restaurant, then gone for a walk along the lake. As the sun climbed, so did the number of joggers on the trail. He avoided them, setting off across the grass, then climbing the rise to the top of this hill. Round about six a.m. he had begun to wax philosophical.

What had brought him here, to this place? Was it his fate to pursue Patterson until one or the other of them died? Had God given him the task? What pushed him to keep going, to keep hoping?

It was absolutely true, provable or not, that Patterson was an unsavory character and unfit for a position of public trust. Larry had seen Patterson leaving the burning cabin, and the cabin up in far northern Michigan, and four times at the lake house, Patterson's alibi provided only by a paid servant.

Scala had gathered thousands of bits of information, adding up to a career built on bribery, graft, and trading favors. He had tracked Patterson's voting history and seen that he always voted for higher taxes, more government control, and exemptions from the same for himself. The man was a chancre.

But was Patterson his responsibility?

Larry shifted uneasily on the bench. Over the years, he'd made choices and they'd seemed right at the time, but looking back, he saw them in a different light. He'd lost his job, lost any chance at a home and family, lost his good name and reputation, by pursuing the man. Was it time to give up? Or had he already paid the price and earned the reward?

There were moral questions as well. For him, not Patterson. Aside from small things like trespassing and impersonating honest citizens, did the end ever justify the means?

He frowned. He really did *not* want to hurt the old lady. He'd spent some time staking out her house and seen her on the porch, a thin, pale woman with a warm smile and kind eyes. The dose was too small to kill her, probably, even if she ate all twelve chocolates in one sitting. Even then, she shouldn't be injured, not permanently.

Each digoxin tablet had contained 0.25 milligrams of drug. If she ate all twelve, all at once, she'd ingest a total of three milligrams of active ingredient. The literature said the dose didn't get dangerous until the patient ingested ten milligrams, but also said caution should be used in the elderly and those with other medical conditions, like cancer.

One dose—one chocolate—would cause cardiovascular effects: a slowed heart rate and a corresponding drop in blood pressure. That might lead to dizziness. She might fall. All the better. A fall would get her to the hospital sooner, to be checked over. If the medicos knew their job, they'd ask her what she'd eaten. Anything out of the ordinary? She would tell them about her birthday and the chocolates. The caretaker could fetch them. The lab test them. The police would investigate.

There was no motive, of course, for Patterson to poison his cousin, except that she was the last member of the family from the olden days, the last person who might know what Patterson really was. But the police would have means and opportunity. When the story hit the media, Larry could come forward with his evidence of other criminal activity. That should be enough to keep Patterson out of office.

So the old lady was safe, unless there was an accident, which could happen to anyone, especially a frail old lady. Scala shoved the idea away. She would be fine. And she'd be doing the world a favor, helping him bring down Patterson.

Larry looked up as his young accomplice drove into the lot and parked an aging pickup truck in one of the slots. Tor bounced out of the vehicle and sprinted over.

"Good morning, Mr. Scala." He grinned. "What are we going to do today?"

Larry smiled and patted the seat beside him. When Tor was settled, as much as any exuberant young thing can be who is on the edge of a great adventure, Larry pulled out a list and a map, and handed them over.

"One of the skills a good investigative reporter needs is to be able to listen in on conversations."

Tor's brow furrowed. "Isn't that illegal?"

"Most of the time, but there are exceptions. Law enforcement officers can do it, if they have a properly executed court order."

Tor nodded.

"It's also legal for one party in a telephone conversation to record the conversation, without telling the person on the other end of the line."

Tor eyes grew wide. "Really?"

Larry nodded. "Also, closed circuit cameras, with sound recording ability, can be used in and around your own property, if there is no violation of other people's rights to privacy. You can get around that by putting up signs warning everyone that the cameras and recording devices are in use. If it ever goes to court, the presumption is that they have consented to being taped."

"Wow!"

Larry grinned. "One of the elements the court looks at, in a wiretapping case, is whether the information is shared with third parties. There are gray areas having to do with *for your own personal use*, whatever that means, and it might include educational purposes."

"So we're going to build a bug?"

Larry nodded. "We're going to build one, and I'm going to show you how to get it into the place you want to record. Then I am going to warn you sternly that what we have been talking about is against the law and you must never do anything of the sort."

Tor grinned. "Got it. Where do we start?"

"You take that map and drive to the store I've indicated. You tell them you think there is a raccoon knocking over your trashcans at night and you want to catch him in the act. You already have the camera and just need the audio. Give the clerk that list. I've written down the price of each component. Don't let anyone talk you into more expensive parts. All we need is on that list and there is no way that shop will be out of stock, so don't let them tell you that, either. Pay them with this." Larry pulled out a small packet of old bills.

"Be polite, but don't volunteer anything. If they push, you can tell them it's for posting on the Internet. Everyone understands cute animal videos."

Tor nodded.

"The cash should cover the purchases and your gasoline and then some. Bring me the receipts." Larry glanced at his watch. "By the time you get up there, the shop should be open. We'll meet back here at noon. All right?"

"Yes, sir. I'll be back in a flash."

"You will not. You will drive safely and under the speed limit. You do *not* want to be pulled over by the police either coming or going. Remember, the idea is to be inconspicuous."

Tor nodded. "Yes, sir, I'll be careful."

"Don't hurry. Take the time to do the job right. If you can get anyone in the shop to tell you how the device works, listen to them. They're the experts. Smile and make eye contact and thank them for their help, then leave. It's just like pretending to be a painter. The secret to not being remembered is to act as if you belong wherever you are."

Tor stood up, his face solemn. "Don't worry, sir. I won't disappoint you."

Larry snorted, then stood up and offered the boy his hand. "Son, there's no way you could disappoint me. Just do your best and we'll deal with any issues that come up." He slapped Tor on the shoulder, and watched as the boy climbed into the old truck and made his way out of the parking lot.

When the truck was out of sight, Larry looked at his watch again. Time to go. He put on his painter disguise, made sure the props for his little stage setting were where he had put them, got into his car, and headed for Chancie Mor.

He parked behind the estate, as before, pulled on paint stained gloves and hat, added a tarp and two paint cans to his costume, and headed for the back door. No one stopped him. No one spoke to him. No one even gave him a second glance. He was in and out in less than fifteen minutes.

* * *

Saturday morning
Mackenzie residence

When Ginny got home from work on Saturday, she found her husband sitting in the kitchen, doing nothing. This was unusual. So was the white face. She set her work bag down and went to him.

"Jim? What's happened?"

When he saw her, he jumped to his feet and wrapped his arms around her, hugging her tightly. Ginny slid her arms around his waist and held on.

"Tell me what's wrong."

"She's dead."

Ginny tried to keep the panic out of her voice. "Who's dead?"

"Marilee."

Ginny sucked in a breath. Marilee was the name of the prostitute hired to corrupt Ian Hunter. She remembered because it sounded like a stage name. Probably was. She remembered, too, that Jim had been sent to warn her.

"Were we too late?"

Jim pulled in a deep shuddering breath. "No. I spoke to her and she listened. Two men grabbed her as she was putting her suitcase in the car. We chased them. There was a crash."

"Oh." His parents had died in a dreadful car wreck. No wonder he was upset.

Ginny disentangled his arms and led him into the den. She sat him down on the sofa, and sat down facing him, reaching out to take his hands in hers.

"Are you all right?"

He shook his head. "No. It could have been you. It might still be." His brow furrowed deeply. "How am I supposed to keep you safe when there are people like that in the world?" He reached for her and she let him settle her on his lap, his arms around her. It could have gone the other way, with him in her lap, if he'd been smaller. The effect was the same. Ginny snuggled close, letting him talk, letting him grieve.

"I've been telling myself that, as deaths go, this one was painless. She was alive one minute and dead the next. And they didn't get a chance to make her disappear. We saw what happened and the police will be able to identify the kidnappers. That should lead us to whoever hired them. It's progress, of a sort."

"Larry will be thrilled."

Jim nodded. He was silent for a moment, then continued. "I've seen plenty of deaths. Some of them are a blessing, some inevitable. But some are preventable. That's when I get mad. I hate to see a life wasted."

Ginny looked up into his face. "You liked her?"

Jim nodded. "I invited her to dinner."

Ginny's eyebrows shot up. "Cocktails for two?"

"No, a family meal with my wife, and maybe Angus, to round out the table."

Ginny laid her head on his shoulder. "You're a good man, Jim Mackenzie."

"I'm a frightened man. I can't seem to stop thinking about how I would feel if it had been you in that van."

Ginny tipped her head back so she could see his face. "I have dreams like that, only it's you missing, or you dead, or you running off with another woman." The last part wasn't true, but it had the desired effect. He smiled.

"Not a chance. You're stuck with me."

"It's a good thing you're the man I want."

He bent to kiss her and Ginny slid her arms around his neck. She could feel the warmth returning to his cheeks, and the moment when the tension in his shoulders began to ease.

"The way to keep me safe," she said, "and you, too, is to find out who's behind this."

He nodded.

"And on the same subject, I got a call today while I was at work, from Detective Tran."

"Oh?"

"She turned up another death."

"Connected to Patterson?"

Ginny nodded. "Maury and a high school rival were fighting over who should be class president his senior year."

"Debate?" Jim sounded dubious.

"Fisticuffs. Maury hit the other boy who fell backward off a nearby cliff. It's unclear whether either boy realized how close they had gotten to the edge. Anyway. A normal person would have tried to help, called out, climbed down to the water, something. Maury is reported to have looked down at his rival disappearing into the lake, then turned and walked away."

"Wow! Who reported it?"

"Maury's sister, to the school counselor, who passed it on to the local police, who included it in their report when they investigated the death. Apparently she had a crush on the other boy, and was in the habit of following him around in the hope of getting him to notice her. Charlotte, as you may remember, is the one death in Larry's collection for which Maury Patterson does not have an alibi."

"I remember."

"This gives him a motive."

Jim chewed on his lip. "Who chose the site?"

"Maury told the police they had planned to use the baseball diamond, which has a chain link fence around it, but there was a game in progress. So they moved to the picnic area. The location is picturesque, with a small stream and a short waterfall. There were some low barriers, the kind that stop cars from driving too far into the park, and there were warning signs, but no fences.

"Tran also wanted to let us know that the forensics team found nothing on the materials Larry supplied for missing woman number three. Nothing that could be linked to Senator Patterson, anyway, just to Larry."

Jim's eyebrows rose. "Is it possible we've been looking in the wrong direction? Just because Patterson is an oily, self-serving, bottom-feeder doesn't mean he's a murderer."

"And Scala's obsession makes it likely that he sees only what he wants to see."

"It could be worse than that. Scala might be the murderer."

Ginny blinked. "How do you figure that?"

"Anyone who knows anything about solving murders knows that lack of evidence is more suspicious than finding the routine DNA we all shed constantly."

Ginny nodded. "And?"

"So maybe he left his own DNA behind because he wanted to be excluded. Maybe he had an alibi prepared. If he was suspected, then dismissed, he wouldn't be suspected again."

"Jim! That's really clever, but it won't fly. According to Tran, the only DNA Larry collected at the scene was his own. Patterson used the lake house for family gatherings and to entertain his political cronies. There should have been lots of DNA on that sticky tape."

Jim sighed. "The scene had been wiped before he got there."

"I think so."

Jim's eyes narrowed. "Maybe he thought of that, too. Wiped the scene down, then brushed his arm to leave his own traces for the police to find and exclude on the same grounds you just did."

"Do you think that's what happened?"

Her husband shook his head. "I have no idea. But I think it's time you and I stopped helping Lorenzo Scala in his quest to destroy Maury Patterson."

Ginny sniffed. "I haven't taken sides, if that's what you think. It's just that none of it makes sense. Even if Scala killed every one of the people he's blaming on Patterson, it doesn't explain Patsy's wedding present. He doesn't know about the candlestick."

"Maybe they're not related."

Ginny wrinkled her nose. "I suppose it's possible. Our evidence is all circumstantial, and hearsay into the bargain. The only thing we can count on is that Scala couldn't have killed Tommy Bryant. Larry hadn't been born yet."

Jim sighed. "I feel as if I'm missing something."

"I know the feeling." Ginny climbed off his lap and pulled him to his feet. "Now darling, it's lunch time. I want to feed you and pick your brain."

"Oh? You think there's something useful in there?"

"One never knows, but Detective Tran's phone call got me thinking, and I have an idea I want to run past you."

"Sounds interesting. What is it?"

"Food first. Brains need fuel as well as puzzles to chew on."

* * *

CHAPTER 34

Saturday afternoon
Chancie Mor

Ginny made soup and sandwiches, supplementing her meal with milk, which she liked, and Jim's with water, which he preferred. She was glad to see his shock had not interfered with his appetite. When he finished, he placed his napkin beside his plate and sat back, looking across the table at her.

"Okay. I'm listening."

Ginny nodded. "You will recall that Jock, the old driver, said Mrs. Patterson, 'buried her troubles at Chancie Mor,' and I assumed he meant that was her base of operations."

Jim nodded. "According to Grandfather, there's been someone taking care of the house the whole time they were living in Illinois. Apparently Mrs. Patterson was back and forth between Dallas and Springfield like a yo-yo."

"So any secrets she might have should be there."

Jim's brow furrowed. "But Patterson is NOT going to let us poke our inquisitive little noses into his mother's business. Or the police. They would need a search warrant and that would take probable cause, which we don't have."

"Not yet."

Jim's eyes were fixed on her face. "What are you thinking?"

"What if Jock wasn't speaking metaphorically? What if

there's a vault on the Patterson estate where Mrs. Patterson put all the things she didn't want anyone else to find out about?"

Jim blinked. "We'd still need a warrant to search the property and it would take someone with blueprints to identify a void."

"I wasn't planning anything that ambitious. Chancie Mor has a historical marker and a caretaker who is allowed to give us access to the public rooms."

"You want to go look around?"

Ginny nodded. "It's a beautiful day and we both have this afternoon off."

Jim's eyes narrowed. "We won't be allowed to touch anything. I know how those tours work. We had lots of them in Virginia."

"I know it's a long shot, but I know the housekeeper and she owes me a favor."

Jim smiled. "All right. I can do with an outing. Let's go see what we can see."

The two of them put on shoes suitable for trudging across the estate lawns, climbed into Jim's BMW and drove to Chancie Mor. Jim pulled up the sweep drive and parked in the shade of an ancient oak. "Okay, now what?"

Ginny put on her most cordial smile and climbed the stairs to the door. When the housekeeper answered, she made her request.

"Jim hasn't seen the house and I've been telling him the history of the Loch Lonach community and how the whole area was fields of wheat and corn and woods filled with deer."

The housekeeper smiled. "The stories I used tae hear from my grandfather! Chancie Mor was th' first house built in the neighborhood, that could be called one. The first wi' gas lighting, a cast iron stove in th' kitchen that burned coal—and had a place where ye could heat water, and a whole row o' outhouses, with carved seats!" She stepped back and let them in. "I'm sorry about th' painters and what not. Th' new Mrs. Patterson was in favor of tearing th' house down, but settled for upgrades and a face lift."

"I thought the place had a historical designation."

"Aye, and there was a stink about doing this much, but the health and safety codes allowed the changes."

They followed the housekeeper as she moved slowly through the major rooms, explaining how the other half lived in the late eighteen-hundreds in a frontier town like Loch Lonach. Ginny expressed her admiration of the beautiful woodwork, the native stone, and the gracious proportions of the original part of the house. They climbed the stairs and examined the tiny bedrooms, with the servant's stair at the back. There were larger bedrooms downstairs, they were told, but they were off limits to tourists, and hadn't been properly cleaned since the old mistress died.

They were then escorted to the kitchen, originally in a separate building, to reduce the chance of fire, now attached to the main house and upgraded. The modern version sported a refrigerator and a microwave.

"They kept chickens and goats, and sheep and coo. The stables ha'e been turned into garages, o' course, but the riding paths are still there."

This was the last stop on the tour and they were standing at the back of the house facing uphill at a winding path shaded by ancient oaks. Ginny smiled. "The trail looks so inviting." She felt a light breeze on her face and breathed in the scent of mimosa. "How lucky you are to have your own woods!"

The caretaker beamed. "Go on, wander where ye will. And if ye want an iced tea afore ye leave us, just knock."

"Thank you. This has been such a treat! I'm so grateful to

you for taking the time to show us around."

The older woman smiled. "I've a great affection fer th' old place. I'm glad as some still feel th' same." She took her leave and went back into the house.

Jim and Ginny struck out along the path. They were soon far enough from the house to no longer hear the cars on the road, just birds and squirrels and insects going about their business. Jim spoke first.

"I didn't see any place in that old house where you could hide a safe."

"Maybe it's in the modern part, where the bathrooms are."

"Or in the bedrooms." Jim nodded. "But we're not going to find anything Patterson doesn't want us to see, not this way."

They walked on for a few minutes, then Ginny noticed a fence on their right hand. They followed it to a stone arch with wrought iron embellishments. Ginny paused and read the inscription.

"Patterson Cemetery, Established 1844." She looked at Jim. "That would be the date of the first burial. Let's look around."

"In the cemetery?" Jim looked less than thrilled at the idea and Ginny grinned.

"A cemetery is irresistible to a genealogist. You wouldn't believe how much fun it is to read the headstones. They give you a glimpse of the dear departed you can't get anywhere else. Come on!"

She pulled him onto the grounds and showed him how to avoid stepping on the graves. "Here's one for you."

> Here beneath this stone we lie
> Back to back my wife and I
> And when the angels trump shall trill
> If she gets up then I'll lie still!

Jim started laughing. "Someone had a sense of humor. Here's another."

Grim death, to please his liquorish palate
Has taken my Lettice to put in his sallat.

Ginny grinned. "That would do for old Mrs. Patterson. Her name was Letitia." She walked on, reading the stones. "This one makes my blood run cold."

Here lies the body of Geordie Denham
If ye saw 'im noo ye wadna ken him.

Jim joined her, nodding. "I see what you mean."
In this manner they moved from the front of the cemetery to the back rows. It didn't take long. It was a private, family cemetery, with not more than three score dead in over a hundred and fifty years. Some of the graves had no headstones, through weathering, or neglect, or vandalism. Some had vaults, some fieldstones.

Ginny found herself reading a series of uprights even more lavish than the ones closer to the gate. Each had a Gaelic name, followed by dates of birth and death, then a series of cryptic alpha-numeric designations. None had lived beyond the age of ten years.

"Look at this, Jim."
He joined her and read down the line. "Cuairt Ghaoth. That means *whirlwind*. Braidseal is *roaring fire*. Uisge Bras Shruth means *waterfall*—no—*a swift moving water*. What are these?"

"I thought they were children's graves, but the names sound more like racehorses. I'm guessing these were dogs, and I think they were American Kennel Club Champions." Each had at least one "CH" in front of a year and what might have been the designation of a particular contest.

"It comes back to me," Ginny said, "that Mrs. Patterson kept Irish wolfhounds. She always had a pair, and I think she showed them. I wonder where the current pair is." She pulled out her phone and took pictures of the stones as she walked down the line. "I had no idea you could read Gaelic."

Jim shrugged. "A bit. Earth, air, fire, and water show up in a number of the old songs."

"Hmm." Ginny concentrated on her photographs. She wanted to show them to a friend of hers who raised dogs and might be able to shed some light on what they were doing in the Patterson Family Cemetery.

She turned the corner at the end of the line, thinking she was done, only to find another line of stones. These were different. There were no uprights and only small flat stones to mark the graves. Each stone had a letter of the Greek alphabet carved on it; alpha through epsilon.

She walked down the line, looking for more stones.

"Jim?"

He left the next-to-last champion and came to join her, looking down at the Greek stones.

"What do you make of these?" she asked. "Placeholders?"

"You mean like they use to mark a fresh grave, until they can put the memorial stone in place?"

"Not one of these is fresh, although they could still be waiting for final markers. Lesser pets, maybe?"

Jim's brow furrowed. "I've buried pets in the backyard, but never felt I had to mark the spot. And these are still inside the pale, where you'd expect to find people, not dogs." He surveyed the area. "This whole setup is screwy."

Ginny walked slowly down the line again, counting carefully, her skin crawling at the idea forming in her mind. "Jim. There are five of them."

He turned to face her. "So?"

"And five missing women."

Jim's jaw dropped. The two of them stared at one another for a full minute in silence, then Jim took her phone and made a series of pictures that showed the location, the way the graves were situated, the relative sizes, and details indicating the length of time since they had been dug. Once that was done, he took her arm and steered her back to the path, then down to the car. They smiled and waved at the housekeeper as they drove off.

"Where are we going?" Ginny asked.

"Grandfather."

On the way to the Laird's house, Ginny called her friend in the dog show business, giving her the names on the tombstones, and was told they were indeed champion Irish wolfhounds.

"I have a question," Jim said. "If it turns out that these are the missing prostitutes, why bury them at all? Why not just dump them somewhere and let nature take its course?"

"Because someone might find the bones."

Jim nodded. "Okay. The only place under Patterson control is the Patterson estate. I get that. But why markers? Why not just let the weeds cover the sites?"

Ginny looked over at him. "To make sure they weren't disturbed. When you see a stone, you know the space is taken."

They explained Ginny's theory to the Laird and watched as he examined the images.

Angus fixed Ginny with his eye. "'Tis quite a theory, lass. Based on Scala's manuscript, is it?"

Ginny nodded.

"And ye'd like tae look inside one o' the graves."

"Yes."

He nodded and reached for the phone. "Ken Muir, please. Ken! Angus. I've a wee proposition tae put tae ye." He explained the situation to the lawyer. When he finished, he put the phone down and turned to face them.

"Ken is o' th' opinion that, as the graves in th' same section of the cemetery are those o' dogs, th' most likely explanation is more o' th' same. 'Tis not necessary tae get a court order tae dig up an animal. 'Tis necessary tha' th' owner o' th' property be present."

"The Pattersons were in Austin last night. We saw them on the news."

Angus nodded. "I'll gie them notice their presence hae been requested."

The next hour was devoted to locating an excavator and driver, a pop-up tent to screen the site from curious eyes, and a specialist who could tell a human skeleton from a canine one.

"We'll also need a videographer, to record the event, just in case," said Ginny.

"And Ken, to make sure everything is done according to Hoyle," Jim added.

"Leave it wi' me," Angus said.

On the way home Jim reached over and laid his hand on Ginny's. "Are you all right?"

She squirmed. "I could be wrong."

He nodded. "Or you could be right. We'll find out tomorrow."

She looked over at him. "I'm beginning to think we owe Larry Scala an apology."

* * *

CHAPTER 35

Sunday morning
Scala's Motel Room

"I'm sorry to get you up so early, Mr. Scala, but Mum insists I show up at church, and the party is right after."

Scala waved away the boy's distress. "No problem. I was up anyway." He had been, too. Trying to figure out how to steer the police investigation in the direction of Maury Patterson, without having to resort to accusing him in public.

"This device was made commercially. Which means it has a serial number and the purchase can be tracked. So if you ever want to do this for real, you'll need to learn how to make the transmitter yourself. It's easy enough to learn. The hard part is controlling the tweezers." Larry handed the device to Tor, so he could examine it closely. The transmitter was only two centimeters in length.

"Wow. So small!"

Larry nodded. "With something this small, the problem is power." He turned the device over and showed the boy how the button battery sat in the slot. "And you won't get any range without an antenna." He indicated the wire projecting from the top of the transmitter and measuring six inches in length. "To get really good reception, this should attach to something that attaches to the structure, like the wires that go to a satellite dish. But even this little one can be picked up from the parking lot."

He slid the device into a waterproof pouch and sealed it with tape. "I've checked this bag for leaks and the thicker the material, the longer it will last. Remember that we're going to hide this in fresh flowers. Someone will add water to the vase at some point, and we want to protect it."

Tor nodded, handing over the bouquet.

Larry undid the package, nestled the listening device in the center, then used more tape to secure it in place. "I painted the antenna wire green so it won't show. We're also going to use a solid color vase, instead of a transparent one." He slid the flowers into the vase and arranged them to cover the wire.

"We'll add water to the bottom, and an aspirin tablet, to keep the flowers fresh. Then we're ready to go."

Larry picked up the receiver. "The last step is to make sure the device is transmitting and that the receiver is tuned into the right UHF setting." He did so, making the receiver squeal. "Now say something."

"This is really nice of you, Mr. Scala." Tor's face lit up as he heard his own voice coming out of the receiver.

Larry grinned. "Your job will be to add these flowers to the table in the reception area, then pick them up and take them away when everyone is leaving, without being noticed. Think you can do that?"

"Yes, sir!"

"Don't get caught using the receiver during the reception. You'd probably be able to argue that no one there had an expectation of privacy, but you don't want it to go to court."

"No, sir." Tor squirmed with excitement.

Larry shook his head. What was it about bending the law that appealed to boys so much? Girls didn't seem so susceptible. Something to do with survival, no doubt.

"When the party is over, take the flowers home. Remove the device. Then give the flowers to your mother. Tell her someone said it was okay. Covering your tracks requires getting ahead of objections. If she sees you with the flowers, she'll ask questions, so make sure she doesn't see you before you're ready to present them to her. Got it?"

"Yes, sir! I can take the bouquet apart in my truck."

"As long as no one sees you doing anything that looks suspicious, that should work. Just remember, there's always someone watching. Cameras are everywhere these days. The secret is to be predictable. You can keep the bug as a reward." He handed the boy the receiver.

"Gee, can I? Thanks Mr. Scala!"

"Now get going. I'll see you at church. And remember! Assume someone is watching and act accordingly."

"I will. Bye."

Scala watched the boy saunter out the side door, carrying the flowers casually in the crook of his arm. He climbed into the truck, put his burden down on the passenger side seat, then pulled out into traffic, moving at an acceptable pace, neither squealing his tires nor creeping along like some little-old-lady. The boy had a real talent for this stuff. Too bad he couldn't ask Tor to take the flowers directly to Patsy's house and see what he could learn by listening in there. But that would be illegal and he didn't want to get the boy in trouble.

Tomorrow he would meet the woman at last. He wouldn't be able to interview her during her own birthday party, but he could ask permission to come visit. Worth a try, anyway. Scala closed the curtain, and headed for the restaurant.

* * *

Sunday morning
St. Columba's Kirk Fellowship Hall

Ginny looked around the Parish Hall thinking that it would be a long time before this event was forgotten. Father Amos had bestowed a birthday blessing on Patsy and the congregation had broken protocol to cheer.

It was standing-room only, so many people had connections to Patsy. So many well-wishers, and not one without a tale to tell. She saw Larry approach Patsy and introduce himself, then smile and leave. Making a date with her, perhaps. Ginny would have to follow up on that. The Pattersons were absent. Still in Austin, perhaps, or in transit.

There was a table set along the back wall, piled high with tributes. Ginny was sure it would take six trips, or at least three cars, to get all the presents back to Patsy's house. She took her punch cup and wandered over to the table, looking at the wrappings and turning over an occasional card.

It was heart-warming, what some of them had written. A last chance to say thank you and goodbye. There was a pretty box marked *Chocolates, Protect from Heat* which turned out to be from Maury Patterson. "To my cousin. Sweets to the sweet. Happy Birthday!" Not very original, but then the old man probably left this sort of thing to his staff. Handwritten, too. Good for him. Ginny moved on.

There were speeches, short ones, and toasts, and a splendid cake that tasted delicious. Ginny stayed for the festivities, then caught Jim's eye. They had an appointment this afternoon. He nodded, then crossed the room to speak to the Laird. Ginny took her leave of Patsy, and headed for the door. Jim met her there.

"It's all set. We have time to change clothes, which I recommend, and pick up a bite to eat."

"Sounds good." Ginny was sure she'd be more comfortable out of her church clothes. She was less sure she wanted to eat. The nerves seemed to be getting to her.

* * *

Sunday afternoon
Patterson Family Cemetery

Jim parked the car on the sweep drive, out of the way, then helped Ginny to her feet. He was being solicitous and she resented it. Well, maybe not. She felt a bit weak in the knees, but was determined not to give in to it.

As many times as Ginny had been in a cemetery, and as many dead bodies as she'd seen at work, she felt unprepared for today. This would be her first exhumation. She pulled in a breath and strode up the drive toward the old stables and the riding path, Jim in her wake.

They had already started, had been at it for at least an hour. She could see the excavator, parked along the back fence, and a large mound of loose dirt beside it. She waited until Jim caught up with her, then slipped her hand into his. He gave it a squeeze.

"Come on," he said.

The tent turned out to be a screen, with two sides open to the air and no roof, but tall enough to stop peeping Toms, even those with long lenses. Ginny and Jim made their way to the far side of the open hole, to join Angus. He was talking quietly with the lawyer. When she got close enough, Ginny could hear their conversation. They were waiting for Maury and Rita to arrive.

". . . dinnae tell them wha' we suspect, just tha' they needed tae be here, tae protect their interests." Angus paused. "Should we hae brought th' police?"

Ken Muir shook his head. "Even if we find evidence of a crime here, it will take a lot more than that to make a case against Patterson."

Ginny caught the lawyer's eye. "Did they object to the search?"

He gave a small shrug. "It doesn't matter whether they object or not. It's in the Home Rule ordinances." He showed her the clause.

> *"Any duly authorized agent of the Loch Lonach Homestead Council shall have the legal right to enter upon the real property of any member of the Loch Lonach Homestead, their guests, assigns, or licensees, for the purposes of emergency, health, safety, management of applicable rules and regulations, or for any lawful reason. Prior notice required except as defined in the public safety statutes described in Section Twelve."*

"Somebody must have seen this coming."

Angus looked at her, a rueful smile playing at his lips. "Th' men wha drew up tha' document understood human nature."

Ginny nodded, then looked around. There were four men in work clothes and hardhats, two of whom were working to attach pulleys to a frame set up over the hole. The other two were in the grave, passing straps underneath the box. They talked quietly among themselves as they worked.

The videographer was monitoring his recording from a laptop set up under the trees. The bone expert was waiting, water bottle in hand. Ginny went over to speak to them.

"Gentlemen."

They nodded without rising.

"Has anyone told you what we are hoping to find?" She frowned. "No. Scratch that. What we're hoping *not* to find."

The bone man's mouth twitched. "Human bones or dog bones." He shrugged. "Though I may need a second opinion."

Ginny nodded, turning to the videographer. "We hope this record will not be needed in any official capacity, but we'd like to be ready if it is."

He nodded. "No fear. Mr. Muir has already explained his requirements." He rose, picked up a hand-held video camera and turned it on. "Whatever the stationary cameras don't get, this will."

"Good. Thank you both for coming." Ginny retired. She got back to Jim's side just as the sound of footsteps reached her ears. The next minute, Maury and Rita Patterson appeared around the edge of the enclosure.

Neither seemed surprised to find the authorities digging in their cemetery. They both looked calm and unconcerned. Ken Muir approached, introduced himself and got Patterson's signature on his authorization papers. Nothing to hide, apparently. Maybe the graves really did contain dogs.

Ginny watched as the box was raised from the depths of the earth. It was maneuvered to the side and lowered onto a pair of trestles set up for the purpose. The men then took up different tools and went to work removing the lid. When they were ready, they slid the top off, set it down out of the way, and moved back.

There was a moment of silence, then everyone moved forward. Everyone except Ginny. The videographer took precedence, making sure he had images of the contents before it was disturbed, then he backed off, his face impassive, his camera panning the people around the box.

Angus and the lawyer peered inside, then exchanged glances and gave way to the bone man. Jim had moved around to the other side of the trestles and was standing quite still, his eyes on whatever lay inside, his face solemn, his expression eloquent.

Maury Patterson had approached with bluster. He was certain the fuss was for nothing. What could they possibly hope to find in a graveyard for dogs? He stepped briskly to the side of the box and looked down.

His face drained of color and he swayed. Jim caught one of Maury's arms and one of the workers hurried to take the other. They led him over to a chair, and sat him down in it. Jim stayed with him.

Ginny's eyes had been on Rita. The third Mrs. Patterson had watched the box as it swung into position and was opened. Rita had lifted her eyes from the box, and found Ginny watching her. They had stared at one another, without blinking, until Maury's attack, at which point Rita moved to his side.

Ginny backed over to the abandoned chairs under the trees and sat down. Jim found her there when Maury had been sent off in a golf cart, to be cared for by the Chancie Mor staff, taking Rita with him.

Jim went down on his heels in front of her. "Are you all right?"

She nodded.

"Do you want to come look?"

Ginny thought about that for a moment, then nodded. "If you will lend me your arm."

Jim helped her climb out of the chair, then slid an arm around her waist. "It's really not bad. The coffin must have been water tight. She's mostly desiccated." He left his arm around her as she peered into the box.

No expense had been spared. The wood of the box was mahogany, carved, and embellished. It was four feet long, three feet wide, and two feet deep. Spacious accommodations intended for a beloved pet. The interior was even lined with fabric, as human coffins are.

Blonde hair, very white teeth, curled up on her side as if asleep. Her clothes were beginning to come apart, but she had obviously not been stripped. Except of her jewelry, if she'd been wearing any.

The breeze shifted the trees above Ginny's head, which, in turn, rippled the sunlight filtering down onto the site. Ginny caught a glint, a reflection of some sort, and peered closer. "She's wearing a watch." Her brow furrowed. "No, it's an exercise tracker. I wonder why they left it on her wrist."

"Maybe they didn't see it. Her sleeve might have covered it."

"A dark shirt, black or navy, and the tracker is black. Yes, I can believe that." She looked across the coffin at Ken Muir. "Can we take it? After the forensic people get finished with the scene, of course."

"Why would you want to?"

"Because I use something similar and the businesses that sell the service keep their records for years. If Reggie can get it to work, we may be able to find out when it stopped recording her heart beat."

"Time of death. Clever. I'll see what I can arrange."

Jim stirred at her side. "It's getting late, love, and I have to work tonight. Let's go home."

"I thought this was your weekend off."

"I swapped shifts so I could have next Sunday off, to attend the play."

Ginny nodded, then said goodbye to Angus and the others. They would be busy for many hours securing the scene, and exhuming the remaining four coffins. Her presence was not needed.

They were halfway home before she spoke. "This changes things."

"It does indeed."

"I don't know whether Tran is going to be pleased or angry with me, now that we have physical evidence."

"That might depend on what the forensic lab finds."

"Yes, but there's more."

"What? More evidence?"

"It should show on the video."

"What should?"

"Guilty knowledge. I was watching the faces. Maury didn't know what we were going to find in that box. He was genuinely shocked to see a woman lying there."

Jim nodded. "I can attest to that."

"Which means he wasn't in on the body disposal. So there's something else we can't pin on him."

Jim frowned. "True. What's your point?"

"Maury didn't know, but Rita did."

* * *

ChAPTER 36

Jim Mackenzie picked up the next chart in line and headed for the exam room. He glanced at the patient's name as he walked, then paused outside the door, to see what had brought her to the emergency room. Syncope, possible fall injuries, x-rays pending.

Jim knocked on the door and entered, finding an RN in attendance on Patsy Olafsson. The nurse looked up.

"BP 142/86, pulse 92, resp 22. Alert and oriented. PERRLA. Sensation intact." The nurse charted the results of her assessment, then moved to help Jim look the old woman over.

Patsy smiled. "Dr. Mackenzie! I haven't had a chance to thank you and your wife for the lovely flowers. I got so many bouquets, and so many presents today. It will take me a month to write all the *thank you* notes. But yours were perfect. How did you know I liked bluebonnets?"

"That was Ginny. You must have mentioned it to her because she made sure the florist would order them in time for your birthday."

"Well, please tell her how much I appreciate her effort, and her remembering. It's been years since I went out into the fields to pick bluebonnets. It brought back such pleasant memories!"

"I'll tell her, but I expect you can tell her yourself on Tuesday. Don't you have another session coming up?" While he chatted with Patsy, Jim was doing his own assessment, looking for evidence of broken bones or bleeding. "Follow my finger." No evidence that she had hit her head, and none of a broken pelvis, but he'd ordered the x-rays to make sure. Sometimes the little old ladies didn't know what hurt until the next day.

He peered into her ears and checked her skull for tender spots, then examined each limb, asking her to move the joints and checking to make sure the nerves were still intact.

"Ouch!" She pulled her hand up to her chest when he released it.

"That hurts?"

"Yes. I think I landed on it."

Jim nodded, adding some additional x-ray views of the wrist. The nurse took the order and entered it into the computer system.

When Jim was done poking, prodding, and listening, he sat down to type up his notes.

"Your hemoglobin and white blood cell counts are both low. I'll call Dr. Weisbrod in the morning and discuss medication changes with him, if that's all right with you."

"Whatever you say." Patsy looked from Jim to the nurse and beamed. "I'm not going to argue with angels sent from Heaven."

The nurse grinned. "Angels, huh?"

"Well, saints anyway. I can see your halos. Bright yellow. They're very pretty."

Jim's head came up. Had he missed something? He went back and looked at Patsy's eyes again. "Let's add a head CT, Marcie, and seizure precautions."

"Do you want to admit her?"

"Not until I see the results, then I'll decide."

"All right. They can do the dig level on the blood already in the lab."

Jim blinked. "She's not on digoxin."

The nurse raised her eyebrows. "Are you sure?"

Jim turned to Patsy. "Are you on any heart medicines? I didn't see any when I was looking at your bedside table, but I might have missed one."

Patsy shook her head. "No. Nothing like that."

Jim looked back at the nurse.

"It's a sign of digoxin toxicity," she explained. "Yellow or green vision disturbances."

Jim nodded slowly. "I've seen it in the literature, but I've never encountered it in a patient before."

Marcie shrugged. "I have."

"Okay. Add a dig level and let's get a twelve-lead EKG." He stood up and patted Patsy's shoulder. "I'll be back when I've seen the results of all these tests. Let Marcie know if you need anything."

Half an hour later Jim was staring at the lab results for Patsy's digoxin level. Elevated, though not critically. Not enough to require the antidote. Enough to slow her heart rate, which would drop her blood pressure, and would explain the dizziness. But how had it gotten into her system?

Jim strode out into the waiting room and looked around. He found Patsy's day shift caregiver sitting in the corner, a magazine in her lap, a worried expression on her face. She glanced at her watch as he approached.

"Violet?"

She looked up, then sprang to her feet. "Dr. Mackenzie! How is she?"

"We're still doing tests. Can you tell me what happened?" Jim sat down beside her and listened to Violet's description of the day. "Did you notice anything out of the ordinary?"

She stared at him. "Everything was out of the ordinary! We went to the party and there were all those people and the cake and champagne."

Jim nodded. "Tell me about the fall."

"She needed to go to the bathroom and I helped her in, then went to get some clean linen. Before I got back I heard a crash. I found her on the floor. I think she hit her head on the tub."

"Did she lose consciousness?"

"No." Violet shook her head.

"Was there anything that looked like a seizure?"

"No."

"Did she say how she fell?"

"She said she got dizzy and her heart felt funny."

"Did she go blue, or complain of pain in her chest? Anything like that?"

"Just the dizziness."

"Do you give her her medications?"

"Yes. I do during the daytime and Priscilla does at night, unless one of us is off, in which case the agency will send another nurse."

"So you know what she's taking."

"Yes, sir."

"And you know how to read a prescription bottle."

"Of course." She looked indignant and Jim hurried to explain.

"Do any of her medications have digoxin in them?"

Violet didn't hesitate. "No."

Jim sucked in a breath. "Okay, one more question. Was there anything she ate or drank today that no one else had?"

"What?"

"The cake and champagne and other edibles at the church

were out where everyone could help themselves. So that pretty much eliminates them as the source. Did she eat or drink anything after she got home?"

Violet had gone pale. "Source of what?"

"Mrs. Olafsson had digoxin in her blood. It made her dizzy. Since she wasn't on a prescription, we need to identify the source. Think carefully. Did she eat or drink anything that no one else touched, maybe after she got home."

Violet's brow furrowed. "Mrs. O. said she didn't want lunch, she was full of party food."

"Okay, so nothing out of her kitchen. Anything else?"

Violet thought for a moment, then her eyes grew round. "The chocolates! She got them as a birthday present. Good ones, too. You know. The kind you have to pay a lot of money for. She ate one and said they were delicious."

Jim nodded. "Violet, will you do me a favor? I need to test those chocolates. Will you go to Mrs. O.'s house and get them and bring them to me here?"

Violet jumped up, tossing the magazine aside. "I'll be right back."

When Violet reappeared, this time with the box of chocolates, Jim thanked her and told her he'd decided to keep Mrs. Olafsson in the hospital overnight. She should check with the agency before reporting for work tomorrow and send the night nurse home, as well.

That done, he considered what to do about the chocolates. He opened the box to find six chocolates nestled in the colored tissue paper. Unfortunately, he couldn't tell how many had been in the original package. It wasn't the kind of box that had indentations for each piece. So he couldn't estimate the dose, unless Patsy remembered how many pieces she had eaten. When asked, she said six pieces. She hadn't meant to be so greedy, but they were delicious. She had paid the price though.

They'd made her feel queasy. Just like when she was a girl and ate too much candy.

Jim explained about the digoxin level in her blood and reassured her that they would take good care of her. But he warned her that they'd have to draw more blood to check on her and that she wouldn't be allowed to go home until the digoxin level was back to normal.

She blinked. "There was a drug in the chocolates?"

"I think so, but we can't know for sure until they're tested and that can't be done tonight." He'd already decided it was a police matter. "Can you remember who gave you the chocolates?"

Patsy nodded. "It was a very generous gift." Her brow furrowed. "But I don't want you thinking I notice things like that. It's just that I know those chocolates and I know what they cost and it was very thoughtful of him to choose my favorites."

"Who sent them, Patsy?"

"Cousin Maury, of course."

* * *

CHAPTER 37

Monday afternoon
Mackenzie residence

Ginny worked a full shift on Monday and didn't get home until close to four p.m. She hadn't spoken to Jim since he'd left for work the evening before. She hadn't tried to call him either, knowing he would be asleep most of the day, and might still be, if he'd had a hard night. But when she got home, she found her husband lying in wait. He pounced as she came through the door.

"Welcome home, darling. Did you have a good day? I hope you're not too tired because I've made an appointment for us, with Detective Tran. Come on."

He turned her around and escorted her into his car.

Ginny gaped. "What's going on?"

"I'll tell you when we get there."

"You haven't forgotten we have dinner with the Hunters tonight."

"I have not."

Jim made short work of the drive to the police substation, announced their arrival, and signed them in. Three minutes later they were seated in Detective Tran's office, with the desk recorder turned on. She looked at the two of them, her mouth twitching.

"Now, Dr. Mackenzie, what is it you wish to share with me?"

"Maury Patterson tried to poison Patsy Olafsson yesterday. With these." He handed the box of chocolates over.

Ginny caught her breath. Poison!

Detective Tran's eyes widened slightly. "What should the forensics team look for?"

"Digoxin. It's a cardiac glycoside. We use it to slow the heart beat and increase the strength of the myocardial contractions. Patsy fell at home and was brought to the ER. We found the drug in her bloodstream. It's not in any of her prescriptions."

Detective Tran folded her hands on the desk. "How did you identify the chocolates?"

"Her caregiver, Violet, remembered Patsy remarking on what a nice birthday present they made."

"And you are accusing Senator Patterson because?"

"The chocolates came with a card saying they were from him."

"I see." Detective Tran turned to look at Ginny, who spread her hands.

"It's the first I've heard of it."

"The card is inside the box," Jim said.

Detective Tran's brow wrinkled. "And what is it you are asking me to do?"

Jim's eyebrows rose. "Search his house, of course. Doesn't this give you probable cause?"

"To search Senator Patterson's house for digoxin? Possibly. But I have concerns about the timing."

Ginny nodded. "We find five women buried in Patterson's backyard on Sunday and he tries to kill Patsy the same day? Is that just a coincidence?"

Jim waved his hand, brushing the objection aside. "The poison could have been prepared weeks ago. The drug is stable at room temperature. And he could not have known we would discover those bodies the same day as Patsy's birthday party. You hadn't even come up with your theory until the day before."

Ginny nodded. "True."

"But?" Tran asked.

Ginny squirmed. "Larry Scala predicted there would be an attack on Patsy. He suggested arranging one."

"Maybe he did." Jim's brow furrowed. "I wonder if his DNA is on the chocolates, or the birthday card."

Detective Tran nodded. "I believe I will need to investigate after all. Thank you for coming in. Dr. Mackenzie, I must ask you to complete a witness statement before you leave, and I will be requesting medical records to support your assertions."

"Of course."

Detective Tran handed them off to another officer who helped Jim pull up the forms on the computer, answered questions, and watched as he signed his statement. After which they barely had time to hurry home and get changed for the planned dinner party at the Hunters'.

Ginny glanced over at her husband. "Are you going to tell him?"

"Huh? Who? Tell him what?"

"Are you going to tell Ian about Patterson, about the bodies in the dog cemetery, and the poison, and what happened to Marilee?"

Jim frowned. "Yes. I'm convinced this whole thing is tied up in that political race. In which case, Ian is the target. And, since he won't back down, I think he has a right to know what Patterson's been up to."

"Patterson—or Scala!"

* * *

Monday night
Hunter residence

Ginny and Jim were seated in the Hunter's living room, sipping after-dinner beverages.

Ian frowned. "Are you telling me he's done this before?"

Jim nodded. He'd explained about the blackmail.

"That's election tampering."

"Yes, but difficult to prove without evidence."

Ian's frown deepened. "How did he get away with it?"

"The reporter asked the same question. He even tried to interview the political rivals, but none of them would talk."

"They were afraid of something. Something more important than their political careers."

"So it appears."

"Why didn't he interview the prostitutes? They could at least have laid the groundwork for the election committees to follow up on."

"Each of the prostitutes disappeared and Scala wasn't able to find out what happened to them." Jim paused, then took a breath. "But we were."

Lola's eyes had grown large as she listened to Jim's recitation. She set her coffee cup down on the table with a rattle, then apologized for the interruption. Ian glanced at her, then reached out and took her hand.

"It was Ginny who figured it out," Jim said. "We found the bodies of all five missing prostitutes buried on the Patterson estate. They were killed and the bodies hidden in a place no one was supposed to look, the canine section of the Patterson family cemetery."

There was silence for a moment, then Ian swallowed. "What about the one who tried to blackmail me? You were going to go talk to her, weren't you?"

Jim nodded. "I met and spoke with her. She packed a bag and was on her way to visit relatives when she was kidnapped."

"Kidnapped!"

Jim nodded again. "We had a tail on her, to make sure she actually left town, and he and I followed the van. There was construction and an accident. Everyone in the van was killed on impact."

"So we can't talk to her, either."

"I did talk to her. She said the photographs sent to Lola were fakes. And she told me she failed to find a chink in your armor. She refused to tell me who had hired her, but when I told her what Maury Paterson has been up to, she paled. She covered it pretty well, but I know shock when I see it."

Ian nodded. "I've heard from the police about those faked photographs. The forensics specialist said there are too many people in the world with that skill set to be able to track down the perpetrator. They're working on the delivery boy angle, but so far no clues there, either." He hesitated.

"I've talked to Angus and he tells me I should level with you. There've been other things." Ian proceeded to tell Jim and Ginny about the attack on his house, about how his car had been defaced with racial epitaphs while parked in the Capital building lot in Austin, about being shouted down at public appearances, and pelted with rotting vegetable matter when he was speaking, and about the social media campaign raging online. "And the death threats come daily."

Ginny felt her stomach clench. She looked at Lola and saw her nod.

"There is one bright spot in all of this," Ian said. "The full force of the law is working to catch these hooligans. There have been several arrests made and a few of the weaker ones have talked."

"Like that one who ended up in the Hillcrest ICU," Ginny

said.

"Yes. The money to pay for all these attacks is coming from Patterson. Not his campaign funds, of course. His personal bank account."

"I thought paid political protestors was a myth," Jim said.

"These people are not hired actors, and hiring someone to organize a protest doesn't rise to the level of criminal behavior. Organizing a drive-by shooting does."

"Can you prove that?" Ginny asked.

Ian nodded. "I've got contacts in the white collar crime world, on the investigation side. They tell me the paper trail is there. What may be tricky is connecting the Patterson estate money to Maury himself. There are a lot of layers of protection in place."

Ginny sighed. "Poor Larry. He never had a chance."

"Larry?" Lola asked.

"Larry Scala, the investigative reporter. He's spent his whole life trying to prove Maury Patterson is a criminal, but he never had the resources. All he had was what he could find out for himself." Ginny shared the parts of Scala's manuscript Jim hadn't yet mentioned. Lola's eyes grew large.

"Patterson killed his own sister?"

Ginny nodded. "His mother covered up for him, and that's not the only time. Larry thinks Mrs. Patterson cleaned up Maury's messes all the way up until she died. And we have reason to believe she started while they were still living here in Loch Lonach."

"Go on," Ian said.

Ginny glanced at Jim and saw him nod. She took a breath. "There is a candlestick with blood on it, Tommy Bryant's blood, and Maury Patterson's fingerprints. Tommy was Maury's first cousin. He died of a blow to the head in the library of Chancie Mor. The death was ruled an accident, a slip and fall, but Mrs.

Patterson hid the other candlestick of the pair, then accused a housemaid of stealing them. We believe Letitia Patterson knew Maury had killed his cousin and she was covering up for him. Very soon after the incident, the family left Loch Lonach and moved to Illinois.

"The bloody candlestick was hidden by the dead child's sister, Patsy. She suppressed the memory of that night for fifty years, but her subconscious got the better of her. She dug it out and sent it to me as a wedding present."

Lola gasped. "Oh! How horrible!"

Ginny gave her a half a smile. "In her defense, Patsy was sleep-walking at the time and didn't know what she was doing. The problem is that Maury found out about it and is now trying to kill her, presumably to keep her from testifying."

Ian's brow descended. "This man must not be allowed to gain a political foothold in Texas."

The other three nodded.

"But how can we prevent it?" Lola asked.

Ginny answered. "I have confidence in the police. It may take a while, but they'll be able to connect Maury to his criminal behavior."

Ian nodded. "I'm sure you're right, but it might not be soon enough. The election is in six weeks."

* * *

CHAPTER 38

Tuesday morning
Mackenzie residence

Jim rolled over, stretching as he rose to consciousness. He'd been dreaming about the sailboat. He smiled. He was looking forward to teaching Ginny how to sail. It was something they could do together. He'd watched as Wade Bryant explained how the steering worked, watched as she moved the tiller and processed how the boat responded. She had a good head on her shoulders, and courage. He had no doubt she'd make a good sailor.

He heard the toilet flush and tucked his hands under his head, waiting for Ginny to come back to bed. She was not a morning person and he knew she'd go back to sleep, if he let her.

When she didn't appear, he opened his eyes, frowning to himself. Had he forgotten an appointment? Something that forced her to sneak out of bed and dress in the bathroom, so she didn't wake him? He threw back the covers and slid his feet to the floor, looking around. No clue in this room, except her dressing gown was gone from the foot of the bed. He slid into his own, padded over to the bathroom door, and tapped on it.

"Ginny?" There was no response.

He was already getting accustomed to her non-verbal

responses in the early hours of the day. Any conversation before coffee was a struggle, but the sound that reached his ears was not her usual mumble.

"Ginny?" He tapped again, then put his hand on the door handle. It opened easily.

She was kneeling on the floor of the bathroom, leaning against the side of the toilet, her head down on her arms, shivering.

"Ginny!"

He grabbed a blanket off the bed and wrapped her in it, then wetted a washcloth and wiped her face before applying it to the back of her neck. When he was sure she was done vomiting, he eased her into a sitting position with her back against the wall. She drew her knees up, wrapped her arms around them, then put her head down and closed her eyes.

Jim, fully aware of how nausea worked, settled down on the floor facing her and waited for her to speak. When she lifted her head and looked at him, he smiled.

"Feel better?"

"Not really. Not yet, anyway."

Jim knew he was breathing faster than usual. He could feel his heart rate jump, the excitement coursing through his veins. And he couldn't stop smiling. "Do you have something you want to tell me?"

She closed her eyes. "Like what?"

Jim lifted an eyebrow at her. "You're planning a nursery and your period was due on the nineteenth."

She opened her eyes, her brow furrowing. "You're keeping track?"

"An occupational hazard. I told you there would be no secrets between us. Not the medical kind, anyway."

She looked uncertain. "I've been under some stress."

"I'm aware of it, but the timing is suggestive."

"You think this is morning sickness?"

"Unless you ate something that disagreed with you, yes."

"Oh, Jim!"

He moved over beside her and took her in his arms. "Darling, wonderful, marvelous, precious Ginny! My love, my treasure, my wife! I'm thrilled! I couldn't be happier!"

She curled up against him. "So soon? We've been married, what, three weeks? I thought I'd have more time to get used to my new life."

"This is part of our new life, making a new life."

She looked up at him. "Three weeks! Is anyone going to believe you managed to get me with child on our wedding night?"

Jim laughed, then kissed her. "Your OB will. She knows you weren't pregnant when you and I did the genetic screening, and she can count. We need to make an appointment with her."

Ginny nodded, then frowned suddenly. "Jim!"

"Yes, my love?"

"Promise not to tell anyone, not even Angus, until I'm out of the first trimester."

"Why not?"

"The book said the first trimester was the most dangerous. Suppose I lose the baby? I can't think of anything worse than having to send back gifts and congratulations."

He pulled her close. "You are *not* going to lose this baby."

"Promise me! I don't want to tempt fate. Chalk it up to superstition, but promise me!"

He hugged her, rocking back and forth with her in his arms. "All right, my love. I promise. No one shall know until you and Dr. Berry tell me it's safe to do so." He held her for a few minutes more, then rose, scooped her up, and carried her into the bedroom, settling her against the pillows. "Stay right there.

I'll be back in a minute."

He strode to the kitchen, located saltine crackers and ginger ale, took them back to the bedroom and set them on her bedside table. "Here, nibble on these."

She gave him a wan smile, then did as instructed, moving slowly, but able to keep them down.

He sat there, smiling at her, thinking about all the changes ahead. It would be a whole new world for both of them. He'd been reading up on pregnancy and parenting, but there was still plenty to learn. Usually, when a woman showed up in his emergency room and was found to be expecting, he was allowed to send her home in the care of her family. This time, *he* was the family.

"Is there any reason you can't stay home today and catch up on your sleep?"

"I have an appointment to help Chris with Patsy this morning."

"I can handle that. You need to rest as much as possible during this first trimester. I won't be able to write you a doctor's excuse to miss work—not if you won't let me tell anyone why—but I can make your days off easier."

She made a face at him. "It could still be a stomach virus!"

"All the more reason to stay home and sleep."

"All right." She snuggled down in the bed, the color in her face approaching normal. Jim tucked her in, made sure she had everything she could want, then dressed quickly and left her, closing the door behind him.

The appointment with Chris and Patsy was for ten a.m. While he was out, he could swing by the drug store and pick up one of those home pregnancy kits. Ginny was right to want confirmation. Most couples spent months trying to conceive.

There were stories, of course, of the exceptional virility of Scottish males. It was said a Scotsman could impregnate a

Incarnadine

woman with just one look, from across the room. And it was scientific fact that wearing kilts, which kept the scrotum cool, increased sperm count and quality, resulting in significantly higher rates of fertility. So why should he be surprised?

He fed himself breakfast, peeked in on her, secured the house, and headed out, feeling ridiculously pleased with himself. The truth of the matter was, he was going to be disappointed if it turned out to be just a bug.

* * *

Tuesday morning
Olafsson residence

Jim watched from across the room as Chris Urquhart reduced the lighting in Patsy's bedroom, gave her a half-dose of the same medication that had triggered her sleep-walking, then began to talk her into a semi-slumbering state. It took him ten minutes.

She had recovered from the digoxin with no apparent ill effects, though it would be another day before her kidneys eliminated all the drug from her system. Jim had noted a lower-than-hoped for glomerular filtration rate on her labs. A result of the chemotherapy, no doubt.

"Patsy, can you hear me?" Chris asked.

She nodded, her eyes closed.

She was fully dressed and sitting in an easy chair, looking better than Jim had yet seen her. The three physicians, Chris, Jim, and Dr. Weisbrod, had put their heads together and, with Patsy's permission, made changes to her treatment regimen. She was no longer on chemotherapy or radiation treatments. They had moved to the palliative stage, which meant they would keep her comfortable, but not try to control the cancer.

Her blood count was rising and with it her strength. It wouldn't last, but it would give her the energy she needed to make her final arrangements.

"You can talk to me," Chris told her. "It's safe to tell me what happened. You're safe. No one can hurt you while I'm here."

Her brow furrowed and she sighed, but her eyes remained closed.

They had discussed, again, whether it was necessary to reach this buried memory and Patsy had listened, then asked that they continue. She felt she owed it to her brother, she said.

"Do you remember sending the candlestick to Ginny Forbes?"

"Yes."

Chris's voice was warm, and slow, and calming. "Why did you send it to her?"

"It was time."

"Time for what?"

Patsy opened her eyes, her mouth trying to form words, but unable to do so. Jim watched in fascination.

"What happened, Patsy?"

She raised her hands in front of her face and stared at them. "What? Will these hands ne'er be clean?"

Jim exchanged startled glances with Chris.

Patsy rubbed a place on her hand, scrubbing at it. "Out! Out, damned spot!"

Jim recognized the lines—Lady Macbeth in the sleepwalking scene.

Patsy rose from her chair and Chris moved swiftly to make sure she didn't fall. She took a step, then another, then faced Chris.

"He's buried and cannot come out o' his grave." Her brow

furrowed, her empty eyes looking around the room. "No, that's not right." She lapsed into silence.

Chris lifted an eyebrow at Jim. "I feel like the physician in *Macbeth*, 'you have known what you should not'."

Jim silently agreed.

Chris gently steered Patsy back to her chair, then pulled his own chair closer. He addressed her again. "Why did you send the candlestick to Ginny?"

She made eye contact with Chris. If Jim hadn't known better, he'd have sworn she was fully awake.

"It had blood on it."

"Whose blood?"

"Tommy's."

Jim caught his breath. Ginny was going to be sorry she'd missed this interview.

"Why did you have the candlestick?"

"I was hiding it."

"Who were you hiding it from?"

"Mother."

"Why did you decide to bring it out of hiding?"

She swallowed, her brow furrowing. "It was time."

"Time to tell the truth?"

She nodded.

"Who told you to hide the candlestick?"

"He did."

"Who did?"

But at this point Patsy closed her eyes and mouth tightly, and shrank from the questioning. Chris tried several variations, but got nothing further from her on the identity of the other person.

"It's all right, Patsy. You don't have to tell me. Let's talk about the other night. Do you remember seeing a face in your window?"

She nodded. "Yes."

"Did the face scare you?"

"Yes."

"Why did the face scare you?"

"He said—he said—"

But here, too, Patsy stuck and could go no further. What's more, she started shaking. There was sweat on her forehead and tears leaked out from behind tightly closed eyelids. "Don't hurt me! I won't tell, I promise!" Her voice had risen at least an octave in pitch and she sounded like a child, a very frightened child.

Chris relented. "It's all right, Patsy. He's not here. He can't hurt you." He talked her back down, into a safe, refreshing slumber, then turned her over to the caregiver, and motioned Jim to follow him into the kitchen.

"I'm going to send a copy of that recording to the Laird. Do you have anything you want to add?"

Jim shook his head. "Is she going to remember any of this?"

Chris nodded. "Eventually. Part of her wants to. Part of her is still afraid of him. And it doesn't count as evidence unless she's awake and in her right mind when she names that other person, whoever he may be. We'll just have to keep trying."

* * *

Tuesday evening
Mackenzie residence

It was dinnertime. Ginny had slept on and off for most of the day, and Jim had hunted up, then prepared, a mild noodle with sauce meal for her, one that shouldn't cause problems. She had no fever and she had not vomited again.

"I'm fine, Jim. I feel fine."

He smiled at her across the table.

"You don't have to fuss over me."

"I want to."

She frowned. "So what have you been doing all day?"

After the meeting with Chris and Patsy, and while Ginny slept, Jim had taken the opportunity to go up to the dry dock and lend a hand on the restoration. He pulled out a list and explained what had been done, what remained to be done, the materials needed, the timeline, and the work the restorer had suggested the two of them contribute.

"I can help with the painting—and organizing the cupboards."

Jim nodded. "You have a gift for it, I know." He wrote a note to that effect on his paper. September! She wouldn't even show three months from now. He would have to have a private conversation with Dr. Berry about what would and would not be safe for Ginny to do. Paint fumes might not make the list.

"Saosainn." She rolled the word around in her mouth. "SOOR-sheen. It's a lovely name for a sailboat. I'm glad you don't want to change it." She smiled at him over her fork.

A name! Well, if it was a boy, that was easy. He'd be Angus James Mackenzie, the Fifth. But what if it was a girl? What would he like his daughter to be called? His daughter! Jim found himself forgetting to eat. A daughter. What was so special about a girl, a baby girl? He found his heart melting at the thought. He put his eyes on his meal and concentrated, giving Ginny a chance to do the same. It would be up to him to take care of them both, mother and child, now and in the future. That included proper nutrition, and a good example of table manners. Jim grinned to himself. Was he becoming his mother or his father, or both?

"Are you all right, Jim?"

He looked up swiftly. "Me? I'm fine. Couldn't be better.

Why do you ask?"

"Because you have a weird expression on your face. Because of the house, and the boat, and learning to be laird. Because you married me. Because I don't want anything to change, and it will, it has to, and it's all going to fall on your shoulders."

He rose from his chair and came around to her, kissing her hands, then taking her in his arms. "I know. I also know not all change is for the better, but this is." He had purchased more than one of the pregnancy tests. The instructions said the best time to try was in the morning, with the first void. If tonight didn't answer his question, they could try again in the morning, but he didn't want to wait that long. "Shall we go test the waters?"

Ginny didn't keep him waiting. And there was no question about the result. It was positive. Unless Dr. Berry said otherwise, they were expecting their first child.

Jim wrapped his arms around his wife and held her, murmuring to her. He brushed her face with his fingertips, smiling into her eyes, his heart racing at the thought of the new life growing within her. A child, *their* child, her child and his.

He slid his hand onto her belly, coming to rest over where the child lay. "It has begun."

She nodded, placing her hand on top of his.

"But, Jim, remember your promise. Not a word to anyone. Not yet."

"I remember."

She leaned against him for a moment, then broke out of his arms, and turned to face him. "Don't you want to hear what I did today?"

"In addition to sleep?"

"Yes, in addition to loafing in bed without a thought for the rest of the world."

Jim grinned. "That sounds like something I should put on my list of things to do, and soon."

"I recommend it."

"Okay, what else did you do?"

"I did some research on Rita Patterson."

"Oh?" Jim followed his wife from the bedroom to the kitchen and helped her to more ginger ale.

"It turns out she comes from a very prominent family, with quite a colorful history."

"Colorful?"

"Powerful, with the kind of connections that can get things done. And there's no shortage of money, which explains her clothes."

Jim was momentarily lost. "Her clothes?"

Ginny smiled. "Never mind, darling. You don't need to know how much her shoes cost. Suffice it to say, she's loaded."

"Interesting. What else?"

"Her father is a very powerful man, with business interests in many states, but none, up to now, in Texas."

"Ah ha! And he wants to expand."

Ginny nodded. "The scuttlebutt from the Edinburgh Homestead is that he's using Maury to gain access to the Texas business network. And my sources say he is working through Rita."

"Wow. So the heiress marries a senator and then the two of them get sent to Texas to establish a branch office."

Ginny nodded. "But wait! There's more! Detective Tran called. She wanted to let us know the digoxin was Letitia's. The police found an almost empty pill bottle in her bedroom. The chocolates were purchased with a credit card issued to Maury Patterson, and it's linked to a bank account also issued to Maury Patterson. Both accounts were set up five years ago and there have been no irregularities. She'll let us know when they find out more."

"So Maury bought the chocolates, laced them with his mother's digoxin, and hand delivered the package to the church." Jim's brow wrinkled. "You know what bothers me about that theory?"

"What?"

"It's not his M.O. He strangled all five girls we found. Well, one had her neck broken, but all died of violence to the throat and neck. Why change what has worked for him in the past?"

"That's easy. Patsy has been protected every minute, and even if he could get to her, he couldn't whisk her body away without someone noticing. He's not in control of the scene this time."

Jim nodded. "Okay. I'll buy that. It was a target of opportunity. He found his mother's pills and decided to use them."

Jim's attention was caught by the red-gold braid cascading over his wife's shoulder, rising and falling with her breathing. A redhead. He hoped the baby would be a redhead.

"That's not what bothers me," Ginny said.

"And what does, my love?"

"Why it was necessary to attack Patsy at all. She's dying of cancer. All he had to do was wait."

Jim brought his mind back to the problem. He'd asked himself the same question. "I think he's afraid Patsy will tell on him before she dies."

"For fifty years she hasn't told anyone what happened that night. Why does he assume she will now?"

"Perhaps it's because, at long last, someone is asking."

* * *

CHAPTER 39

Wednesday noon
Mackenzie residence

On Wednesday morning, Ginny went to work, putting in a half-day on the preceptor training project. It was shaping up nicely. She would have months of shake-down to do before the program could be considered ready for automatic implementation, and she was being required to keep records and write up the results as part of the price for a flexible schedule. But it was looking good and she was getting positive feedback from the participants.

She tossed her keys onto the table and went in search of her husband. She found him in the kitchen, helping himself to lunch. He looked up and smiled at her.

He had risen early and fed her with ginger tea and toast—in bed—this morning, and it had helped enormously. Useful to have an educated man around the house. According to the experts, the morning sickness would get worse, peak around the seventh or eighth week, then taper off and be gone in time for the second trimester. Something to get through and something to look forward to. In the meantime, here was the father of her child, smiling at her. She smiled back.

"How'd it go?" he asked.

"Fine. No problems with the nurses and no problems with

my stomach."

"I'm glad to hear it." He set a plate down on the table and indicated it was for her.

Ginny sat down and inspected the soup and salad. Perfect! She helped herself to a slice of bread from the basket and dug in. "Ummm. Delicious!" She smiled at him over her spoon. "What have you been up to while my back was turned?"

"They delivered the garage and are in the process of setting it up. By the time the concrete is dry enough to park on, we'll have a roof as well."

"So progress is being made."

"On that project, yes."

Ginny lifted her head. "Not elsewhere?"

Jim sighed. "I've been trying to figure out how we can connect Patterson to all of these incidents."

"One will do."

"True, but Mrs. Patterson must have had good legal advisors. Maury is as slippery as an eel when it comes to prosecution."

Ginny waited for him to elaborate.

"Grandfather has been in touch with the Illinois lairds, all of them, and gotten polite regrets. They are all familiar with Patterson. He's a lost sheep after all. And he's been accused many times of all sorts of crimes, but nothing ever sticks."

Ginny wrinkled her nose. "If the locals can't pin anything on him, I don't see how we're going to." She shook her head. "Every way we turn we hit a dead end."

Jim sat back in his chair. "Maybe not. After what I heard Patsy say yesterday, I'm convinced she knows who killed her brother."

Ginny caught her breath. "She said something! Tell me!"

Jim grinned. "You're incorrigible, you know that?"

"I know, but you were warned and married me anyway, so

tell me what happened!"

"She admitted to Chris that it was Tommy's blood on the candlestick. And she admitted that someone—a male someone—had scared her, threatened to hurt her. That was as far as we got."

"But it's progress!"

"Chris wants to meet with Patsy again, but neither of us is free this Friday, so he's going to have to wait, or proceed without us."

"He's recording the sessions, isn't he?"

"Yes."

"And he's a doctor."

"Of course."

"So all he needs is someone to sit in and make sure there is no misconduct on his part. Violet can do that."

Jim lifted an eyebrow at her. "What a prurient mind you have."

Ginny sniffed. "Standard operating procedure, to protect the innocent."

"True." Jim sighed, then shook his head. "I feel as if I'm missing something."

"Whatever it is, darling, it will come to you. I have faith."

"Sweet of you." Jim cleared his dishes off the table. "That's all I can think of at the moment. Dinner at four?"

"Yes and two a.m. lunch at the hospital."

He came over and took her in his arms. "Which leaves us five hours before getting ready to go to work." He bent to kiss her. "I want you to take a nap."

Ginny leaned against him and considered his advice. She had never been a fan of napping. She was too afraid she'd miss something. But it would be a big part of her life once the every-two-hours feeding schedule began. It might be a good idea to get in some practice.

"Only if you come with me."

His dimple flashed. "I'll lower the portcullis and raise the drawbridge."

"And I will shutter the sun."

She lifted her face to his and closed her eyes, surrendering to his wishes and to the warmth of his embrace. Their lips met and she could hear bells. Bells? A bell. The doorbell!

* * *

Wednesday afternoon
Mackenzie residence

The doorbell rang again, but Jim didn't let her go. "Ignore it!"

Ginny kissed him. "I can't do that. It might be Himself."

"I don't care who it is, send them away!"

Ginny giggled, pushing herself out of his arms. "Come on. You can be my bouncer." She led him to the front door, then peeked through the viewfinder.

"It's Larry!"

"Let him get his own girl."

"And he has someone with him."

Jim stopped nuzzling Ginny's neck and looked up. "Who?"

"A young man, a stranger to me."

Jim sighed, then let her go. "All right. Let them in."

Ginny opened the door and smiled at the visitors. "Good afternoon."

The young man blushed and shuffled his feet. "Good afternoon, Mrs. Mackenzie."

Larry lifted an amused eyebrow. "This is my assistant, Tor McLeish. The laird graciously assigned him to help me in my investigation. May we come in?"

"Of course." Ginny stepped back, then gestured toward the

kitchen. "May I get you something to drink?" The day was warming up.

"Yes, please," said Tor. "No, thank you," said Larry.

Ginny ignored Larry, seated them all around the kitchen table, then produced a pitcher of iced tea. She focused on Tor first. "I'm so pleased to meet you, Tor. Himself speaks very highly of you."

The boy blushed scarlet, hiding a grin in his glass, then seemed to remember his instructions. He sat up straight, made direct eye contact, and blurted out, "This is a great opportunity for me. I'm learning so much!"

Ginny blinked, but her smile never wavered. "Oh? What have you learned?"

The boy gestured expansively. "Mr. Scala is teaching me how to be an investigative reporter!"

Ginny smiled at Tor. "So what does an investigative reporter do?"

"He talks to people and asks them questions, polite-like, and low-key, so as not to spook them. And when they answer, he writes it all down so he can use it later."

"I see." Ginny shot a glance at Larry.

"And we take pictures and we write down the date and time and location and make sure we spell the names right, and get permission so if it gets published, no one can say we cheated."

A sudden qualm seized Ginny and she had to fight to keep it out of her expression. "Who have you been talking to, then?"

"Oh, everyone. We're investigating what Loch Lonach was like fifty years ago. That's like ancient history, but there's some as are still alive and remember."

Ginny looked at Larry and found him looking like the cat that ate the canary. "Tor?"

"Yes, ma'am?"

"Did you introduce Mr. Scala to everyone in the clan?"

The boy grinned. "Yeah! It was great! They dinnae want to talk to him, but they were all willin' to talk tae me." He swiveled his head. "No offense, Mr. Scala."

"None taken."

"Anyway, I explained about the school credit and then they let us record what they said, and take pictures, and write down whatever I wanted. And Mr. Scala told me what to say so I didn't forget anything."

Out of the corner of her eye Ginny saw Jim's hand cover his face. He had seen the implication. She fixed Larry Scala with a jaundiced eye. "I assume you have a reason for bringing this to our attention."

Scala nodded. "We found something."

I'll bet you did, Ginny thought. "And what was that?"

"We interviewed a sweet old lady who used to work in the Patterson household. She was dismissed under a cloud of suspicion that has never yet been cleared away. She maintains she is innocent and she wants justice."

Tor's eyes shone. "This is gonna make a great paper for school. My teacher's always telling us we need to be champions for those that don't have anyone else to fight fer them."

Jim made a motion as if to rise. "Tor, let's go in the other room and have a little man to man chat." Ginny stopped him.

"No. Tor is entitled to hear this and we need his cooperation if we are to protect the innocent."

Jim paused, then nodded and sat back down.

Ginny again focused on the young man. "Tor, none of what you are about to hear can leave this room. Innocent lives depend on your ability to keep the secret. Do I have your promise?"

He was struggling, his face alight with the honor of being trusted by the Laird's grandson and his lady, and by the thought of something important enough to need his cooperation. Something a lot bigger than a school paper. Ginny saw his face fall as he reached this point.

"Will I still get to write the paper, and get the credit?"

"Yes, but not yet. Himself will make sure your teacher knows we asked you to wait."

Tor's eyes flicked from her, to Jim, to Scala, then back to her. "Yes, ma'am. You have my word."

"Thank you." Ginny now turned to Scala. "You spoke to Hannah McLachlan."

"Yes, and she has a theory."

"That's all it is, a theory. She has no proof."

"I don't need proof. I've got her statement, and she's willing to testify under oath."

"If you ask her to come forward and make a public statement, she might not live to do it."

Ginny saw Scala start, then his face hardened. "That's what police protection is for."

"The police can only offer protection if a credible threat has been made. None will be. They will kill her secretly, out of sight of her family."

"You do it then. You've got cops around Patsy's house."

Ginny nodded. "And we will do the same for Hannah." She nodded at Jim, who rose and left the room, pulling his phone out of his pocket as he went. "But it shouldn't have to be necessary. You are forcing our hand."

Larry leaned closer. "You forced me. I told you someone else would have to die before we could catch Patterson in the act."

Ginny glanced at Tor. He was paying close attention, a heavy frown topping sharp, clear eyes. She looked back at Scala. "I told you we were not willing to risk another life, and that you were to let Detective Tran take care of the situation."

Larry snorted. "The police are worthless. They couldn't find their—"

"Mr. Scala!" Jim's voice erupted from behind Larry's chair, cutting him off before he could utter something inappropriate.

Tor grinned. "I reckon I know that one already. Go on."

Ginny lifted an eyebrow in Jim's direction. Young Tor McLeish looked to have quite a future in the clan.

Scala did as told. He leaned toward Ginny, then found Jim's hand on his shoulder and relaxed back into the chair. "You never mentioned a candlestick."

"What candlestick?"

"Don't toy with me. Hannah McLachlan says she told you there was a pair of candlesticks on the mantle when the party began, that they both disappeared before she was sent in to clean up, and that there were blood splatters on the mantle where no blood should have been." His eyes grew cold. "I have been after that man my whole life and you withheld critical information from me."

Ginny frowned. "I don't know what Hannah may have told Detective Tran, and I don't know what Detective Tran may have made of her story. But I do know that I have been told this is an ongoing police investigation, and no one is supposed to be talking to the press."

"That is an admission."

"Not on my part. Hannah McLachlan is a bitter old women with a blood feud against Letitia Patterson. There are newspaper accounts of the accusation and you are welcome to read them, as I have done."

Larry gave her a hard look. "I'm going to write this up and see that it appears in every media outlet on the face of the planet. I promised the old woman I would, and I always keep my promises. But, I want to talk to Patsy Olafsson first. You're going to make that happen." He leaned forward. "You owe me."

"Patsy is still under a doctor's care. We'll need his permission."

"Her oncologist won't have any objection."

"Her psychiatrist."

Larry paused, then nodded. "Okay, and he can be present, it won't matter to me, but sooner, rather than later."

"Patsy may be on the point of remembering, if she's handled carefully. Why don't you wait and see what she has to say?"

Larry hesitated, then shook his head. "I've waited my whole life. I'm not waiting any longer."

"It won't hurt you to delay a little while. As long as the information gets into the hands of the voters before the election, you'll have accomplished what you set out to do."

Larry rose, giving her a hard look. "I'll have the first draft of this story finished by this evening, and I backup my work as I go, so don't get any funny ideas. Also, I'm going to let everyone know the exposé is coming. I'll give you three days to get me in to see Patsy Olafsson. After that, I send the story in without her." He looked at the boy. "Coming, Tor?"

Jim stepped in. "No. Tor, please stay behind. I would like to have a word with you. I'll drive you home."

Scala shrugged, then let himself out the front door. Ginny closed it behind him, then rejoined the men in her kitchen.

"Well!" She dropped into a chair. "That was fun."

Tor was fidgeting, waiting to find out what kind of trouble he was in. Ginny let Jim take over.

"Tor, you made a mistake, but it was an honest one. The only reason I want to point it out to you is so you won't make it again."

Tor gulped, but said nothing.

"That stranger could not have found out about Mrs.

McLachlan and her candlestick theory if you hadn't opened the door for him. You vouched for him, telling everyone he was helping you. They opened up and talked to him, because you implied it was safe to do so."

Tor dropped his head into his hands. "I'm sorry. Mr. Mackenzie told me—" He stopped.

"What did the Laird tell you?"

"That I was to stay with him and report what he did, and keep him away from Senator Patterson, if possible."

"It was Mr. Scala's idea to interview everyone for your paper?"

Tor hung his head. "Yeah."

"Son, look at me."

Tor looked up at Jim under lowered brows, without lifting his head.

"You were used by an unscrupulous man who saw a way to get past one of the safeguards in place in this community. We don't talk to outsiders. There's a reason for that, and there should have been some in the community who remembered it."

"There were. About half wished me well, then moved off."

"Well, I'm glad to hear it. Now Tor, here's what I want you to learn from today's lesson. If a stranger seems eager to do you a favor, suspect his motives. Ask yourself, what's in it for him? If you can't figure that out, don't cooperate."

Jim sighed. "It's a wicked world. We do our best to keep the Homesteads free of the worst of the corruption, but it still slips in."

He rose and dropped his hand on the young man's shoulder. "Let's go tell the Laird what's happened, then I'll take you home. And you'll make sure not to talk to anyone about any of this. There are two old women in danger, and it's up to you to help us keep them safe."

Tor nodded. "Excuse me, sir. Will I ever find out what all this is about?"

Jim smiled at him. "If you prove trustworthy, I expect something can be arranged."

Ginny followed them to the garage and waved goodbye, then retired to the bedroom to try to get some sleep. Ten minutes later, she gave up, rose, and went to the den. Scala's plan to publish was a very bad idea. He was right, just as Hannah was right, that the accusation would hurt Patterson at the polls. Patterson must know it as well.

Scala had managed to alienate his media contacts. They might not take his calls, and they might trash his copy, but Scala didn't need them. All he had to do was put the story up on the Internet and those who wanted to believe him would.

If that happened, there would be no reason for Patterson to kill either Hannah McLachlan or Patsy Olafsson to shut their mouths. But until then, both had to be considered targets.

Ginny turned the TV on, hoping to find something that would take her mind off Maury Patterson. What she found was that someone had firebombed the police station.

* * *

CHAPTER 40

Thursday wee small hours
Hillcrest Medical Center

The primary topic of conversation during the drive in to work, and among the staff at the hospital, was the fire at the police station. The news coverage was on every channel, with updates throughout the night. Rumors flew like the sparks themselves. "It was a bomb," someone said. "No, arson," said another. The gossip raged long after the blaze was put out.

"Dr. Mackenzie!"

Jim pushed his chair back and leaned around the corner. "Yes?"

"ST segment elevation, chest pain, elderly female."

Jim tossed his pen on the desk and hurried to assist. He examined the patient, found her in the throes of what was probably a mild coronary, oversaw emergency protocol for the situation, arranged interventional radiology care, called in a cardiothoracic surgeon who happened to be in the building, and handed the thrombolytic therapy, dilation and stent placement over to him. It was only when he addressed himself to the charting that he looked at the patient's name.

"Hannah McLachlan?" He hunted up the triage nurse. "Tell me what she was doing when the symptoms started."

The nurse looked at his log. "Watching TV."

"Anything in particular?"

"Yeah." The nurse grinned. "Her daughter said a commercial came on for some politician and the old woman went ballistic. Started shouting at the TV, saying she was going to make sure he never got elected. The daughter says she may have over-reacted a bit."

"What was she doing up at midnight?"

"Watching the coverage of the fire. Woke her daughter with the shouting."

Jim smiled. "Thanks." He strode back to his office and put in a call to Ginny.

"Hey, doll."

"Doll?'

"Sugar lips?"

"I hope no one is listening on your end, mister, because you are crossing the line into sexual harassment territory."

"But you're my wife."

"That's no excuse. I'll let it go this time, but you'd just better mind your Ps and Qs, my lad."

"Yes, ma'am."

"Now, what can I do for you?"

"You will not believe who just showed up in the emergency room. Hannah McLachlan."

Jim heard the sharp intake of breath on the other end of the line. "Is she—?"

"She's going to be fine. She just had a little heart attack this evening when Patterson showed up in an election cycle commercial on her TV."

"Oh the poor woman, and her daughter!"

"Her daughter's going to be fine, too. Hannah is in interventional radiology having a stent put in."

"Well, that's a relief. Did you call me just to share?"

"No. I want to tell you what I want, then you can tell me

why I can't have it."

"Go on."

"I want to put her in protective custody here at the hospital. That will mean one of the isolation rooms, with an armed guard, private nurses, and a roster of known and reliable staff—no strangers."

"Wow! Angus has the authority, of course, but it's going to cause trouble and hard feelings."

"One of the good things about working in a private hospital is never having to say you're sorry to the staff. They're used to getting jerked around."

"You know very well that the staff here is happy and loyal, but it will be a logistics nightmare. I suppose you want me to arrange it?"

"Please."

"Okay. Give me twenty minutes. I'll call you back."

* * *

Ginny hung up on Jim and called the house supervisor, asking her to come to Ginny's office for a private chat. Susan Reed had been one of the ICU nurses on night shift before taking the positon as Night Nursing Supervisor. Ginny knew her well and they were friends as well as colleagues. For this reason, Ginny could level with her.

"So that's the situation. Can we get two twelve-hour people to work private duty back to back for the next two days? They would need to be able to read an EKG, and spot trouble, though I don't think they're going to have any. What they need to be is stable, solid, and sea-green incorruptible."

Susan nodded. "I have three or four that would fit. I'll call to see who can come in. Can I offer them bonuses?"

"You'll need to clear that with Himself, but I'd bet he'll say yes. And the isolation room?"

"We have six empty at the moment. If I need it, I'll bump her, but I won't do that without letting you know."

"Okay. The nurses can draw the labs. I don't anticipate x-rays. EKGs can be done via the monitors. We can let her family prepare her meals and bring them in. I'll explain to them how that will work. Pharmacy is a weak point. If someone really wants her dead, switching a medication to one with a poison in it is just too easy."

Susan's brow furrowed. "The anterooms have dedicated crash carts, and computer controlled access to the drug and supply dispensers, for billing purposes. We can add anything the docs order before anyone knows who is going into that room. If she needs something special, the automated system can deliver meds to the airlock of the isolation room. It was set up that way. And chemo processing can seal items so they can be examined for tampering. That just leaves the preparer to watch."

"All good ideas. I think I'm going to ask Dr. Mackenzie to oversee the drug juggling."

Susan grinned. "I'll look forward to working with him again, however briefly."

"You do know we're married now?"

Susan sighed. "I know. I'll behave."

"You'd better!"

Susan hurried off to make the magic happen and Ginny called Jim back. She explained what they'd come up with and asked him to make sure any necessary medications came in anonymously.

"I've called Himself," he said. "So we've got clearance. And he's sending over a security detail for tonight. They'll work out a schedule in the morning."

"Okay. Have we forgotten anything?"

"I hope not, though I'd be happier if Scala was the one being locked up."

"Me, too." There was a sharp intake of breath, then silence on the other end of the line. "Jim? Are you still there?"

"Yes." He sounded strangled.

"What's wrong?"

"I—I'm not sure I should tell you."

"Jim! You're scaring me!"

"Are you in your office?"

"Yes."

"I'll be there in five minutes. Stay put."

Ginny hung up the phone, swallowed her heart, then fixed her eyes on the clock. She jumped to her feet and threw herself into his arms as he came through the door. "Talk to me, Jim. Tell me what's going on."

"Nothing bad, I hope." He hugged her, then drew in a deep breath, steered her over to a chair and sat them both down, knee to knee. He took her hands in his. "Do you remember what happened when you went to Austin for that conference last December?"

Ginny's eyes narrowed. "Which part?"

"You remember that I came after you."

"Yes." Ginny's eyes widened. "The Sight! You've had another vision."

He nodded.

"Tell me!"

"It was very much like the last one, a riot in progress and shouting. This one had gunfire and a bullhorn. I couldn't hear what was being said, but I could see landmarks. That riot was taking place outside the Loch Lonach gates."

"Outside the gates?" Ginny frowned. "How could it be outside the gates? The gates are never closed."

"Well they were this time." He swallowed, then continued.

"Ginny, I saw a man die."

She stared at him for a moment, her heart in her throat. "Who?"

"I don't know. I couldn't see his face, just what he was wearing." Jim shook himself, then rose to his feet, drawing Ginny up with him. "Come on, it's lunchtime. I'll feel better with some food in my system, and coffee."

Ginny closed her office door and followed him to the elevator. When they were alone in the car, he gave her another hug.

"Don't worry. It wasn't me, or Angus. That much I know."

Ginny shook her head at him. "Of all the miserable gifts God could bestow, this has got to be the worst. To see a death and know you can do nothing to stop it."

Jim nodded slowly. "They say knowledge is power. Maybe there's a way to use it."

"Well, if it involves going anywhere near the gates, promise me you'll resist the temptation. You can phone it in to the police. Tran would listen."

"So she would." He looked down at her. "All right. I promise I won't play hero."

Ginny's breath caught in her throat. She reached up and threw her arms around his neck hugging him tightly. "I don't mean to be selfish, but I need you, Jim, alive and well, now more than ever. We need you."

She saw the smile spread across his face, his lips first, then his brow, then his eyes. "Don't worry, my love. I haven't forgotten." He was kissing her when the elevator doors opened.

* * *

Incarnadine

Thursday afternoon
Mackenzie residence

Jim was scheduled to work the night shift again. When Ginny had fed him and seen him off, she climbed the stairs to her office and settled down to answer a question that had been bothering her. Where did one get a coffin large enough for an Irish wolfhound?

She had the pictures she'd taken during the exhumation, several of which were of the box itself. She'd captured a logo displayed on the silk lining of the lid, the sort of thing that would be visible in a showroom when the coffin was open. She enlarged the logo and ran it through her image matching utility. It came up sweetly.

"Patterson." The name of the company was Patterson Pet Supplies, and it was located in Springfield, IL. Ginny could not believe this was a coincidence, so she pulled up the About the Company page and looked at the owner's name. Naomi Holloway. Okay, no clue there. Ginny picked up the phone and dialed the number. The clerk answered on the second ring.

"Hello," Ginny said. "I'm calling from Texas and I was wondering if I could speak to Naomi Holloway, please."

"This is Naomi. How may I help you?"

Ginny had been wondering the same thing. "I saw a casket, for a dog, quite recently and it had your logo on it and it was absolutely lovely." No lie there. "It was for a big dog, an Irish wolfhound. Do you still carry those, the caskets, I mean?"

"Yes, we have a supplier we order them from. I'm so sorry for your loss."

"Oh! No, I don't have a dead dog, but I know someone who shows Irish wolfhounds and was wondering if you supplied the casket I saw. It was on the Patterson estate in Dallas, Texas."

There was no hesitation. "You mean Letitia Patterson?"

"Yes."

"She was my mother-in-law for a while. We supplied all the caskets for her show dogs. Bizarre names she gave them. I couldn't get my tongue around them."

"They were in Gaelic."

"Oh, well that explains it."

Ginny sucked in a breath. "Do you by any chance have records of when you sold coffins to Letitia?"

"Yes. It's all computerized, to make the new orders easier to fill. Just type in her telephone number, you know. Though I understand someone else will have to take over, now that she's passed on."

"Yes, and we're trying to identify all the vendors and such. Is this a good telephone number for you?"

"This is the store number. Let me give you my personal number as well." She rattled off the digits and Ginny jotted them down.

"I'm sorry, I didn't get your name."

"Ginny Mackenzie. Here's my number and email. Feel free to use them if you think of anything that can help us get all this stuff sorted out."

"I'll pull the records and let you know the dates Letitia bought coffins. That's what you wanted, right?"

"Right. Thank you. Goodbye."

Ginny hung up the phone and reflected that doing business with an honest person was an absolute joy. They weren't suspicious of your motives and they acknowledged facts without fuss. And the facts in this case included that Maury Patterson's ex-wife had no idea what Letitia had been doing with those dog coffins.

Her next call was to Wade Bryant. She found him almost recovered from his stroke, with a residual limp, but no speech or memory deficits. He remembered Ginny immediately and confirmed that Letitia Patterson had been a good sailor and that she had taken the boat out alone a few times, but he had no idea what the dates might have been. Ginny volunteered any help Wade might need, emphasizing that it was no trouble and she would be glad to arrange assistance. Wade said he would think about it, then hesitated.

"What can I do for you?" Ginny asked.

"Is there any chance you could get tickets to *Macbeth,* the play the theatre group is putting on this Sunday? I know it's really short notice and they may be sold out, but I've got some grandchildren that would really like to see the sword fighting, and Patsy tells me she'll be in it. One of the witches, I gather."

"I'll call the producer and get back to you."

"Thanks."

Ginny dutifully called Alan and got a promise of four tickets to be held at the "Will Call" window. She relayed this information to Wade, then added that these tickets were a gift, a thank you for all his help with *Saosainn.*

Her tasks done for the moment, she was left with the evening to herself. Jim would call later, if he wasn't too swamped to say goodnight. In the meantime she could do what she wished.

She rose, crossed the hall and stood in the doorway of the nursery. There was so much to do, to be ready, but she shied away from the thought. She hadn't been kidding when she told Jim she was superstitious about planning on having a baby. She'd seen too much, heard too many things in her professional career. It seemed to her that if anything could go wrong, it would. Murphy's Law. She turned away and went downstairs to watch TV.

* * *

CHAPTER 41

Friday afternoon
Mackenzie residence

On Friday, Ginny waited to start her day until Jim had been fed and had retired to his bed. Her first stop was her obstetrician, Dr. Berry. She'd been lucky to get the appointment and had jumped at it, even though it meant she'd miss Chris's next session with Patsy.

It was long and tedious, including as it did numerous tests and a lot of teaching. Ginny's specialty was ICU nursing, not obstetrics. She was nervous and wished Jim were with her, to hold her hand, but he needed his sleep and she would be able to talk to him this afternoon. Later on, she'd also want her mother, but for this first appointment, she relied on her friend, into whose hands she was committing herself and her unborn child. She sucked up her courage and smiled.

Dr. Berry was going over the findings with her. "You will remember from school that this is a presumptive diagnosis. The pregnancy is not confirmed until the baby's heart begins to beat. You are four weeks from conception, so it's too soon to be absolutely sure. But we're going to treat you as if we are. Because I am."

Ginny left the office with instructions for prenatal vitamins, how to handle the nausea, and what she should eat for the next nine months. She swung by the bookstore and found a planner aimed at pregnant mothers, and a baby book, which was tempting the gods, but she slapped down her fear and bought it on spec.

She dropped her purchases at home, peeked in at her husband, grabbed a bite to eat, and headed for Detective Tran's office. The detective greeted her at the door and waved her towards a chair, then settled down behind her desk.

"Thank you for making time to see me," Ginny said.

"You have concerns?"

"Yes. Larry Scala is threatening to publish the story of the bloody candlestick, the one Patsy sent me as a wedding present. He believes he can prevent Maury Patterson from being elected, that the voting public will not want a child killer making decisions for them. He's probably right."

"I agree."

Ginny took a breath. "But there's a problem. As much as I'd like to see this end with Patterson withdrawing from the race, Larry is a loose cannon."

"Please clarify."

"He's not credible. His media contacts may be polite, but they won't trust him. He's been wrong too many times."

Tran nodded.

"He's been going around talking to people who can give him information about Maury as a child, and he's still trying to get an interview with Patsy Olafsson, but Dr. Urquhart won't allow it. He says it might hurt his efforts to break down her mental block about the night Tommy died."

Again Detective Tran nodded.

One of Tran's charms, Ginny reflected, was that she listened without trying to hurry you. She continued her narrative.

"This has stirred up a lot of gossip and I find it hard to believe Maury Patterson, or Rita, or one of the Pattersons' staff hasn't heard it. If I were in Maury's shoes, with his history, I wouldn't hesitate to eliminate the people spreading the rumors."

Tran frowned. "Even if what you say is true, Senator Patterson will not be able to eliminate the entire community. He will have to be content with rebutting the accusation and letting the gossip die down."

Ginny nodded. "Patsy is probably safe. We have guards with her twenty-four/seven. Hannah McLachlan had a heart attack Wednesday night and is isolated at the hospital, surrounded by trusted staff members. But Larry is free and stirring up trouble. I've been wondering if you might be able to find an excuse to put him in protective custody."

Tran's brow furrowed. "Has anyone made a direct threat against him?"

Ginny shook her head. "Not that I know of."

"Then I am afraid I cannot accede to your request."

Ginny sighed. "He's going to get himself killed!"

"Perhaps not." Tran opened a folder on her desk, extracted a sheet of paper and passed it over to Ginny. "Mr. Scala was seen on the surveillance camera footage at the chocolate shop. This image was compared with the sales receipts."

Ginny caught her breath. "This is Larry?"

"The credit card was issued to Senator Patterson, but with a fictitious address. Deposits to the bank account, to cover the purchases, were all made in cash. No signature was required as all transactions were completed online."

"Wow. He's been planning this for a long time."

Detective Tran nodded. "You are aware we got an anonymous tip that the poison could be found at Chancie Mor?"

"No, I hadn't heard that."

"We searched and found a pill bottle, a drug crusher,

digoxin fragments, and a syringe with dissolved drug residue inside. However, the person who left these items behind made a mistake."

Ginny held her breath.

"The only chocolate residue was on the needle. There should have been trace amounts of chocolate on the countertop. There was none."

Ginny was thinking furiously. "You think Larry poisoned Patsy."

"Either Mr. Scala or Mr. Scala and Senator Patterson working together, but Mr. Scala alone is the more likely."

"Are you going to arrest him?" If he was in jail Maury couldn't get to him. Probably.

"We are still sifting through the forensic evidence. Mr. Scala does not have a clear motive for attempting to kill Mrs. Olafsson."

"To frame Maury!"

"We are considering that possibility. But the fact remains that it is Senator Patterson who would benefit from the death of his cousin before she regains her memory."

So Larry would remain at large, fomenting trouble, and sticking his neck out. Ginny sighed to herself and made a mental note to pass this information on to the Laird.

Detective Tran raised an eyebrow. "There is something else you may find interesting, about the candlestick."

"Oh?"

"You will recall there was a fire at the police substation on Wednesday evening."

Ginny nodded. The news had said arson was suspected, but that there had been little damage and no injuries.

"The fire was set as a diversion. During the evacuation and confusion, the evidence locker was breached. There was only one item taken, a candlestick."

Ginny gasped. "Not—?"

"No. The thief appears to have been unaware that there were two candlesticks in the box. Whoever it was took the one on top, the one you found hidden on the boat, not the one with the blood on it."

"Someone wanted to get rid of the murder weapon!"

Tran nodded. "The incursion was subtle. We were not meant to realize that anything had been stolen."

"Then how did you catch it?"

"The arsonist failed to eliminate all of the surveillance coverage. The evidence locker has night-vision back-up, in case of power failure. The intruder was disguised as a fireman. He cut the lock off the access point, pocketed it, and replaced it with the same model, with a different combination, of course."

"An insider?"

"We think not. There was a simultaneous computer attack, from the outside, also tied to the fire and meant to be blamed on the damaged wiring. Many files were lost."

Ginny's eyes widened. "Including those related to the investigation of Maury Patterson!"

"Correct."

Ginny leaned back in her chair, thinking. Larry wouldn't want to suppress the evidence of Maury's crime. If he was in possession of the candlestick, of either of them, it would be on the news.

"I'm guessing the Pattersons hired someone to break in and steal the candlestick. There's enough money and Rita has connections. If there was no evidence, Maury could deny the rumors and move on."

Tran nodded. "That is my theory."

"And Rita broke into my house looking for one or the other of the candlesticks. If her people can erase all the files in an investigation, they can also read them. She must have known that I brought the first candlestick, the bloodied one, to you. That means she was looking for the second."

"We were able to use the tread database to identify the make and model of the shoeprint found in your house. We have requested a warrant and will see if any of Rita Patterson's shoes match."

Ginny rose, and held out her hand. "Let me know how I can help."

"I shall. Thank you."

Ginny hurried home. It was too soon to wake Jim, but she could phone Angus. She slipped up the stairs and into her office.

"Sae th' Pattersons were behind th' fire, aye?"

"It appears so, and they took one of the candlesticks, the clean one, as it turns out."

Angus chuckled. "'Twill do fer evidence o' theft, I warrant. And Scala poisoned Patsy."

Ginny could hear the disapproval in his voice. "Again, it appears so. Tran is moving forward on both investigations."

"Weel, 'tis all verry interesting, but if wha' Scala says is true, Patterson may weasel out o' th' charges an' be elected in spite o' us."

"Not by intimidating Ian Hunter. And that's another thing I wanted to talk to you about. The debate is tomorrow. I think we should plan on trouble."

"Aye, lass. I agree. Wha' did ye hae in mind?"

* * *

Jim was fascinated. He kept putting his fork down and staring at Ginny as she told him about her visit with Detective Tran.

Ginny sipped her ginger ale. "Stealing the evidence implies guilty knowledge. Maury is afraid Patsy will denounce him when she gets her memory back."

"So we need to keep an eye on her. What about Hannah?"

"I think Tran is right. With the evidence gone, all Hannah has is her theory. Maury can tell her to prove it, and she won't be able to. So, the mud can be slung, but it won't stick. I think a clever campaign manager could handle it."

"I agree," Jim said. "If we want Patterson to withdraw from the race, what we have to do is figure out how to prove he killed those prostitutes."

Ginny's brow furrowed. "How do we do that?"

"Paper trail. We need to follow the money."

Ginny nodded. "Letitia bought the dog coffins and I've got the vendor sending me the details so we can compare dates." She told Jim about how she found the supplier and the owner's relationship to Letitia Patterson. "But I don't believe Naomi Holloway was in on it."

"It would be safer for Maury that way. One less potential witness."

"Is there any chance we can locate the men who did the kidnapping Larry photographed?"

"According to Detective Tran, they are no longer in the country."

Ginny sniffed. "Disappeared, did they? Just like the women!"

"Which may mean there are more bodies to be discovered."

"Or they are living in some comfortable country that doesn't have an extradition treaty with the U.S."

"It's possible. Okay. What else?"

"Ian said he was working on proving Patterson's money is behind the attacks. So is Detective Tran. But Ian was right about the timing. We need proof *now*, so we can make sure Maury doesn't win that election."

"You aren't willing to use innuendo and slander?"

Ginny squirmed. "I'm considering it. Larry is right about the power of the press. The problem for us is that we can't back up any accusation and that lays us open to libel charges. The only people we hurt if we go down that road are ourselves."

"Maybe Patsy will remember who killed her little brother in time to testify."

Ginny sighed. "I've been hoping so, but it won't help."

Jim's brow furrowed. "Why not?"

"Because I've remembered something. A blow to the back of Tommy's head hard enough to crack his skull would dent the silver, even a weighted base. And there were no dents on the candlestick Patsy sent to me."

Jim frowned. "I need to see that autopsy report."

"Yes, but what I think you'll find is that it was Letitia Patterson who delivered the fatal blow."

"Which means Maury can't be accused of killing Tommy."

"Right. He skates again."

Jim shook his head. "There has got to be something we can use to show the voters how corrupt he is."

"Larry's been working on it his whole life, but Maury knows how to cover his tracks. I doubt if we'll be any more successful."

"Maybe Larry has the right idea."

Ginny sighed again. Discrediting Patterson in the eyes of his constituents might work, but was iffy at best. They needed another way to make sure he didn't win, one that would assure Ian Hunter a victory at the polls and she had no idea what it would take. Something for her subconscious to chew on.

In the meantime, there was her visit to Dr. Berry to discuss. Ginny smiled at her husband and changed the subject.

* * *

CHAPTER 42

Saturday morning
Alan Bean Auditorium

Ginny stood just outside the entrance to the auditorium, her eyes scanning the crowd. She had already inspected the inside of the building.

The security features were discreet, but properly deployed and staffed. Angus had recruited two dozen active military to operate the metal detectors. Reggie had provided another dozen to watch monitors and report trouble. The Loch Lonach police force was in evidence, as were members of the Dallas police who had ties to the Homestead. In addition, Angus had arranged roving spies in plain clothes to wander the building and grounds, reporting back as needed.

The media were confined to the back of the auditorium and had all been vetted. They were free to say what they wanted, but they were being filmed as well as filming and might face incitement charges if there was trouble.

Signs in and around the building warned all comers that they had no expectation of privacy during the event. They also warned that anyone disrupting the proceedings would be promptly and forcibly removed to jail. As part of the process, each person signed a waiver stating they understood the restrictions and would abide by them.

Ginny watched another bus pull up. It disgorged an additional one hundred plus demonstrators, armed with placards, tee shirts, and determination. They joined the throng already straining the police barriers.

The first to arrive had done so early. Three busses full of constituents from other parts of the district had turned up before breakfast and, in an effort to show goodwill, been fed by the Homestead staff over at the Cooperative Hall.

More had arrived throughout the morning. The parking lot was full of people milling about. Reggie had anticipated this and installed huge monitors along the colonnade. They would display the debate to those who were unable to get a seat inside.

"Good morning Mrs. Mackenzie."

Ginny turned to find Maury Patterson standing beside her, surveying the crowd and smiling. She nodded.

He waved at the throng and they cheered, chanting, "We want Patterson! We want Patterson!"

"A lovely day for a debate."

Ginny could have used a tornado or two at the moment, but she kept her temper. "It is."

The Patterson supporters were a varied bunch, recruited, as she could see, from the numerous ethnic groups that inhabited District 17A. Conspicuously absent were the Scots. They were already inside, seated, and waiting politely for the debate to get underway.

Patterson turned toward her, his smile devoid of warmth. "As you can see, Senator Hunter does not carry the entire district."

The placards bore messages of frustration and anger. *Give us what we deserve! We demand free housing and education! Medical care should be for everyone, not just the rich!*

"What I see is people who feel aggrieved. There are already

channels for addressing such concerns."

Patterson lifted an eyebrow. "This country was founded on the idea that the people should dismiss a government that isn't in their best interests and institute a new one."

She turned to look at him. "The current government was founded on the idea that citizens have duties as well as rights."

"True, and governments owe duties to their citizens." He swept his hand over the crowd and was greeted with a roar of support. "The old order changes."

Ginny frowned. "Maybe, but first, you have to get elected." She turned on her heel and went back inside.

Jim was leaning against one of the interior walls, talking to Angus. He smiled when he saw her and waved her over. She gave him a hug, but didn't bother to report her conversation with Maury Patterson.

"Where's your mother this morning?" Jim asked.

"She and Dr. Urquhart had a date with her backyard."

Jim grinned. "That should be fun."

Ginny caught a frown out of the corner of her eye and turned in time to see Jean approach Angus. His brow descended and he raised his phone to his ear. Ginny could hear a few words as he strode past them on the way to the front door.

"Close and lock them. Aye! That's wha' I said. Close th' gates!"

Ginny turned to look at Jim and saw his eyes grow round. "You are to stay here," she said. "You promised!"

He nodded, then tightened his grip on her. Ginny glanced at her watch. Fifteen minutes to start time.

The candidates were backstage, getting made up for their TV appearances. The wives were seated in the front row. They would be introduced to the crowds.

Rita was scowling. She turned around and said something to

the two Scots sitting behind her. They had been talking to one another, as was most of the crowd, and they did not appear to appreciate being told to be quiet. Ginny leaned towards Jim.

"I wish I knew what they were saying."

"They were talking about me."

Ginny jumped, then realized Larry Scala had come up behind her. She looked at him. "Oh?"

"I was talking to them earlier. They wanted to know what my opinion was of Patterson, since I'd been studying him my whole life."

"What did you say?" Jim asked.

Larry lifted an eyebrow. "I told them the truth, that there have been some inconsistencies and a number of investigations."

Rita Patterson had disappeared, probably headed for the restroom as the debate was expected to last for two hours. Ginny decided that was a good idea and excused herself, following Rita's lead.

She located the nearest Ladies' Room and joined the line. A minute later, Rita strode out of the restroom and turned toward the stage entrance without a glance to right or left. Ginny watched her pass a trashcan, one of the large, open barrel types, without breaking stride.

The gesture was so smooth Ginny wasn't sure she'd seen it. She moved quietly out of line and sauntered toward the barrel. She glanced down, saw a phone, reached in, and retrieved it. The SIM card had been removed, and the battery. The phone was dead.

Ginny pocketed it, concluded her business, then went back to stand with Jim again. The debate had started. Angus was making introductions and everyone was listening closely. Ginny looked around, to see if anything untoward was happening while all eyes were glued to the stage.

She whispered to Jim. "Where's Larry?"

"He got a text message and took off. I sent Tor to follow him."

"Good idea."

The Master of Ceremonies was introducing the candidates and their families. Normally this job would fall to the Laird, but Angus had delegated the honor so that he could remain on hand in case of trouble.

Wally and his mother rose, faced the cameras and smiled, to the accompaniment of polite applause. When they were seated again, Rita Patterson was introduced, to murmurs of appreciation and one promptly suppressed wolf whistle.

The opening statements were done and the questions had begun when Ginny became aware of the sound. The crowd outside was growing louder. She could hear shouting, then something smashing to the ground, then a roar of anger. Jim's face was turned to the back of the auditorium. He took a step in that direction and Ginny grabbed his arm.

He looked down at her and smiled. "Don't worry. I'm not going anywhere near the gates."

"Well, wherever you're going, I'm going with you."

He nodded and led her up the staircase to the command center located in the light booth. Here they found Angus directing traffic, his face grim. He caught sight of them and motioned them over, pointing at the camera feed trained on the crowd outside. There was a full-scale riot in progress.

"Who brought in the baseball bats?" Ginny asked.

"Ain o' th' busses brought in a full load o' trouble-makers armed wi' bats. They got in afore we could close th' gates. We've called fer backup."

"There are people being hurt." Jim's face was a mask of fury as he watched a woman clubbed to the ground.

Angus nodded. "Aye. There's a helicopter on its way tae tak' ye tae Hillcrest. Ye'll be needed there."

Jim nodded, removed Ginny's hand, and headed for the door.

"And ye, lass. Ye'll be in charge o' the First Aid station."

Ginny tore her eyes from her husband's retreating back and faced Angus. She nodded.

The high school gym had been turned into an emergency staging area that morning. It was all set up and ready to go, part of the plan she and Angus had discussed yesterday. Ginny followed Jim down the stairs, pulling out her phone and calling in the volunteers.

She reached the main floor and caught up with Jim. He was watching the crowd. The disturbance outside had managed to breech their defenses. There were shouting matches and fights breaking out all over the auditorium. She took a step closer to her husband and he slipped an arm around her.

The auditorium was a nice one, with tiers of seats and boxes along the wall. Ian Hunter was at the podium. He had stopped speaking and was looking up at one of the boxes. Ginny watched as he suddenly leaped to one side, rolled as he hit the boards, then scrambled off stage, Lola's scream drowned by the sound of the shot.

The police closed in, wrestling the shooter to the floor of the box and taking the weapon. Officials hustled Patterson offstage and grabbed Lola and Wally, covering them with their own bodies. Rita had disappeared.

Jim's mouth was open. "He's been hit." He took off for the stage, Ginny right behind him.

They found Ian on the floor behind a massive beam designed to hold up the ceiling. He had a hand over his ear and blood dripping onto the floor from between his fingers.

"Let me look," Jim said. The light was poor, but it was enough to see that it was only a graze.

Ian grinned crookedly. "Scalp wounds bleed like the devil. Too bad he wasn't aiming for my heart."

"You wouldn't have liked that," Jim told him. "Even with a bulletproof vest on, you can break ribs." He helped Ian to his feet. "I'm headed for the hospital. You can ride with me."

Ginny waited until she had seen the two men safely into the helicopter, then went in search of Lola. She found her in a concrete-lined room beneath the stage.

"Are you all right?"

Lola's eyes were huge. "How's Ian?"

"The bullet nicked his ear. He's on the way to the ER to get stitched up. And you're coming with me, you and Wally." Ginny put an arm around Lola's waist and steered her out the back door and into a waiting police cruiser which took them to the high school. Ginny metaphorically rolled up her sleeves, deployed her troops, and got down to business. An hour later she paused to make a phone call.

"Chris? I am so sorry to bother you, but there's been an attack on the Homestead, at the debate. I've got a lot of hysterical people on my hands. Is there any way you can help?"

"We'll be right there."

"Thank you!" Ginny gave him directions to the gym. She was relieved to see her mother arrive with the psychiatrist. Sinia was always a great help in a crisis.

"I'm going to open my classroom for Chris to use as a counseling center," Sinia told her. "Come get me if you need to."

There was a monitor in the corner of the gymnasium. Inevitably someone remembered it and brought up the news. Ginny watched, as fascinated as everyone else at the extent of the violence, the rising death toll, and the state troopers rounding up the criminals.

"Not here," someone said. "I can't believe it happened

here."

Ginny shut her mouth and went back to work. What were the odds Patterson was behind this disturbance, too? And how was she going to prove it? More deaths! Patterson was going to have a lot to answer for.

* * *

By two p.m. the gym had stopped being a first aid station and become a morgue. One of the wounded had come off the bus. He had been questioned by the police within Ginny's hearing, and protested that he'd had no idea what was planned. They were given baseball bats and told to smash windows and dent cars, not to use them on people. When he'd seen the others aiming at people's heads, he'd tried to leave, and become a victim himself.

Ginny's task now was to see if she and the remaining volunteers could identify any of the dead. The injuries made it hard at times. Baseball bats can shatter facial bones. They were going through pockets, hoping for identification of some sort. About half had a driver's license or other ID on them. The rest would have to wait until it was known whether or not their fingerprints were in the system.

Ginny was moving methodically down the line when she came to a body that didn't fit the pattern. She recognized him immediately. Someone had stepped on his face, and his clothes were filthy, but this man had not been battered. He'd been shot.

Ginny knelt beside him and for the first time that day began to cry. That lovely voice silenced by a wicked man's ambition. Was this Scala's destiny? Was this death ordained before he was even born? He could have chosen to give up, to abandon his pursuit. It was tempting to believe that his obsession had killed him, but that wouldn't be true. Someone pulled that trigger, and that someone was a murderer.

Ginny wiped her face with her hands, then dug in her pocket for a tissue. When she had herself under control again, she called Jim.

"How's it going?" he asked.

"Scala's dead."

There was a brief silence. "How soon can you pick me up?"

"The pros have started to arrive. I can turn the responsibility over to them right now."

"When you get here, come in, and let me know."

"All right." She hung up the phone, handed responsibility over to the Medical Examiner's office, then made her way upstairs to her mother's classroom. She looked through the window in the door and watched for a moment. Chris was almost nose to nose with a child of ten, whose mother held him in her lap. Her own mother was sitting on the floor, rocking a toddler while she listened to the child's father talk, the mother conspicuously absent in this tableau. Ginny slipped away.

* * *

Saturday evening
Jim's car

It had taken some doing, but Ginny had finally run Reggie to earth and handed over Rita's phone, explaining how she had found it and suggesting it be treated as evidence. Jim had left his car in the parking lot when he flew off in the helicopter, tossing the keys to her before he boarded. She gathered up her stuff, got in his car, and drove over to the hospital.

The long summer day revealed the extent of the

devastation. The baseball bats had been effective, smashing windows and breaking lamp posts and fences. Cars parked around the auditorium resembled those destroyed by a hail storm. Street signs had been bent in half, traffic lights torn down, mail boxes crushed flat. But the worst was the blood.

She slipped quietly into the ER lobby and was admitted to the back by the triage nurse. Jim was in his office. When he saw her, he gave her half a smile, signed the medical record he was working on, and followed her to the parking lot. Once the car was in motion, he took a breath.

"Ian's fine. Most of the people who were brought to the ER will be, too. Broken arms and collarbones. Bruises. Some missing teeth. We admitted six for head injuries, and another eight for knife wounds."

Ginny nodded. "The count was twelve dead when I left the gym. There may be more. Head injuries. Crush injuries where the crowd trampled them. Gunshot wounds. *A* gunshot wound."

"Larry."

Ginny frowned. "I've been thinking about it all afternoon. Do you remember when he told us those men were talking about him?"

Jim nodded.

"And Rita was annoyed with them?"

"Yes."

"And then she got up and left the auditorium."

"I remember."

"She came out of the Ladies' Room and dropped her phone in the trash. I saw her do it. I retrieved the phone, but the SIM card and battery had been removed." She frowned. "I think she called someone and that someone met Larry at the gate and gunned him down."

Jim's brow furrowed. "Then it was Larry I saw at the gates?"

Neither of them questioned the Second Sight. It was a legacy from Jim's mother and had been proven reliable.

"I think so. I think she laid a trap for him, promising him something he couldn't resist, because of what she overheard those two men say. I don't think she realized he was a threat to Maury's political ambitions until then. She had to use her own phone, and then ditch it, so no one could trace the call."

"Reggie may be able to."

"And if he finds something, we can turn it over to Detective Tran." Ginny nodded. "Which would suit me just fine. But none of this gets me any closer to figuring out how to stop Maury Patterson." It seemed unbearable that Patterson was getting away with using violence to sway the voters, that he might actually be elected and given power over the Homestead.

She reached up to brush a tickle away from her cheek and found it wet. "Is this the end of us, Jim? Is it our destiny to be destroyed by the evil outside our gates?"

He took a deep breath. "There've been plenty of times in history when the wicked were in control and the innocent suffered. But those times ended, usually because the innocent fought back. The police are investigating. The clan is rebuilding. You and I are caring for the injured. We're not giving in. And if it comes to a fight, we're ready."

She reached over and took his hand. The Scots were doughty fighters, always had been. And the women fought alongside their men. But, always, there had been casualties.

"Let's hope it doesn't come to that."

* * *

CHAPTER 43

Sunday morning
Olafsson residence

When Ginny's phone went off during church the next morning, she almost didn't answer it. She kept the device on silent mode, because of her job, but she felt she'd had enough excitement for a while and wanted an hour or two of peace before tackling life again. Not gonna happen.

As soon as she could gracefully slip away, and after arranging for her mother and Jim to carpool, Ginny left church and drove to Patsy's house. The message she'd received sounded urgent. When she arrived, she found Violet waiting at the door.

"How is she?" Ginny asked.

"Very upset. She wants to talk to you." Violet escorted Ginny into Patsy's bedroom, then left, shutting the door behind her.

It was obvious at first glance that Patsy'd had a bad night. Her eyes were puffy and red, and her skin sagged. Ginny leaned over and kissed her cheek. She found the old woman trembling.

"What's wrong, Patsy?"

"Sit down, dear. I need to tell you everything."

Ginny obeyed.

"Dr. Urquhart was here on Friday and whatever he's been doing, it must have worked. I was watching all that violence yesterday on television and it felt real, as if it was happening to me. Last night, I dreamed about how Tommy died. When I woke up, I remembered everything."

Ginny caught her breath. "Can you tell me?"

Patsy nodded. "We were playing in the library at Aunt Letty's house, Tommy and Maury and I. I don't remember what the game was, but the boys had toy swords. I think I was the maiden locked in the tower and they were fighting over who would get to rescue me." She took a breath.

"Maury was bigger and stronger and had longer arms, so he was winning, but Tommy was ferocious. He was having a great time, poking at Maury, and telling him he was dead. Maury kept insisting he wasn't, since he'd 'killed' Tommy first, but I don't think Tommy understood him.

"Maury got mad and tried to take Tommy's sword away, but Tommy dropped his and caught hold of Maury's. Somehow, he managed to get the sword out of Maury's grip. He scooped up the other sword from the floor and ran over to the fireplace, holding both swords over his head and taunting Maury. I don't think he had any idea what he was doing.

"I watched as Maury ran over to Tommy, who tried to run away again, but Maury caught hold of his shirt. Tommy turned his back to Maury, both swords held tight against his chest, and he was yelling that Maury couldn't have them. It was clear to me that the game was no longer fun. I could see that Tommy was just about to give up. But not Maury. He reached up and took a candlestick off the mantel. I remember watching the taper fall out and break on the bricks. Maury swung that candlestick and hit Tommy on the back of his head and I saw blood. I think I screamed."

Patsy covered her face with her hands. "I wasn't paying

enough attention. I was supposed to be taking care of my baby brother. If I'd been a better sister, he wouldn't be dead." She started crying.

Ginny rose and wrapped her arms around the old woman's shoulders. "That is not true! No one could have expected what Maury did! You are *not* to blame." She took a careful breath. "Wasn't there someone who was supposed to be with you, an adult?"

Patsy nodded. "She had a sick headache and had to go lie down."

Ginny gave it another minute then asked, "How did you end up with the bloodied candlestick?"

Patsy lifted a tear-stained face to Ginny's. She swallowed. "Tommy hadn't moved. He just lay there. Maury looked up and saw me. His face was terrible. Cold and angry and fierce. He came over and thrust that candlestick into my hands and told me to hide it where no one could ever find it again." She gulped. "He said if I ever told anyone, even my mother, he would kill me, too."

"So you ran home and put the candlestick in your grandfather's chest, up in the attic."

Patsy nodded. "How did you know?"

"We found traces of blood inside."

"My dress had blood all over it. I didn't want to wear it again. I threw it into the garbage can out back, got into bed, and stayed there until they found me." She looked at Ginny. "I kept my promise. I never told a soul."

Ginny gave her another hug.

Patsy wiped her eyes, then took a breath. "I have two favors to ask of you, dear."

"What can I do for you?"

"Stay with me for a while."

"Of course."

"And take my place in the play this afternoon. I don't think I can face a crowd."

Ginny's brow furrowed. "But you've worked so hard to get ready."

"I know, but I don't think I could remember my lines. My head's too full of Tommy." She looked at Ginny, her eyes filling again. "You know the part, you've been helping me. You can stand in for me."

Ginny thought about it for half a minute, then nodded. "Of course I will." She settled down in the chair and listened as Patsy poured out all her memories of the little boy they had lost. Ginny offered to call Dr. Urquhart for her, but Patsy shook her head.

"Later. I feel you have a right to hear it first, because you were so kind about the genealogy, and because you made it possible for me to remember Tommy."

Ginny listened and soothed and persuaded Patsy to eat something, then took her leave. "If I don't go now, I won't have time to get into your costume and run through the lines. Are you sure you don't want to come?"

"I'm sure. I just don't have the heart for it."

Ginny nodded. "Do you mind if I let a few people know you've got your memory back? Himself, and Jim, and Chris."

"I don't mind if you tell, but I'd rather not have visitors this afternoon. I didn't get much sleep last night."

"Okay. You sleep and I'll tell you all about the play later."

Patsy nodded, a wisp of a smile tugging at the corner of her mouth. "Break a leg."

Ginny ran for the car, asking Violet to take over and to let Patsy sleep, if she could. Also, to call if either of them needed anything. She jumped into Jim's car and drove home, climbed out of her church clothes, stuffed a sandwich in her mouth, and corralled Jim, explaining what was up. They made it to the

auditorium with just enough time to prepare, Jim feeding
Ginny her cues, and Ginny trying to fight down sudden panic.
Why on Earth would anyone want to be an actor?

* * *

Sunday afternoon
Alan Bean Auditorium

Ginny was watching the play from the wings. As a girl, she'd
been taken to *Shakespeare in the Park*, but Texas on a summer
evening has other things to offer youngsters. She had never
paid much attention.

Even so, she was disgusted to find that Maury Patterson,
cast as Banquo, was wearing a wire. He had a prompter feeding
him his lines. He hadn't even bothered to memorize the
pronunciations! Ginny stifled a snort. After all, this was
amateur theater. All the players were volunteers. And Banquo
was bound for the role of corpse, so what possible harm could
it do if he blew his lines? It might even turn an *aye* vote to a
nay. That could be useful.

Hecate, Patsy's role, wasn't scheduled to appear on stage
until Act Three, Scene Five, so Ginny had plenty of time to
rehearse her lines. Alan had, quite sensibly, chosen a
shortened version of the play and omitted the intermission, so
the entire production would run for just under two hours.
Ginny found herself caught up in the backstage magic, then in
the story itself.

Macbeth, hearing from witches that he will be king, decides
to make sure this prophecy comes true. When the King of
Scotland, Duncan, comes to stay in Macbeth's castle, Macbeth
sneaks in, kills him as he sleeps, then blames it on the servants.
Duncan's sons run off, leaving Macbeth to claim the throne.

Macbeth has also heard from the witches that it is Banquo's descendants, not his, who will be kings of Scotland. Macbeth decides the way to change this prophecy in his favor is to kill Banquo and his son, Fleance. Too squeamish himself to kill again, he hires murderers, who botch the job, leaving Fleance alive.

The rest of the play shows Macbeth's descent into madness and his death at the hands of MacDuff. He is killed in a sword fight, the same one Ginny saw rehearsed by Alan and Ian. She was looking forward to seeing it again, in costume this time.

Her own part was limited and contained none of the well-known quotes from the play, but that didn't bother her. The casting did, a bit.

Banquo was supposed to be a noble and honorable Scottish lord, Macbeth a traitorous, greedy, ambitious man ruled by his wife. To Ginny's mind, Maury Patterson fit Macbeth better than Banquo. But it was Alan's production and no doubt he'd needed to take whatever help was offered.

Ginny heard Macbeth telling his wife he would visit the witches again, and prepared for her entrance, accompanied by thunder produced backstage by the shaking of a sheet of metal hung from a wooden frame.

"Why, how now, Hecate! You look angerly."

"Have I not reason, beldams as you are, Saucy and overbold? How did you dare . . ."

Having delivered her lines, Ginny exited, but didn't go far. She would be needed again, and soon.

"Double, double toil and trouble. . ."

Ginny slipped onstage. *"O well done! . . ."*

She faded into the shadows to watch the apparitions. These were done with digital images on a smoke screen of mist, their voices reverberating through the hall. Ginny was impressed and so was the audience.

The phantoms were followed by a procession of Banquo's descendants (local high school boys) and Banquo himself (Patterson in his ghost costume). They faded into the back of the stage, oozing through a cleverly wrought curtain of black streamers. And then it was time for Ginny to leave as well, following her witches off, stage right.

She turned right, intending to take her costume off and watch the rest of the show from the back of the auditorium. There was a bit of a hallway, and a slope down toward the bowels of the theater, with dressing rooms and staging areas along both sides. She squeezed past props that would be needed for the remaining scenes.

A hand came out of the darkness and grabbed her arm, pulling her into one of the anterooms.

"What?"

She gasped as the arm threw her against the wall and an apparition of her own took hold of her throat, squeezing, choking her. There was light filtering in from the hallway, enough to show her who it was. Maury Patterson. Her eyes widened. An old man, but so strong!

She didn't want to hurt him, but if she didn't break free soon, she would die and Jim would be furious. She wedged her right arm between them, pushing toward his face. When she was in position, she struck. Her knee landed in his groin with a muffled thump, the two costumes padding the blow. But it did the trick. He was startled and recoiled an inch or two.

In that moment of surprise, she brought the heel of her hand up as hard as she could, landing just at the base of his nose. She slammed into the cartilage, jamming her hand upward, bringing tears to his eyes, and forcing him to let go.

She lunged for the door, made it, and stayed upright by clinging to the woodwork. She stared at Patterson, watching blood drip from his nose onto his costume. He stared back, a

MAGGIE FOSTER

puzzled expression on his face. Ginny pulled her headdress off and tried to speak, but no sound came out, just a rasp.

"You're not Patsy!" He moved toward her.

Ginny turned and ran, her legs betraying her. Stumbling, she grabbed at the walls for support. And it wasn't just her legs that were failing her.

She was having trouble seeing. Black spots swirled in front of her eyes. Her hand fell on the sheet of metal used to produce thunder. She recoiled, then grabbed and overturned it, throwing it at Patterson, and making the most awful racket. Someone was sure to hear that! Someone did.

Three people appeared out of the gloom and tried to shush her, demanding to know what she was up to, interrupting the actors like that. Ginny pointed at Patterson, who had been advancing toward her, the skirt of his costume held to his bleeding nose.

"Stop him!" She was croaking, but audible. "He tried to kill me! Stop him!" They surged toward him, Ginny in their wake.

* * *

Maury had been stunned to find that his careful planning had fallen apart. Instead of a dying old woman, easy to silence, the costume had hidden a young woman, able and willing to fight back. He heard her accusation.

He headed for the back door, but others had come to investigate. They were between him and the exits. He turned and hurried across the back of the stage, behind the flats. But again the crew prevented escape. They were asking in stage whispers what was going on? Why the noise? Didn't he realize the play was in progress?

He turned again, but now there were men forming a wall between him and the rear of the building. He backed up, tripping over cables and props. They were closing in. He headed in the only direction that remained open to him, onto the stage.

There were gasps at his appearance, and puzzled whispers. The three weird sisters tried to ignore him, still chanting, as if he were part of the scene. He looked over his shoulder and found someone close enough to grab his shroud. He snatched the fabric away and darted toward center stage. If he could get to the stairs, he could leave down the center aisle, as if it had been planned that way.

He shoved one of the witches out of his way and lunged toward the edge. She shrieked, grabbing his robe to keep herself from falling off the stage. He tore it from her hands, stepped on the hem of his costume, lost his balance, and fell backwards onto the cauldron.

The noise rang in his ears and his head hurt. His skull must have hit the cast iron hard enough to set the metal vibrating. No, cast iron didn't ring. The ringing must be in his ears. He could still see, sort of. He was on his back on the stage, staring up into "heaven," the roof of the stage where they keep the catwalks and scenery and engines necessary to create illusions.

Had Macbeth gone to Heaven? Had Banquo? The real-life Banquo had been just as guilty as Macbeth. The Banquo of Shakespeare's play was a lie from first to last. A lie made up to flatter an ambitious king. He knew that much, from school.

He tried to blink, to clear his vision, but nothing changed. Ambition. He'd chosen ambition and a powerful life in the ruling class. Like Macbeth, he'd seized power and used it to make sure he would keep it.

It had not been hard, though he'd been lucky. He'd been born lucky. One has to be born into the right family and he'd been lucky in his choice of mothers. He'd been born to rule, like Macbeth. His mother had seen to that.

He remembered the interview, after the death of the harlot on the Upper Peninsula. Leave everything to Mother. Keep your hands clean. You must be innocent, so that you can do good in the world. You have a destiny to fulfill. The masses don't know what's good for them. You will tell them and I will make sure they listen.

His mother's face rose before his eyes and he saw that she was old, as old and ravaged as one of the weird sisters. Cold, too. Her breath felt like ice on his cheek.

Her face faded, but the cold lingered. The colored spot lights hanging from the rails in "heaven" were fading, too, being replaced by bright white lights, and the pain was dying. That was supposed to mean something, but he couldn't remember what. Besides, it didn't matter. He had fulfilled his destiny. He had been king.

* * *

Ginny knelt beside Patterson, trying to get his attention, to get him to respond to her, to look at her, to move his hand, anything. Jim slid an arm around her and raised her to her feet, taking her place at the injured man's side. He lifted the man's eyelids, and tried to elicit reflexes. Nothing.

The actors stood around the cauldron, in horrified silence, their numbers swelled by the curious. Ginny felt a stir of air and looked up to see Ian, in full battle dress, pushing his way to the front of the crowd. His face hardened as he took in what had happened.

"Sic semper tyrannis," he said, then turned on his heel and strode off.

Alan marshalled his actors. He gave orders to the crew to close the curtains and to the cast to take the performance forward, to finish the play out front.

Ginny heard a commotion and turned to see Rita Patterson fighting her way to her husband's side. She was white as his sheet, horrified. "No! Get up, you fool!"

Jim had his phone to his ear. Ginny heard him tell the 9-1-1 operator what had happened. Then his arm was around her and he was guiding her off stage and into one of the dressing rooms, checking her over, asking someone for ice.

The rest of the afternoon was a blur. Policemen came and investigated the death. The audience was asked to write down what they had seen, then released to go home. The body was removed to the morgue. By the time the officials released Ginny and Jim, the sun was setting.

Jim took her home and fed her soothing drinks and soup. Her throat was sore and bruised, but it seemed there was no permanent damage. She could breathe and she could swallow. What remained was shock.

Break a leg, Patsy had said. Patterson had broken his neck.

* * *

CHAPTER 44

Monday wee small hours
Mackenzie residence

Ginny sat in front of her computer and stared at the screen. The device wasn't ideal for the task, but she didn't have butcher paper in the house. She'd have to get some tomorrow.

She heard Jim coming up the stair, but stayed where she was. She was only sorry she'd waked him, not that her teeming brain was keeping her awake.

He stepped up behind her and peered over her shoulder, resting his hands on the arms of the chair, one on either side of her, and leaning forward. She could feel the warmth of sleep on her neck and cheek and see the fur on his arms ripple as he shifted his weight and brought one arm up across her chest, holding her close.

"What are you working on?"

"I'm trying to do what Larry couldn't, find real evidence against Maury Patterson."

"At three in the morning?"

Ginny sighed. "I couldn't sleep."

He kissed the top of her head, then looked around. "We need another chair in this room, one with wheels."

Ginny smiled. "There's a chair in the nursery."

Jim stood up, fetched the chair, and set it down beside her, so he, too, could see the computer screen. Ginny made room for him.

"You realize Maury can't be prosecuted posthumously."

She nodded. "I'm just trying to make sense of all this."

"Okay. Talk it out. Tell me what you're thinking."

Ginny took a breath. "The first solid evidence was the bodies in those dog coffins. They suggest a crime was committed, several in fact. In Texas, the person who takes possession of a body is required to file a death certificate within twenty-four hours. That didn't happen, not here and not in Illinois. And if you intend to transport the body between states, say from Illinois to Texas, you are required to obtain a burial-transit permit. There are none on record."

She took another breath. "It's legal to bury someone in a family cemetery on private property without embalming, if you do so within twenty-four hours. The driving time between the Patterson lake house and Chancie Mor is just a little over ten hours."

Jim nodded. "Doable, even in a van, even with stops for meals and gas."

"There are additional statutes dealing with the type of coffin, but the dog coffins fit the description, so no problem there. The inventory we got from Ms. Holloway tells us there was a purchase made each time Maury was due to face the polls. Which brings us to the exhumation. Maury didn't know what was in that coffin, which means he was not involved in the disposal of the bodies."

"At least not the one we watched being opened, the fifth prostitute, the one Larry didn't get to see because he was being arrested for trespassing."

"She was also the one wearing a fitness tracker, which gave us the presumed time of her death. Her heart rate shot up to over two hundred for about three minutes, then slowed down, then stopped." Ginny frowned, imagining that death by strangulation.

"But I've found proof it could not have been Maury Patterson who killed her. He and his bodyguard stopped at the gas station before heading home. Maury got out, was recognized, and posed for photos. There was one with two teenaged girls in bathing suits, flanking him, complete with date/time stamp. It's been pinned to the bulletin board in the gas station ever since. It's evidence Maury could not have killed that fifth girl."

Jim was silent for a moment, his brow furrowed. "He could have paid to have her killed."

Ginny nodded. "I think it's clear *someone* paid to have these women killed, then delivered to Chancie Mor and buried in the back forty. The question is who? I can't find anything to point to one person or another. All I know for sure is that Rita was in on it."

"Okay, what else have you got?"

"Against Maury? The candlestick. Patsy witnessed the blow and saw her brother go down. She recalls Maury thrusting the candlestick into her hands and telling her that she should hide it and tell no one or he would kill her, too."

"So Maury thought he was responsible."

"Did you ever find that autopsy?"

"Still working on it."

"Charlotte's death was investigated and dismissed. Even if we could persuade the authorities there was enough doubt to re-open the investigation, Patterson is dead, so they wouldn't waste their time." Ginny swung around and faced her husband. "So I got nuthin'. Except a bad case of guilty conscience where Larry Scala is concerned."

"Yeah, me too."

Ginny reached out and took Jim's hand. "Larry's death is not your fault."

Jim's brow furrowed. "I should have warned him."

"You didn't know who you'd seen in that vision."

"I should have recognized his clothes."

"Even if you had, you know he wouldn't have listened to you, right?"

Jim sighed, then nodded. Very few people understood how the Second Sight worked and even fewer trusted it.

"Reggie told me he's working on a lead. Something about that phone I pulled from the trash. Maybe he'll find something we can use."

"He's dead. Ian Hunter is running unopposed. The Homestead is safe. Why do you have to prove who killed whom?"

Ginny shook her head. "If Maury didn't do it, then someone else did. That person should be caught and punished."

"Okay." Jim nodded, then rose, drawing her to her feet and into his arms. "Come to bed, love. Your brain will work better in the morning."

Ginny nodded, flipped out the light and let Jim take her downstairs. He settled her beside him, his arms around her, and was soon breathing deeply. Ginny was glad of it. At least one of them would get some sleep.

She lay still, thinking about the problem. She was missing something. That was the only explanation. She needed to figure out what, and where to look. Because there was a solution to this puzzle somewhere. She just had to find it.

* * *

"Jim? Are you ready?" Ginny stuck her head into the bedroom and saw her husband adding a black armband to his outfit. He was in classic kilt this afternoon. Ginny was in black. They were going to a wake.

"Almost. Give me a minute."

"I hate funerals."

"This is not a funeral. It's a party where the guest of honor can't spoil the fun."

Ginny snorted. "The guest of honor will not be present. The medical examiner isn't done with him, yet. But there will be a widow and maybe even his children. I haven't heard."

"Does he have children?"

Ginny nodded. "Three by the third wife."

Jim's eyebrows rose. "Three wives? How did he manage that? I can barely handle one!"

"Jean says the first wife died young, of cancer. The second was either infertile or very, very careful. They were divorced after ten years. The third is Rita and she stands to inherit the entire Patterson fortune."

"So, perhaps not grieving as much as lesser mortals might."

Ginny sighed. "She seemed genuinely distraught yesterday. Let's give her the benefit of the doubt."

"Okay. I'm ready."

Chancie Mor had been opened for the event and the caterers must have been busy all morning, the house was packed with people. After signing in, Ginny found herself face to face with Rita.

"I am so sorry for your loss."

Rita made a lovely widow. Her outfit was impeccable; chaste, elegant, and made of the best raw silk money could buy. Her face showed evidence of damage to her makeup and her eyes were red. Convincing grief. And her words were gracious and well-bred, something Ginny had not expected.

"Thank you for coming."

Ginny wandered through the crowd, speaking to those she recognized, being introduced to strangers. It was a good turnout, the result of Maury's political connections, no doubt.

There was a table covered in cards and letters, and flowers everywhere. Conspicuously absent were Rita's children, and any musicians. Ginny had never yet been to a wake where there wasn't singing, and usually dancing, to celebrate the life that had been. Considering the number of business discussions going on, albeit in low and respectful tones, Ginny was sure the topic that occupied most of the minds present was the money that was about to change hands.

Ginny wandered through the front rooms, then made for the library. She and Jim had seen it when they were given the tour, but she wanted to look again at the room where Tommy Bryant died. She stood in front of the fireplace, Patsy's words echoing in her mind. Tommy, with his back to Maury, trying to run away. Maury with his hand on Tommy's shirt, preventing escape. Then Maury reaching up and grasping the candlestick, bringing it down on the back of Tommy's head. Tommy falling, bleeding, not moving.

"Here you are."

Ginny started, and turned to face her hostess. "I hope you don't mind my wandering off. It was a bit crowded in the front rooms."

"Not at all. I feel the same way, only I can't escape, not for long." Rita smiled crookedly.

"Will you be staying in Texas?" Ginny asked, making conversation. "You have a house in Springfield, I think?"

Rita nodded. "Yes, my home, and the only home my

children have ever known. I'll stay there at least until the last one is on his own."

Ginny nodded. "And Maury? Will you take him back to Illinois?"

"We were thinking of burying him beside his mother."

At her own request, Letitia Patterson had ended up in the graveyard behind the Auld Kirk, rather than beside her husband in Illinois. She was Homestead, after all.

"Not in the family plot behind the house?"

Rita looked surprised, then thoughtful. "I wonder if they'd let me do that. He would have liked the symbolism. Shall we go pick out a place for him?" She gestured for Ginny to precede her out of the room.

Ginny was no stranger to murder mysteries and Rule Number One for the heroine was to avoid being alone with the suspected murderer. But that was fiction. Even if Rita was involved in the deaths, she hadn't killed any of those women with her own hands. And the suit she was wearing was too tight to conceal a weapon.

Rita was still talking and Ginny thought she sounded very much as Patsy had done, in need of a sympathetic ear. Plus, Ginny wanted answers. Perhaps the grieving widow would let something slip. All Ginny had to do was listen, and stay out of reach.

Rita ushered her out the back door and onto the path that led to the cemetery. "Letitia was a remarkable woman. You'll recall I told you how much she and I had in common, in addition to Maury, of course."

Ginny nodded. "I remember."

"She asked me to take care of her son, and I promised to do so. In exchange for which, Letitia promised to let me have the estate."

Ginny felt her skin crawl. Why was Rita talking about her

inheritance? Surely that was none of Ginny's business? "I expect you'll inherit whatever was Maury's."

"What was actually his, yes, but the bulk of the estate was tied up. She didn't trust me. Oh, she *liked* me, but she recognized herself in me. So she put a condition on the promise."

They had reached the cemetery and Rita was holding the gate open. Ginny felt an impulse to run, but if she did that, she wouldn't find out what Letitia Patterson was holding over Rita's head.

She entered the cemetery and turned right, walking along the front row and looking at the arrangement of the graves. "Here's a spot that might do."

Rita followed her over and considered the suggestion, then nodded. "Front and center. Yes. And we could put the stone facing out toward the house." She wandered on, looking for other options.

"Any way, what she did was put a stipulation on the bequest. I would get everything if Maury died a natural death." She resumed walking, her eyes sweeping the graveyard. "Nothing on this row. This one is too narrow. The roots of this ancient oak have taken over this quarter of the field. Maybe farther back."

"You don't want to put him among the dogs, do you?"

Rita faced Ginny again. "Why not? She valued those dogs as much as she valued her son."

"Which reminds me," Ginny said, trying to bring the conversation back to a more normal level. "What happened to the two Irish wolfhounds she had when she died?"

"They're in Illinois," Rita replied. "Such outlandish names! The kids have re-named them *Sirius* and *Orion*, both of which they can spell."

Ginny smiled. "Much better, I'm sure."

Incarnadine

"For us, yes." Rita's eyes narrowed. "She would not have approved." She moved toward the exit, stopping when she was between Ginny and the gate. She turned to face Ginny.

"She was always telling me how to behave, what to do, in the kindest possible manner, of course, dear." Rita mimicked Letitia's voice and Ginny felt a penny drop in her mind. She caught her breath.

"It was her! Letitia, not Maury!"

Rita gave her a nasty smile. "Are you just now figuring that out? You must be stupider than you look." She reached down and grabbed a shovel that had been lying in the dirt. She swung it at Ginny.

"*You* killed him. *You're* the reason I'm not going to inherit a fortune. You and that bitch of a mother of his."

Ginny jumped back, stumbling on the uneven ground. "What? No!"

"Oh, yes! He was trying to silence you." She advanced toward Ginny.

"He thought I was Patsy." Ginny backed away from the shovel.

"Patsy would have died quietly. You raised the roof, shouting and sending everyone to corner and capture him."

Ginny's eyes dilated as she saw the hatred in the other woman's eyes. "It was an accident," Ginny said. "He tripped and fell."

Rita lunged and Ginny jumped back again. She was wondering if there was any way she could call Jim on her cellphone. It was in her pocket, but she didn't dare take her eyes off Rita. She had a panic button on the phone, too, for the police, which she might be able to hit, but she needed to see the screen to aim for it.

Rita snarled. "Falls are specifically prohibited. I think the old woman expected me to push him off a cliff."

Like the high school rival. Letitia must have known about that incident. Ginny pulled her phone out, still watching Rita, but it was a mistake. The other woman lunged and caught Ginny on the arm, knocking the phone to the ground.

Ginny turned to run and found herself on the edge of the first exhumation. No one had filled in the holes, yet.

With a howl of fury, Rita swung again. Ginny ducked under the shovel, slipped, and fell to the ground, her feet scrabbling in the loose dirt. She had gotten dust in her eyes and mouth and nose. She coughed and sputtered, trying to wipe her eyes so she could use them, but Rita was too fast.

The shovel slammed into her side and Ginny cried out as the blow fell. Then she was falling. Rita had pushed her over the edge, into the grave.

Ginny tried to climb out, but found she couldn't raise her left arm. She reached up and tried to get a grip on the edge of the grave, using her right hand. Rita stamped on it, and began shoveling dirt as fast as she could go.

Ginny wrapped her throbbing hand across her aching side and looked around. The walls of the grave were almost as hard as concrete, the roots from the grass anchoring the clods in place. She could find no footholds and her fingers proved useless. She needed leverage.

The dirt from the exhumation, dry to begin with, had lain out in the summer sun. Each shovel-full dumped into the grave raised a further cloud of dust. Ginny reached out blindly with her hands and caught the shaft of the shovel, hanging on for dear life. She used it like a rope to pull herself up the wall of the grave. Rita responded by letting go. Ginny and the shovel fell back into the hole.

It knocked the breath out of her and Ginny lay still for a moment, just long enough for Rita to find another shovel and go back to work, dumping dirt on top of her. Ginny got to her feet and backed up against the wall, wondering how high the pile had to be to hold her weight. She had no intention of being buried alive. As long as she could stay on top of the dirt, she could climb out, but it was already over her ankles.

She dragged her feet out of her shoes and tried again to climb the wall, this time using her shovel to make indentations in the dirt. This worked, but Rita had the high ground and used her shovel as a weapon, to prevent Ginny from raising her head above the edge of the grave.

Ginny considered trying to hit Rita's ankles with her shovel, but the angle was wrong, and with one arm disabled, Rita would certainly take the weapon away from her if she tried.

Rita was breathing hard, shoveling hard, not wasting her breath on further explanation. Ginny paused for a moment, trying to think.

"She manipulated you."

"So what?"

"She didn't treat you as an equal."

Rita ignored her.

"She expected you to take over for her, to take care of Maury, but she didn't trust you. Which was ridiculous, because you were every bit as powerful and well connected and ruthless as she was."

Rita paused. "Maury was an idiot. Always running to Mamma to get his marching orders." Rita resumed shoveling.

Ginny coughed, trying to catch a breath of clean air. "And when she died, you expected Maury to turn to you, to listen to you, just as he had listened to his mother. Because that's what Letitia had told him to do." Ginny put a foot on the growing pile of dirt, sinking into it, but gaining a couple of inches toward the lip of the hole.

"Wouldn't you know the fool would decide to grow a backbone just when we most needed him to shut up and do as he was told."

"You warned him to stay away from Patsy, but he wouldn't listen."

"No, and I'm tired of listening to you!" Rita raised the shovel, intending to bash Ginny's head in with it. Ginny ducked, lost her footing, and rolled down the dirt pile to the bottom of the hole, expecting more dirt to follow, but instead she heard a gasp, then a cry.

"Let go of me!"

There was a scuffle going on topside, with grunts and heavy breathing. Ginny climbed the dirt pile again and peeked over the edge. Rita was on the ground with Jim kneeling on her, holding her still while he wrapped his sporran strap around her hands. He used his belt to do the same with her knees.

Ginny took her shovel, rammed it into the wall, then used it as a step to help her climb out of the grave. When she stood on the grass again, Jim looked at her and raised an eyebrow. "You are covered in dirt."

"Not as much as she intended."

Jim rose to his feet and came over, brushing some of the dirt off her head. He pulled a handkerchief out of his sporran, moistened it, and went to work on her face.

She looked over at Rita, who had managed to roll over and sit up. "It was Letitia who arranged all those killings, and paid for them."

"Of course. Except for the last one. I did that. Not that I got credit for it. She would never have admitted she was losing control, but she was. All her people were too old. So I took over." Rita's face flooded dark red. "She owes me! So help me, I'll break that Codicil if it's the last thing I ever do!"

* * *

CHAPTER 45

Tuesday morning
Makenzie residence

Jim had taken her straight to the emergency room, as soon as the police arrived to take custody of Rita. Chest x-rays (with appropriate abdominal shielding) had revealed two hairline fractures of the fifth and sixth ribs on the left side. The injuries to her hand, where Rita had stomped on it, turned out to be tissue-only. She had inhaled a lot of dust and was coughing up dirt, which hurt her side, and there were miscellaneous scrapes and bruises as well. But the worst of the whole episode was that the ER doc had insisted on doing an HCG, which meant Ginny's pregnancy was now part of her chart and anyone with access would know about the baby.

Jim had smiled at her distress. "It's privileged health information. No one is going to talk, for fear of consequences."

The parts of her that had needed bandaging had been washed at the hospital. Jim had taken care of the rest, and that included washing her hair, which was a chore. She had grumbled at his inexperienced touch. "Maybe I should just cut it off,"

"Don't you dare! I love your long hair."

"I won't be able to raise my arms to braid it for weeks. Who's going to do that? You?"

"Yes."

"But you don't know how."

"You'll teach me."

He hadn't scolded her, hadn't berated her, hadn't told her what a fool she had been to follow Rita to the cemetery.

She had asked him, on the way back to Chancie Mor, "How did you find me?"

"I was looking for you."

"Out the window?"

"Yes, and then using the locator app on your phone."

Of course.

The ER doc had given her a prescription for a mild pain killer. After checking with her OB, Jim had written her one for something that would actually work. Even so, it had been a bad night.

She poked at her scrambled eggs. "I hate it that redheads need more anesthetic than normal people."

"It's a curse, I know." He set a cup of hot ginger tea down in front of her. "The next few days are going to be hard. I've cancelled my shifts – and yours – so I can be here with you."

She looked up into his face. "Jim, I'm sorry."

He reached out and stroked her cheek. "I got there in time to hear some of your conversation. I'm pretty sure you could have talked her down, but I wasn't prepared to take the chance."

Ginny's mouth twitched. "I'm glad you weren't. I did not want to face that shovel again."

"I'm glad she wasn't able to knock you unconscious, toss you in that hole, and bury you for real."

Ginny sniffed. "Give me some credit. I wasn't letting her get that close. I've always thought the heroines who are induced to peer at the exotic plant deserve what they get when they are conked on the head from behind. She tried, but I saw her coming."

Jim laughed. "It's a step in the right direction. Now, if I can just teach you to stay away from women with weapons."

"It was a shovel."

"And the last one was an alligator."

Ginny nodded. "Well, at least it wasn't a gun." Because, if it had been, she'd be dead.

* * *

Tuesday mid-morning
Mackenzie residence

On Tuesday morning, Jim, Ginny, and Himself gathered in the Mackenzie's living room to hold a post-mortem. Angus began.

"'Tis over then."

The other two nodded.

"I'd as soon not hae th' man deid, but it may be just as weel."

"He killed his sister and he tried to kill me, thinking I was Patsy!" Ginny scowled.

"Aye, an' he were guilty of many other crimes besides murder."

"What's going to happen to Rita?"

"'Tis early days yet, and th' woman hae her faither's resources tae call on, but they found th' stolen candlestick in her possession, an' she attacked you, and there's more than one as will say she arranged th' attacks on th' Homestead. 'Tis unlikely she'll escape prison."

Jim nodded. "She and Letitia Patterson, between them, are responsible for the deaths of those five prostitutes. The police have Larry's photographs of the van and the men, and my testimony to the abduction of Marilee. It's only a matter of time before they find the connection. And there's something else. Remember that niggle at the back of my brain I couldn't pin down?"

"Yes."

"Well I got my hands on Tommy Bryant's autopsy yesterday. It says the first blow wasn't the one that killed him. There was a second."

Ginny nodded. "It took me forever, but I finally figured that out. If Tommy had hit the back of his head by falling, he would have to have been facing Maury. But according to Patsy, he was facing away from Maury. He should have hit that coffee table face first."

"Mrs. Patterson must have found him unconscious and mistook him for dead. She needed to explain the head injury so she turned little Tommy over and dropped him on the edge of the coffee table."

Ginny's brow descended. "What kind of a mother could do that?"

"One determined to protect her son."

"I think she took it too far." She shook her head. "Rita's no relation to any of us, but her children are. What's going to happen to *them*?" Ginny was expressing the general feeling that blood was blood and the Scots had an obligation to take care of their own.

Angus frowned. "Th' youngest is twelve. They're auld tae be brought up wi' us, and their parents both rejected th' Homesteads. I think 'tis best they stay in Illinois, wi' their grandfather. Th' estate, howe'er, will be under our control. 'Twas a condition of Letitia's Will."

"That 'dead man switch' she included, to make sure Rita didn't kill Maury the minute her back was turned."

"Aye. I expect th' heirs will sell as soon as they may. They'll hae more use fer the money than th' legacy."

Ginny nodded. "The candlesticks will go to the insurance company and be put up for sale."

Jim smiled at her. "Would you like to buy them?"

Ginny feigned horror. "Heavens, no! Let someone else have the job of cleaning them!"

Jim turned back to Angus. "What about Larry?"

"His body will be returned tae his family, in Illinois. 'Twould be a kindness, I think, if ye will write wha' happened, and explain tae them." He looked at Ginny, who nodded.

"Yes. I want to explain that he was right all along, a knight errant whose quest was fulfilled. Patterson was defeated and the crime ring behind him exposed. They should be proud of him."

Both Jim and Angus nodded.

"And Tor needs to be told how important his contribution was," Jim added. "He saw Larry murdered and was able to give the police a description of the man. They caught him before the day was out."

"Aye. I'll arrange wi' his teacher tae gie him credit, withoot giving awa anything as should be left unsaid. A good lad, that one."

Ginny was glad Tor would get his promised reward. The boy had become a man that day, and that sort of growing up was hard on anyone.

"Th' challenges tae th' Loch Lonach Home Rule hae been withdrawn, and Ian ha' a clear path tae his Senate seat. He'll hae some trouble pleasing all o' his constituents, wha with th' promises Patterson made tae them. There's work tae be done there, but he's up tae it."

Angus frowned. "Th' council ha' voted tae go ahead wi' construction on th' perimeter defenses. 'Till be a challenge tae secure th' grounds, but 'tis needed."

Ginny sighed. "I hate the thought of living behind walls."

Angus looked at her. "Th' gates will be open tae any as come wi' good will." He put his hands on his knees and pushed himself to his feet. "And now, I'll leave ye young people tae carry on. I've got a Homestead tae deal wi'"

Jim saw him to the door. Ginny heard her husband offer his services to his grandfather, and heard the Laird's reply.

"I'll let ye know, lad. But fer now, ye've enough tae keep ye busy, wha' wi' that wife of yours."

All other questions answered, there remained one more hurdle. Ginny sighed and pulled out her phone.

* * *

Tuesday evening
Mackenzie residence

When the doorbell rang, Jim answered it, admitting Chris. He performed the host duties of ushering the visitor into the living room and offering a drink. Ginny smiled and gestured Chris toward a seat.

"Please make yourself at home." She swallowed. "Thank you for coming to me. It will be a while before I can get around on my own."

Chris nodded. "I'm happy to make house calls, in a good cause." He sat down across from her and caught her eye. "Do you want Jim to sit in?"

Ginny frowned swiftly. "I don't know. Should I?"

"You two are a team. I think he deserves to hear what he's gotten himself into."

Jim had been hovering, glass in hand. He gave it to Chris, then took a seat facing both of them, making a triangle of the conversation.

Chris took a sip of his drink, his eyes on Ginny. "How may I help you?"

She frowned. "You see what a mess I've made of this candlestick business. Six weeks of misery and I can ill afford the time. I have so many responsibilities."

Chris nodded.

Ginny swallowed and continued. "I promised Jim when we got married that I'd give up investigating. He was very gracious, and also skeptical." She glanced at her husband. "He offered to help, to keep an eye on me, I think. And it's a good thing he did. Otherwise I'd be at the bottom of one of those erstwhile graves in the Patterson family plot."

"I'm not so sure of that," Jim volunteered. "You hadn't even gotten mad, yet. You were still trying to reason with her."

"Well, *she* was mad. Crazy, actually, to try to kill me during her husband's wake. She should have waited until dark."

"Target of opportunity. She hadn't planned it."

Ginny nodded. "I know." She took a sip of her ginger ale. "Anyway." She turned back to Chris. "Maybe it's the Scottish Play, or maybe it's the changes going on in my life, but I've been think a lot about fate and destiny and choices.

"What I want to know is whether it's my fate to stick my nose in where it's not wanted, or can I walk away?"

The corner of Chris's mouth twitched. "Have you read any of the research going on in the field of evolutionary biology?"

Ginny shook her head. "Why?"

"There's new evidence about how societies are formed, and how they manage to survive. Encoded in the human DNA, as it turns out."

"Successful traits survive, unsuccessful ones are eliminated."

Chris nodded. "You may already know there's no society on Earth that hasn't got the concept of the Golden Rule."

Ginny recited what she had learned in kindergarten. "Treat

others the way you want others to treat you."

"Scholars call it 'reciprocity.' As it turns out, societies that take care of their own reproduce more successfully." Chris leaned back and crossed his legs. "The research is interesting. They've found genes that play a role in moral behavior. The theory is, once humans needed help—to bring down a big game animal or get the crops in—the tendency to selfishness had to be controlled. Individuals who could work with others passed on their genes because they got enough to eat."

"Okay." Ginny was listening, but couldn't see what this had to do with her problem.

"Eventually, the concept of fairness emerged. Those who worked got fed. Freeloaders got driven off. Think about that for a moment—morality hard-wired into the human psyche." Chris paused.

Ginny couldn't help remembering some of the people she'd known who had not outgrown the toddler stage.

"But there are two sides to that coin." Chris continued. "You have to be able to do both. Lay aside your aggression—cooperate, and live. Then take up arms and fight—defend your crops and family, or die."

Ginny was reminded of the fierce loyalty of the Scots, their reputation for clannishness, and their tendency to distrust outsiders. It was a strategy that had served them well over the centuries.

Chris looked from her to her husband. "There are a few behaviors no society will tolerate. Murder is one of them."

Ginny's brow furrowed. If something showed up in every society, it had survival value. A lot of it. A universal ban on murder implied it was bad for the birth rate. So a murder in the community would trigger a strong response against the perpetrator.

"You're suggesting the need to eliminate murderers is hard-wired into human beings."

He nodded. "Inherent and instinctual. Like a knee-jerk reaction, it isn't under conscious control."

Jim frowned. "Then why hasn't murder been eliminated long ago?"

"It's not that simple, of course. If you're a farmer and the neighbor decides to take what is yours, you need to be able to fight, or you die, and your genes die with you. You need to be able—and willing—to kill your enemy."

"Basic survival."

"Yes, but it goes deeper. The research suggests that, because of this need, an aptitude for waging war is also encoded in human DNA."

Ginny snorted. Armed combat was a way of life for the Scots, always had been. If they weren't fighting foreign wars, they were stealing each other's cattle.

"Okay, we're a quarrelsome people responding to instinctual demands intended to produce more babies. How does this explain me?"

Chris smiled. "The ability to kill for a good cause is the same ability that results in murder. We're all born with it. Even a mild-mannered grandmother can kill a dog attacking a baby."

Ginny was momentarily distracted by the memory of a gray wolf with his teeth in Jim's arm, but Chris was still speaking.

"Evolutionary forces may have been selecting for cooperation, but they couldn't throw out the baby with the bath water. So Mother Nature tinkered with the DNA, trying to find a mechanism for controlling unproductive violence."

Ginny laughed. "Unproductive violence! That's a really good description of football."

Chris smiled. "Some would say it's a good outlet. The point is, evolution uses trial and error. The genes for cooperation coexist with the genes for annihilation. Some combinations prove more successful than others."

"Okay. I'm with you so far."

"Me, too." Jim said.

"Because of the complexity of the problem, there's not just one gene involved. There are many, and the expression of the genes—the traits—exist on a continuum, from none to a very great deal."

"Okay, still following."

"Remember that murderer who shouldn't exist?"

She and Jim both nodded.

"One of the theories being considered, using known inherited conditions as a model, is that he, or she, got a bad combination, or a damaged copy of the cooperation gene. It would mean a genetic predisposition to antisocial behavior, and that's not a popular concept."

Ginny lifted an eyebrow. "It wouldn't be."

"The opposite may also be true. Some of Mother Nature's lab rats would get a double dose of one or more of the genes predisposing them to stronger than usual pro-social conduct, including the need to hunt down and destroy murderers." Chris caught Ginny's eye and held it. "That's what I think happened to you."

Ginny stared at Chris. "You think my DNA compels me to solve murders?"

"To engage in pro-social behavior. I spotted the trait the first time we spoke. You have a stronger than average instinct for justice."

Ginny's shoulders sagged. "So I'm doomed to a life of chasing criminals?"

"I said the instinct was there. I didn't say you couldn't choose your response to it."

Ginny's brow furrowed. "This only started last fall. Shouldn't a trait like that have shown up sooner?"

Chris nodded. "It does. We see it in small children. When one takes another's toy, the first child protests. He knows it's not right to steal."

"We're supposed to learn to share our toys."

"Yes. Cooperation supports survival." Chris' eyebrows drew together. "But it requires the members of a society to come together and establish a set of rules. They must cooperate in deciding what matters. Once that's done, they must also cooperate by following the law, for the good of the group. What's more, those who don't obey must be punished. If there's no punishment, the result is anarchy, and societies can't survive chaos. That's where the prosocial individuals come in."

Ginny was thinking hard. "This doesn't sound like me. I've never been the slightest bit interested in causes."

"Haven't you ever fought for someone you thought was being treated unfairly when you were a child?"

"Of course." Ginny flushed. "But no one ever thanked me for butting in."

"How about as an adult?"

Ginny squirmed. "Well, yes. It comes up all the time at the hospital. Nurses are supposed to be advocates for their patients."

Chris nodded. "And you didn't allow Charlie to get away with murder."

"How did you find out about that?"

"Greg Gordon confided in me when I asked him what was eating you."

Ginny was struggling to wrap her head around the idea. "I've always known I hated anything that wasn't fair, but life isn't fair. Grownups have to accept that."

Jim set his glass down, rose, and moved over to sit beside her on the sofa. He slid a finger under her chin and turned her face, so that she was looking at him.

"I knew there would be things about you I'd discover after we were married, and I'd already made up my mind I would love you no matter what. All I ask is that you temper righteousness with mercy, at least where I'm concerned."

Ginny felt her heart melting. "Always."

Chris had one more thing to say. "It's a part of who you are, Ginny. Whether you like it or not, you'll feel the need. You can act on it, or ignore it. That's up to you. But you'll never escape it. You are hard-wired for justice."

"And I—" Jim bent to kiss her. "—wouldn't have it any other way."

THE END

GLOSSARY

Ain – own
Ane - one
Aye – yes
Bairn(s) – child / children
Bonnie – handsome
Canna – cannot
Ceilidh – party
Coo - cow
Dinna – did not / do not
Doesnae – does not
Ghillies – flexible, lace-up dancing shoes, akin to ballet slippers
Gied – gave
Gloaming – the time of day immediately following sunset
Guid – good
Hielan(d) – Highland, of or from the Highlands of Scotland
Ken – know
Kith and kin – friends and relatives
Mony - many
Nae – none
Nay – no
Nicht – night
No – not
Noo – now
Oot - out
Sae – so
Slàinte – ("slahn - shu") – Good health
Tae – to
Uisge-beatha – "water of life", aka "whisky"
Wee – small
Wee dram – an indeterminate amount of whisky

THE GHILLIE KNOT
LOCH LONACH MYSTERIES, BOOK SIX

Someone is hunting redheads.

Ginny Mackenzie's red hair is unusual in the general population, but not among the Scots. Her long braid is also not that uncommon. Lots of women have long hair. Combined, though, she falls into a small subset of women with long red braids—and it just may get her killed.

THE LOCH LONACH COLLECTION

The Loch Lonach Mysteries
- *The Arms of Death:* Loch Lonach Mysteries, Book One
- *The Swick and the Dead:* Loch Lonach Mysteries, Book Two
- *Viking Vengeance:* Loch Lonach Mysteries, Book Three
- *Final Fling:* Loch Lonach Mysteries, Book Four
- *Incarnadine*: Loch Lonach Mysteries, Book Five

Loch Lonach Short Stories
- *Dead Easy*
- *Duncan Died Dunkin'*
- *The Aviemore Cabin Boy*
- *Fifteen Minutes*
- *Out on a Limb*

Loch Lonach Men in Kilts Clean Romances
- *Sae Deep in Luv, Sinia and Chris*

Award winning and addictive, every book is a five-star read!

To find out more about the **Loch Lonach Mystery Series** and the **Loch Lonach Men in Kilts Romance Series** visit
www.lochlonach.com

REVIEWS REQUESTED

BOOK REVIEWS help readers find new books and authors find new readers. If you enjoyed this novel, please take a moment to leave a REVIEW on Goodreads.

I read each and every one and appreciate them all. You can also FOLLOW me to receive updates on my WIP (work in progress), new or upcoming releases, sales, promotions, and giveaways. Looking forward to hearing from you!

Slàinte, y'all!

goodreads
https://www.goodreads.com/book/show/55032176-incarnadine

ABOUT THE AUTHOR

MAGGIE FOSTER is a seventh-generation Texan of Scottish descent. In addition to being steeped in Scottish traditions and culture, she has spent a lifetime in healthcare as a nurse, lawyer, educator, and redhead. Her interests include history, genealogy, music, dancing, travel, dark chocolate, good whisky, and men in kilts, not necessarily in that order.

You can contact her at:
maggiesmysteries@gmail.com or
Maggie@maggiesmysteries.com

Website – www.lochlonach.com
Goodreads – www.goodreads.com/maggiefoster
Facebook – www.facebook.com/lochlonach/
Twitter – www.Twitter.com/maggiefoster55
Instagram – www.instagram.com/scottishsleuthsofdallas/

Six Virtual Ways to Support Your Favorite Author

Buy their books
Write reviews
Recommend on Goodreads
Request at your library
Post pictures holding their books
Sign up for the e-mail list

Made in the USA
Middletown, DE
11 August 2023

36576179R00249